The enemy ship was billowing steam from side vents now, a clear sign that there were fires within and its hull was compromised.

It fired a battery of projectiles and energy streams towards me, but my dancing pinprick of a fighter craft eluded them all.

The enemy's huge battle ship was faced with a single-Maxolu skycraft, and it was losing. I felt a surge of triumph.

And then I saw that the enemy vessel was descending, and landing. It burned the grass in a field and touched down with no jolt, and the side of the craft opened up and I saw far below me — in the image magnified by my mask-eyes — a single figure step out.

I increased the magnification on my eyes still further; and was surprised to see that the figure emerging from the ship was a female warrior carrying a sword. Was this a challenge?

The enemy battleship lifted into the air once more and flew off. The warrior remained, alone, on the ground. The message was clear: a one-on-one combat was being proposed.

I plunged downwards, with a jolt of joy that was like falling off a cliff.

By Philip Palmer

Debatable Space
Red Claw
Version 43
Hell Ship
Artemis

PHILIP PALMER

HELLSHIP

www.orbitbooks.net

Orbit
Hachette Book Group
237 Park Avenue, New York, NY 10017
www.HachetteBookGroup.com

First U.S. Edition: July 2011

Orbit is an imprint of Hachette Book Group, Inc. The Orbit name and logo are trademarks of Little, Brown Book Group Limited.

Library of Congress Control Number: 2011925236

ISBN: 978-0-316-12513-0

10 9 8 7 6 5 4 3 2 1

Printed in the United States of America

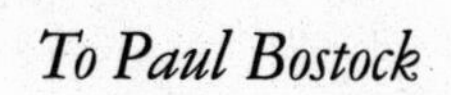

To Paul Bostock

BOOK 1

Sharrock

I could see flames in the night sky; and fear for those I loved burned in my soul.

I had been riding for five days and five nights through the red and lonely desert. My throat was parched, and my skin was like ash. And I had been dreaming, vividly, of the pleasures I would soon enjoy: a lazy bath in warm and perfumed waters; a slow massage of my angry muscles; a richly sensual copulation with my beloved wife Malisha; a long draught of rich wine; and, finally, a deep, soul-enriching sleep on a mattress filled with shara feathers.

All these dreams ended when I saw the glow in the sky. The clouds above and beyond the gnarled escarpment of grey rocks were bloodied by red flame; white floating pillows now transformed into ghastly red carcasses.

And I knew that my village had been torched.

I dismounted my cathary and knelt, and put my ear to the soft sound-conducting sand. And I waited, until my mind and ears were in tune with the planet and its hidden truths. And then I heard:

A faint humming noise, like the murmur of blood running along a warrior's veins, and I guessed that it was the sound of a skyplane hovering.

Shrill receding cries, remote, celebratory, in a language I did not recognise.

The hooves of riderless mounts, aimlessly pit-pattering.

The low moans of warriors and wives and husbands and children; sad cries of dying grief that mingled agony with impotent rage.

I heard also, faintly but unmistakably: the soft, hoarse death gasps of throats scorched by sun-fire blasts; the pants and grunts of those enduring brutal wounds; the wretched sobs of wounded children; the despairing howls of mothers cradling their lost beloved.

A massacre.

I took out a shovel from my saddle-pack and dug a deep hole in the sand. Then I took my cathary by the reins and led her down into the hole, and coaxed her to lie down. The beast whinnied and kicked, but I stroked her mane and whispered in her neck-ear and calmed her. Then I lay beside her, still whispering, and the winds swept sand over us, and before long we were buried deep and invisible.

After four days buried in the sand I crawled my way out. The cathary was in a coma by now, and I gently massaged the creature's heart until her eyes flickered. I drank from my canteen and spat the water into her moisture holes. And then slowly the cathary got to her feet, and shook her head, and whinnied, and was ready to ride once more.

It took two hours for me to ride through the teeth and gaping jaws of the rocky escarpment and reach my village. The flames had died down by now. The bodies that had burned so fiercely as to light the evening sky were now but charred corpses. The shrubs and trees whose blazing leaves and bark had sent daggers of flame to falsely dawn the sky were now no more than patches of ash. The tents were still intact—no fire could ever harm *them*—but the mountains and foothills of the dead stretched before me, like the remnants of a bonfire in an abattoir. Too many to count, too blackened to recognise.

And all were dead now. No moans, cries, whimpers, sobs. This was a village of the dead, and all those I had known and loved were gone.

I was sure beyond doubt that my wife Malisha was trapped

somewhere in the decaying mass of suppurating flesh. And I supposed too that my daughter Sharil must be one among the many black and silently howling tiny bodies I witnessed inside the tents, whose impregnable walls had kept out the flames though not, tragically, the heat. This was a systematic slaughter. There would be no survivors; only those wounded beyond hope of recovery would have been left behind.

I could see plainly that the warriors had all died in combat, and I counted more than a hundred of them. Their bare faces were frozen in screams, and their swords were gripped in hands, or had fallen close to their bodies; but no traces of gore could be seen on their sharp and fearsome blades. No glorious battle this, but a long-distance act of butchery.

My friends, all. All but a few were wearing body armour, and this puzzled me. For I knew that only a long and sustained burst of sun-fire rays could burn the hard-weave plate in such a way. And the warriors of my tribe were too swift and agile to be trapped in the path of such deadly beams for that long. But all were dead anyway, sundered into pieces by a fast-moving beam of power that could incinerate bodies encased in armour *in an instant.* And dead, too, were the husbands and wives of warriors, and the daughters and sons of warriors. And dead too were the Philosophers, forty and more or them, small and helpless and beautiful as they were, caught up in a battle they were unable by temperament to participate in and slain like ignorant beasts.

Which tribe could have done this thing? The Kax? Or the Dierils? Or the Harona? All had sworn peace in the days after the Great Truce. But truces could be broken, and there was no underestimating the guile and malice of these island tribes.

Or could this be an act of revenge by the exiled Southern Tribes, who long had hated our peoples of Madagorian for expelling their vile nation from our planet? I had lately spent six months in the decadent and perfumed city of Sabol, on a mission that almost cost me my life and the future freedom of our entire race (and yet, let it be known: Sharrock was not defeated!) And so I knew only too well how hated we were by these fat and effete Southerners, with their technology and their "mechanoids" and their passion for ceaseless expansion through space.

Could they have done this? Did they send their sleek and powerful space vessels to wage war upon their former home? Surely they would know that such an act of barbarity would incur our deepest wrath, and their own inevitable destruction?

I realised I was weeping. Not for my dead wife or my murdered child, for *that* grief lay deep in my heart and would torment me until my dying day. No, I wept from shame, that I had not taken my place with my fellow warriors and died in glory. Instead, I had buried myself in sand and lay there like a corpse until all those who were slowly dying had agonisingly perished, and their attackers were long gone.

The shame ate at me like a double-edged knife carving a path through my innards; but I knew I had done the right thing. Sometimes, a warrior must be a coward.

I filmed the carnage carefully with the camera in my eye and then inspected the sands where the battle had taken place for forensic evidence; for the performance of this vital task was my purpose in surviving. I found no enemy bodies, even though some of our warriors had clearly fired their projectile weapons and sun-fire guns in the course of the bitter conflict. In places, the red sands themselves had been burned by the crossfire; and the rock escarpment and the grey mountain ridges were pitted with bullet holes and heat scars.

I surmised from all I had witnessed that the village had been attacked by stealth fighters of some kind, armed with weapons more powerful than any I had ever encountered, and with armoured hulls that were impervious to the rifles of our warriors and our anti-skycraft cannons. Our warriors would have had only minutes to prepare for battle; that would explain why they had not taken to the air in their own fighter jets.

I knelt before the body of one of the dead warriors who had been killed but not burned, and recognised him as Baramos, a noble warrior indeed. Baramos's guts had spilled from his body and sandworms were eating them. I ignored that and took out my thinnest dagger and thrust it into Baramos's skull, and split the bone open. Then I used the tip of the blade to root inside Baramos's inner ear until I retrieved the dead warrior's pakla.

This would provide the scientists and Philosophers in the city with all the information they needed; every word uttered between the warriors in the course of the battle would be recorded here.

Baramos had been, I recalled, as I gouged the pakla out of his brain, a magnificent fighter and a fine scientist and (so his wife had often bragged) an astonishing lover and also (as I knew from my own experience) an inventive and poetic story-teller.

I spoke a prayer for the dead, and then I called my loyal cathary over to me, and I stroked the creature's mane and kissed its snout with genuine fondness.

Then I took out my second largest dagger and slit the beast's throat, and stood back as blood spouted from her slit artery. Her knees buckled, and she sank to the ground, staring at me; and then she died.

I regretted the death. But I dared not leave the creature here, where it would, as hunger assailed it, be bound to feed upon the corpses of the dead. That would be a sacrilege; the carrion birds could and would do their worst, but no cathary should ever eat the flesh of a Maxolu.

The ground shook beneath me.

I was startled, and almost lost my balance. I looked up, and saw the skies were black.

A distance-missile and skycraft battle was in progress, I deduced, above and inside the city, which I estimated was 234,333 paces away from my current position. The missiles that were being dropped on the city must be enormous, because they were sending shudders along the planet's crust. And clouds of black smoke were now billowing in the sky to the northeast of me, a clear indication that high toxicity weapons of some kind were being employed.

I muttered a subvocal prayer to release the hidden doors of

the skycraft hangar; and stood back as the sands shuddered, and parted, and the skycraft deck was exposed.

But at that moment a sandstorm sprang up, with an abruptness that shocked even me, and I was flung upwards and backwards, and battered with sharp grains of red sand. I rolled over, letting my body go loose to avoid injury, then clambered to my feet and ducked down low with my back arched and my hands clutching my knees; and tried to walk towards the hangar. But the blasts of the gale were too strong, and I was once again snatched up by the teeth of the snarling wind and sent tumbling like a broken shrub-branch along the desert dunes.

Finally, I managed to hook my wrist-grapple to a deeply buried rock, and my flight was halted. I turned over and lay face up as if I had been staked to the sand to die. A streak of lightning shot across the sky above me, like a three-pronged spear. The clouds were bright silver moons now, as countless missiles exploded in mid-air and seared their softness with angry flares. The ground shook again.

Was this, I wondered, the end of me? Was Sharrock finally, after all his many adventures and countless terrifying brushes with angry death, to be defeated?

No, I thought.

Never!

I waited until there was a brief lull in the battering gale, then I detached my grapple and crawled on my belly over the sand, my eyes shut tight as the wind ripped at me with dagger-stabs of blinding pain. I felt as if I were climbing up a high mountain made of turbulent seas, as the soft sand moved beneath me and the wind tried to tear the skin off my body.

The world above was red whirled sand; and the ground below was treacherous liquid-softness; and thunder roared; and my veins could feel the pulse of electricity in the air as the lightning flared.

And I dug deep into my soul, until I touched that part of me that will never *ever* be defeated; and I crawled, and crawled, into the sharp teeth of the savage spitting storm.

Eventually, I reached the dip in the sand that marked the hangar deck's opening, and I tipped myself over and fell downwards into the sand mountain, and slowly slid to the bottom. I was now entirely buried in sand, with grains in my nostrils and ears and eyes and no way to see. But the sand was slitheringly soft, and I was able to slide my way through it, not breathing, and not opening my mouth or nostrils for fear of suffocating on sand-grains. It took me thirty minutes, almost to the limit of my lungs' capacity, before I reached the side of the hangar bay, guided throughout by my infallible sense of direction and mental map of the hangar area that allowed me to "see" precisely where I was without the use of eyes.

Once I had touched the wall, I fumbled with my hand until I found the clicker that turned on the hangar's fans; and then I clicked it.

And I was now *inside* a sandstorm, clinging on to a rail like a cathary-breaker clutching his mount's silky mane as a tornado of red sand grains rose up and around me and then flew upwards into the sky like a comet.

And when the world was clear again, I coughed like a dying beast, and tried to spit but my mouth was too dry. The fans continued to whirr, creating a single oasis of calm air within the swirling sand all around. And I opened the store cupboard and clad myself in armour, slipping into the soft but impregnable bodyweave that yielded to my body's every muscled contour, and fitting the black mask tightly on my face so that I became a shadow with no visible eyes. Then I chose the fastest of the fighter jets that were parked on the deck inside invisible-wall overcoats; shut down the invisible-wall with a signal from my pakla; and clambered in.

I sat in the cockpit, buckled up, and spoke the silent prayer that would tell any friendly pilots or skycraft controllers nearby that my craft should be accorded urgent passage.

Then I started up the skycraft's engines and it bucked instantly upwards, then soared effortlessly into the air like a stone hurled by a warrior up at the moon. I flew over the massacre site, hovering above the mounds of the dead below me, and wondered if I should use a missile or an energy-beam to burn the rest of the flesh off the corpses' bones.

But that might, it occurred to me, attract the attention of the enemy. I did not even dare to send a message from my pakla to the city with news of the massacre, for fear it would be intercepted and used to home in on my position. No, I would have to deliver my message in person.

I switched my engines on to full and the skycraft ceased hovering and leaped forward through the air like a wild maral pouncing and snatching a bannet from the sky before swiftly fleeing its victim's brutal mates.

The speed-weight crushed me to my seat. And as I flew, I had a moment of reflection on what I had lost; my friends, my village, and my two deep and abiding true loves: Malisha, my wife, so truthful, so funny, and so passionately loving. And Sharil, my daughter, three years old, sweet, and mischievous, cursed with my own dark roguish features, yet blessed—nay thrice-blessed!—with her mother's beauty and wit, and radiant smile.

For a moment, I recalled these two and I felt their presences.

And for a longer moment still I was appalled at their evermore absences.

But then I had no more time to mourn.

I took the plane up high, out of the atmosphere, until I could see the cratered pockmarks of our purple moon and the unmistakable towers of our lunar city. But I realised that the towers had all fallen, and the moon was pock-marked a thousand times more than usual. Then I banked and ripped downwards through the sky of Madagorian, and proceeded at a fast diagonal towards the capital city, Kubala.

Then I saw it.

It was one of the enemy's skycraft, without a doubt. A vessel larger than a battle-plane, and bizarrely coloured in varying hues, and shaped, extraordinarily, like the stem of a harasi tree. It was invisible to my matter-sensors, and the dazzling sunlight on the hull made it opaque to ordinary vision too. But the faint heat emanating from the craft was clearly visible to me through my enhanced-vision mask-eyes.

I smiled, in anticipation of vengeful victory, and launched my missiles.

Then my craft kinked, in a savagely fast manoeuvre that was designed to avoid any return missile fire.

The Philosophers had dreamed the single-seat skycraft to be winged creatures that embodied air and speed and grace; they were to be supple beautiful flying-machines that merged with the minds of their pilot, so that flesh and machinery beat with a single heart. And our warrior-scientists had followed the Philosophers' dreams precisely and with unmatchable skill.

And so my craft, a tiny dot in the air, was now as much sky as sky-plane; it was a bird and a cloud and a raindrop; and yet it was also a killing machine with near unquenchable reserves of bombs and missiles and devastatingly powerful fast-fire guns.

And my sky-craft had another eerie power; it was able to change direction abruptly and swiftly without the effects being felt by the Maxolu warrior in the cockpit. So that when I piloted the plane, I could fly faster and more unpredictably than any bird that had ever lived.

I and the plane-that-was-part-of-me skidded across the sky, and reversed and looped, and plunged towards the ground, and recovered from the plunge, and accelerated at a speed so near to light that time itself, as measured by the skycraft's clock, very near stood still.

All the missiles achieved direct hits, for my aim was unerring; but the enemy vessel clearly had some kind of protective invisible-wall, so the explosions splashed harmlessly off its hull.

Then I flew beneath the enemy ship and extended my craft's nose spike and I flew directly *into* the other craft. The spike penetrated the hull, and I fired a fusillade of delayed action missiles into the vessel, then snapped the spike, and flew like the heel of a skate upon ice across the blue sky and watched.

The enemy battle-ship jerked out of control as the bombs exploded inside it. It veered wildly from side to side, then started to fall from the sky.

Then it vanished.

And reappeared behind me and I saw it through my all-around mask-eyes and I fired a hail of burning gas through the rear of my craft and saw flames burn the enemy's hull, and was once more dancing around the sky.

The enemy ship was billowing steam from side vents now, a clear sign that there were fires within and its hull was compromised. It fired a battery of projectiles and energy streams towards me, but my dancing pinprick of a fighter craft eluded them all.

The enemy's huge battle ship was faced with a single-Maxolu skycraft, and it was losing. I felt a surge of triumph.

And then I saw that the enemy vessel was descending, and landing. It burned the grass in a field and touched down with no jolt, and the side of the craft opened up and I saw far below me—in the image magnified by my mask-eyes—a single figure step out.

I increased the magnification on my eyes still further; and was surprised to see that the figure emerging from the ship was a female warrior carrying a sword. Was this a challenge?

The enemy battleship lifted into the air once more and flew off. The warrior remained, alone, on the ground. The message was clear: a one-on-one combat was being proposed.

I plunged downwards, with a jolt of joy that was like falling off a cliff, and landed my craft on the seared grass. I knew this might be an ambush, but I had to take the risk. For according to the laws of my world, any battle and war can be decided by single combat, no matter what the sizes of the respective armies. But now I wondered: would these enemy warriors hold to such values?

For I had, of course, realised by now these were no ordinary warriors; they came from elsewhere, from some other planet around some other star that existed far away in the universe of stars that encircled us at night.

My enemy were aliens, and they had invaded my world.

I stepped out of my craft. I removed my mask, so I could taste the cold morning air on my cheeks, and shook my long hair. Then I took my sword and scabbard out of the cockpit-pouch, strapped it over my back, and walked calmly towards the alien warrior.

The warrior was female, as I had already seen. But, close up, she looked like no female I had ever before beheld. She had fangs, like an animal, which protruded from her mouth; and no ear-flaps. In the centre of her forehead was a third eye. She was large—twice as large as myself—and powerfully muscled. And she wore no body armour but was clad in tight bright yellow animal-hides that left her legs and stomach and arms bare. Her hair was bright scarlet and streaked with silver and blew in the wind. And her skin was pale, more white than red, and entirely lacking in soft ridges.

The contrast in our sizes was almost comical; I was a dwarf beside this giant. She was without doubt a magnificent specimen of her species, warily graceful, with bulging shoulders and arms and stocky legs. And there was a steely look in her eyes that assured me she knew well the bitterness and the joy of combat.

I stared up at her appraisingly and without hate; for hate will slow the warrior's hand and eye. "What tribe are you?" I asked.

"You do not know my tribe," the warrior replied, in a husky low voice that made my flesh tingle with the eerie unfamiliarity of its tone.

"What is your name?" I continued, patiently.

"Zala," said the warrior. "And yours?"

And she stared at me impassively, unafraid to meet my eyes.

"I am," I said proudly, "Sharrock."

She stared at me, unimpressed.

Hiding my disappointment at her lack of response to my, by

all objective criteria, legendary name, I added: "You are, I take it, not from our lands."

"I am not."

"Tell me then, whence do you come?"

She was still staring into my eyes; shamelessly, and in my view arrogantly. I felt a flash of rage and stifled it.

I would kill her first; and *then* I would savour my wrath.

"Far away," she said, in what sounded to me like sad tones. "Another planet, around another star."

"As I had suspected," I told her, formally. "For your ship is like nothing I have ever seen. Your appearance is hideous and strange. You are an alien."

"In your terms, I am."

"Why do you wage war upon us, you whore-fucking, turd-eating monster from afar?" I asked her, with ritual invective.

She laughed.

"Answer my question, o withered-hole!" I insisted, and she laughed again.

"We come," she said with open mockery, "o pathetic-male-with-a-tiny-prick-that-I-will-eat-and-feed-in-morsels-to-my-female-lover in order to conquer and destroy you."

"Why?" I said, stung at her unfamiliar insult.

"Why not?" said Zala the female warrior, tauntingly.

Once again I had to bite back my rage; for I truly despised this warrior's lack of respect for tradition. Her people's war with my people should not have been fought like this! A formal declaration should have been made, and hence due warning given; poems should have been spoken, songs composed, regrets expressed. All this should have been done, to create a war that would have been ennobling for all concerned.

Instead, they had simply ambushed our valiant warriors, massacred our defenceless families and Philosophers, and left them all to rot.

"Which planet do you come from, you tainted-by-vulgarity-and-laughed-at-by-small-children shit-covered harlot?" I said.

She grinned, clearly amused by our social ritual of rhetorical abuse. "It has a name," she said casually. "You will not know it. It is far away. Your astronomers will never have seen it. All you need to know is I am a warrior of a once great world. Will you fight me?"

"I will."

"If I kill you, your world is forfeit," the alien warrior said arrogantly.

"Very well," I said calmly. "And if I kill *you*?"

"That won't happen," said the alien warrior Zala and she lunged forward with her long curved sword, the hilt clutched in both her hands.

I dodged easily and drew my sword from its scabbard on my back with one hand and swung it fast at her and she recoiled and barely dodged it, then I wove forwards to the left and then to the right, ducking and rising in a single flow, then thrust the tip of the sword towards her bare midriff. But she leaped in the air and danced on the flat of my blade and kicked my head and somersaulted over me then plunged her sword back and over her own head at me, without turning around.

I was awed at her speed, but evaded the blow and swept my own blade a thousand times in the air in a series of continuous movements. Zala countered each sword-strike with a speed that impressed me, for we were both fighting faster than the beatings of a baro bird's wings.

But I was stronger, and the next time she leaped in the air I leaped high too and clutched at her face with my fingers and plucked out one of her eyes.

We both landed, swords held upright and clashed steel once again. Blood dribbled out of her empty eye-hole. Her face was a cold mask of hate. I felt a surge of joy; this was glorious combat.

Then her blade went through my heart and I exulted, and with my dagger I sliced off her hand at the wrist and stepped back. I grunted in pain, and also in delight. For her severed hand and blade were now trapped in my chest, with the tip of her sword protruding from my back. But my second heart was easily able to sustain my body. And now the alien was fighting swordless and one handed, with scarlet blood gushing from the bloody stump of her right arm.

But Zala just laughed and drew her second sword, and I lunged again and she dodged and stabbed my leg and so I butted her face and swung my own weapon in a rolling pattern of cuts that shook sparks from her blade. Then with my left hand I stabbed once more with my dagger and slashed at her throat so powerfully it severed her head, and the head fell off her body and bounced on to the sands.

And I paused, and for a moment allowed myself to relax; but her head continued to laugh.

I was shocked at this; then I realised that the head must have its own blood supply. And, too, the headless torso was still holding its sword and was undeterred by the loss of its head; with speed and bravado it leaped at me and carried on fighting, blind yet unerringly accurate in its sword strikes.

I was on the defensive now; the headless torso had renewed strength and was able to somehow perceive where my body was and even anticipate my moves in ways I could not fathom. And all the while the head on the sand laughed, as its body fought me; and I forced myself to ignore the absurdity of it all and lost myself in battle-lust until my blade swept down and rent the warrior's body in two.

The two halves of the alien warrior's torso twitched on the sand, blood gushing, organs spilling out. The battle was over; or so I thought.

But then the right half of the warrior lifted its sword again, and tried to stand up. And the left half of the warrior drew a knife and rolled in the sands, trying to get upright with only one foot.

The warrior was still not dead. Still not dead!

I brought my sword down and split the head into two halves. Blood splashed, and I could see the grey folds of the creature's brain. Her tongue was split in two, but her two separated eyes were staring at me and still she was laughing, even though it was a gurgle and not a real laugh.

"Die you devilish fucker-of-evil monster!" I screamed.

The two halves of the head spluttered with delight.

I lowered my sword. I was defeated; no matter what I did, I could never kill this creature.

"What will happen now?" I asked. But the sundered head could no longer speak. And there was, I felt, sadness in her remaining eyes.

And at that point, Zala's head started to shimmer before me, and I realised I could see through her face and sundered smile to the sands behind. Then her head slowly vanished, and her body too, like mist dissipating in the morning heat.

I marvelled at this magic. What powers did these creatures have? And what utter, taunting, disgusting malice. This was not war, it was mockery.

I looked around.

The alien battle ship had not returned. And in the distance, a false bright red dawn on the horizon revealed that the city itself was ablaze.

And I saw that the sky above me was now black with single-Maxolu fighting craft; but they weren't fighting, they were just spiralling aimlessly. There was no battle being fought, merely the sad savouring of abject defeat. I had a sinking feeling of despair.

The ground below me shook again. But these weren't bombs exploding in the distance; this was an earthquake.

And I realised that the sand beneath me was hot; my feet were seared with heat through my boots. I cleaned the blood off my sword and dagger, then sheathed them.

The ground shook again. I braced myself.

Then the ground erupted. The sand was scattered into the air and the rock below was exposed, and it split before my eyes, and red liquid lava poured out of the rents. The earth's hot crust was erupting out of the ground directly beneath me.

And at the same time lightning once more ripped across the sky, vast forked bolts that stabbed the air and made it scream.

And a loud roaring sound filled my ears, and then a wind sprang up from nowhere and knocked me off my feet. I staggered upright and saw hot volcano-spew rolling towards me like tides in a raging ocean. The sky was empty now, all the Maxolu craft had been obliterated by the savage winds. The air itself shimmered with heat, as if it were ablaze; and hail rained down on me and burned my face.

I knew now that my world was dying and there was nothing I could do to save it.

A river of lava flowed fast towards me, and engulfed my knees and thighs, and burned off my trousers and boots and the flesh of my legs and arse beneath, and I tasted ash and my own blood as I accidentally bit my tongue. My skin was hot and my body hair was sparking, and waves of heat oppressed me like a pillow used to suffocate a convicted coward.

I howled in despair. I could not run, or move in any way. My legs were ablaze, the flesh was turning molten.

Then the red-hot volcano-spew engulfed me, up to the chest, then up almost to my neck. I thought about my wife, Malisha, and my baby girl, Sharil. And I mourned their deaths, as my tough flesh began to burn, and my bones were seared with heat, and my eyes stung with ash that turned my tears into hailstones.

Sharrock defeated? I wondered.

Never! I vowed. But in my heart I knew I was doomed.

And then—

BOOK 2

Jak

My name is Jak. I was, once, a Trader.

And this is my story.

The green-hided soldiers led Cantrell and myself through dark moist corridors of rock until we emerged into the FanTang Council Chamber.

The Chamber was high-ceilinged and awesome; it was a huge hall set within a cavern hewn out of a mountain. Its white marble walls were inlaid richly with gold and silver and precious stones, and the pillars and pilasters were decorated with bas-reliefs carved with remarkable delicacy and beauty, notwithstanding their brutal content.

The air was toxic, a blend of oxygen and gaseous cyanide, and I breathed in deep draughts, savouring the thrill of inhaling certain death with no actual peril. Cantrell stared at me sourly.

"Let me do the talking," I said.

"Here they come," said Cantrell.

The FanTang leader stepped up before us. He was at least a basal taller and broader than the other FanTangs we had met. His green porcupine hide was ridged with spikes, and he had glittering eyes on every part of his body except his head.

"Ears?" I whispered.

"That was covered in the briefing," snarled Cantrell.

"I wasn't listening. Ears?"

Cantrell sighed. "Where your girlfriend's nipples are, those are its ears."

And so I stared at the monster's nipples; they were as sharp as a dagger's point. I counted six of them; and I wondered, idly, if this creature's aural organs could also lactate.

Then I lowered my head, and scraped my right foot on the ground five times, the FanTang ritual for greeting.

"You did hear *some* of the briefing then," Cantrell hissed.

I cast him a brief but brilliant smile; then looked at the FanTang leader, lowered my head, and scraped my foot on the ground five times once more. Hello, *again.*

But the FanTang leader did not move. His three advisers did not move either. They glared fiercely with body-eyes that appeared to be made of glass; and their open mouths dripped saliva through fangs on to the cavern floor. And I noticed that the spikes upon the bodily carapace of the FanTang leader were stained with what looked like red-celled blood.

"We wish you to hear us," I said, in fluent FanTang, and the FanTang leader's glassy eyes all blinked, in unison.

I took the translating pads out of my sack—having reached the limits of my idiomatic FanTangian—and knelt, then crawled on my hands and knees to the FanTang leader. I held out the translating pads.

The giant FanTang took the pads.

I touched my own chest with my hands. The FanTang copied the gesture and the adhesive pads gripped his breasts and then the listening pads were in place.

"We wish you to hear us," I said, in Olaran, which was then translated into the FanTang's language by the listening pads.

"Can you in fact hear and comprehend us?" I said.

The FanTang leader was still. "I can hear," he said in his own language, and the translator did its job, and I heard the worlds in Olaran.

I crawled back on my hands and knees to rejoin Cantrell.

"Mission accomplished," I said grinning.

"How does this work?" the FanTang leader asked, querulously.

"It's a translator," I explained. "It translates."

"We have seen this device before," said the FanTang leader. "You sent swamp-wolves into our camps and they spat these things on to our bodies and the wolves howled at us and we understood them and marvelled, and then we slew them."

"And what did they say?" Cantrell asked, dryly.

"Don't," the FanTang leader admitted, "Kill. Us."

Cantrell sighed, disapprovingly, and the translator turned the sigh into words: "[Disapproving exhalation.]"

The Fan Tang leader was startled.

"We sent the swamp-wolves," I explained smoothly, "to prepare the way. We know that you are afraid of us."

"We are not afraid of you!" roared the FanTang leader.

"We come from deepest space, in ships that spit fire, and you are right to be wary of us," I said diplomatically.

"We are not wary of you!"

"You blew up," I said impatiently, "all our scout ships with your nuclear missiles. In our culture, that counts as 'wary.' "

"Wary, perhaps," conceded the FanTang leader, "but not afraid."

"Our ships were piloted by robots," I said. "Non-living creatures, not alive. You did us no harm. We bear you no grudge."

"You are our enemy, it is therefore your duty to hate and destroy us," the FanTang leader rebuked me.

It was by now apparent that these creatures were small-minded, ignorant, bloodthirsty savages; nonetheless, I persevered.

"We are not your enemy, we are your friends," I said, as carefully and clearly as I was able. "We come not to fight war, but to make peace. We do not wish to conquer, we wish to trade."

"What," said the FanTang leader, "is this word 'peace'? And what is 'trade'?"

"Peace is the opposite of war."

"Surrender is the opposite of war," the FanTang leader explained.

"No, not-fighting is the opposite of war," I said. "Collaborating. Being-friends-ing. Concord. Not killing each other."

"These parent-fucking monsters have *no* fucking idea," Cantrell muttered sourly.

The FanTang leader roared, but in a cheerful way; I realised it was a laugh. "Parent-fucking, that is a good phrase. We can adopt that in our own language," the FanTang leader said gleefully.

"Trade means we give you what you want, you give *us* what *we* want."

"We want your deaths," said the FanTang leader, and took out a stick that was tied to his belt, and shook the stick so it became a sword, and struck off my head.

{I woke, in agony. I forced myself back down on to my couch.}

"That won't help you," Cantrell said mildly.

Blood poured out of my neck-stump; I made it congeal. My heart stopped beating; I made it beat again. I opened my eyes and found I was on the floor staring up at an odd angle at the entourage of green, angry, aristocratic FanTangs.

"We come in peace," my head said mildly.

The FanTang leader jerked in shock.

My torso sat up. My hands picked up my head and put it back on my bloody shoulders. The broken blood vessels rejoined; the neck healed, leaving an ugly scar. I stood up.

"You can survive the loss of a head," said the FanTang leader, marvelling.

"Can't you?" I said, mockingly, and took out my ray gun and fired it, a flech to the right of the FanTang leader's skull-protrusion.

A chunk of the marble column behind the monster vaporised, with a sharp hiss. I fired again, and the rock-table vanished. I fired a third time, at the feet of the FanTang leader's monsterly advisors, and a hole appeared in the ground beneath them and they leaped for safety.

("Good shooting," murmured Cantrell.)

"If we fought a war," I explained gently to the FanTang leader, "you would lose."

"Yeah! You parent-fucking bastards!" added Cantrell, viciously.

The FanTang leader emitted a sad, pathetic howl. He looked around helplessly. "I am humiliated," he said, feebly.

"Not so," I said calmly, and handed the monster the ray gun. "Look. A gesture of trust. We come in peace. Here is my magic weapon. I give it to you to show that I trust you. We come in peace, which is not-war, which is better than war, which is—"

("Quit while you're ahead," murmured Cantrell.)

"All we want to do, you see," I said patiently, to this savage green-hided brute with skin like lava and no control whatsoever of its salivary glands, "is trade."

"You give me your weapon!" said the FanTang leader, marvelling, holding the ray gun as if it were a—well, as if it were a deadly weapon of extra-FanTangian origin that had just been given to him as an unexpected present. "That shows much respect! And trust. And—"

He pressed the button on the side, and the gun fired.

"And folly!" the FanTang leader roared, delighted by his own rhetoric.

The blast ripped me into pieces; I flew through the air and landed in fragments, and my blood gushed on to the floor messily.

Then the monster pointed the ray gun at Cantrell, and fired again.

[I woke, in agony again. I took a moment to recover my wits. All was going according to plan.]

I returned into my shadow body. It was a perfect simulacrum of my real body, accessible to all the senses including touch. But it was, at the end of the day, no more than a computer simulation, which I could easily control with the power of my thought.

And so this time I allowed my pools of blood to coagulate and merge until they stood upright and formed a human silhouette. My severed limbs slicked across the floor and reformed and rejoined, and my arms then placed my head back on my body, until I stood before the monsters as a flaccid blood-emptied sac of skin. Then I opened my mouth...

...and I drank my own blood-silhouette, like a squelched fruit travelling backwards in time; and resumed my normal shape.

Beside me Cantrell did the same. The two of us tottered on wobbly legs, regaining our balance, then stared as terrifyingly as we could at the FanTang leader and his associates.

"We ask you to surrender," I said, using the only relevant term this creature seemed to grasp.

The FanTang leader gaped; the flow of saliva became a flood; and I screamed: "SURRENDER PARENT-FUCKER OR YOU DIE!" while beside me, Cantrell grinned approvingly.

"I surrender, o mighty one," said the FanTang leader humbly, and cravenly.

"We ask for your sword, you defeated and abject, um, defeated creature," I demanded; and the FanTang leader took his sword from his belt, and shook it until the blade grew and gleamed, then handed it to me, hilt uppermost.

I hefted the sword. It was light, but powerful. I guessed that small-worlds technology was involved. This was, despite the aliens' brutality and grotesque salivation, a pretty sophisticated culture.

"We ask for, nay, we demand, your life," I said, with what I felt was considerable aplomb; and I swung the sword and lopped off the FanTang leader's head.

The creature roared, and fell to the ground and died in evident agony, green blood spouting from its head-less torso; while the head itself rolled slowly across the cavern floor until it hit a wall.

"We now offer the hand of friendship," I said, icily, to the surviving FanTangs. "Rebuff us again, and you will all die." The FanTang advisers bowed their heads, in a clear gesture of submission, clearly reassured that I was finally talking their language.

"How do we," one of the advisers said humbly, "trade?"

[Back in my simulacrum-tank, I grinned.]

My shadow-self, stained with splashed blood, bent and twisted where my body hadn't properly reformed, still managed to retain its customary dignified demeanour.

"I shall," I said coolly, "explain."

"Come on, stretch," said Averil sternly.

After five days in the simulacrum tank, I was stiff and muscle-wasted and yearned to lie down and die. But I pushed myself hard, stretching my leg muscles, shaking out my shoulder muscles, and turning my head — with a satisfying crack of my neck vertebrae — in a perfect circle, to get it nicely limber.

"Swivel those hips," Averil ordered, and I swivelled my hips so that my groin exchanged places with my arse, and vice versa.

"And back!"

I swivelled my hips swiftly back to their normal position, and blinked, seeing stars.

"Floor jumps!" I dropped to the ground, pushed up and down, jumped into the air, and made an X shape with my arms and legs.

"Hold!"

I held my position, hovering in mid-air, breathing through my diaphragm to keep my air-sacs inflated.

"And land."

I landed.

Sweat bathed my muscular body now, and I could see that there was a sparkle in Averil's eyes. She was an exhilaratingly intelligent woman, squat and powerful, with a shrewdness in her features that made my heart skip.

"Run on the spot."

I began running on the spot, my legs arcing high with each pace, and Averil followed suit. We ran side by side to nowhere, with an effortless stride.

I could see the dampness of her strong shoulders. I could see her muscles moving beneath her smooth skin as she ran. I knew her game, and I was enjoying it.

"Okay, stop," said Averil, "and rub down."

I grabbed her, and touched her all over with my hands.

"Rub *yourself* down, I meant!" she said laughing.

I kissed her lips. My tongue flicked into her mouth.

"Not here, there are cameras," she protested, mildly, kissing back.

"I disconnected them."

"You disconnected them huh?"

"On the offchance."

"On the offchance of what?"

"On the offchance of this."

I fumbled with her leotard, slipped the catch, and it fell away from her body. She was naked, her body was hot and flushed and soft. I kissed her breasts, then put my hand between her legs and touched her sex, its hardness and softness, and its pulsing heart. I slipped out of my own leotard and stood before her naked; and with her gentle fingers and warm palm she caressed both of my erect cocks.

"Yes!" she moaned as I entered her, and then she screamed, and her body gripped me, and her muscles squeezed me, and her kisses dampened my cheeks.

"I love you," I murmured, gently, as her passion grew, and she screamed, and swore, and her body bucked and spasmed until finally she came, with adorable violence.

Averil lay panting in my arms. And I savoured the pleasure, the unique joy, of being able to liberate *her* joy.

"That was fabulous," she conceded.

I smiled. I had made my female happy.

I was content.

"Let me see," said Chief Trader Mohun, and I opened the casket.

"Jewels," I said, passing over an elaborate chain embedded

with precious stones and tiny golden ingots carved with complex shapes and soft white things that looked to me like the teeth of FanTang infants, though I chose not to enquire too deeply.

"Fabrics," I added, and passed over a sheet of softest silk, made from the webs of Blaga-sized creatures called Shibbols who were kept in underground FanTang farms where they wallowed in excrement and never saw the light of day.

"Weapons," I concluded, and showed Mohun a selection of swords, axes, knives, bolas, hurlable metal spikes and throwing darts, all moulded and carved with impeccable artistry.

"We can sell these to the Kala," Mohun said, beaming, for avarice was the candle that lit his soul. "They love weaponry of all of the sharp, nasty and stabby varieties. And body parts, too of course."

"I know," I said, smiling nostalgically. "I've seen—"

"You've seen their diamond eyes?"

"I've sold their diamond eyes. Wrested from the corpses of slaughtered Banzoi. They are, indeed, beautiful artefacts; eyeballs that can be worn as jewellery."

"I like the Kala," said Mohun, thoughtfully.

"They are indeed," I concurred, "easily duped, and often overpay by huge margins."

"And what's this?" Mohun said, inspecting the air-image of an evil-looking body-ridged monster with hundreds of dead staring eyes and skin like food that had been hidden and forgotten about centuries ago.

"The FanTang mummify their dead."

"Ah," said Mohun delightedly, as if I had bathed him in Magola oil with soft hands that had never known a hard day's work.

"They use a kind of resin that turns decaying flesh into, well, decaying flesh that doesn't actually smell. The effect is striking. A perfect ornament for the hallway or courtyard."

"Perfect! They'll sell their mummies to us?"

"Not willingly."

"But we have small print that will cover it?"

"Our print," I assured him, "is so small that microbes can make necklaces of our Os."

"And what do they want in return?"

"Wealth, power, and the ability to smite their enemies and conquer the universe."

Mohun roared with laughter. "Predictable. What can we actually give them?"

"I think they'll settle for technology that will allow them to geo-engineer the other planets in their system."

"We can offer that," Mohun conceded.

"And they also want access to our shadow-self technology."

"Also not a problem."

"And they've guessed we have a way of travelling instantly through space. They want us to teach their scholars the essence of rift theory."

"Out of the question."

"That's what I thought. How about showing them how to teleport?"

"Yeah, I guess we can do that," said Trader Mohun, with a sly smile.

"Good," I said, riffling mentally through my notes. "Their animals are edible to Type 430s. Their plants are delicious, apparently, if you have a second stomach."

"All very satisfying," said Mohun. "We'll set up a trading post. Have you signed the contracts with them?"

I shook my head. "Not yet; give me a few days more."

"I have every faith in you, Trader Jak. A drink?" said Mohun.

"Always," I avowed. Mohun poured two thimbles of rich-juice. We sniffed, then swallowed, then slammed; and I felt a familiar pin-prick in my eyes and a pounding in my brain.

We each took a deep breath, as the rich-juice entered our brains and sent our thoughts into violent paroxysm.

And then tranquillity descended upon us. Our moods became mellow. And we engaged, for a quarter hour or more, in chit-chat about our favourite colours and textures and smells; and reminisced about the soft touch of Madyouran silk upon one's body, and the tenderness of the Laumarax star-flower, and other such memories.

"They are, the FanTangs I mean, an appalling species in many ways," I told Mohun. "Violent. Warmongering. Scornful of other species. And yet all the indications are that they will honour a deal; and, with sufficient intimidation from us, will refrain from trespassing on other planets in the Olaran Trading Zone."

"And if they don't?"

"Oh the usual precautions," I said. "One cannot be too careful."

The celebration banquet was, as one would expect from a Trading Fleet as sophisticated and cultured as our own, magnificent.

It was held in the Banqueting Dome of the Court Ship, a glass-shelled room which offered a spectacular view of the stars around us.

I wore my Fogan life robe, made of silk from the finest queen Fogan-spiderbirds. The robe had once been a shawl that was wrapped around the new-born me; at which time it bonded with my spirit so it would always be perfectly attuned to my moods.

Tonight the robe was cheerfully scarlet and blue and bejewelled and dazzling, and swept behind me as I walked. I wore a tight tunic over my muscled torso and my legs and arms were wrapped in wool plucked from young Mantrian Shaals.

"You look wonderful," said Averil, who wore a rich pure-white Drax-hide gown, her hair pinned back to highlight the smoothness of her high forehead. Slyly I ogled her acuity; she was indeed sublime.

"Kiss my lips," I requested, and she did; my lips were lightly coated in electrically-charged jewel dust and sent sparks into her tongue. Beneath my robe, my entire body was coated in the same dust, which kept me in a permanent state of sensual excitation.

"A good day's trading," said Chief Trader Mohun, as he ushered me to my seat at the banquet table. I admired the arrangement of the dishes—a thousand tiny portions in a pyramid that hovered above the table. As each course was eaten, the pyramid would re-form into ever more appealing new shapes.

I sat, and looked around, admiring the beauty of my fellow Traders and the majesty and understated authority of the assembled Mistresses of the Fleet.

However to my dismay I saw that there were—seated directly opposite me, like black thunderclouds in a clear blue sky—two grim-faced Space Explorers. Dressed in drab grey synthetic-fabric tunics with no bodily or facial adornments and not a trace of, well, *finesse.* The younger one was pretty enough—though hardly beautiful by the standards of the Court Ship—but his companion was old and bald with eyes like black holes. This wizened old spacefarer had skin like withered hide, and a scowl that made me shudder. I conjured up my most charming smile, and vowed to never let myself become so decrepit.

"I am Trader Jak Dural," I said to the Space Explorers, "and it is an honour to encounter such famed adventurers; I've read so much of your exploits."

The old one glared; the younger one beamed.

"Do you even know," the older one said, "who we are?"

"It's on the tip of my tongue," I said sweetly, checking my factology via murmur-link.

"I am Morval, once I was Assistant Chief Trader to the Empress," said the one whose name, I now knew, was Morval.

"I recall your name; the honour is all mine," I replied.

Morval! One of the most legendary arseholes in the history of the Olaran Home Court!

"My name is Phylas," said his young companion, and flicked his tongue so I could see he did at least have a jewelled stud embedded in it.

"You have, I take it, been many years in the wastelands of space?" I asked.

"That's what we do," said Morval grimly.

"I'm hoping," added Phylas, "for advancement into the Trader Fleet one day."

"Once your suspended sentence has lapsed," added Morval, cattily, though it was hardly a surprise to me; only the old and the criminally disgraced would serve with the Explorers.

"Is it a crime I would have heard of?" I asked brightly.

Phylas scowled, and his youthful good looks were marred. "Forgery of alien artefacts."

"Skilfully executed?"

"Apparently not."

"Then you deserve," I said, uncharitably, "everything you got."

"I gather," said Morval, "that the negotiations with wretched FanTang have been successful?" He had, I noted approvingly, changed the conversation with some degree of tact.

"Early days," I said modestly. And Morval grunted, with open scorn.

"This system was one of my most appalling missions," Phylas admitted. "I found it . . . well, appalling in many ways."

"They boiled us alive," Morval informed me. "Or rather, our simulacras. It was a test of course. When we survived, they agreed to meet our trading team."

"They're a monstrous species," I agreed.

"Cruel," said Morval.

"Treacherous," added Phylas.

"Vicious," clarified Morval.

"Barbaric," muttered Phylas, further clarifying what did not need to be further clarified; I realised these two had spent a great deal of time together in deep space.

"Bloodthirsty," Morval countered.

"How," Phylas burst out, "can you do business with monsters like these?"

I was amused at his naïvety. "What would you rather do?"

"Isolate them!"

"Then they'll never," I pointed out, "improve."

"Ah," said Phylas, the light of insight in his eyes. "So we're really using trade as a way of making barbaric civilisations more... civilised."

"Define civilised," I said coolly.

"Not eating your young, or enslaving a rival sentient species."

"Fair definition," I conceded. "But our job is not to conquer, or to manipulate societies."

I sipped my wine, and felt a glow as it slid down my inner throat, then entered my outer throat, and then proceeded downwards into my stomach where I tasted and savoured it again.

"Our job," I explained, "is to make the universe a better place, through the fairer distribution of its treasures and its artefacts of sentient-created beauty."

And I showed them the jewel that hung around my neck; a diamond the size of a Toowit's egg; a gem of the rarest beauty.

"Jewels," said Phylas. "It's all about jewels?"

"Pretty much," I admitted. "Plus fabrics, objects of artistic merit, music, novels, films—mainly, though, jewels."

And I selected and ate my first morsel of food from the aerial display; a crustacean paste spread upon the liver of a snowbird. It was, as I had anticipated, sublime.

The second bottle of wine surpassed the first; it had a rich tang like the bass notes of a stringed larura mingled with the promise of sunshine on a cloudy day.

Indeed, each course was a joy to be savoured a dozen times in each of my taste organs. I gorged myself, and drank until my vision swam. Then I circulated around the table, conversing with a wide variety of Traders and Mistresses and crew.

All agreed the mission looked to be a triumph, and Mohun had already selected the Traders who would remain in the permanent trading post.

Yet, despite the pleasant company, and the sensory epiphanies of the food and the several buckets of alcohol I consumed, I carried a stone in my soul. For whenever I looked at Averil, I saw she was aglow; and I inwardly wept.

When the meal was over, the singing and music began, and the table sank into the floor. Cushions replaced our dining chairs, and some brave souls swayed in time to the rhythm of the tabadrums, moving like birds trapped in viscous air across the sway-floor.

I joined Averil and hugged her hips with my palms, and kissed her temples, and admired the diamond around her neck, which was glowing in time with her heartbeat. It was the pair of my own diamond; the two stones began to glow in synchrony.

"What are you thinking?" Averil asked, playfully.

"About how wonderful you are," I told her.

"Flatterer."

"It's true."

"All males are flatterers."

"And all females are angels."

"Liar."

I smiled. "I worship you, you know that?"

Averil smiled, and picked a fruit from a floating-tray and ate it with a flamboyant swallow. "I know," she said casually, and her hand brushed her hair, drawing my attention to the vastness of her exquisite brow.

And still, she glowed.

The ship's Commander approached us. She too was wearing an exquisite white gown, and exuded effortless authority.

"Congratulations," said Commander Laeris.

"Thank you Commander."

"They're a vile bunch, the FanTangs, aren't they?" the Commander said, laughter in her voice.

"I've rarely seen viler," I smiled.

The Commander kissed Averil on the temples, courteously, and the two of them basked in the joy of being female.

"He's quite a catch," the Commander teased, and Averil burst out laughing, and her skin glowed even more brightly.

And my spirits sank, further than—I have no metaphor for how far they sank—and I felt bleak melancholy sweep over me.

For, you see, honoured listener to my tale, whoever you might be: the females of my species always glow in the hours after passionate, love-filled sexual congress.

And yet I had not fucked Averil since *yesterday.*

Two of the ship's most distinguished females stood on the stage and began to sing, unaccompanied, a melody of eerie beauty. I listened, and watched, wallowing in awe, yet sick with despair.

And I stared at Averil with desperate intensity as she listened to the delightful ditty; rapt and focused, visibly appreciating each tiny nuance; and I marvelled at the lustre of her intellect.

She glanced at me, with an unexpected look of regret. Then her eyes flickered to one side and her glow increased in radiance.

I followed her gaze.

Mohun.

Mohun!

The Chief Trader was a hundred years if he was a day. His face was old as parchment. He was physically fragile. How could she prefer *him?*

I left the Banqueting Dome and walked back to my cabin. I sank into my bed, and wrapped the sheets over my face and mouth and tried to pretend I was hibernating, as my ancestors used to do.

Mohun!

My pain had an echo; for, many years before I met Averil, I had been married to a stunningly intelligent and percipient female. And she too had betrayed me.

My beloved was called Shonia, and I had asked her to be my bride when we were holidaying in the Olaran city of Pandorla, on a narrowboat on the river Kal. Amusingly, she claimed to be shocked by my effrontery in proposing to *her*, and pretended to slap me with rage. However, she misjudged both the distance between us and her own strength, and managed to swipe me off the boat with a single powerful blow. Still laughing, Shonia dived in after me and the two of us swam to shore, followed by the angry curses of the boatman.

We had been equals, back then. Shonia had refused to be bound by convention; and when we married, she allowed me equal rights and status. She had even tried her utmost to give me sexual pleasure, despite the frustrating limitations of our species biology. (We Olaran males, you see, cannot achieve orgasm; it is nature's way of keeping us in our place, as my mother always said.)

For a whole year my soul nearly burst with joy. I believed I was the luckiest Olaran male in all of history; for I was in love, and I knew that the female I loved also loved *me*.

And then one day I had woken to find Shonia asleep and glowing, and I had realised this wasn't my glow. She was connecting, sexually and spiritually, with another.

A month later I received a note from Shonia revoking our marriage, and asking me to leave our family home. I never saw her again. And that's when I signed up for the Trader Fleet. To forget my grief.

Now it had happened for a second time.

And, after this second betrayal, my old grief had returned and merged with my new grief, to create a doubly-grieving knife (a metaphorical knife, I hasten to add, though perhaps I did not need to) that jutted from my soul.

"I beg pardon," I said formally to Averil.

"You are forgiven."

"I have proved an unworthy partner for you," I said.

"Another has proved more worthy," said Averil, concluding the divorce ritual. Then she grinned. "Oh come on Jak—is this really such a big deal?"

"To me it is," I said stiffly.

"In this day and age? Many Olarans don't mate for life any more. We could just be lovers."

"I could not endure that."

"They call them 'fuck-friends.' "

"I could never be that. I love you, Averil."

My words resounded like off-key notes.

"I know you do," she said.

"Then I must leave the Fleet."

"That's your choice."

"I will join the Explorer ship," I threatened.

A wild gamble on my part; it failed utterly.

"Whatever," she replied, casually.

"I could be killed," I pointed out. "It's a dangerous universe. We may never see each other again."

"That's too bad," said Averil in bored tones.

I sighed, forlornly.

"Averil, I shall think of you always," I said, with undimmed ardour.

"No doubt," said Averil pleasantly, "you will."

I packed my possessions into a box. Holos of my parents. A key-ring with all my metal-mind storage files, from childhood on. My identity pass. My bank folder. It was not much, after a life in service. I was well-off, admittedly, but I'd stock-piled no treasure, and I'd never been assigned my own planet. All the money I'd earned at trading, I'd spent on my women. First Shonia, then Averil.

I should have been more cunning, I realised. There were many males who kept their independence by embezzling from their own earnings before passing on their pay to their wives. I had never pursued that route; I was too much of a romantic.

Or, I mused, too much of a fool.

Mohun snorted. "You're throwing your fornicatory life away," he pointed out.

"I care not."

"You have talent."

"What do you care—you betraying son-of-a-slattern!" I sneered.

Mohun forced a smile; but I could tell he was hurt by my words.

"But you are still my friend," I added, and the relief shone in his eyes.

"Listen Jak," he said to me softly. " I cannot deny that your former wife Averil has a truly gorgeous mind and lip-smackingly apt judgement. And I am, of course, privileged to be hers."

"Indeed you are."

"Indeed I am."

Mohun was holding back his tears; and I respected that. For if he had wept, I would undoubtedly have done so too; and we would both have been lost.

"However, I should stress, my dear friend," Mohun continued, "that my love affair with Averil and your consequent humiliation were not my choice, nor my desire."

I nodded, to acknowledge that eternal truth; females choose males.

"I shall never see you again," I said, and walked out of the Chief Trader's cabin, to begin my new life.

BOOK 3

Sai-ias

I felt so very sorry for him.

He was, like all the new ones, angry; and savagely so. And bitter; unreachably so. Possessed by a wild desire to take revenge for what had happened to him and his people; and deranged, too, by grief and sorrow, at the loss of everything he had ever known.

And, as was always the case, he vented these feelings upon *me.*

"You murdering daughter-of-a-pustulent-rapist-who-fucks-whores bitch!" he roared, and then he spat at me, a rich mouthful of acidic spit that stung the soft skin of my face and left a sticky residue on my cheeks.

"You malice-tainted shit-eating-sloshy-farting father-fucker, how could you do it? How could you do it?" he roared, accusingly.

I yearned to touch him, and to soothe his rage; but I knew that my—from his perspective—monstrous appearance made my very presence an ordeal to him.

"Monster! You're uglier-than-a-two-headed-mutant-baby monster!" he angrily told me, as he paced around his confining cabin.

"If you say so," I replied, in the mildest of tones, but that just enraged him all the more.

All in all, my heart burst with sympathy; I knew just how this poor, sad creature felt.

For I had once felt that way myself, many years ago. And I remembered my rage then, and marvelled at its absence now.

"Let me explain to you," I began gently.

"I'm going to fuck you with a spear in your throat and your eyes and arsehole!" he screamed.

"I wouldn't like that," I informed him, "very much."

"Evil-bitch-that-even-a-fat-arsed-Southerner-wouldn't screw! Festering cock-meat!" he screamed, spittle falling from his mouth. He was quite hysterical now, and entirely oblivious to the gentle irony of my last comment.

"Later," I said, kindly. "I will explain it all, later."

"I don't know how you can tolerate that foul-mouthed creature," Fray said to me.

"At least," I said, as tactfully as I could, since Fray was legendary for her indolent refusal to help her fellow captives, "I'm doing something to help the poor unfortunate soul."

"You think so?" sneered Fray, with that tone of hers which implied only a fool would say such a stupid thing.

"I do," I said softly. For it is my self-appointed role: I greet the new ones, teach them the ways of our world; and thus I ease the pain of their transition.

"You sad pathetic arse-sucking beast," Fray said to me, shaking her head bewilderedly. And then she roared, a powerful rising roar that deafened me, a raw hoarse trumpet sound that embodied all her rage, and pain, and grief.

I took a moment to let my hearing return to normal.

"He'll come to terms with it," I said, quietly and sensibly, "the same way we have."

Fray roared again, implying she had by no means come to terms with "it," and the sound made my skin prickle with fear and regret.

I watched the sun go down. It was a beautiful sight. The yellow orb became a red staring eye; its gaze swept slowly across the landscape, shedding a scarlet radiance on the white snow-capped mountains and the calm blue lake. As I watched, ivory clouds were metamorphosing to become daubs of orange upon an orange-black sky.

The richness and beauty of this setting sun effect was, as it was every night, awe-inspiring.

Then the sun was switched off, and pitch-darkness swathed my world. I lit a torch, and its faint beams cut a tiny slice out of the night. It was time to retire to my cabin.

That night I told my cabin friends a long and, in my opinion, delightful story about my mother. She was — or rather had been — a wonderful creature, full of warmth and love, and I had never seen her flustered or angry. (Except of course, at the end, as she embraced me, her only surviving child, in those soul-wrenching minutes before she died.)

And this was the hilarious story of my mother's journey to the seabed to fetch pearls from the jaws of the vast and fearsome kar-fish. It was the day of the tenth anniversary of my birth, and when she arrived at my party, bloodied but triumphant, she was able to shower me with the richest of gifts: black pearls that sang and were warm to the touch; shards of coral-fish-fragments that caught the light like a rainbow; and live seabites that I could hold beneath my tongue, and which made me feel as if I were (as my distant ancestors had been) a lazy seabeast swimming through the oceans, allowing food to drift effortlessly into my mouth.

That was my mother! She'd risked her life to make me happy that day. And such kindness, in my opinion, is a rare and a special thing.

There was gentle applause when I finished my story.

"You loved your mother?" asked Fray.

"I did," I told her.

Fray snorted.

Her species, I knew, had no concept of maternal love. One time Fray had told us, with relish, a story about how Frayskind mothers loved to eat their young; and she'd gone into considerable detail about how enjoyable it was to crunch upon the bones of newborn Frayspawn, and to munch the skulls of toddlers who had, in some unspecified way, been errant. Our response to her tale had been unamused, and indeed hostile.

Fray had, I recalled, been extremely offended at our narrow-mindedness and lack of empathy for her culture's moral values.

I watched the dawn. The sun was a rich and glorious ball of fire, as it always was. And its red rays lit the waters of the lake and made them ripple like flames furiously flickering, as they always did.

I looked at the Tower, standing bleak and eerie on its craggy summit that loomed upon the island at the centre of our world's only lake. And I felt a breeze on my face as the wind was turned on, and the fields of purple grass began to sway.

I drank from the well of life, and it was rich and refreshing, and cold. I tipped the dregs from my cup over my face and felt my black hide moisten.

"You must eat," I told the prisoner softly, for the hundredth time. It is one of the most important things the new ones have to learn; the necessity of eating both regularly and well.

"Eat," I said, but he ignored me.

"Please, I beg you, eat," I implored, but his eyes were blank and he did not move.

Then he turned to me, and his face became a sneer, and once again he spat at me (clearly a gesture of disdain in his culture), and he screamed, with spectacular fury: "Fuck your puckered-arsehole, you soul-stealing fucking bitch!"

And I could tell he yearned to be able to attack me, and mutilate my body, and perhaps even kill me; but he dared not, for my every tentacle was larger than his single torso.

He was, to my eyes, a quaint and tiny creature; very prone to rages, and gifted with an extraordinary breadth of eloquent invective. Most of his insults cast aspersions on aspects of my femininity—for my voice to his ears was unmistakably female—or my inability to practise monogamy, or the size and condition of my sexual organs. Often, he ascribed to me a fondness for eating my own excreta, which in fact I do, so I wasn't too offended by *that* one. And, on other occasions, he indulged himself in vivid fantasies about my demise.

One of his favoured insults, as I recall, was: "May your small-brained children eat your mouldering-fucking-flesh so they can shit it out and feed it to the fucking Baagaa [rodent-like creatures who were indigenous to his planet]!"

Another classic taunt was: "You're just an ugly mother-raper-whose-children-ought-to-turn-into-mutant-freaks-so-they-can-fuck-your-arse-then-eat-you-alive!" Or rather, this is how it came out in translation; in his language, he later told me, all this could be expressed by a single one-syllable word; a miracle of linguistic economy, in my opinion.

He also, and often, encouraged me to "swallow the cock of a Sjaja [a large furry animal indigenous to his planet] and choke to death on it."

His language was, all in all, deplorable, even after being toned down by the translating-air. But I had no linguistic taboos, so his words did not hurt me.

"If you don't eat," I explained to him eventually, "you will be in pain. You will suffer intestinal disorders. Your body will start to consume its own fat reserves. You will not die, but you will wither away." At this point he began screaming and weeping, but I continued:

"Your skin will be like parchment," I told him. "Your heart will be hard as a stone. Your blood vessels will scar your body like blue streams in a rocky desert. And this process cannot be reversed. Eat, or the flesh will fall off you and it will never grow back."

"I don't plan to live that fucking long!" he said savagely.

"Show me your arms."

"Fuck away, you bitch-with-a-withered-arsehole-that-stinks-of-death!" he sneered.

"Show me."

He hugged his arms tightly to his body. I gently but firmly pulled one arm away and looked at the wrist. It was gouged and ugly and full of pus. The teeth marks were still visible. But the artery had resealed and there was no trace of infection in the wound.

"You must understand," I pointed out to him, "that you cannot die."

"What have you turd-fucking monsters-from-Hell done to me?" he asked, with desperation in his tone.

I had, I must confess, become fond of the poor wretched creature by this point. Though his ranting did annoy me somewhat; and I found him, to be candid, rather ugly, although these things are of course highly subjective.

He was a thin biped—a morphology I used to loathe, though I was becoming used to it—with two eyes in the front and one mouth; and, at this very moment, his face was wet, which I knew from considerable experience of this species-type indicated a show of emotion.

Then, as his face dampened still further, he lay down and curled his body up in an unnatural posture which I presumed to be defensive and defeated. So I waved my arms and blew soft air on him through my tentacle-tips, and was appalled when he began to scream.

I withdrew a few paces and, still in my gentlest tones, explained the truth about our lives, the thing that we all of us have to face.

"Your body has been improved," I said. "Your rejuvenation powers have been enhanced. A bullet cannot kill you. A knife cannot kill you. A broken neck cannot kill you. Age cannot kill you. Disease cannot kill you. But if you do not eat, you will become a living skeleton and the pain will drive you to the brink of insanity."

"This is evil beyond evil, you creature-who-should-never-have-been-born!" he roared.

Then he began to writhe and spasm, and he howled in horror, fists tight-clenched, tortured by the fact that his formidable (by small biped standards) physical strength could not be used against an enemy such as this: his own body.

"You must," I told him sternly, "eat, or you will regret it, bitterly and self-reproachfully, for all eternity."

That night, Quipu recited to us a poem; it took six hours to perform, using a complex system of calls and responses between his five garrulous heads. His poem was extremely good but a little repetitive. It was the story of a god who played tricks with all his creatures by disguising himself as various exotic animals indigenous to Quipu's home planet. The final trick was when the god arrived on Quipu's world disguised as an alien invader.

We all roared with laughter at that.

I watched the dawn. It seemed to me that the dawn was a slightly different colour every day, though Quipu told me I was deluded.

I felt a breeze on my cheek.

"Enjoy your day," I said to Lirilla, as she hovered next to my head, also savouring the dawn, and cooling me with the rapid beating of her multi-coloured wings.

"I shall," Lirilla replied, in a voice so soft it was like a memory distantly recalled.

After five hours of cutting and biting with my claws and teeth, I fabricated a perfect stone, and then I carried it on my back from the quarry to the Temple.

The path was long, and winding; I passed herds of grazing creatures dawdling in the fields, savouring the sun on their variously coloured hides; I skirted the swamplands, where drowsy mud-beasts were wallowing, occasionally splashing each other with shit and mud; and finally I reached the Great Plain, where stood the Temple of the Interior World.

It reached, by now, almost to the clouds; a double-cylinder 8 shape with oval windows built, brick by brick, out of carved rock, modelled on a constellation visible from the night skies of my own home planet. The rays of the sun shone down upon the polished surfaces of the stone; it gleamed white in the soft light, a squat beast with its head striving to angrily butt the sky.

I placed my perfectly-shaped stone down on the grass for just one moment, and admired the beauty of the magnificent edifice we had conceived and built: a doubly circular obelisk set amidst rich grassland, with the snow-capped mountains in the distance peering down at the child of their rocky loins.

And I felt *proud;* just for a moment; the very briefest of moments.

And then I clambered up the side of the Temple until I reached the top and levered the stone into position. And I spat the fast-mortar I had been carrying in my mouth into the thick join between stone and stone, to secure the block in place.

This trick of mine always annoyed Fray. There were cranes and ramps that were specifically designed to allow workers to raise up the stone blocks, and hordes of skilful builders of various highly dextrous species standing by to mortar the stones into position. I was, Fray argued, spoiling it for everyone else by "showing off."

I did not care; this was one of my rare moments of purely selfish joy.

From the top of the Temple I had a perfect high view of my entire world. I savoured it for a while, till Fray screamed at me to come down and stop being such a forsaken-by-good-manners turd-mountain braggart.

I visited the prisoner again. He had not eaten, nor had he drunk his water of life. His skin was paler than it had been when he first joined us. He looked terrible. He wasn't pleased to see me.

I watched as Fray ran across the savannah. Her hooves thundered, her vast bulk blurred; she could run faster than any land animal I knew of on this world.

Fray's savannah however was small, and not very plausible. When she reached the forest, she stopped abruptly, and tossed her head, and staggered around in half-circles to come to terms with the fact she was no longer running like the wind; and then she roared to the skies.

Lirilla laughed. She hovered next to my cheek, a whirlwind of colour and grace, lit by the sun.

Above us, Cuzco was flying loops in the air, with extraordinary grace. Fray snorted, getting ready for another run.

"Tell that fat fuck," I said to Lirilla, of Fray, "that she's a useless lumbering fat fuck." This was a phrase I had learned from Fray; among her kind it is considered a term of endearment. (Or so I have been led to believe; for it is what she so very often calls *me.*)

Lirilla vanished, and was back in the beat of a wing.

"She says that she has seen great steaming mounds of shit more active than you," Lirilla told me.

"Cruel," I observed.

"I think she meant it kindly," said Lirilla, anxiously.

"Tell her," I said, "that she's an awkward dim-witted loose-bowelled cart-carrier." And Lirilla vanished; and flew across the savannah so fast it was as if she were rifting through space; and whispered in Fray's ear. From my vantage point, I could see Fray snort and roar and crash her hooves on the ground.

I looked up; Cuzco, the orange-bellied giant, was flying on updrafts of warm air, not moving his six wings at all; like a cloud made of golden armour held up by hope and poetry.

And Lirilla was back, whispering in my ear. "Watch this," she said, quoting Fray.

I saw Fray begin another run across the savannah; hooves pounding; dust rising up in clouds; her ugly ungainly body turned into pure graceful motion as she traversed the savannah with extraordinary speed. Finally, she came to a halt, steam billowing off her hide, and pounded her hooves on the ground and stood up on her three back feet and roared.

"Tell Fray," I said to Lirilla, "that for someone who is so-clumsy-she-falls-over-her-own-huge-tits-all-the-time, that was not at all bad."

"Tell me your name."

The prisoner shook his head, stubbornly. Three days had passed, and I was making little progress with him. But I was still patient. It takes time.

It always takes time.

"Tell me your name." My voice was gentle; I was using my sweetest tones to make it clear that I was on his side, and that I cared.

"Why are you doing this to me, you bitch from Hell?" he said, in calm fearless tones that betrayed his underlying panic.

"Because I want to be your friend," I said.

He blinked. "How could that be possible?" he said accusingly. "You destroyed my entire world!"

"Not I. They. I am like you. A captive. A slave."

He considered this assertion; clearly considering it to be an outrageous lie.

"You are an evil ugly loathsome vomit-inducing monster," he pointed out. "Are you telling me my enemies are even worse than *you?*"

"I am not," I suggested, "so very bad."

He stared at me, his angry features trembling. His skin was soft, reddish in hue, marked with diagonal ridges, and it undulated slightly when he spoke.

"You're really not my gaoler?" he asked, eventually.

"No." I replied.

"You were captured as I was?" he said.

"Indeed."

He considered this. "If that is so, perhaps I have wronged you," he conceded.

"It was an easy mistake to make; I just want you to know I am here to help you."

"Then I thank you for that," he said courteously.

"So, what *is* your name?" I asked him.

"They call me," he said proudly, then paused and uttered, as if bestowing a precious gift, his name: "Sharrock."

And he stared at me, clearly expecting a reaction.

"In my world," he added proudly, "I am—" But then he broke off, and did not conclude his train of thought.

For there no longer was, of course, a "his world"; and no one would ever again sing songs about him and his heroic exploits, whatever they might have been.

"My name is Sai-ias," I told him gravely.

"What language are we speaking?" he asked, quietly; his spirits clearly dashed.

"It is not a language. We are not speaking. Or rather, we speak, but the ship transforms the sounds, via invisible translators in the air, into patterns of meaning in our minds."

"The air does that?"

"It does."

"How is such a thing possible?"

"I do not know," I admitted.

"And who is in charge? Who controls this ship? Who are our masters?"

"I do not know."

"How can you not know?"

I sighed, through my tentacle tips, and patiently explained:

"I was captured, as you were, by a spaceship. I have never seen my captors. Other slaves explained to me what I had to do, and how."

"So you don't know who these creatures are? The ones who destroyed my planet?"

"My people called them Ka'un. In my language, that means 'Feared Ones.'"

"What do they call themselves?"

"I don't know."

"Where do they come from?"

"I don't—"

"I get it. You don't know. Have you asked? Did you try to find out? Do you know where on the ship they dwell? Do they look like you, or like me? What are their intentions? Do they have weaknesses? What is their purpose in attacking worlds like mine? Can we negotiate with them in any way?"

"They dwell in a Tower which no creature can approach. That's all I know about the Ka'un," I said.

Sharrock stared at me, intensity building in him like molten rock in a volcano approaching eruption.

"Then Sharrock," he said, in the tones of a person making a

vow that will change his life, "will find all the answers to all these questions, and more. And then he shall study the flaws and weaknesses of these accursed creatures. And then—"

"Then you shall wreak your wrathful vengeance upon the Ka'un?" I intercepted.

"Yes," he admitted. And with some chagrin, he said: "You've heard that said before, I take it?"

I sighed, through my tentacle tips.

"Many times," I told him.

A little while later Sharrock, with heart-broken eloquence, told me his tale. The dark and terrible story of the End Of All Days for his species.

He was a brave and proud warrior, he told me, and he came from a brave and proud and noble family. His people were exceptionally gifted at science and engineering, as well as being courageous fighters. He was, I learned, at some length, incredibly proud of his people and their status among the other tribes on his planet.

He also told me that on his planet there were two biped species living as one family unit: his kind, comprised of warriors of either gender and their spouses, guided by a Chieftain such as himself, but all equal in law and status; and the three-gendered Philosophers, who were small, tiny-tailed creatures of remarkable kindness.

The Maxolu warriors, he explained, were as clever as they were brave; and when they weren't in combat, or stealing from other tribes, they were hunters, and farmers, and masters of mathematics and science.

The Philosophers, by contrast, knew little of science, and less still of war; but they had the gift of dreaming great things. And out of these dreams, Sharrock's people had created skyships and spaceships and satellites and devices that make it possible to fly without experiencing the effects of acceleration.

I understood very little of all this but I knew it made Sharrock calmer to talk, so I let him talk.

Philosophers on his world, he continued, were treated like honoured guests, or small children; they weren't expected to work, or to fend for themselves. All they had to do was dream; and those dreams were inspired, and had yielded an endless succession of extraordinary inventions and discoveries and concepts. In consequence, his own people were the masters of their solar system, and also of all the habitable planets within two hundred light-years of their sun.

I marvelled at the power of their Philosophers' dreaming; and it gave me a strong sense of kinship with these now-extinct creatures. For my people too once knew how to dream.

Although their technology was advanced, he explained, Sharrock's people were nomads. They lived in tents in the desert for large parts of the year, and loved to feel the desert sandstorms on their flesh. But even so, their cities were magnificent; and they could build machines of great complexity that could walk and talk and think, and kill at a distance; or could convey objects from here to there in less time than the blink of an eye. And they had become, through the manipulation of their own biology, extremely long lived.

Sharrock talked too about the historic rivalry between his people of the North, and the Southern Tribes who had occupied the equatorial zones and who, after a long battle the details of which held little interest to me, were banished into space, where they had created an empire of many planets. Shortly before the End of All Days, Sharrock had been on a mission in Sabol, the capital planet of this empire, a place steeped in luxury and decadence where (as he explained it) fat and effete Southerners lived inside machines, oblivious to the joys of the natural world.

He then explained to me how—after acquiring without purchasing some priceless artefact or other, which now of course was worthless—he had returned home to find his village laid waste, and his people dead.

He had then, he told me, taken to the sky in some kind of vessel and after various adventures had fought with a large alien female with red hair streaked with silver.

My heart sank when he told me this; I was confident I knew who it was he had fought, and I hoped I would be able to keep the two of them apart.

Sharrock had then been engulfed in lava as the planet began to fall apart; and had lost consciousness, only to wake up inside the bowels of the Hell Ship, his burned limbs and body miraculously healed.

He had subsequently witnessed his planet's destruction through the glass walls of the prisoner-hold of the Hell Ship; a place I knew only too well. Trapped and alone, he had seen his sun flaring, like a wounded beast spitting bile and entrails from its shredded guts; he had seen comets and asteroids crashing into his planet's atmosphere; he had seen earthquakes and volcanoes devastate his world with their hot burning horror; and then he had seen the planet itself break into a million parts like carved and coloured glass shattered by a blow.

The image haunted him, and I understood how he felt. For I, too had seen my world explode into many parts, and the memory of it has never left me.

"Let me tell *my* tale," I said to Sharrock.

"My kind," I told him, "are not warriors. We do not—or rather we did not—have weapons. And nor did we believe these creatures from space would hurt us. By the time we realised our error, our planet itself was in the process of being destroyed; racked with earthquakes and terrible storms."

He listened carefully, but with a certain detachment. It was clear that in his mind what happened to me could not in any way compare to what had happened to *him.*

"And I was captured, and held in a spaceship, just as you were, and saw my planet fall into pieces, just as you did."

"How do they do that?" Sharrock asked. "The earthquakes? To do that requires a radical sundering of the planet's structural integrity." His features were alert; he was thinking hard now, and it made him look like a hunter eyeing his about-to-be-captured prey. "Bombs fired into the planet's core? Missiles made of un-matter?"

"I do not know."

He nodded, absorbing the sheer depths of my ignorance. "I think so," he said. "Un-matter would do it. You know what un-matter is?"

"No."

"The opposite of matter; when the two collide, Poof!" He clapped his hands, to demonstrate the explosion resulting from the happening of whatever he was talking about. "Or maybe a collapsor sun. You know what that is? A sun so massive it collapses in on itself?"

"We have no such concept; I have heard talk of such things though, from my friends on this ship," I said.

"The physics is formidable," said Sharrock, grinning with relish, "but the engineering is simple. Put your un-matter or your mini-collapsor in a big missile, fire it into the planet's crust; set it to detonate when it reaches the liquid outer core. Bang!" He clapped his hands; so skilful was his storytelling that I could see the very same image that *he* was seeing. "The planet is gone. Brutal. Our Philosophers have dreamed of such a weapon; but even the Southern Tribes would not be so entirely fucking evil as to do *that.*"

"The Ka'un," I said, "are undeniably that entirely fucking evil."

He nodded. "Continue," he said, as if I were his servant, and he my king; and I did.

"My planet was lost to me," I told him, "and no more can

be said of that. And then I came to the Ka'un ship, and I was shocked at what I encountered."

I had his attention fully grasped by now; and I needed him to heed these words. For those who do not comprehend how it was *then*, cannot exist *now.*

"It was," I said, "back then, so many years ago, a bleak and barren world. The lake was stagnant, the grasses were knotted with weeds that stank like corpses. My fellow captives slept outdoors, and every night when the sun was switched off, the blacker-than-black night was filled with screaming."

For a brief moment, I allowed myself to touch the memory of those days; and it seared my soul.

"And so I learned," I said, "in those early years, the way to survive. And this I must now teach you."

"You may," said Sharrock, "endeavour so to do."

"The way to survive is this: *do not fight.* Do not rage. Do not yearn for vengeance."

Sharrock smiled; and I recoiled at the power of his hate.

"How can you say that?" Sharrock said scornfully, his skin glowing scarlet, his eyes glittering, his muscles bunched. "You slack-cunted bitch! You coward-who-would-comfort-his-mother's-rapist! Vengeance is all there fucking is!"

"No! You must surrender your hate," I said, and my normally gentle tones were strident now. "Thoughts of revenge will gain you nothing; they will merely poison your soul." I knew this well; so very many of my friends had been consumed by hate and implacable rage.

Sharrock thought about what I had said, sifting it like evidence in a murder trial. "How can I give up my dreams of revenge?" he said, more baffled than angry now.

"You have to."

"No!" he roared.

"Remember this," I said, "life is worth—"

"I don't want to hear your fucking platitudes, you black-hided monster!"

"Then I shall cut to the gist of it. To live here," I explained firmly, "there are several simple rules that you must follow."

"Whose rules?"

"Rules we live by."

"No one tells me," said Sharrock, "how to fucking live!"

"Rules you *have* to live by," I insisted. "For know this: you must from this moment on abandon all abstract ideals like 'freedom' and 'justice' and 'happiness.' These concepts belong to the past; our only future is one of shared regret.

"And embrace, too," I said, with a wisdom acquired over aeons, "*joy:* joy in our world; joy at being alive, and at being together. Each day is precious, to me, and to all of us, for the moments of joy that it harbours."

And I paused, anxious to hear if my logic had prevailed with this arrogant, war-mongering fool.

And, for a moment, Sharrock did in fact look pensive; he nodded slowly, as if considering my words, and met my gaze calmly.

But then Sharrock spoke:

"You," said Sharrock, in rage-filled tones, "are nothing but a fucked-up-the-arsehole drinking-piss-and-thinking-it-tastes-like-wine conniving-with-the-enemy and sucking-the-cock-of-the-creature-who-killed-your-mother-and-your-father piece of shit!"

And I sighed, once more, from my tentacle tips, regretfully.

Clearly, my work with Sharrock was far from over.

Jak

And so, as I have already narrated to you, I left Mohun. And soon afterwards my ship the Explorer 410 slowly accelerated past the planet of Varth, leaving behind Kawak and his herd of savage predators.

I was Master-of-the-Ship, serving under Commander Galamea, and the ship's officers included the two Space Explorers I had met at the banquet, Morval and Phylas.

The ship was a small, squat working vessel with a hull streaked with stripes and pock-marked with small asteroid scars. The quarters were basic; I had a cabin smaller than my wardrobe on the Vassal Ship. There was no banqueting dome; we ate in the canteen, with food malignly designed by the ship's computer brain to be nutritious, but not appealing. It was, all in all, a place of horror.

It took a week for Explorer to reach the outer limits of the solar system. Averil would soon depart with the main Trading Fleet, with her new lover Master Trader Mohun.

I thought of her often.

In fact, incessantly.

Indeed, for every moment of every day, I was haunted with memories of her achingly intellectual features, her lusciously perceptive smiles, and her casually neglectful glances when I performed for her some great service or other.

But I had made my choice: I would lose himself in my work. And I was no more a Trader. My job now was to lead the Explorer craft into the depths of uncharted space; where, in time-hallowed fashion, we would search out new and alien civilisations, in order to get the better of them in sly negotiations.

"Welcome to my ship," I said to Morval.

His old, withered, bald head scrunched up in a scowl more ugly than—well, I had never seen anything more ugly.

"I have been on this vessel," he pointed out, "for two hundred years."

"It's my vessel now," I reminded him, courteously.

"I'm aware of that." The scowl became a sneer; hardly an improvement.

"We should be friends," I told the old Trader generously.

"I have, as a point of policy," said Morval, "no friends. My friends all abandoned me when I was banished by the Chief Artificer."

"I always admire an Olaran," I said, "who can harbour a grudge the way a father raises a child; with love, care, and the passage of decades."

"Ah, Master-of-the-Ship your wit is so... entirely adequate," said Morval, bitterly.

"Let me make a wild surmise; you were passed over for promotion?"

"I was."

"Because of your sullen attitude and melancholic disposition," I suggested.

"And my abundant lack of youth and beauty."

"Then clearly," I suggested, "I am better qualified; for young I am, barely forty years, and many consider me beautiful. But you shouldn't in any way feel—"

"This is a godsforsaken Explorer ship! We don't need a pretty boy Master! We need someone who knows what in fuck's name he's doing!"

"And you would be that someone, I take it?"

"I would be, and I am." And Morval stared at me with his dark haunting deep-set eyes. "The previous Master-of-the-Ship," he pointed out, "died of shock when his simulacrum was eaten alive by sentient slugs, after he and I had spent two years trapped in an alien forest."

"I'm used to danger."

"You have no idea," Morval told me, with evident glee, "what danger really is."

I stood in the bleak, spartan Command Hub of my new ship, with grey walls all around, no porthole, and four brushed-Kar-goat-leather (I mean the common variety of Kar goat, not the rare beasts with skin like a baby's arse) seats for the ship's officers and our Commander. One of these seats was currently occupied by Star-Seeker Albinia, who was linked by a cable which stretched from her shaved head to the ship's brain; and hence existed dreamily in a world of her own.

"You're used to better," sneered Morval.

"My Vassal Ship," I said politely, "had wooden furniture, shaped and whittled intricately by a Master Carver, and a ship's wheel made of gold and titanium."

"Frippery!" said Morval. "Explorer steers the ship, Albinia sees through its eyes; what's a ship's wheel supposed to do?"

"It made me feel," I pointed out, "important."

Phylas grinned at me as if I'd made a great joke; he was, I realised, a shameless ingrate.

"Any chance of a view?" I asked, and Morval grunted again, with even greater disapproval. But I glared: Pardon me, direct order? And he yielded.

"Albinia," Morval said, "give us your eyes." Albinia responded without speaking, and the blank grey wall ahead of me became a panoramic view of the space outside our ship.

"Background music?"

A dark dense thrilling chord pitched at almost subliminally low levels filled the small cabin; that, and the stars, gave the spiritless space at least *some* sense of atmosphere.

Morval grunted and scowled, clearly caught up in a crescendo of disapproval, but I ignored him.

"My bunk," I said to Phylas, who stood shyly beside me, "is it considered acceptable on such vessels?"

"It is the largest bunk on the ship."

"Except for the female quarters."

Phylas snorted with amusement. "Except, obviously, for the female quarters."

"What is the Commander like?" I said. "Give me fair warning. Is she firm? Fair? Disciplined?"

"She is fierce."

"Ah. Fierce."

"She is a former Admiral in the Olaran Navy; she was discharged for excessive, um, brutality."

"Against who?"

"Against the Stuxi."

"The Stuxi," I pointed out, "tried to destroy our home world; they were flesh-eating savages who murdered millions before we forced them into a truce."

"Even so, a military tribunal found her too brutal."

"Ah."

"I believe also that she considers me an idiot," Phylas admitted.

"And does she have grounds for that?"

"Occasional comments of mine have not always, um, accorded with common sense."

"You really are," I said kindly, "a child, aren't you?"

"Aye Master."

"Morval. Tell me about the ship. What weapons do we have?"

"Six gen-guns; twelve light-cannons, three negative matter transporters, and a disruptor ray," Morval said.

"Engine capacity?"

"Four point two kais. With booster engines, and stay-still wraparounds. In a crisis, we flee to the nearest rift and escape." Morval's tone was brisk now; when it came to the business of the ship, he clearly knew his stuff.

"Show me how the stay-still does its job."

Phylas conjured up his phantom controls, and pressed an oval; and our three bodies shimmered as the inertial haze surrounded us.

Then Phylas pressed another oval and the ship suddenly flipped over. Albinia of course was strapped to her seat; but Phylas, Morval and myself remained hovering in air, in the same position, though we were now upside down in relation to the Hub floor and control rigs.

Phylas pressed a third oval and we were right way up. "An alternative," he said, "to seat harnesses."

"Seat harnesses have always worked for me," I said testily.

"I find," said Morval, "they chafe."

Phylas pressed the oval again. The ship flipped again. I was upside down, again.

"Oh, boy," I said, delighted.

"Initiate the space drive," said Commander Galamea.

We were ready to rift, and Commander Galamea had joined us in the Command Hub. She had made no comment about the wrap-around space panorama that now dominated this small room, but had quietly asked Albinia to cut the background music.

Galamea was a lean, strongly muscled female; her eyes burned with a blue light that betrayed many years in rift space; she did not look as if she knew how to smile, nor did it seem likely she would welcome instruction in that art.

"I am proud to serve, o exalted mistress," I said.

"Just 'Yes Commander' will do," Galamea said tersely, and I recalled how the military hate any display of courtesy and eloquence.

"Yes, exalted Commander," I replied.

"Disreality is achieved, Commander," said Morval.

"The slippery-sands-of-chaos envelop us," said Phylas.

"Explorer is content," said Albinia, dreamily. The cable that connected her to Explorer hung loosely out of her shaved head; her eyes were closed; her mind entirely in tune with the ship's computational brain. She was, I noted in passing, the most ravishingly clever-looking Star-Seeker I had ever seen.

On my phantom controls, I could see that we were getting random readings across all vectors, as a consequence of the flux of chaos being generated.

A certain amount of time elapsed, but no one knew how much, or whether it was a longer or shorter passage of time than usual.

"A rift has emerged," said Phylas eventually.

"I see it," I said authoritatively, though in fact I saw nothing; just a jumble of incomprehensible graphs and equations on my phantom control screen.

"Can we predict the destination?"

Albinia moaned, as she tried to analyse the data flux and find some notion of what lay beyond the rift in time and space.

"No," Albinia eventually concluded.

"Morval?" asked Commander Galamea.

"I see no trace of disruptive nothingness," Morval said, slowly reading the data on his phantom control screen as if was a novel of which he was savouring the sentence structure.

(In passing, I marvelled at the nerve of the man; pretending he *understood* the data!)

"Phylas?"

"The ship's engines are showing no potential signs of imminent spontaneous detonation," said Phylas, comfortingly.

I looked at Commander Galamea as she made her decision. She was pensive, almost absent-minded.

Finally, she nodded her assent. Travel through rifts via disreal projection was a hazardous business; we all needed a few moments to prepare for the possibility of never becoming our actual selves again.

I took her nod as my instruction. "Proceed with space leap," I instructed.

Phylas moved the sliders on his phantom controls; the ship's drive was restarted; the disreality beams were dimmed. And the Explorer flew—instantly, so fast that it arrived before it left, *almost*—through a rift in space.

As we flew, the Command Hub tilted violently, first this way, then that, until we all were all upside down relative to the harnessed Albinia and the Hub itself. But the stay-still fields kept our bodies immune to the effects of violent oscillation, and the phantom control displays patiently followed us to our new positions.

Albinia moaned with joy as she entered the rift; and I knew that she could sense, with every part of her skin and body, what it was to be not-real. And even we, who did not have her direct access to Explorer's sensors, could feel the *strangeness* of the moment.

We emerged from the rift.

Morval assessed the data on his screen.

"We are—nowhere," he said.

"No traces of organic life," Phylas confirmed.

"No habitable planets," Morval added.

Albinia's eyes snapped open. "Explorer," she said, "hates this place."

"Try again," said Galamea.

"Reduce our probability once more," I said tensely.

"Yes, Master," said Albinia, and closed her eyes again.

A few moments of idle nothing passed; I yearned to have my ship's wheel back. There was no romance in pressing ovals on an illusory screen.

Then I felt the strangeness come upon me again.

"Probability is reducing, Master-of-the Ship," said Phylas, reading the data off his screen. "And reducing more. And more. And more," Phylas added.

I knew, though I did not fully comprehend, that the universe is a rocky reality built upon slippery sands of disreality; this was the heart and truth of Olaran science. And only the Olara—or strictly speaking, the Olara *women*—knew how to control this process.

And so, whilst remaining motionless, Explorer began the long process of reducing its own likelihood, until the new rift appeared, and had been, and was, and will be again. (Though all this made much more sense in mathematical form, so I am reliably informed.)

And thus Explorer vanished, and reappeared elsewhere; and the ship's computational mind swiftly calibrated where it was *this* time.

Again we detected no traces of life; the process recommenced; Explorer vanished, and reappeared, a million light years further on; and then did so again.

We were taking our ship out, far out, into regions of space never yet charted.

"We have a possible trace of organics, Master-of-the-Ship," said Morval, eventually, and the ship halted and its probability rose.

All of us on the Hub forced vomit back down our throats; the stay-still wraparounds weren't *that* good.

"Let us proceed," I said calmly, and the ship's true engines fired up, and Explorer began its slow journey towards its destination.

Albinia was communing deeply with Explorer. Her eyes were closed; her expression rapt. She was lost in a whirl of data from sensors that could perceive the mass and chemical constitution of stars a million baraks from here, and could feel like a touch of skin on skin the crash of microparticles against her ship's hull.

It felt wrong to stare at her; a violation, like watching a lover asleep. But yet I continue to gaze; I could not stop myself.

For whenever Albinia was in her trance, she had a beauty of mind and spirit that haunted me. Her eyes twitched under closed lids, her lips moved involuntarily. Her face flickered constantly with emotion—fear, regret, anticipation, joy.

She was, in a word: sublime.

"We're here," said Phylas.

"Ease her out," I said.

"We have readings from six separate planets," said Morval. "This culture has colonised its entire planetary system, but their main focus is on Planet Five, the gas giant. No traces of shifting sands scars. Their Fields of Force signature is sixty-three point four. A nuclear haze, they're a messy bunch."

"Albinia," I said. Her eyes flickered and then opened. She took a gasp.

"Am I done?" Albinia asked.

"You're done," I said softly.

"Good," said Albinia briskly, and her face was a neutral mask again. I retreated at the touch of her inner authority.

"We think they're pre-interstellar, recovering from a relatively recent nuclear war," said Phylas.

"What will we call them?" asked Albinia.

"Morval?"

He clicked an oval. "The next name on the list," he said, "is Prisma."

"Then Prisma it is."

"Explorer doesn't like them," Albinia said.

"Why not?" I asked.

"She didn't say. I just felt it. She fears this place, and these people."

"They're primitives," teased Phylas. "What is there to fear?"

"Primitives," Morval reminded him, "once obliterated all of Caal, and all eleven Trader ships in the area."

"We would never be," said Phylas arrogantly, "so easily duped."

Explorer glided through space, propelled by sub-atomic interactions in seventh dimensional geometry, or some such thing; the truth is, I can never recollect the detail of these tedious technical matters. The light from the system sun made the ship's hull glow; I admired the image of our ship haloed with radiance on my panoramic wall-screen.

Explorer passed a pock-marked asteroid.

This solar system was, I noted, quite beautiful. There were brightly coloured gas giants with multiple rings, comets with tails, and from our angle of approach we could see all seven planets of the system in a single gaze, clustered like a family of unruly children of every different size and age.

There is nothing finer, or so I thought then, than the moment of initial approach; that first glimpse of an alien stellar system, with no hint as to what might lie within.

"Our gen-guns are being charged," said Phylas matter-of-factly.

For a moment I didn't take in his words. Then:

"What?" I said, startled.

"The ship is taking evasive action," Phylas explained.

"Oh by all that's joyous," Morval muttered to himself, "this Master-of-the-Ship has *no* idea."

"Cease," I barked at the old man, "sarcasming."

I could see, on the panoramic wall-screen, that Explorer was now weaving and zagging through space, in bewildering randomised patterns.

I was uncomfortable. It was proper protocol for the Ship's Master to be informed in advance of all decisions made by the vessel's computational mind; but on this occasion I was being ignored.

For a moment, I felt a surge of annoyance; for in truth, I hated being sidelined like this. I understood of course that my role as

Master was largely ceremonial; and that all major decisions were made by the Mistress Commander and the Star-Seeker and the ship's computational brain. But this was an ugly reminder of a truth I generally preferred to, well, ignore.

However, I hid my irritation between a mask of bonhomie, charm, and self-deprecating wit; as I always do.

"Why?" I asked courteously, with my favourite irresistible smile, "are we doing all this?"

"Missiles have been launched by Explorer; power beams are being fired by Explorer; the intended target is the asteroid," said Phylas, ignoring my question.

"Yes but why?"

"You'll find out," said Morval with grim pleasure, "soon enough."

I followed the progress of the attack on the wall-screen: our ship in space, the orb of the planetary moon looming before us; the flaring colours of the gen-gun missiles, and the pillars of energy from the light-cannons arcing a slow progress towards the asteroid. It was a stately dance of colour and light set against a black cloth of night.

I assumed that the enemy were attempting to attack us; but Albinia had still told me nothing. Her lips moved silently as she and Explorer waged space war. I was tense; for the truth was, I had never been *quite* so close to combat before. In all the battles in which I had played a role, I had been part of the rapidly fleeing Trader fleet, protected by Navy and Explorer vessels.

Now, I was in the front line and I could die.

I saw, on the screen, our missiles flying closer and closer to the asteroid. While, on my phantom control display, a bewildering series of graphs and equations flashed before my eyes, though I had no idea what meanings they conveyed.

"Now," said Morval, somehow managing to guess what was about to occur.

And at just that moment, the asteroid erupted. And a flock of black triple-horned warcraft emerged from it, hurtling towards us.

"Two hundred and forty-two enemy drone missiles," said Phylas.

"The radiation trail indicates dirty nuclear bombs," added Morval.

"They're attacking us!" I summarised, in a cheery fashion; playing the fool with my usual panache.

"Forgive me," said Albinia, dreamily. "I thought it better to act first, and inform you of my decisions later."

"Very wise, beloved Mistress," I said generously, concealing my anger.

"Sarcasming is not a word," Morval reminded me, with his usual long memory.

"It has a ring to it," I said defensively.

Commander Galamea arrived on the Hub, in a blaze of implicitly-rebuking-the-rest-of-us-for-being-so-lazy energy.

"Master-of-the-Ship, report!" she barked.

"Morval, brief the Commander please," I said, sneakily.

"Explorer seems to have detected an imminent attack, we have no more data," said Morval, which irked me, because I could have said *that* much.

Albinia groaned, lost in communion with Explorer.

And, just as the last of the enemy drones emerged from the artificial asteroid, Explorer's missiles began to silently detonate. It was like a birthday sky-fire display against the blackness of space.

Moments later, a haze appeared on the screen; and the enemy drones began to slowly fall apart, like dancers breaking away from a tableau into separated solos. There were no subsequent explosions as these craft broke up; these were merely objects sundering into their myriad pieces as if changing their minds about existing.

I realised that our gen-gun missiles were not just kinetic, they also harboured atom-disruptor particles. The snarling swarm of enemy drone bombs were being destabilised at sub-atomic level.

"What information do we have about this civilisation?" asked the Commander.

"Hostile?" guessed Morval.

"Type 3, post-nuclear, pre-shiftingsands, the home planet is the gas giant fifth from the sun but they also inhabit five other planets and twelve satellites and those comets are in fact space stations with tails," said Albinia, with her usual calm dreamy certainty.

"Explorer is preparing to fire again," said Morval.

And thin rays of energy erupted once more from the gen-gun tubes.

And before long, the panoramic wall-screen showed nothing but empty space, and the faint wisps of former menace that was all that remained of the enemy fusillade.

"See this," said Morval, somehow once again miraculously anticipating the action.

A juggernaut of a spaceship was emerging from the hollow asteroid. It was clearly expecting an easy passage behind its escort of killer drone bombs. Instead, it was met with a withering hail of destructive energy from Explorer. The juggernaut shimmered, like a firebird on a midsummer night about to explode; then abruptly dematerialised.

And I looked at Morval, puzzled. How did he manage, time and again, to predict so accurately what was going to happen?

Explorer glided deeper into the stellar system, until it reached planet Five, the home of these unpleasant sentients.

It was a gas giant, with six natural rings and a larger artificial ring which Explorer identified as a space defence system.

And there we waited. We had already demonstrated that we (or rather Albinia in communion with Explorer) had powers beyond the imagining of these beings. The rational response would be for them to surrender unconditionally, in the hope of averting further fatalities.

That seemed, however, unlikely.

I reclined in my Master's chair, watching it all on the wall-screen. "How many times," I asked Phylas, "do the wretched aliens try to kill you when you appear?"

"Always."

"Not always," corrected Morval.

"There was that time—"

"That was a feint. They greeted us in peace, and ambushed the Traders a century later."

"How did you know—"

"I always know what you will say," said Morval.

Phylas glowered; hurt at being shut out from his own conversation.

Commander Galamea prowled the deck.

"Explorer, progress report," said Galamea.

"Wait and see," said Albinia dreamily.

We waited.

And then an image appeared on our panoramic wall-screen; Albinia had made contact with the aliens' leader. He was a squat, asymmetrical, slimy and undeniably ugly creature, with no visible eyes and a mouth that went up instead of across.

"Greetings," I said. Explorer had of course been intercepting all the radio traffic from these creatures since we arrived in their system, and had gathered enough information about their language to run a translation facility.

"You speak language our," growled the alien.

"Apparently not that well," I conceded. "We come in peace, and so forth; and we wish to trade."

"You kill have of hundreds our people," said the alien.

"Albinia," I snapped.

"Give us time; their language has a weird syntax," Albinia said defensively.

"We did not destroy your warriors and their spaceship," I explained carefully. "We have merely concealed them in another dimension, from which we can retrieve them easily if you prove you are peaceful. And now we wish to negotiate."

"You hold people our hostage!" roared the alien.

"Indeed we do."

"Smart is thinking," said the alien, evidently reassured. "Down welcome planet ours."

"I would be delighted," I said.

Our landing craft emerged like a child being birthed from the hull of Explorer, and rocket-propelled across the expanse of open space. The shadow-selves of Albinia and I sat side by side in the cockpit and watched the view. I was close enough to smell her skin, and hear her breath, if she had been possessed of skin and breath.

It occurred to me that I had certain clandestine personal reasons for wanting Albinia on this mission with me; and I was delighted at my own unsuspected subterfuge.

Our craft reached the outer atmosphere of the bright purple gas giant; and we looked down at the swirling winds below.

"Are you still inhabiting Explorer?" I asked Albinia.

"Yes."

"Whilst operating the simulacrum."

"Yes."

"And do you have, perhaps, enough reserves of consciousness remaining to engage in idle chat?"

"No."

"As I feared."

The landing craft descended; we were held in position by our stay-still fields, as the vessel rocked and shook. The hull was being buffeted by powerful gales and seared with toxic gases, but the craft's force-mantle protected it entirely. The electronic eyes on the craft's hull looked deep into the wild screaming madness of the atmosphere, and Albinia saw it all too.

"How do they endure this place?" I marvelled, using a murmur-link to connect directly to Albinia.

"It is, strangely, magnificent," Albinia said and smiled. And then the smile faded and she was, once more, off in a world of her own, barely aware of me.

I looked at the view from my tiny porthole, a maelstrom of heat and burning gases, and I felt nauseous. Outside the craft, the pressure was so great it would crush a space suit and condense an Olaran body to the size of a crumb, if we had been so foolish as to go for a walk.

Thus, through air as thick as ice, we fell downwards, until, finally, we were in the midst of the alien flock.

These creatures—the Prismas—were spawned of gas and plasma, yet somehow (the physics entirely eluded me) nevertheless existed in squat asymmetrical solid and eyeless form that could survive without a spacesuit in the atmosphere of a gas giant.

According to Phylas, these strange beings could act like suns—creating metals out of their own substance, and then weaving them into spaceships. Thus, their drone ships were spawned like eggs; and their "missiles" were not mere artefacts, they were in effect, cells discharged from the Prisma host bodies.

"Can understand us you?" said a voice over our radio net. I looked outside the porthole; and I could see a hundred Prismas hovering in the air like fat turds with mouths all around us. This was as near as our species could get to each other; the Prismas could not survive in our atmosphere; and we would not be able to see or hear a thing in *their* atmosphere. So we would have to talk to them from within the landing craft.

"Yes we can," I said, peering out and wondering which Prisma I was talking to.

"Living are creatures you?"

"We are living creatures."

"You travelled space have? Through."

"We have travelled through space."

"Whole tendrils of a are you?"

"We are not tendrils of a whole; we *are* the whole. We are creatures of flesh and blood. We do not exist as you do, as creatures of gas and, er, stuff."

"Impossible."

"It is possible. There are many varied kinds of life."

"Rocks are you. Excreta are you. Are worthy not to talk with us."

"We have to talk with you. We owe you this."

"Where is the planet from which you come?" said the Prisma. Our translator was, I noticed with some relief, finally getting the hang of the creature's syntax.

"Far far away. You cannot reach it."

"Can it be inhabited by our kind?"

"You cannot reach it."

"It *can* be inhabited by our kind?"

"No, and you cannot reach it."

"You have no idea who we are. We are the most powerful and fearsome creatures in all the universe."

You are, I thought to myself, a bunch of arrogant fucks; and then I realised my murmur-talk device had translated this into speech.

I switched off my communicator and turned to Albinia.

"What do you think?"

"Something is happening."

"What?"

"I don't know. Something."

I turned on my communicator and spoke again to the Prisma:

"We are here to trade; do you understand that concept?"

"You have come from far away; how? What ships do you possess? Are you long-lived?"

"We give you a thing; you give *us* a thing. It's called trade. Do you understand this concept?"

"We have sent spaceships into farthest space; they have never returned. Can you explain this?"

"Well, it's a dangerous universe out there."

"We are the most fearsome species in existence; no harm could come to creatures such as us. Our voyagers were told to conquer and destroy and then return to fetch us. That was ten thousand years ago; and they are late. And we are full of wrath."

Albinia and I exchanged glances; this wasn't looking too promising.

"Be that as it may," I continued to the Prisma, "let's talk a bit more about this concept of 'trade.'

"You see," I continued, getting into the swing of it now, "you have the ability to create metal artefacts with the power of your thoughts, and we could maybe sell stuff like that. Whereas we—"

"Perhaps the journey was too long, and they died. We long to travel swiftly among the stars, rather than being trapped at sub-light speeds. Can you do that? Journey faster than light?"

"We can."

"Can you teach us how?"

"We could certainly give you some hints," I temporised.

"Then we can 'trade,'" said the Prisma.

Albinia patted my arm. I switched off my communicator. "Yes?"

"Firstly, these creatures are a bunch of dangerous fucking lunatics," she pointed out, quite accurately. "Secondly, I'm detecting some kind of weapon. Don't know what. It involves the planet, and the sun, and a fleet of—something nasty. I think they're aiming to attack Explorer again."

"What should I do?" I asked her, for though I was Master-of-the-Ship, I trusted her judgement totally.

She thought, for a brief moment, with her merged-with-Explorer face, then a cold look came upon her.

"They're bastards; let's fuck 'em," she said.

And so we fucked 'em.

I triggered the self destruct switch.

And our landing craft exploded; and obliterated into particles so small they could not be assimilated by the Prismas.

And then a searing wave of heat from the explosion ripped through the alien creatures, sundering them into a billion wavelets.

And then—as I was later told—in orbit above the planet, the Prisma battle fleet emerged from the shadow of their moon and launched a massive attack upon Explorer.

At the same time, Prisma drone ships leaped from hiding places amidst the gas giant's rings and rained missiles and heat-energy upon Explorer, drenching its forcefields.

However, Explorer's shields deflected the enemy's beams and missiles with ease; and it then counter-attacked, using its disruptor ray at full capacity; and the entire Prisma fleet was obliterated in an instant.

And all that was left was a swirl of random atoms in space.

For such is the power of Olara; we do not seek war, but when we fight, we always win.

At about this time, I woke up on my simulacrum bench. And I staggered to my feet and saw that Albinia's skin was close to burning point; steam was rising from it. The simulated experience of being burned alive on the planet was manifesting as actuality on her real body.

I doused her with cooling spray, just as she woke up, and screamed with agony. Then I cradled her, as Phylas entered.

He turned ashen at the sight of Albinia.

"She'll be fine," I snapped. It had been my idea to take Albinia with me on this mission; but to risk the life of a Star-Seeker was, in retrospect, a reckless and a foolish thing. I knew it myself, and I desperately hoped no one would be vulgar enough to tell me so.

I carried Albinia to the sick room and placed her in healing stasis. Then I returned to the Hub.

"What's happening?" asked Commander Galamea. "Explorer isn't moving."

I am not—well, said Explorer, forlornly, via our murmur-links.

"Manual operation," I said, and spoke directly to Explorer: "Your human half is unconscious. She has been injured. Seal the system."

Injured, how? said Explorer's voice.

"Psychosomatic sympathetic burns. We died, down there, and we felt it here."

"Your fault," said Morval, cruelly. "You jeopardised the life of our Star-Seeker. You—"

I should have known it would be *him.*

"Explorer: these are my instructions," I snapped. "Bomb the gas giant, kill as many of those ugly big parent-fuckers as you can. Then seal the system. Get us out of here."

"I need to—" Commander Galamea said.

"DO IT NOW," I screamed, and Explorer heard my voice of command, and on the wall-screen I saw plumes of cloud start to emerge from the gas giant. Teleported bombs were exploding on the planet's surface.

Explorer accelerated; but the stay-still fields were not in place so we were scattered like ritsos, and I flew across the room and crashed into Commander Galamea. We gripped each other, just as the stay-still came on; and for a few awkward moments we were held aloft in each other's arms, as if swept up by an imaginary wind.

Then Explorer slowed down, and the stay-still fields were released, and we dropped to the ground like stones off a bridge.

The Commander and I staggered to our feet, bruised by each other's bodies. Then, carefully avoiding eye contact, we studied the panoramic image around us of the stellar system of the Prismas.

"Show the barrier in false colour," I said, and Explorer changed the screens so that they revealed the shape of the invisible barrier in space that now encaged the Prismas; a shifting-sands-wall that would trap the Prismas, irrevocably and for all eternity, in this little bubble of space.

Galamea whispered to me: "You were wrong, of course, to take Albinia."

I nodded, to acknowledge that I knew she was right.

"Nevertheless," Galamea said, "that was a good first mission. You were fair, but decisive."

"They were a bunch of evil bastards!" I said angrily.

"No," said Galamea, kindly. "Not evil, not bastards; these are aliens. We can't judge them by our own ethical and cultural standards."

"Even the Stuxi?"

Galamea thought about that. "Actually, they really *were* evil bastards," she admitted.

Later, I recorded the summary in my log for the mission: **No potential for trade. Danger Rating 4. Alien hostiles Quarantined, in perpetuity.**

Later still, I went to visit Albinia in the sick room. Her flesh had peeled off, she looked like a corpse. But she was awake. She fixed me with a scornful glance; there was no trace of the absent, dreaming Albinia. This was a cold hard woman, looking at me as if I was a nobody.

"I apologise," I said, "for your pain."

Her raw skin twitched, which I took to be a sneer. "It was my decision; it is my pain; do not presume to pity me," Albinia told me coldly.

"Yes Star-Seeker," I said, and my dawning love for her received a brutal jolt.

And thus the months passed, and then the years. I remember that period fondly now, as a kind of golden age. Though at the time it seemed to be mostly drudgery and terror, alternating with moments of love-sick anxiety.

So many missions. So many evil aliens! So many unscrupulously bargained contracts of trade!

That was my life, the all of my life, before it changed. Before the events that—

But no. I'm getting ahead of myself.

"Are you sure there's life down there?" I said sceptically, looking at the panoramic wall-screen image of the slime-covered festering oozing planetary surface that was beneath us.

"Explorer says yes," said Albinia.

"All right then," I said. "Phylas, suit up; and let's get going."

Our shadow-selves materialised in a field of green grass. The sun beat down upon us.

"Nice weather," said Phylas, cheerily, and I shot him a filthy look. Phylas, I had learned during our many missions together, was possessed of the boundless optimism of the utterly stupid; his naïvety was almost as vexing to me as was Morval's bleak melancholy.

"*There are storms*," Albinia/Explorer informed us.

A six-legged faun sauntered up to us, and nuzzled me with its snout. I patted it; and it was soft and warm to the touch.

And my mood mellowed. Phylas was grinning still, yet it no longer irked me. Indeed, I ventured a grin of my own, which he easily outmatched.

"I like this place," I told Phylas.

Phylas laughed out loud. "Indeed so! It reminds me," he said.

"Of what?"

"Of when I was a boy. My father used to take me hunting. We'd shoot our native grazing animals with a home-made bow and arrow. It was a rite of passage; I was born on the planet of Darox, you know. We had our own—"

I realised that Phylas was now holding a wooden bow, and a quiver full of feathered arrows; a highly unexpected shadow-self conjuration on his part, or so I mused.

"This is meant to be," I pointed out, "a serious mission."

"Live a little!" said Phylas. I envied him his youth and his foolishness. And I wondered, where had each of mine of those gone?

"*You need to move out of that swamp,*" said Albinia. "*There's a strong probability that the sentients are located in the hills above you.*"

Swamp?

Phylas drew back the arrow, as the faun skittered away. His aim was true; the arrow took the beast through the neck and it fell.

I stumbled backwards, towards the river. A narrowboat drifted past me, with my beloved Shonia on board, in a beauteous white robe. I blinked.

"Dream of me!" my first true love cried.

I tried to speak, in order to summon Albinia's help; but my vocal cords were frozen. I blinked again.

"It's exquisite," said Phylas, as we walked through the palace, admiring the gem-studded walls and the rich hangings and the seductive beauty of the incense fumes in the air.

"It reminds me," I said, searching for the memory.

"Ah glory," said Phylas, for a harem of radiantly intelligent Olaran females were now approaching us. They were clad in robes as rich as—as—

I took out my knife and I severed Phylas's throat. Then I thrust the blade through my own forehead, so it impaled my brain and severed my—

[I awoke on the couch, with a blinding headache. Explorer began recalibrating my connection with my shadow self but—]

I bit my finger and screamed with pain, and lunged off the couch. I ripped the contacts off my skull and body. And I stood there panting.

Then I looked to Phylas. He had sunk back into his shadow-self; so I brutally ripped the contacts off him and he screamed and looked at me.

"Bliss!" he roared.

"Illusion," I pointed out.

We staggered up to the Command Hub.

Albinia had already surmised that this was a planet inhabited by telepathic slime; Explorer's instruments informed us that this continent-wide intelligence was able to manipulate the thoughts, emotions and sensations of all who walked through its muddy oozing bogs.

"Why didn't you rescue us?" I accused.

"You looked as if you were having," said Albinia, "fun."

I wrote up the experience in my log, and concluded: **No potential for trade: Danger Rating 3: System Quarantined; review in 100 years.**

Commander Galamea was curt, and clearly angry with me, I did not know why.

"Set course," she said, and Albinia sank into a trance-like state.

Phylas and Morval attended to their phantom control displays.

I realised that the Commander's skin was pinking; and it dawned on me that she was in heat.

"Commander," I said softly.

She glared at me.

"If you need any—" I hinted.

"What?"

"Help?"

She glared even more.

"Help with what?"

"If your mood is... I realise that when a female is..."

Her glaring intensified.

"You want to fuck me?" she asked, savagely.

"If you need me to," I said helpfully,

"I will never," Galamea said, "need a male ever again!"

Her body was trembling with repressed passion; I was awed at the strength of will she was displaying in refusing my offer.

And baffled, too; for all she had to do was indicate her sexual state, and all of us males would do our duty. Grudgingly, perhaps; but even so!

So what, I wondered, made her so bizarrely reluctant to ask?

We shadow-suited up, Galamea and I.

I had a bad feeling about this. But it was the Commander's idea; she wanted to experience a mission with me.

I lay down on the shadow couch. I closed my eyes.

And then I opened my eyes and found myself standing on a planet full of dark gloom. I could hardly see my way to walk.

Galamea switched on her helmet-torch and we made our way through a dense mass of pointed stakes. This was, I realised, a field of sorts.

"*The nest is to your left, six thousand baraks,*" said Albinia/Explorer.

"Why the darkness? I thought it was daytime," Galamea asked.

"*I have no data on that.*"

"Are there thick clouds?"

"*I have no data on that.*"

My shadow feet left no tread; but my motion must have triggered a trap. A stake impaled my body, from my arse to my scalp. I tried to wriggle free.

"Split yourself," said Galamea bluntly.

"I can't."

"Split yourself!"

I split my body in half and Galamea picked up the pieces and stuck them back together. My shadow self reformed.

"*Here,*" said Albinia/Explorer, and I switched on my own helmet-torch and the field was illumined. We saw around us leafless trees haunted by shadows. The shadows were the nocturnals who were the primary sentient species on this planet. The secondary sentients were trees and our chances of trading with them were approximately low to zero.

"Do you have any concept," Galamea said to me, in quiet tones, as we were waiting for the shadows to approach.

"Of what, Commander?"

"Of how it feels. To have no power over your body."

"I do not follow."

"Last week. When I was in heat. You so courteously offered to . . . fornicate with me. When I was, as you were aware, in heat."

"I would have been privileged to assist you, Commander," I said, cautiously. I had never been spoken to so candidly by a female before about this delicate matter. Even my lovers had never referred to the monthly imperative of their biology, except in terms of their needing it, and needing it *now.*

"I did not want you to do so," Galamea said bluntly. "I mean—what I'm trying to say here Master-of-the-Ship Jak—is that I didn't want you to fuck me, at such a time, and in such a way."

I was piqued at that.

"Why not?" I asked.

"Because I don't want to be," she pointed out, with anger modulating her normally calm tones, "just an *animal.* Unable to control my brute lust. Nor frankly do I savour your selfless pathetic obedience. We need to be more than prisoners of our own biology, Jak! We have—don't we see—the potential to be so much more!"

"Whatever you say, Commander," I said, my casual tone belying the fact I was affronted at her words.

Pathetic? Obedient? Was that really how she saw me?

"Do you have the faintest idea what I'm saying?" she asked me, sadly.

"Not really," I admitted

"Then forget we had this conversation."

"It's forgotten."

The shadows lifted from the trees and hovered above us. A slow hissing sound surrounded us.

"Can you translate?" Galamea asked Albinia.

"*Not yet.*"

We waited patiently for Explorer to decode the linguistic patterns in these creature's malign hissing.

"Are these shadowy bastards a hive intelligence?" I asked.

"*I have no data on that*," said Albinia/Explorer.

The shadows hovered high, and when I looked up at them, at the black clouds that blocked the sun, I realised that the clouds were moving.

"These creatures block their own sun," I told Albinia/Explorer.

We stood in that field for fourteen hours, but Explorer never managed to decode the aliens' strange hissing language.

And so the system was abandoned, but not quarantined. The mission was a failure.

But Galamea's words stayed with me.

And many years later, after she was dead, it occurred to me what she had really been saying that day in the field of trees and shadows.

She had been asking me to *change.* To stop serving her blindly; to cease treating her with craven adoration; to treat her, in short, as an equal. All this, I eventually realised.

Too late.

BOOK 4

Sai-ias

"Where are you talking me?"

"Not far. My cabin is here. Down the corridor," I said.

Sharrock stepped anxiously along the circular corridor, struggling to keep his balance because of the steepness of the slope. The corridor was large enough to accommodate my bulk and that of Cuzco and the other "giant" sentients, as we are called. Sharrock was dwarfed by it, like an insect clambering across the hide of a huge and grossly fat land animal; or, indeed, like Lirilla dancing upon the backside of Fray.

He slipped, and fell, and scrambled back to his feet.

"Take care," I advised him.

"I tripped," he said angrily, "on that fucking slime trail you leave wherever you've fucking been."

"It is an outpouring of my essence, not a 'fucking slime trail,' " I told him stiffly.

"You fucking corpse-fucking slime-leaving freak," Sharrock sneered.

I slithered on.

The circular tunnel expanded into a large circular atrium, and I spoke the code and a door opened in the wall. I slid inside and Sharrock scrambled behind me, and we arrived in my cabin, the largest on the ship, which also was a perfect sphere.

Sharrock stood and looked around and his breathing became irregular, and I guessed this was a visceral response to what he saw before him.

"These are my cabin friends," I explained.

His face was calm, his demeanour relaxed, as befits a warrior; but I could tell that, beneath the mask, Sharrock was filled with fear.

"Hello there," said Cuzco.

"Hi," added Fray.

"You look like shit," said one of Quipu's heads—the leftmost one, Quipu One—unhelpfully.

"Welcome," said Doro.

"Hello," said Lirilla.

"I am privileged," said Sharrock, with nary a tremor in his voice, "to encounter such noble creatures."

Cuzco snorted with contempt; and Sharrock flinched, as smoke seared the air and Cuzco's eyes radiated hate.

"In my world," Cuzco said softly, "you would be carrion."

Sharrock stared up at Cuzco, fearlessly. "You really are one ugly son-of-an-arsehole fuck, aren't you," he said marvelling. And Cuzco's eyes blazed scarlet with rage and his back-body thrashed and his body-horns grew into long spikes, and his scales rattled, and all at once the huge circular room seemed too small to contain us all.

Sharrock continued to stare, with no trace of fear; ready to fight or to die; his body a veritable masterpiece of composure.

And finally, Cuzco gave ground: his body shrank, his back-body stilled, his scales became silent, his horns sank back beneath his armour, his eyes turned green again. And his tongue lapped the air, and we could see the jagged tongue-spikes which Cuzco, in the old days, would have used to suck the blood and the life out of any errant or impertinent biped.

But those days, as even Cuzco now acknowledged, were gone.

"Sit," I said to Sharrock, gently.

That night, Fray told us a tale we had not heard from her before.

"This is the story," she told us, in her booming low voice that always for me evoked the thudding of hooves on a lonely savannah, "of how my world was born. It is a story told to me by my mother, and her mother before her. It is our origin story."

I curled myself up comfortably, and breathed air scorched by Cuzco's breath, and kept an eye on Sharrock, who, I noted, was rapt and exhilarated as Fray eloquently spoke.

"We were born of the wind, so my mother said," Fray told us. "The wind that blew from the north and crashed in great tumult against the mountains of the south. And then the wind's angry tongue licked the rock, and the rock roared with pleasure, and split, and a grey wet mess of flesh was birthed. And that was us. The Frayskind.

"We were born of the union of the wind and the mountains; and our father the wind is still our friend. That is how we learned to hunt. We were slow and heavy and all the other creatures could hear us thundering after them, for we were never the fastest of beasts. But we begged the wind to howl and roar, and the grasses were whipped wildly by its gusts. And the animals we stalked could not smell us, for the wind conveyed our stench swiftly away, and they could not hear us, because the sounds caused by the wind were so deafening. So we thundered towards them and caught them unawares and ate them in our great jaws, and when we had digested them we farted loudly and long, to return the favour to the wind.

"And the mountains are our mother, and when the great Majai hunted us and killed us by the thousands, we took refuge in the womb of the mountains. Rents appeared in sheer cliff faces and we clambered inside the caves and we made our homes there for many hundreds of years. And while we were gone our father the wind roared and ripped the planet apart and all the land animals died, including the Majai, and when we returned we were the only large land animals left alive and we were able to eat the thick grasses and the rich vines without any competition or threat from other predators. Thus were we saved by our mother the mountain.

"And to this day, I worship the wind, and revere the mountains. And I fart loudly, and long, when I eat. This is our origin myth. And," Fray continued, crisply, "it is based to some degree on historical truth. For the archaeological records show that in the ancient eras our planet was racked with terrible storms that destroyed all the major life forms apart from us, the largest land animal, and the clumsiest. But we survived because we cowered in caves and scrambled among rocks and when we emerged the wind was stilled and the land was fertile again.

"I am an atheist; I do not believe in the god of wind, and the goddess of mountain. But I love this story. It has poetry and beauty."

"It's a fine story," agreed Cuzco.

"Aside," said Quipu One, "from the farting."

The sun rose; I watched with delight. And I felt a surge of anticipation. For today was Day the First; the day on which I explore the rich and varied habitats of our world.

Ours is, it cannot be denied, a small planet, easily traversed in a matter of hours if you can swim the seas, which I can. Or if you can plunge through the murky suppurating swamplands, which I can. Or if you are nimble enough to traverse the thick forestlands, which I am. The mountains are steep, and few land creatures can clamber up their sheer cliffs, but I am one such. And the valleys are dark and gloomy and raging torrents fill them, but I am easily able to ride the stormy waters and descend the waterfalls.

Day the First has always been my favourite day; I simply travel, from one end of my world to the other. And I am always tired by the time I retire to my cabin, where every night I desperately strive, but fail, to sleep.

That night, I brought Sharrock once more with me to my cabin. And he listened, with intense attentiveness, as Doro told his tale.

Doro talked, with quicksilver speed, of the joys of metamorphosis.

"I am this, or Icanbethat," Doro said.

"Stone rock sand sea plant animal twig bug bird metal or anything at all ifithasthesamebodymassasIdo. You all know this," Doro added, still speaking so fast that I was never truly sure if I had heard him speak at all.

"Look, look at me, look at me as I change," he said, and Doro became a shimmering ball of light; it took a real effort to realise he still existed in solid form beneath the glittering rays.

"And look, looklooklook again." And Doro became a crack in the floor, a complex pattern that was like bared raw mortar and that would be overlooked by any except the most attentive or paranoid seeker-of-life.

"And again." And Doro became a shadow; the shadow of one of Quipu's heads.

"And again." And Doro became a sound in the night, and for some reason we could not see him, we could just hear his Click Click Click as he echoed past us.

"I have no stories to tell," Doro said. Rock, shadow, noise in the night.

"For I *am* the stories that I tell." Crack in the floor, flash of faint colour.

"I am any thing and I am allthings." A twig; a cloud in the sky.

"Am I real?" Doro was no longer there.

"Or am I not?" And Doro was there again, a small shiny rock once more.

"Is this in your mind?" A miniature lake, set amidst mountains.

"Or do I, yes do I, no askyourselfthis, *can* I, really transform myself so?" A diamond, glittering.

"Or perhaps it is both: I am inyourmind, and reallytrue, both at the same time?"

Doro shapeshifted; and spoke, and teased; and delighted; he was a magician. In truth, we knew nothing of him: he seemed to have no inner life, no philosophy, no ideas, no curiosity. But he was articulate, and certainly intelligent in his own peculiar way, and in the service of his own peculiar purposes; and the marvel is that no creature could ever hunt or kill a creature like Doro. He was unfindable, elusive, unkillable.

Only the Ka'un could ever hurt one such as Doro.

"Is this Doro?" A rock. "Or *this*?" A plant. "Or *this*?" And Doro became a small, angry lizard-like creature with a forked tongue and staring eyes.

"Or this? Is *this* Doro?"

As I led Sharrock back to his cell that night, he quizzed me on my friends, and their worlds, and their powers. He was animated; full of joy.

But it was, I feared, the wrong kind of joy.

"With the strength of Cuzco, the power and speed of Fray, the shapeshifting magic of Doro, there is nothing we could not achieve!" he ranted.

"You want to declare war on the Ka'un?"

"Of course. Would you expect anything else—of *Sharrock*?"

"It cannot be done," I explained.

"Of course not," he said soothingly, his eyes ablaze. "I would not dream of challenging the authority of our gaolers. I am happy indeed to be a slave." I recognise the deceit in his words; he was humouring me.

"I had hoped," I said sadly, "that meeting my cabin-friends would have taught you to be like us."

He smiled. "I yearn to be like you Sai-ias. Your humility inspires me."

His tone was warm, his words were gracious; yet I knew contempt for me was in his soul. I found myself resenting this puny creature's arrogant sense of moral superiority. I was old, and wise; Sharrock was by comparison just a *child.*

"I have much more to teach you," I told him.

"I look forward to it with 'joy' in my heart," said Sharrock, smiling even more broadly, whilst tauntingly throwing my own word back at me.

I ushered him to his confining cell. Sharrock lay down upon his bunk and I stared at him a moment: his disproportionately large arms; his torso deeply striated with muscle patterns; his long black hair; his piercingly blue eyes. Sharrock had a way of being still in a fashion that conveyed boundless inner energy; he reminded me of the many four-legged predators that stalked through the forests, who lived only to hunt.

I sighed, from my tentacle tips, sadly but philosophically; then I closed and locked the door.

Day the Second dawned.

For me, this Day is always an arduous delight. The Temple reaches nearly to the clouds now, it is a magnificent achievement and a beautiful one, and it will soon be finished. The final curved stones will be placed at the summit; and the rooms within will be decorated with the names and images of those beloved and mourned by our most gifted artisans.

But every ten years, to my infinite regret, it is decreed that the Temple is imperfect and must be demolished, brick by brick. And so we demolish it, brick by carefully hewn brick, until the ground is bare and the rocks have been returned to the quarries and smashed into fragments; then we begin again. A new Temple, identical to the first, is build with new bricks, and fresh labour; until magnificent imperfection is once more achieved; and then the Temple is once more destroyed.

This has happened, by my reckoning, at least twice ten thousand times.

I watched the sun rise over the Tower.

The Tower was a soaring magnificence of brooding tallness; its walls were made of grey brick mortared with gold; and it shimmered in the sun like the light in a lover's eyes, or so I am told.

It was, without doubt, a creation of great beauty. And yet, forgiving though I am by nature, I hated the Tower with all my soul. For it was the fortress of the Ka'un, where our oppressors dwelled. The sight of it was a daily reproach to all of us; a reminder of their power, and our utter helplessness.

No one could ever reach the Tower. Many had tried, and failed. I knew all their names; they numbered scores of thousands; all doomed by the Tower's wrath.

The Tower was there to mock us; it was a clear token that the Ka'un could never be defeated.

Nor, as I knew well, was there any way to escape from the Ka'un and the planet-sized spaceship they used as our prison. Many had tried that too; including myself.

For when I had first arrived on the Hell Ship I was full of a child's blind rage at the killing of my parents and my people. And when I was told that my enemies dwelled in the huge Tower on the lake, I swam out to it in fury, determined to confront them; and was caught up in a huge storm. And, battered and appalled, I found myself entirely unable to reach the island's shore, because of an invisible force barrier of some kind which surrounded the Tower.

So I returned to land and brooded; and then was told there *was* a way off the ship: through the hull-hatch in the vessel's glass belly. Here it was possible to throw waste objects off the ship—such as bodies—and I excitedly made one of my fellow captives explain the mechanism of the hatch, and its inner cavity that was used to prevent air from the ship from billowing out into space.

And so one day I crept to the glass belly and entered the hatch; and secured myself in the inner cavity; then opened the outer door and toppled out of the ship into deep space.

This of course would have meant certain death for most species; but not for my kind. For we were once creatures of the sea who then journeyed to the land; and then over many years we made a second journey into space, in which bleak environment we can comfortably survive. So my plan was simple; soar off into the vastness of the universe and travel until I found another planet inhabited by my own kind. It was an idiotic plan—I was but a child after all!—for as I now know huge distances separate each star; and in any case, I had no notion around which suns the remainder of my people dwelled, or how to reach there.

But I didn't care. I would rather, I recall angrily thinking to myself, die free than live a slave.

But the Ka'un were far smarter than I; and I soon discovered that their entire spaceship was surrounded by an invisible force barrier, of the same kind that encircled the Tower. Thus, after two cold and futile days trapped in space, I was forced to come clambering back on board and never spoke of it to anyone.

We could not fight; we could not flee, so I was sure that the only way was my way: Live each day, and enjoy it as best you can.

And to encourage my new ones into that contented and calmly resigned state of mind, I treated them gently at times, but at other times with implacable cruelty. For only in this manner were they able to learn the hard lessons that they needed to learn.

Kindness alone does not work; I have tried it and it has always failed.

Thus Sharrock, a nomad, had been deliberately kept by me trapped in a small confining cabin for many cycles. It was making him claustrophobic and desperate; he was by now talking to himself, and occasionally (as I could glimpse through his door) he became engaged in imaginary conversations with his lost loved ones. And so revenge was daily becoming less important to him than having at least *some* measure of freedom.

It was all proceeding according to plan. And when I was with him, Sharrock's rages were fewer; his language was becoming less coarse and offensive; the spittle associated with his ranting tirades was far less often spat in my direction. And so I decided he was now ready to venture out into our world, where he would discover what his life *really* had to offer.

I opened my eyes, after several hours of not sleeping, and I sighed.

Around me were the bodies of Fray and Quipu and Cuzco and Lirilla, all like me savouring the pleasure of pretending to sleep, in the dimly lit spherical cabin that was our home and womb.

There was no trace of Doro; then I noticed that Quipu had six heads. I was amused; Quipu hated that particular jest.

I left my cabin and made my way through circular corridors until I reached the confining cells. I could look through the metal of the door—though prisoners could not look out—and thus I could see that Sharrock was practising his combat moves, in the slowest of motion.

I spoke the codes that Gilgara had taught me so long ago, and the door slid open. Sharrock waited inside patiently, motionless now, poised for action.

"What do you want?" he said, puzzled, for I never came to him at this hour.

"Come with me," I said.

I led Sharrock down another long corridor, past the numerous unoccupied cabins. Once, or so Quipu believed, the ship was equipped to carry colonists by the million, and these cabins were the lonely remnant of that time.

Finally, the white corridor walls came to an end and a single black wall was before us, blocking the way. "I am Sai-ias, four five six oh two one seven, let me through," I told the wall, and it became a door, and opened.

I stepped through, and Sharrock followed. Then he blinked, and looked around.

The sun was rising over the empty lake; the clouds were stripes of scarlet-and-orange splendour; the silhouette of the Tower on its rocky summit loomed blackly against the dappled-redness of the sky. And I wondered once again if the colours of the dawn today were slightly different to the colours of yesterday, and the day before.

I noticed that a flock of aerials were hovering, warming themselves in the sun's beams. And I glanced at Sharrock, and I decided that, despite his air of unimpressable contempt, he was awed at the sight.

"Is it an illusion?" Sharrock asked, with open astonishment.

"It's a construction," I qualified.

"The sight of it could, in some creatures, lead to a sensation of dizziness," Sharrock conceded.

Then Sharrock stepped forward, still blinking in the glaring light, staring up at the empyrean. And that clever-thinking look came upon him again, as he analysed what he saw and tried to make sense of it.

"Artificial downwardness," he speculated. "Whirling-force creates a . . ."

"I know nothing of such matters," I explained warily.

"Downwardness is the compression of space," Sharrock explained, getting into his stride. "It's what keeps us on the surface of a planet. It's why fruit falls. Whirling-force is—"

"I know nothing, and care nothing, of such matters," I informed him, courteously.

"It's a fuck-my-grandmother-if-you-have-a-cock-of-steel hell of a trick," Sharrock said, admiringly. "How big is it?"

"In the units of measurement used on my planet," I said, "It is a breath, or a tenth of a hope. According to the measures more commonly used on board the ship, it is one hundredth of one millionth the size of a yellow dwarf sun. Approximately the size of a typically-sized sea on what I am told is a 'median sized' planet. It's possible to circumnavigate our world in five hours," I added, "if you are a flying creature. Nine, if you ride the rails; and Fray can run it in less than two days, though that is exceptional."

"A planet the size of a small ocean, but the people live on the *inside,"* Sharrock said. There was respect in his tone; and I knew he was consciously learning all he could about his captors and their technology.

My eyes absorbed the view, for I took great joy in the image of my interior world. It was hard not to believe that the sky was about to fall down upon us; hard, too, not to marvel at the genius of a species that could build an entire planet to contain their slaves on the *inside* of a spherical spaceship.

"What's that? The blurring?" asked Sharrock.

"Storms," I explained. "Vast typhoons that prowl the northernmost reaches of the interior planet. Sometimes, the storms escape and entire mountain ranges are ripped to pieces, and the lake is sucked dry of water."

"Why? Why build an artificial planet that has such terrible storms?" Sharrock asked.

"It may be, I am told, a design flaw," I lied. The Ka'un loved to see things being destroyed: how could he not guess *that*?

"And how many different species exist here?"

"Many," I said evasively; some find a tally of the number of defeated civilisations demoralising.

"And none of them are from my planet."

"None."

"Everyone died?"

"Everyone," I explained, "except for you."

Sharrock's face was pale, almost pink. It became moist again.

"Let us explore," I said, brightly.

We walked down to the lake and I dived into the waters and returned with a mouthful of wriggling fish that I spat out and gutted with my claws and offered to the startled Sharrock.

Sharrock stared at the eviscerated fish anxiously. "Are these not intelligent creatures, like you and I?" he said, warily.

"No, of course not," I said. "I know all the sentients by name. But many of the fish in the lake, and the aerials in the skies, and a few of the grazing species, are just dumb beasts; and they multiply without restraint. We have to keep their numbers down. We sentients, however, cannot breed. Although the Kindred keep trying."

"The Kindred?"

"The giant bipeds. There are a thousand or more of them, all the same species. Twice the size of you, with claws on their fingers and with one more eye than you have. They do not mix."

"And how many other 'bipeds' are there?"

"Three hundred and four, of the hairless and tailless varieties such as yourself. You will be able to get to know them soon," I said; though that was a lie.

"Good," Sharrock conceded grandly, as though I were his subject; this was I realised an annoying habit of his.

Above us, dumb birds and smart aerials flew. The trees nearest us were purple sentients and were admired by all of us for their extraordinary intellect and wisdom. I warned Sharrock not to eat the berries, for that was tantamount to eating the gonads of a great philosopher. Arboreals of all sizes and colours perched in branches and swung from branches and seized every opportunity to stare curiously at the newcomer. Sharrock looked around at it all, appraising, memorising, undoubtedly awestruck.

"I'd like a swim," said Doro, and Sharrock looked around, baffled.

I slithered across to the rocks, and picked up Doro—who was, as always, perfectly camouflaged. And I held him in the tips of two tentacles.

"How is he doing?" Doro asked.

"A talking rock?" Sharrock said sceptically.

"You've met Doro once before," I explained. "The night I took you to my cabin."

Comprehension dawned in his eyes. "The shapeshifter. I encountered another species like that once, while on a mission in the Lexoid Galaxy."

"That is a tale I would love to hear."

"And so you shall," said Sharrock, with charm.

I hurled Doro into the waters of the lake, where he became waves.

Sharrock smiled. He was, I could tell, starting to enjoy himself.

My strategy was working.

"This tastes good," Sharrock said, a little while later, chewing on the fish I had caught for him.

"It has no nutritional value," I admitted. "The Ka'un alter the cells of these fish to be non-poisonous to all species, but our physiologies are so different we can't hope to digest the flesh. It is the gloop we eat daily and the water from the well of life that truly feeds us."

"The water?"

"It contains foodstuffs and minerals and hormones in solution form, and is able to alter its molecular structure to suit the needs of each of us."

"Water can do all that?"

"The water and the air are what keep us alive."

"How so?"

"They just—do," I explained.

Sharrock laughed; and crinkled his eyes. He was, I realised, using his charm on me again.

"Perhaps, dear Sai-ias, you could explain in just a little more detail?" he said, and there was a courtesy to his tone I had not heard before.

I remembered all I had been told, by the technological sentients like Quipu. "The air," I told Sharrock, "doesn't just translate our words, it transforms itself so that we can breathe. It transmutes itself to give oxygen to one species, methane to another, and so forth. Somehow, the air knows how to be the *right* air for each of us, no matter how different our worlds."

"The air—*knows this*?" said Sharrock.

"Yes."

"That's—" said Sharrock, and could not find a word for it.

"And it also, so I'm told," I continued, "carries with it light. The sun is not the sun, it is merely air shaped in a ball. And when the air of the sun grows tired, the light gets redder and we call that sunset."

"Air can do all *that*?"

"In this world, yes it can," I explained.

"Such marvels are—beyond belief," said Sharrock, and I could tell he was plotting and scheming again. "But this air—the Ka'un created it right? It has, perhaps, micro-particles that carry information? So each molecule of air functions like a miniature artificial mind? Like a...a...data engine, but at a sub-atomic level?"

"Perhaps," I said, cautiously.

"You have no idea what I'm talking about, do you?" said Sharrock.

"No I do not."

"Amazing."

"Why is it amazing?"

Sharrock's mouth made a shape, common to many bipeds; a smile.

"I'm not considered to be a great scientist among my kind. I'm certainly not a Philosopher," Sharrock explained. "But these are basic concepts, that every sentient creature must be aware of. Surely?"

"Not me," I admitted.

He was silent for a while. I could tell his spirits were high; he was convinced he had discovered some secret that could be used to destroy the Ka'un. The usual delusion.

And so, as we sat there, I realised that it was time for me to proceed to the next stage of my strategy; to save this poor wretched creature before hope wholly destroyed him.

Thus, once we had eaten and digested, I began to speak to him softly, whilst bathing him in a persuasive spray from my tentacles that would, I knew, render him more pliable and less aggressive.

"This is what will happen," I explained. "In a while we will walk down to the forest. You will find there a place to live. And there also will be creatures for you to live with. They will teach you the ways of this world; and they will be harsh ways. I will visit you when I can. But I can help you no more; this must be your home now."

"You're leaving me?" Sharrock said, drowsily, with only a trace of fear in his voice.

"I will see you as often as I can," I said. "But though you and I can be friends, we can't be—close friends. Our bodies are too different."

"And what do I do, when I'm given this new home?"

"You must learn," I told him, "to love the little pleasures. You can fish, and forage, and hunt; and bask in the sun; and savour the Rhythm of Days."

"That is no kind of life," Sharrock said, through his sleepy haze, "for a warrior!"

"Ah, you warriors, you are so brave," I said, flatteringly.

"I am," he said, drugged yet proud, "among the greatest of warriors!"

"You must forget all that," I said soothingly. "Forget your old ways. Live for the moment."

"The greatest," he murmured, "of warriors."

And I sighed, from each of my tentacle tips, sorrowfully.

I dared not tell Sharrock the truth, not just yet; that there is indeed a place for warriors on the Ka'un's ship.

For some nights, the night does not end. And a deep dreamless sleep descends upon us.

And when we wake, we find that some of our most fearsome fighters have disappeared. They have been conveyed, in a fashion we do not comprehend, away from their cabins while the rest of us slept. And of these, the Vanished Ones, some never return. And others, like Cuzco on so many occasions, do return after a passage of months or years, but horrendously scarred and battered, or with limbs that are weak and recently regrown.

And these Vanished Warriors have no recollection of what has occurred to them, and no inkling as to how they sustained their injuries.

At first, many of us assumed that the Ka'un were "experimenting" on the Vanished Ones, to advance their knowledge of alien biology; such ruthless behaviour is, I have learned, common among many technological species. Others believed that the Vanished Ones were being tortured for information; though since all of us had lost our worlds, it was hard to say what information the Ka'un might need from us.

But as time went by the truth forced itself upon us all. The Vanished Ones always had one thing in common; they were strong, or armoured, or fierce, or terrifyingly large, or from species which made a religion of the art of war.

Or to put it in bolder terms: those who go missing are the warriors supreme of the Ka'un's Hell Ship. And it became obvious to all of us what they do.

They fight, and vanquish, and destroy, and capture fresh slaves.

Thus, these warriors unwillingly serve the evil that is the Ka'un. They conquer alien worlds; their memories are swept clean; and they are returned to us.

This, I knew, would be Sharrock's fate; his warrior skills would make him irresistibly attractive to the Ka'un. I did not warn him, however, of what was in prospect for him; for who could bear to know they were cursed with such a terrible fate?

Lies, sometimes, can be kinder than truth.

"This will be your home now," I told Sharrock, as we stood in the shadow of the scarlet carola trees that marked the boundary of the forest region.

He stared at me accusingly. "Did you drug me?" he asked.

"I calmed you."

"My rage," said Sharrock, incredulously, "has gone. I feel content."

"That is good."

"My rage has gone. I feel content!" He sounded like a child who has had a toy stolen by a sibling.

"You will be happy here." A silver-furred arboreal dropped from the tree-top and joined us, scamperingly.

"This is Mangan," I said. "He will be your companion and your mentor now."

Mangan danced, and snarled; and his eyes flickered hatred.

"Why," said Mangan, "do we have to put up with this hairless fucking freak?"

"He is my friend," I said soothingly. "Protect him."

Mangan cackled, and scratched his balls, and spat green phlegm, and began to—I need describe no more. Mangan truly was the foulest of beasts.

Sharrock looked at the silver arboreal warily, and with an

expression of considerable distaste. "*These* are the creatures I must live with?"

"Treat him well," I said to Mangan, who merely cackled, and stared with hate at the fresh meat I had so generously provided him with.

I unfurled my cape, and I seized the ground with my tentacle tips and hurled myself into the air away from them. Sharrock called after me; but I continued to seize and fly, seize and fly, and I did not look back.

Sharrock

I felt an overwhelming sense of relief when the monster departed.

This black-hided brute has pretended to be my friend; but I know that she is no more than the hapless pawn of my gaolers. Her soft words—for her voice is melodious and beautiful without doubt—have been used to lull me and deceive me. She has preached acceptance and forgiveness; but as a warrior, I could never accept, or forgive, those who have wronged me so utterly.

And so to be free of her gave me a great sense of liberation.

I looked about me, and became attuned to the sounds and the sweet smells of the forest. I could hear screeches and howls and clicks and roars and bellows and grating noises. There were very many creatures here, and none of them were familiar to me. The trees also were strange—some with bark as hard as marble, some soft to the touch. The plants which covered the forest ground were equally diverse and bizarre and their leaves and flowers spanned the rainbow of colours, with some shades of green and purple I had never seen before. There were no insects; that was strange. The air was mild, quite warm; the sun cast a steady heat but never moved.

Once Sai-ias had left, Mangan had fled too. As I had suspected, this was a creature who knew nothing about honouring one's word. But this too filled me with relief; I had no intention of being trapped in a forest, and certainly not in a small cabin, with a bunch of monkeys.

Instead, I resolved I would live alone, in this forest; I was a creature of the desert, but I was sure I could easily adapt. And I found that I liked the colours, and the scents, and the cacophony of sounds of this alien landscape.

For months I had lived in a cage of metal, occasionally released from captivity only to spend hours in the company of garrulous monsters of astonishingly vile aspects.

But now, after all those months of close captivity, I could smell flowers in the air, I could hear creatures crying and howling and singing, my senses were exhilaratedly alive. And I felt—no this could not be!—yet it was—I felt *content.* Fulfilled.

I could of course never be *truly* happy on this world. But I did at least relish being alive, in the forest, with all my senses engaged to the full.

And so I walked carefully through the avenues and alleys of trees, treading a path through wild shrubs and knotted ground vines, over mossy carpets of green and scarlet, and past plants with barks that resembled obsidian and others that seemed to be clad in soft velvet, and others stranger still.

And then my instincts flared and I rolled to the ground and turned around, to see that a serpentine creature had dropped from the branches behind me. It was clearly enraged that it had failed to land upon my head; it snarled viciously; its fangs were large and it spat venom that I dodged swiftly. And then it lunged at me. I had no weapon, but I stood my ground, and caught the creature in my hands, and strangled it to death.

Then I ripped the creature to pieces with my teeth and made a weapon out of its hide and fangs.

I moved onwards. It occurred to me I was still wearing the clothes I had on when my planet was attacked—leather tunic, leather trousers, a gold-mail vest, and silver bracelets around my wrists; and I now wondered how that was possible. The lava would have burned all these things off my body, as well as destroying my flesh and organs. So how was I alive? And how could my clothing still be wearable? And what had happened to the space armour I had put on? Why in other words were some of my clothes intact, but not all?

I decided these could not be my actual clothes. They must have stripped the clothing off the corpse of another warrior of similar bulk, cleaned it of blood, and dressed me in his garb. My body was then, or so I speculated, rejuvenated by means unknown to me; but that was hardly difficult to achieve. My own kind have rejuvenation therapies that allow us to restore a broken warrior to full health within months; it was no wonder these technologically advanced aliens could do better.

I sniffed my clothes and my theory was confirmed; these were not Sharrock's. The leather of the tunic smelled of leather; not of me. I had worn my own garments on a myriad adventures; they were steeped in my stench.

And now a new adventure had begun. My planet was gone; my people were gone; I was alone on a hostile planet, which is actually a ship, surrounded by aliens who are monstrous beyond belief, ruled by unseen devils who all fear but none dare defy.

It was, I resolved, time for Sharrock to show what he could really do!

For I remembered the time—

A figure dropped to the ground behind me; I interrupted my reverie, and turned in a single easy gesture. It was the silver-skinned monkey, Mangan, glaring at me with his evil eyes.

"Greetings," I said.

"You are to be our cabin friend, I gather," said Mangan.

"That was the stated intention of the monster Sai-ias," I said. "But I am happy to live alone."

"That is not an option, cock-brain," said Mangan, cackling.

"I will live alone," I said calmly.

"You will do as Sai-ias requires," Mangan insisted.

"I think not," I said smiling.

Mangan cackled again. He was a vile creature. And then, to my shock and dismay, he hunched down and he shat, like the most vulgar of beasts. Then he captured his column of shit in one hand, and squeezed it into a tight compact ball.

And then he threw it at me. It was so fast I did not have time to dodge; and the shit-ball was remarkably hard, harder than any stone. I felt the dampness of my own blood trickle down my cheek.

But I ignored the provocation.

"My people were killed, I will take revenge somehow, I will live alone," I explained patiently.

Three other monkeys dropped to the ground beside Mangan. One of them had a sharpened stick, and I relaxed, hefting the home-made fang-weapon in my hand.

I sensed another home-made missile about to hit me from behind, and this time I was ready; I rolled easily to the ground; the shit-ball flew past me, but a second ball of excrement from an assailant I hadn't spotted hit me on the side of the head.

I cursed; the months of captivity had sapped my warrior reflexes.

Fortunately, however, this particular ball had been inadequately compacted; it was soft, not hard; thus, I had sustained no damage. My head however, felt damp and sticky and I touched it with a finger. The smell overwhelmed me.

However, I laughed uproariously, to show I could take a joke.

"Do you have a hole where you ought to have a cock?" asked Mangan, provocatively.

"Not so," I said cheerfully.

Mangan cackled, then he turned his back to me, and then he—

At this moment, I am bound to relate, I foolishly lost my temper.

Jak

Albinia closed her eyes. I watched as she sank into a trance.

Her worry lines faded, her angry look disappeared. She was, once more, radiant.

I could see on my phantom control display the images she beheld via Explorer's riftscope. Glimpses of planets and suns and black wildernesses of space and U shaped galaxies and oval galaxies and spilled-milk galaxies and fast-whirling galaxies and exploding stars.

"Three civilisations in subsector 412, planet O431," said Albinia, through her trance.

We saw, on our display screens: stars, then planets, then seas, then fields, and plains, and savannahs, forests, mountains, cities, walkways, flying vehicles, temples, houses, shops and, finally, images of three kinds of sentients.

Furred bipeds with three arms, living in the cities.

Scaled polypods with tusks, dwelling in the savannahs.

And feathered aerials nesting in clouds made of excreted webbing, above the forests.

"Three Grade 2 civilisations on one planet?" I asked.

"It looks that way." Albinia murmured.

"Any of them aggressive?"

"Perhaps. Perhaps not. Can't tell."

"Any artefacts? Jewellery? Artworks?"

"Too soon to say."

"Do they have shifting-sands technology?"

"Yes. Maybe. No. I don't know."

Albinia's head twitched. She was seeing the not-real as well as the real; visualising shards of possibilities that existed on the other side of the rift, of worlds and civilisations that might in fact not exist.

"Set the coordinates," I said.

"We have an incoming message," said Phylas.

"Take the message, then get ready for rift flight," I said.

A face appeared on the screen; I recognised it as a FanTang.

(This memory comes to me now laden with such terrible ironical agony; for those loathsome murderous creatures did perhaps deserve to die. But not *us*; *we* did not deserve it! Not all of *us*.)

"We wish you wealth and health, and success in all your dealings," I said formally to the FanTang.

"You betrayed us!" roared the FanTang, with the hysterical rage so typical of his species.

"We may," I admitted, "have out-negotiated you. It's a cultural thing: we see no harm in it, you see."

"You brought death and destruction to our planet!" roared the FanTang.

I hesitated.

And then continued to hesitate.

"What are you talking about?" I eventually asked, baffled.

"Earthquakes have ravaged our land! Fires from the sky have—"

The transmission was interrupted.

I blinked, totally at a loss. "What was that about?"

"I have no idea," said Morval.

"A hoax?" suggested Phylas.

"A trap?" suggested Galamea.

"No," said Albinia. Her eyes opened. "Explorer has accessed other such messages, sent to other Olaran vessels. We have also made contact with the Fleet. There is a story is emerging about what has befallen the planet of the FanTang."

"And what is that?" I asked, impatiently.

"Apocalypse."

The sun of the FanTangs had exploded. Or rather, to be more precise, it had flared to an exceptional degree; coronal mass was billowing forth, and a vast proton swarm had radiated into the stellar system, where it was wreaking terrible havoc on the various planets and asteroids and space towns where the FanTang dwelt. Our sensors told us that there were now no traces of organic life in the entire stellar system.

And the home world of the FanTang was a fireball. As we flew our cameras closer, we could see that the forests were ablaze. Volcanoes were spewing their hot lava into the atmosphere. Even the seas burned. *The seas?*

"How can that be?" I asked. "The oceans on fire?"

I and the rest of the ship's officers were watching camera images transmitted from Explorer via Albinia's mind; images that were being filmed by robot scouts that flew through the cloud and into the depths of the inferno.

"It's possible," said Phylas, "but only if—"

"Do we have the technology to do such a thing?" I snapped.

"No," Phylas conceded.

The robot scouts flew down closer. We could see lava spurting out of cracks in the planet's crust. The cities were wrecked, and entire mountain ranges had been demolished after devastating crust-plate shifts ripped the planet apart. FanTang military aeroplanes had fallen from the sky like snowflakes ablaze, and the remnants of futile missiles were scattered on fields and plains wherever we looked. Mushroom clouds from nuclear explosions billowed and their clouds merged to form an ugly grey shell in the sky.

And the streets of the cities and smaller settlements were covered in corpses, and already-whitening skeletons. All the dead were FanTang or Jaimal, and many wore heavy body armour or exo-skeletons.

The people of this planet were warriors and they had marched into battle against some implacable foe. Billions if not trillions had died; yet our cameras did not see the corpse of a single enemy combatant.

It was carnage; token of a defeat so absolute it beggared belief.

"That's a Trader craft," said Morval, and the scout ship flew lower and we saw the wreckage of a Trader vessel on the ground, its complex bottle-curves shattered by some hammer blow. There were corpses lying near the wreckage. They were clearly Olaran.

"Retrieve the bodies," I said, and the scout ship levitated the corpses and swallowed them in its hull.

"Who did this?" asked Galamea.

The image on the screen began to flicker.

"What's wrong?" I said.

Albinia screamed, and screamed, and her eyes snapped out of trance, cutting her link with the metal minds.

"The planet," she murmured.

Phylas changed the sky-eye image, and now we saw hovering in mid-air a more distant view of the blackened smoking globe of the planet of the FanTang.

"The planet's going to blow," said Phylas, taking the readings.

Pillars of flame started to burst upwards from the planet's surface. Black clouds gathered and dispersed, then re-gathered. The blue of the seas and the red of the fields slowly vanished; until nothing could be seen except a black haze of smoke that mingled with the mushroom clouds.

"The sun!" screamed Phylas, and an image of the sun appeared before us.

The sun was changing colour, and its corona was flaring even more wildly, expelling gobbets of plasma like the vomit of a dying Olaran. I looked at my instruments and saw that we were being drenched in solar radiation.

"Supernova?" I said.

"I believe so," said Phylas.

Now, the process seems wearily familiar; then, it was a horror like nothing we had ever seen.

After hours of devastating volcanic activity and earthquakes that ripped the land to shreds, the planet itself *shattered*—it broke into a million parts, as if struck a terrible blow, and the fragments drifted in space.

And then, in a ghastly slow ballet, the moons too detonated, one by one; like spools of cable unwinding, leaving sad haloes of light behind where once life had dwelled.

And finally, the sun of the FanTang turned supernova; an eruption of light like a universe birthing; a vision of nature's fury such as I had never seen before.

Ten years previously I had travelled to this stellar system and raged at the ignorance and brutal violence of that wretched species, the FanTang. Now they were a memory; their bodies interstellar debris; and I was chilled at the breathtaking malice of such an act of planetary genocide.

"The FanTang," Albinia announced, "left a dying message; they blame us for their downfall."

"No one will believe that," said Albinia.

"Some may," conceded Morval.

"They accused us of betraying them; ambushing them; and destroying their planet," said Albinia.

"They were," I said excusingly, "wild with grief."

"The Trader Post was also destroyed; five hundred Olarans dead," Albinia added.

Morval made a strange exclamation; more howl than word.

"How is that possible?" Morval said. "Our space defences are—"

"The Olaran Court believes there is a aggressive species currently active with technology comparable to our own," Albinia concluded.

"That conclusion is inescapable," said Galamea coldly. She had fought in the war against the Stuxi; she more than anyone knew what was at stake here.

For our entire culture, our entire civilisation, is founded on one thing: undefeatable military might, based on science far beyond the imaginings of most sentient species. The Stuxi came close; but even they were, ultimately, easily defeated by our astonishingly powerful weapons of destruction.

It was our military power than ensured that no species could invade us, or defeat us, or threaten our trading links. But now, at a stroke, that had changed. And we were vulnerable.

I felt dizzy; as though standing on a high cliff top, staring down into an abyss.

"Whoever did this," I said, calmly, but with utter conviction—for I knew the ability of our kind to birth a grudge, and to nurture it, and then to wreak the most terrible vengeance—"they shall pay."

Sa-ias

I was travelling fast across the plain, throwing myself upwards and forwards with my tentacles, like a bullet with arms, when I heard a roaring sound above me. I tried to swerve away, but I was too slow and a great weight came crashing into me.

Cuzco!

His claws lashed at me, his great jagged tongue jabbed me, his six wings enveloped me and prevented me from propelling myself forward.

"You fucking cunt-eating cowardly fucking seamonster!" he screamed at me, and his foul words flew on the wind as our bodies encoiled and rolled.

I screamed at him to stop but he wouldn't heed me and we continued to tumble along the ground.

At the last moment Cuzco broke free but I carried on hurtling onwards and gouged a huge trench out of the grey earth with my arse and back segments.

Cuzco's assault had knocked the breath out of my lungs. I was dazed. I clambered myself upright on to my twelve feet and I glared at Cuzco.

"Was that your idea," I asked, "of a joke?"

"Oh," said Cuzco, "yes."

And Cuzco bared his face at me; and mocking laughter consumed his features.

I sighed, from my tentacle tips; I loved Cuzco, but even so, I had to concede that he could be an annoying bully sometimes.

"That stupid fucking biped of yours," he said tauntingly, "will never last. He'll be in Despair and out of the hatch in less than a year."

"We'll see."

Cuzco's features were consumed with hilarity. "He doesn't stand a swamp-fucking chance!" he crowed, and I raged at his cruel mockery.

And yet I feared his words were true.

The Rhythm of Days consumed me, as it always did.

And then, on a Day the Ninth, just three cycles after leaving Sharrock with the arboreals, I travelled to see him, once again using my tentacles to fling me fast through the air.

I saw that the camp I had helped him to make in the forest was deserted. I stood by the trees and called his name and saw no trace of him.

And so I called up to the aerials flying above and they descended, and I asked them courteously for a favour.

And then I spread my cape and they gripped my carapace in their claws and lifted me up into the air. Up I rose, their sharp talons gripping my soft skin, their wings beating; a hundred aerial creatures with scales and feathers and furs upon their wings, some with double heads, some with none, some as large as clouds, some as tiny as a biped's skull; and they flew me up, above the tree line; then higher still; and patiently waited until the winds were strong enough to support me.

Then I thanked them again, and the aerials released me, and flew off, no doubt relieved to be no longer lifting my considerable bulk. I was now gliding on updrafts of air, undulating my cape and extended body to remain stable.

And from my aerial viewpoint, I peered down at the forest canopy, looking for the haloes of the arboreals who were supposed to be Sharrock's cabin friends.

It took me a while to remember the knack of ignoring visual input so that I could focus on the mesh of body heat and personality that defined each sentient's halo. The four I was looking for had strongly defined haloes—they were angry, spiteful creatures, and that made them easier to find. They were: Mangan, who I had introduced to Sharrock, Tara, Shiiaa, and Daran.

But there were hundreds of arboreals down there, and it was hard to focus on haloes as my body bucked and kinked in the wind. But I persevered: and so slowly and carefully, as the black shadow of my body fell upon the green and yellow forest canopy below, my eyes analysed the blurry patterns of hundreds of bodies in motion.

Eventually I was confident I had found my four. They were travelling fast, running up and down trees and swinging from branch to branch. They were chasing something; and then I saw a fifth halo and recognised it as Sharrock. They were playing with him.

This was exactly what I'd feared; the foul-mouthed, arrogant, always-angry Sharrock had riled the vicious little bastards.

I began to glide downwards towards the canopy. I furled my cape to make my body smaller then released my hood so it dangled above and behind me, slowing my fall, allowing me to control my descent.

Then I tightened into a hard ball and crashed through the canopy, breaking branches and shattering tree trunks until I landed safely on the ground.

I was now back to my usual size, a moist-skinned jet-black sea creature in a forest; feeling out of place and claustrophobic. But I owed it to Sharrock to rescue him.

I called out Sharrock's name; no response.

I called Sharrock's name again, but still he did not show himself. So I peered through the trees, looking for his halo, and saw that he was near. He was running along the ground, frenziedly and fast; clearly he was not agile enough to swing from branch to branch.

He had been doing this, I guessed, for about thirty-four days; and yet his pace was unfaltering and fast.

I charged forward and crashed a path through the thick forest, towards Sharrock's fleeing body. I could hear screaming and cackling near him. On I thundered; I was too large to weave between trees so I simply ran at them and pushed the trees over, leaving a trail of destruction behind me.

And as I ran, I called Sharrock's name, and his halo moved closer and closer, and I could tell that he was tracking me, trying to reach me. And finally, I emerged into a clearing, and he broke from cover and ran towards me.

As he ran, projectiles rained down from the trees and crashed into his body, exploding like bombs and coating him from head to toe in a slimy brown slurry. The blows were powerful and I could hear bones breaking, but Sharrock's run did not falter. He ran towards me, and rolled, and stood up behind me, using me as his shield.

The projectiles, I realised, were balls of shit; Sharrock was stained with the juice of them, and I was glad I had no olfactory sense.

"You evil fucking bitch!" Sharrock shouted at me. He was out of breath. His arm was crooked and he favoured one leg; I guessed he had been beaten badly, perhaps several times. One of the arboreals had eaten his nose, and the bloody mess on the front of his face was still damp and unhealed.

"Oh Sharrock," I said, "I'm so very sorry."

"You fucking should be!" he roared. "These bastards have been chasing me for an entire fucking [unit of measurement on his world]. You treacherous cock-with-contagious-boils! This is all your fucking fault! Get me out of here!"

I sighed sorrowfully through my tentacle tips; for there was really no cause for such extreme language. I considered myself to be unoffendable, but even I was starting to get annoyed.

Meanwhile, the arboreals leaped down from the trees and hopped around, elated at the success of their great joke.

"I cannot," I said.

"They tried to fucking kill me!"

"You must have provoked them," I said sternly.

He looked at me, with horror and rage. "No I did not!"

"Did you tell them," I asked, "that they are inferior to you, mere ignorant simians without any culture or grasp of sophisticated concepts?"

He hesitated; no doubt startled that I knew him so well. "Well perhaps," he said. "But not in those exact words."

"What were in fact your exact words?"

"I told Mangan," said Sharrock recalling the moment with evident relish, "that he was nothing but a tree-fucking ape, and that on my planet we cook the brains of such ignorant branch-swinging hairy-arsed shit-hurling ignorant fucking savages!"

I sighed again, and in fairness he had the grace to look abashed at his own misguided eloquence.

"You insulted them," I said. "And this is their way of asserting dominance over you."

"Over *me*!?!" roared Sharrock. "On my planet, we feed hairy-cocked beasts like this to our fucking pets! You evil fucking whore-shit! You led me into a trap. You knew what would happen to me!"

"I knew it was possible. But you should not have not been so discourteously provocative," I advised him.

"You should have warned me how vicious these evil fuckers are!"

"I sedated you," I pointed out, "prior to leaving you in the forest. Surely that was warning enough?"

At that moment, Mangan strode towards us, his three legs moving in an odd rhythm, his silver fur matted, his big staring eyes blinking. Mangan's four arms were huge, and he carried spiked clubs made out of tree branches in each hand.

"You fled, you hairless foul-tongued coward," he sneered at Sharrock.

"I am no coward! However, I would like to try," said Sharrock, in an unexpected attempt at diplomacy, "to be your friend."

Daran threw another shit ball, rather sneakily; and I batted it away with one tentacle.

"This is wrong," I told the arboreals. And they cackled and danced on the balls of their feet, entirely unrepentant.

"I regret my words," said Sharrock. "I have insulted you, and for this I deserve all you have done to me. For Sharrock is," and at this moment he literally hung his head in shame, "humbled, and defeated."

The arboreals cackled again. Mangan was starting to look mollified. For one exhilarating moment, I began to think that Sharrock was capable of behaving like a sane and civilised sentient.

And then Sharrock screamed: "Ha! I jest! Sharrock? Defeated? *Never!!*" And he pounced.

And then I realised that for all this time he'd been trying to get the four arboreals to descend to ground level. In the trees, they had the advantage; down here, he had a fighting chance.

And so he dived forward and rolled, like a bird in flight, and unbalanced Mangan with a foot swipe, and as he did so his elbow connected with the huge arboreal's ribs. He broke two of Mangan's arms in moments and then he had one of the clubs in his hand, and as the other three arboreals leaped at him he lashed out and in a series of swings so fast they defied the ability of eyes to see, he smashed their heads into pulp.

Mangan was back on his feet, and locked one hand around Sharrock's neck but Sharrock had a knife made of serpent's fangs concealed and he hacked Mangan's arm off then buried the knife in his brain.

Shiiaa recovered from her battering, and got up, and lunged; her skull was caved in but her three knife arms were swinging. However, Sharrock leaped above Shiiaa's head and landed behind her, then delivered two savage kicks to the arboreal's twin spines, shattering both, and then broke her neck with a single savage twist.

But then Tara's tail whipped up and caught Sharrock by the neck and lifted him in the air.

"Stop," I said, but Tara ignored me so I spat at her; the spit congealed and wrapped her body in a tight web. Tara choked and fell to the ground, unable to move, snarled in white congealed spit that was stronger than metal. And Sharrock broke free of the tail and fell to the ground.

"Nice one, bitch," he said, when he'd got his breath back.

"Climb on my back," I told him.

I ran out of the forest with Sharrock clinging on to me, ramming through undergrowth and trees, hoping that I was not hurting any sentient plantlife in my clumsy progress. And then we emerged into the light, and I crashed down upon my lower segment on the purple grass of the savannah.

"I was defending myself," Sharrock said, angrily.

"You picked a fight," I informed him, accusingly.

"They were treating me like a slave."

"You *are* a slave, and you should learn to be more polite."

"You fucking betrayed me!" he roared, spittle rolling down his jaw again. "You put me with a bunch of fucking apes. Why didn't you let me go and live with creatures who actually look like Maxoluns? The hairless bipeds. I know they exist. I saw them, the tree-huggers saw them too. They are creatures much like me!"

"The hairless bipeds," I said, calmly, "have swords of metal. You would have fared far worse."

Sharrock was silenced by my words.

"You mean, you knew," he said, in calmer tones, "that I was going to get the fuckhood beaten out of me by those fucking apes?"

"Yes."

"And you still let me go there?"

"For your own sake," I explained to him, "For you have to

learn to hold your tongue, and be more respectful of your fellow captives."

"No fucking way, not ever! I'm a warrior!" he ranted.

"You've made four bitter enemies now. They will hate you for all eternity."

"I killed at least two of them," he bragged.

By this point I was tempted to give way to anger at his naïvety. But I restrained myself. Sharrock was so new; he had so much to learn.

"No you didn't," I explained in my calmest tones.

"Don't utter such fuckery! No one could—" he began to say, but I interrupted:

"Their injuries are survivable. Mangan will grow his arm back, and his brain cells will very likely heal after such a minor fang-stabbing, as will Shiiaa's broken neck and snapped spines. And when they are all recovered, they will seek you out and batter you to a bloody pulp. But unless they entirely pulverise your brain, you too will heal, after months of agony. And then, consumed with rage, you will take your revenge upon *them,* and they will be beaten and bloody and in pain. Then *they* will heal, and—"

"I'm guessing you don't approve of all this wretched backing-and-forthing," he said quietly.

I sighed, from my tentacle tips, and noted with approval that Sharrock did finally seem a little embarrassed.

"These creatures are not your enemies," I said. "We are all of us in this together."

Sharrock made a sharp exclamation—it was his version of a laugh, I realised. But there was no humour in his tone.

"Fuck your anus!" Sharrock said viciously. "Those tree-fuckers bit my nose off! They broke my arm, my legs, then they tried to take my intestines out with a sharpened branch. Those shit-eaters deserve to die by choking on the barbed cock of a [untranslatable]!" Sharrock concluded, spitting with rage again by now.

"Make peace with them," I said.

"Never!"

"You can't," I told him, "go on like this."

He glared at me.

"Sai-ias, you mean well," Sharrock said, icily, with what I felt was odious condescension. "You have a good soul. But the truth is," and now Sharrock's contempt for me shone through in every syllable, "you are nothing but a fucking coward."

Sharrock's scorn was hard to bear; but bear it I will and must.

For I have learned, over many aeons, to ignore the disdain of others, as warriors shrug off ghastly wounds without showing even a flicker of pain.

This is my tale; the tale how I shaped my world.

I was but a child when the Ka'un invaded my home world; just fifteen years old, two or three years away from my metamorphosis.

And I remembered how we young ones were amused when the alien spaceships first appeared in the sky. We made a game of swiftly dodging their bombs as they crashed to the ground, scattering earth and terrifying the land animals. And then we ran home and told our parents.

My parents comforted me, and told me we would be safe. But they did not fight, they fled, using flying ships to convey us at speeds faster than sound, as far away as we could get from the alien ship. And when the bombs continued to fall from the sky, we and millions of our kind took refuge deep in the earth's crust. We would, my mother said, wait it out. When the enemy tired of destroying our cities and houses, such as they were, we would emerge and rebuild our planet. Or we would find another planet. It would be easy enough.

But when the earthquakes began my father was crushed by a

wall of rock that collapsed on to him. He cut himself free, knowing he could, eventually, regrow his lost limbs. But he was worried now.

Then poison gas came through the rock and my brothers and sisters died in agony. My mother nursed them all, stroking them with her tentacle tips and mouth and thus absorbing the poison into her own body. And then she too died, while holding me in her tentacles, exhaling deadly air upon me, killing me with foolish love, for by then she had lost her senses with grief.

My father found me in time and sucked out the poisoned air out of my lungs and into his own body, dooming himself but saving me. Then he wrapped me in protective shielding, and placed me in a space capsule. And he fired the capsule into orbit, with a course set for another of the worlds occupied by our kind, so that one of us at least should live.

When he said goodbye, my father vowed that I would live a happy life, and that these invaders would not find it so easy to invade our other planets. For mind-messages had been sent with instantaneous effect to all my people—to those living on alien soil and also those who lived on artificial orbiting cities and those who chose to slowly drift in space, living on the energy from distant suns—to warn them that the ways of peace must come to an end. We must, as a species, resort to war, using all of our formidable powers.

All this he told me; and I marvelled at the rage in his voice, and the anger-fuelled expansion of his normally compact body. And I sorrowed for him, and for my dead mother; they were kind and full of joy and I loved them, and they will live for ever in my memories and in the depth of my soul.

Then, as I grieved, a child forced to confront evil for the first time, my father sealed the capsule and I was shot out into space in a cylinder of metal that was, my father hoped, to be my home for the next one thousand years.

However, his plans failed; and I was captured by the alien invaders as my craft made its way out the atmosphere. I lay in semi-sleep and woke abruptly when I felt my capsule lose all its momentum in a moment.

And later the capsule was broken open and I was confronted by an ugly tiny creature with two legs and fur, which I later learned was clothing. This was a Kindred; but at the time I thought it was a Ka'un.

I clambered out of my capsule to confront the creature, and lashed at him with my tentacles; and found he was made of air. A projection.

I realised I was alone inside a huge room shaped like a globe, made of some kind of glass; and beneath me and all around was the blackness of space, and the stars. And shining in the midst of the emptiness of space was a planet, my own planet; which our people had called Tendala. I knew this view of Tendala well; for I had flown in orbit around her many times; and as I looked now at the planet in space, I saw the oceans that I had swum in, and the mountains I had climbed.

I was confused, and frightened, and baffled. My confining shell was large and had no features and no visible doors; and because the floor too was made of glass it felt as if I were floating in space.

And, there, from my vantage point inside the glass belly of the Ka'un spaceship, I saw my planet start to break into pieces.

It was an impossible yet haunting image. I saw none of the terror and destruction that must have existed on the ground—the cities and forests burning, the seas racked with storms, the volcanoes erupting. All I saw was a beautiful blue globe breaking apart like smashed glass, and fragments the size of entire countries tumbling into space.

And my soul was rent with pain.

I knew I would never seen my loved ones again; never again would I feel the winds of Tendala, or swim in the Parago Seas, or watch the beauteous birds of Tharbois in colourful flight. Child though I was, I knew by now that these monsters took joy in the extermination of other sentient beings. And I knew them to be, by our own moral code, "evil."

But though I was full of rage back then, my anger eventually, over the ensuing months, dimmed into a calm acceptance.

I was, I admit, grievously disappointed that others of my kind did not come to rescue me; but I did not resent them for this failure. Perhaps, I mused, they had decided to forgive the alien invaders? For forgiveness is the way of my species. We will, if absolutely necessary, fight; but continuing hatred is not in our nature, and indeed runs counter to our philosophy of life.

So I did not, as many Kau'un captives do, wallow in thoughts of vengeance. Nor did my captivity terrify me; and the prospect of spending eternity as a slave caused me little grief. For my kind are long-lived, and patient, and we endure.

And yet!

Even now the memories of the horrors that I saw in those early years on the Hell Ship cause me pain. The savagery! The cruelty! I arrived, a fresh slave, and was greeted by a slavering mob of creatures of all shapes and sizes, with claws and beaks and horns and soft pulsing flesh and hard scales and thick hides, creatures who flew and creatures who crawled and creatures who walked on a hundred legs and others who were nightmares made manifest. And all these monsters taunted and mocked me. And then they advanced upon me in a ruthless mass and savaged me, and tried to rip the outer shell off my three segments with their teeth and claws and horns and feelers and feet. One of the creatures spat acid upon my skin. Another wrapped its coils around me and tried to crush my body into a state of suffocation. And then one of them, a giant flying biped, picked me up in its claws and carried me up to the summit of the mountain range, over bleak and terrible terrain, and there he dropped me from a great height upon the sharpest crag. And I tried to fly away to safety, but my cape was shattered and I could not see because my eyes had been pecked out, and I could not hear because small worms were crawling in my brain and affecting my ability to sense my surroundings or to think.

When I hit the rocky crag the wind was driven out of my

body and my carapace was cracked and my heart ruptured and my back spine was shattered.

And I was in agony for many months until I managed to drag myself down from the mountain. And then I hauled myself across the grasslands in the baking heat, until I found a well full of soothing water and dived in. And this, I later learned, was the well of the water of life; and these waters healed me.

Within months, I was restored to health; my spine was restored; my eyes grew back; my wounds healed; though my fear of my fellow captives was undimmed.

Carulha was the dominant warrior on the Hell Ship back then. A giant red polypod with spear-like protrusions on his flesh and a hundred bony arms that could cut and sever flesh and a thousand snake-tails that could spit venom and lash like whips. Carulha had led the mob that tortured and taunted me. And when I was healed, it was Carulha who sought me out and told me the laws of my new world. I must obey him, and him alone; for I was *his* slave, just as he was the slave of the Masters of the Ship. And I must, he told me, at all times use my strength to intimidate and humiliate the smaller bipeds (though not the Kindred) and the arboreals and the sentient aerials and the multi-legs and the swamp-dwellers, for that was the way of things on this ship.

I refused.

So Carulha went away and when he returned he once more led a mob of huge and deadly creatures. I can remember them now: Sairyrd, the hairy three-legged grey-skinned breaker of bones. Marosh, a serpentine with wings and teeth that could rip and tear in all the many mouths that ran the length of her slithering body. And Tarang, a creature with no fixed form, who oozed and shapeshifted and had the power to hurt by absorbing the bodies of her prey into her own soft sucking loathsome body. And more, many more. The bipeds fought too, for they served Carulha then, not the Kindred as they do now; and though they were small, they were armed with bows and spears and knives and wooden machines that could hurl rocks and balls of fire. The arboreals also joined this army; they were agile and guileful, and used their teeth and tails to maim and hurt at Carulha's behest. And the aerials flocked at his command, and could peck out the eyes of a helpless new slave in a matter of seconds.

This was the mob that for the second time faced me. But this time, I was no longer a child; for I had been prematurely metamorphosed into my adult self through pain and grief. Thus, my strength and powers were enhanced a thousandfold, as is the way of our kind.

And so, sorrow in my heart, adulthood forced upon me, I defended myself.

After six hours of combat, I left behind me a trail of broken bodies and screaming, agonised monsters, and slept that night by the shores of the lake, watching the sun go down above the Tower. The wind was cold.

I missed my world.

Naturally, once I had proved my superior strength, Carulha and the others left me undisturbed. And that made me glad; and yet also broke my soul. For it is not in my nature to be alone, and unloved.

And even though I now enjoyed a protected existence, Carulha and his gang continued to hound and humiliate all the other slaves; and everything I saw brought me fresh torment.

For in those days, the lives of the slaves on the Hell Ship were truly dark and desperate. We were our own worst enemies, there was no comfort to be got, and no comradeship, and no kindness or compassion, and, most appallingly of all, no routine.

And those facts made me, deeply and wretchedly, sad.

And indeed it makes me sad even now, looking back, to remember how when I was a new slave, no one helped *me;* no one trained *me.* And there were no cabins either, not back then. No sanctuary, no friendship, just savagery.

Thus, in my first few years on the Ship, I lived in a state of perpetual disgust with the ways of my world. For all was hate! In the days, the slaves would fight and rip each other limb from limb, with pointless brutality. And at night their bodies would lie still and bleeding before they, slowly and painfully, began to heal.

And also, every night, after all the bickering and warring, we Ka'un slaves would lie on the grass while the sun set; and we would be filled with terror as the sheer blackness descended. A night so dark that nocturnal animals were blinded; a night where nothing moved, and no sound carried, and creatures possessed of echo-location were as helpless as those with eyes. A night of total and terrifying silence.

Then, after a few hours, screams would rend the night. As the absence of all light sent creature after creature to the brink of madness, or into the arms of cold Despair.

Then, eventually, the sun would rise, and cold light would leach across the land. And we would see before us the forests of the Despairing: dead and petrified figures that stretched as far as the eye could see, their warm bodies turned to icy stone, their screams of agony preserved for all eternity in rock. Such are the consequences of the bodily apocalypse we call Despair.

I was shocked the first time I saw this happen; and awed that the Ka'un were able to punish the weariest spirits by changing the very physical constitution of their bodies. No one could understand how they did it.

But I came to understand the reason for it: since the existence of Despair forces us all to be not just obedient, but also *hopeful* slaves. Knowing as we do that Despair will be our lot if we ever lose our precious will to live.

And the cruellest thing is that those who die of Despair never truly die; their minds are trapped alert yet helpless for all eternity in bodies of stone.

That is what makes the punishment so terrible. There is blind and remorseless cruelty; and there is what the Ka'un do to us, with their curse of Despair. It is, in my view, as different as day is to night.

Our days back then were largely spent disposing of stone

corpses through the hull-hatch in the ship's glass belly. I had no friends. We all lived separate lives, mistrustful of each other, cruelly hating.

Then one day we woke, and a hundred of us were missing.

Some returned, many cycles later, with limbs that had been regrown, or new heads, and with no memory of what had happened to them. And some never returned again.

And this is when I first realised what we slaves were *for*. Some of us were merely scorned chattels, but many served as the warrior army of the Ka'un.

Furthermore, every time we woke from our dreamless sleep, new ones had appeared in our world. Single or several samples of newly captured sentient species. And they arrived full of terror and pain; and were immediately plunged into a world of even greater terror and pain. Carulha used to brag that every new slave needed to be made to feel as *he* had felt, after the death of his world. The agony of others, he would argue, in his few coherent moments, was the only way to honour the lost dead of his magnificent, arrogant species.

But I believed Carulha to be a brute, as terrible in his way as the Ka'un. His wretched kind, I mused, deserved their fate; it was the rest of we slaves who should be pitied.

And so I resolved to change my world. Instead of fighting, I would make peace. Instead of hating, I tried to spread love.

And this I did. For many long frustrating months.

And I was mocked for it; and despised for my innocence and my foolishness. For I spoke to all I met about the need for love and a new world order. I begged them all to share tales of their past, and to find a commonality in our sentience. I explained that hate and anger will simply feed more hate and anger. And I told them that we needed to accept the frailty and folly of our captors. Not to *condone* their crimes, but rather so we could forgive them, and thus exalt our own souls.

I spoke to each creature on the ship in such manner, over the space of hundreds of cycles. I told stories of my own people's history to illustrate my point that violence is an evolutionary dead end. And I conjured up a vision of a world in which all of us would exist in amity and harmony.

For a long while I was ignored; but eventually my words began to take hold. I acquired a following; several of the more vicious predators broke with Carulha and began living their lives according to my principles: routine, comradeship, storytelling, love.

And Carulha was enraged by this. He regarded it as treachery, a threat to his authority.

And so once more his army of bullying cruel monsters gathered to destroy me. To rip me, as they bragged, "limb from fucking limb," and then to hurl me from the hull-hatch.

They met me on the Great Plain. And there I stood—all alone, for my allies had abandoned me as Carulha approached. I was faced with an encircling army of nearly six hundred giant sentients, two hundred or more hairless bipeds, six thousand many-limbed predators, and all the arboreals. Only the Kindred did not deign to fight me, for they refused to have any part in the workings of our world.

I will admit that I was afraid; for I did not want to hurt anyone, and yet I knew that I would have to.

"No fucking speeches," yelled Carulha, "die, you fucking cunt!" and the battle began.

And thus for the second time in my entire life, I fought.

And I slew them by the score, and ripped them limb, as Carulha had put it, from "fucking" limb. I smashed the aerials out of the sky with my tentacles and I ripped open the bodies of the giant sentients and tore the arboreals and bipeds and the many-limbed predators into pieces with my tentacle-claws that moved so fast that none could see their motion—thus my foes would abruptly and inexplicably split into many parts, gushing scarlet blood.

All this I did and more. And when it was all over, I threw Carulha's dismembered body out of the hull-hatch, and the bodies of Marosh, Tarang, and nearly three hundred others. They would not die—I knew this for a fact, as I had known and understood so much from my very first moments on the Hell Ship. The same way that I had known that the waters of the well of life would heal me faster and more fully than allowing nature take its course.

No, they would not die; but their souls would live for eternity in the ripped remnants of their bodies, drifting through the emptiness of space.

And when the surviving slaves saw how I had vanquished Carulha, they swore their loyalty to me. They told me that I would be their new master!

But I refused their plea. For I would not be worshipped. I would not be obeyed.

I would, however, I insisted, be listened to.

And so they listened. And I used my newly acquired power to change our world. And this I have done; all the good that exists on my world, the clear blue waters of the lake, the comradeship, the use of cabins, the division of labours, the fertile plains, the Rhythm of Life itself—all this I caused to be.

Sharrock had no knowledge of all this; he arrogantly assumed I was merely a gullible and docile pawn of the Ka'un.

But in fact, I had *defied* the Ka'un, without them ever realising. I had turned their nightmare slave ship into a place where sentients of many species could live, and love, and share the joy of friendship.

So I have done; of this I am proud.

I found Cuzco on a crag, on Day the First, looking down at our world.

"The views," he told me, "are wonderful up here."

I looked at the views. They were indeed wonderful.

"Are you brooding?" I asked him.

"Fuck away," Cuzco advised me.

"You are."

"I am, indeed, you ignorant ugly monster, brooding," he conceded.

I sat with him, in silence, for an hour.

"I'm still worried," I said eventually, "about Sharrock."

Cuzco snorted. "No need; he's doomed. Forget the little cock-faced biped, for he'll be marble soon enough. You *worry* too much, Sai-ias."

"But I care about him. And it was a hard time for all of us, remember? The first few years. You must have—"

"You are so fucking pathetic!" Cuzco raged at me, cutting off my words. "You're like a fucking mother to the new ones! You'd feed them the food from your mouth if you could. You sad ingratiating suck-arse! You can't coddle creatures like this. Fly or die, that's the way of the world."

"I helped *you.*"

"No one helped me."

A lie, of course. Cuzco had also been an angry, bitter new one; I had spent many hours trying to teach him how to bank down his rage, and to find the moments of joy concealed in the bleakness of his life. Now, of course, he denied that he had ever needed me, or received any help from me; such was his pride.

"He reminds me a little of you, in fact," I ventured.

"Go fuck a cloud!" said Cuzco. "He's a biped. I'm a—a—" And he used a word that the air could not translate, but I knew it meant he had status. He was a giant among beasts, even on our interior world.

And, indeed, I often felt that Cuzco was a truly magnificent creature. He was a land giant with the power of flight; his armoured wings made him somehow lighter than air, and so he was able to effortlessly dance among the clouds, though he weighed more than Fray and myself put together. And his body was beautiful, in its own eerie fashion: he had two torsos, linked by bands of armoured flesh, and orange scales that glittered in the light. And claws on his haunches and torsos that could, when he so chose, be as delicate as hands. And no head; his face was on the breast of his left body, and he had features that were expressive and flexible and eyes that seemed to me to twinkle with delight when his mood was cheerful; though that was, in all honesty, not often.

"I fear Sharrock is harbouring a secret plan," I admitted "He thinks he knows a way to defeat the Ka'un."

"Perhaps he does."

"You know he doesn't. It's folly."

"I once," said Cuzco, "had ideas like that."

In his first year on the ship, Cuzco had, like me, attempted to attack the Tower. And to do so he had gathered a formidable army of aerials who had joined Cuzco in his attempt to breach the Tower's invisible barrier from above. But storms had battered them and Cuzco's six wings had been ripped off him so that he crashed like a rock in the lake, and the savage gusts of air had ripped the entire flock of aerials into shreds. Blood had rained upon us all that day; blood and beaks and feathers and scales and fragments of unrecognisable internal organs that pelted downwards and left our bodies soaked and stenched. Many of Cuzco's followers were still mutilated after their mauling by the storm; and none of the aerials ever spoke to him now.

"Perhaps you could talk to him," I said. "Counsel him to be—"

Cuzco stood up and his hackles rose, and terrifying spikes emerged from his body.

"I will tell him nothing of the sort! What do you take me for, you cowardly colon-full-of-shit? You do not comprehend," said Cuzco, "what it is to be a warrior!"

"I comprehend it totally."

"My kind were masters of all creation! We vanquished all the lesser breeds in our galaxy, and we were proud of it!"

"Your words bring you shame. You are nothing but a monster, Cuzco," I told him, wearily.

Cuzco snarled; and then he stood; and leaped off the cliff top; and with grace and majesty he flew above the clouds, a patch of orange blurring the blue sky.

"Monster," I said sadly, knowing it was true. If I'd met Cuzco in any other setting, he would have been my enemy, not my friend.

BOOK 5

Sharrock

I was tired of running; I had been running for days; yet still I ran.

I knew that in the trees they were faster than me; so I seized my moment and broke through into a clearing, and knew it was just a few more minutes to the lake—

But then I whirled and saw that the wretched monkeys had me surrounded. They had clubs and knives; there were a hundred or more of them. An army. They cackled and screamed with delight; and were clearly convinced I was not capable of causing them any further trouble, with the odds so heavily in their favour.

They did not, it seemed, know Sharrock!

I clutched the stone in my hand, relaxed my body, and calculated the distance between myself and Mangan and his regiment of tree-huggers. My eyes quietly scanned the mob. I identified the dominant beasts who needed to be slain first; and then I cleared my throat so I could deliver a battle-roar to confuse and paralyse the more timid ones.

I also considered how I could use the monkeys themselves as weapons; using the bodies of the dead ones to club the live ones, whilst using my teeth to bite and sever arteries. I recalled the time on Latafa when I was faced with a baying mob of two hundred highly trained four-armed centurions, and slew them all. All in all, I concluded, my task here was difficult, but by no means impossible. For as the historians of Maxolu all agree—with only those two irksome exceptions—I am indeed the greatest Northern Tribe warrior of all time!

The monkeys roared more rage, and started to slowly move towards me. I thought for a few moments more. Calculating all my options. Plotting my various potential battle moves.

Then I quietly let the stone drop out of my hand.

"Do your worst," I said calmly.

And they did.

Sai-ias

I laid Sharrock's bloodied body down upon the grass, and I bathed him in water from the water-of-life well; oozing the healing moisture on him through the spiracles in my tentacle tips.

"Can you speak?"

He grunted, and opened his mouth; inside was a bloody void. As I'd suspected, his tongue had been ripped out. His torso was bruised and bloody, and I suspected there was severe internal damage. They'd also eaten one of his eyes.

He grunted as the water drizzled on to his naked body.

Just as I'd feared, Mangan and the arboreals had taken their revenge.

For twelve cycles I tended to Sharrock; nursing his wounds, talking to him; telling him stories. His wounds healed, and his tongue grew back quickly; but he was not communicative even when he did speak.

After six cycles he was able to walk.

After ten cycles he made a sword out of a tree branch; the wood was tough and the point was viciously sharp. He killed a non-sentient grazer and skinned it and fashioned himself a scabbard. He used the hooves to make knuckle guards, to help him with hand to hand combat. For days he collected stone remnants at the quarry and from then on always carried a bag of stones and a sling.

"Will you take revenge?" I asked him.

"You want me not to?" he said mockingly; for his tongue was now regrown.

"I want you to forgive them," I said.

"You know I cannot do that," Sharrock said sternly.

"Please, Sharrock. For me?"

"Never!" he snarled. "Those branch-fucking savages tricked me. Ambushed me! I was trying to do as you told me, live in peace. But they attacked me anyway."

"And now," I said sadly, "you will attack them?"

Sharrock looked at me; his pale blue eyes were calm. And he never, I noticed, felt the need to blink as many bipeds did.

"No," he said, calmly. "These weapons are just for self defence. I gave a beating, I took a beating. Further violence would be folly, so now I'm done. From this point on, I embrace the way of peace."

"You really mean that?"

"I really mean it," Sharrock avowed.

I felt so proud.

Over the next twenty or so cycles, I got into the habit of spending the early mornings with Sharrock by the lake side.

He loved to fish; he had fashioned lines and nets and captured dozens of fish each day, all of which he released back into the water. And he was a gentler spirit now, after the mauling from the arboreals. A status quo had been achieved; indeed, Mangan and Shiiaa and the other arboreals occasionally invited Sharrock to share their cabin at night, and there they told each other tales. Sharrock had passed, and survived, his brutal initiation.

Sharrock talked often to me about his family—his love-partner Malisha and his daughter Sharil, and Malisha's brothers Tharn and Jarro, and their love-partners Clavala and Blarwan, and their assorted children—with love and tenderness. And he told some delightful stories about the stupid things that young

Sharil used to do, and the even stupider things *he* used to do to make her laugh.

And I told him that I had been merely a child when I was taken by the Ka'un. I had never had sex, or known adult love; my adolescence ended when I was captured by alien invaders and brutally beaten by the then occupants of the Hell Ship.

He was clearly shaken by that story; it affected him sorely for days.

I talked to him also about Cuzco and his warrior code, and I tried to get him to see how unutterably foolish it was.

"My people were not like that," Sharrock protested. "Cuzco is just a savage; from all you say, no better than the Ka'un. But we were a cultured and a civilised people."

"Truly?"

"Truly."

"Then tell me; how many Maxoluns have you killed in single combat?" I asked him,

Sharrock was shaken by the question. "Hundreds," he admitted.

"And in war?"

"Thousands."

"And you feel no guilt?"

"None."

"You should."

"Perhaps I should," Sharrock conceded.

He was silent for a while, made pensive by my words.

"How can that be?" I asked him. "How does a child become so ruthless a warrior?"

"When I was eleven," he said, "I was sent into the desert, to spend three days and three nights alone. And," he said, his eyes sparkling at the recollection, "it was hot. Fierce hot, with air that scorched the lungs. I drank water from roots. I hid from predators, including the great Sand-Baro. And I fought the Quila. These are four-legged creatures, the size of my hand, with vicious teeth, who live in the sand itself. And every dawn on our world the Quila would emerge from their sandy burrows and bask in the sun and feed on the flesh of unwary creatures who strayed their way. I killed six thousand of them before my father came to fetch me."

"And what did that teach you?"

"Ha! That Quila will die, if you hit them hard enough with a club. And furthermore, if you judge it right, they will squirt blood from both ends." He laughed bitterly. "It taught me nothing. No, not true, it taught me how to survive."

"Yours is a brutal culture."

"I'd never," admitted Sharrock, "thought so, before I met you."

"Imagine," I told him, "a world where sentient species collaborated, and helped each other, and cared for each other. Where discovery mattered more than victory. Would that be so bad?"

"Not possible."

"We achieved it. My people."

"Then the Ka'un came and your people didn't know how to fight," Sharrock taunted me.

"At least we lost a civilisation," I said. "You lost—what?—a barbarism?"

Sharrock's features were pale with shock; my words had hit home.

"Perhaps," he said, and I marvelled at his courage in accepting that his entire life might have been founded on moral error.

And so, buoyed with confidence at Sharrock's new attitude, I decided he was finally ready to learn the real truth about our terrible world.

"It is time," I told Sharrock, "for you to meet your own kind."

Sharrock and I travelled up past the lake to the mountain ranges, and thence into the deep Valley where the smaller bipeds and the Kindred dwelled. The air was darker here, and clammy in the throat, and the high ground was just rock without any covering of soil. But the valley itself was rich and fertile, and twin rivers trickled and gurgled their way through it.

I had built these rivers with my own teeth and claws and the help of all the giant sentients. We created channels that were pumped with waters from the lake; and to our delight, the lake could refill itself by some unknown automatic means, so the rivers always flowed.

And further down the valley there were fields, fresh ploughed, and grazing animals on the grasslands. We proceeded on a pebbled path down a steep slope, as giants walked below us; I, slithering down on my segments, Sharrock running along beside me.

And at the gateway to the village of the Kindred, we were greeted by Gilgara, their chief warrior: a bearded colossus who was twice as tall as Sharrock, and who, like Sharrock, had upper arms as large as his head and strongly defined muscles upon his torso.

Sharrock bowed, clearly impressed by Gilgara's military bearing and physique, and avariciously eyed the metal sword that the giant wore in a fine leather scabbard.

"You have weapons?" Sharrock said.

"Forged with fire; the metal comes from walls in cabins that we have pillaged," said Gilgara.

"Impressive," said Sharrock, respectfully.

Next to Gilgara was Mara; a glowering female warrior with one eye larger than the other. Mara peered at Sharrock, and a smile grew.

"Fresh meat," Mara said, looking at Sharrock, and Sharrock's own smile faded.

Sharrock then started to warily look around him. There were twenty or more Kindred warriors strolling out of the village to join us, each twice as large as he, wearing furs and hides over their shoulders and groins, leaving legs and arms and midriffs bare; and many were ornately tattooed.

And there were a considerable variety of smaller hairless bipeds too; some with three eyes, some with two, or five; some with two arms, some with four, some six arms, some eight; some with soft skin, some with tough hide; some were grey in colour, many pink, some blue, some purple, quite a few black, many were bronzed, and a handful of exceptional specimens had colourful striped skin. But all were of a similar morphology to Sharrock; comprising minor variations of what I firmly believed was an archetypal biological form.

And some of these small bipeds wore loose shackles with chains at their feet, to prevent them running away, and bore a haunted look. While others wore rich leathers and strode proudly; but still wore metal shackles around their upper arms, and kept their eyes averted from the members of the Kindred.

Sharrock was studying it all, with that attentive and curious look on his face; I knew it would not take him long to work out the power balance here.

"These peoples live side by side?" he whispered to me. "The giants and the similar-to-Olarans?"

"In a manner of speaking," I explained. "The smaller bipeds are slaves to the Kindred."

"Slaves?"

"They have no freedom; they fetch and carry; they are flogged if they disobey; slaves," I clarified.

The sharp and angry intake of breath from Sharrock alarmed me.

"We came here," I explained to Sharrock, "for you to see this, and to absorb the lessons it holds about the reality of power on this world, and then to leave."

"Have you brought this squalid wretch to join us?" asked Gilgara, interrupting our private conference with arrogant brusqueness; as if we were the food on his plate that had dared to converse.

"Not so," I explained, "Sharrock has come merely to pay his respects."

"He must stay. All bipeds live in the Valley," Gilgara said fiercely.

"Fuck away," I said calmly. "This one is protected by me."

"You'd live with this monster, not with your own kind?" roared Gilgara to Sharrock.

Sharrock stared up at the giant warrior. "Why do so many wear metal bands on their arms?" he asked.

"Each band bears a name; it denotes the master of the slave," Gilgara said, matter-of-factly.

"We are all captives here," Sharrock said calmly. "But none should be slaves of—"

Gilgara spat at him; it was a vast gob of green, and I admired the giant's aim; it struck Sharrock on his forehead, and dripped down his face; but Sharrock's stare did not falter an instant.

"We are the Kindred," said Gilgara. "We are no creature's slaves. We serve the Leaders of this ship freely, and voluntarily."

It took Sharrock a few moments to comprehend what he was being told. He looked at me; I waved my tentacles to indicate agreement, and realised that made no sense to him, so I said: "That is so."

"The smaller bipeds, however," said Mara proudly, "*are* slaves, And you shall be too."

"Never!" Sharrock said angrily.

Mara drew her finely forged metal sword, and pointed it menacingly at Sharrock. Gilgara did the same, in a swift gesture as fast as lightning spanning the sky. Sharrock tensed, ready to fight.

I caught Sharrock with a tentacle and threw him on my back. Then I tentacle-flipped away.

The Kindred did not give chase; they knew me too well.

"The fucking bastards!" roared Sharrock.

"I wanted you to see for yourself."

"This is why," said Sharrock, piecing together the parts of a puzzle that, until that moment, he had not realised *was* a puzzle. "This is why you put me with the arboreals, not with others more akin to my physical type."

"Nine hundred cycles ago, the Kindred enslaved all the biped species. I was unable to prevent them."

"Why would they do such a thing? To their own kind!"

"The Kindred are the Kindred; they have no 'kind.' "

"And I am the only 'biped' who is free?"

"Yes."

"Why? What makes me so special?"

"You are under my protection."

"You mean, you'd fight for me?"

"No," I conceded. "But the Kindred rely on me; I make their rivers flow, and their crops grow; I discourage rebellion among the giant sentients; I keep the world from falling into anarchy and Despair. The Kindred rule the Valley. They have biped slaves to dominate; and so they are content. We other sentients keep apart from them. We lead our own quiet lives."

"Well, that's going to change," said Sharrock, quietly smiling now.

"No, it will not change."

"Just watch, sweet beast. Now Sharrock is here, the world will come to its senses, and freedom will prevail!"

"No! We cannot have freedom! Things must not change," I said angrily, "For what we have achieved here is precious beyond all measure: it is *equilibrium.*"

And Sharrock stood up; and his eyes shone with fury; and spittle came from his mouth when he spoke, so great was his wrath.

"Sai-ias, hear this!" said Sharrock, and I knew I was in for a poetic rant; a common foible amongst battle-worshipping warriors.

"I have come to know you Sai-ias, and I know your heart is full of love," said Sharrock, with his usual withering condescension; oblivious to the fact I am old and wise, and large enough to keep him in my mouth for years on end and yet not notice his presence when I dined.

"And yet you are a fool," Sharrock continued; and his voice had a rich timbre, as if he were addressing a hall of drunken wastrels who needed to be inspired to commit acts of glory. "You allow yourself to be used by these monsters, these Ka'un! You preach obedience; but that is just servitude. You teach acceptance; but that is just another way of making slaves more docile. And worst of all, you all—"

I was bored by now; so I picked him up with one tentacle and shook him as a child shakes a toy that has lost its rattle in the hope it might yet make *some* kind of rattling noise.

Eventually I dumped Sharrock on the ground. He was dazed, winded, dizzy, and began vomiting profusely.

"All the biped slaves on this world," I told him coldly, "volunteered to be so. They prefer it that way. You may despise that decision, but you will respect it. Or else, I shall carry you to the valley of the Kindred myself; and watch as they bind and shackle you and put a whip to your back!"

This was an idle threat, in fact; for, however much he vexed me, I could never be so cruel to him; but I hoped that Sharrock would not realise that.

Sharrock finally managed to get back to his feet. He staggered a little, getting his balance back. He spat the last of the vomit from his mouth. His eyes were out of focus, and he was in shock; but his body was, I knew, resilient, and he would recover swiftly.

Yet though he was now standing, he did not seem to me to stand as tall as before. And when his eyes refocused, they had lost their piercing stare.

"Why would anyone," he asked, with a bafflement like that of a child discovering that her parents are fallible, "*choose* to live as a slave?"

I had no answer to give him.

The Days passed.

Day the First.

Day the Second.

Day the Third.

Day—

"Come," said Lirilla, and I came.

I found Sharrock in the centre of the grass amphitheatre. He was unconscious; one arm was ripped and bloody; there were savage sword wounds in his torso; and both his eyes had been gouged out. Fray stood by, scratching the ground with her hooves.

"What happened?" I asked, after a few moments of feeling overwhelmed with sorrow.

"The aerials called me," said Fray. "They found his body high on a mountain crag. I clambered up, and carried it here."

I touched my tentacle tip to Sharrock's throat; no pulse.

I lifted his body up with one tentacle and put it in my mouth. And I breathed in through my spiracles, and out through my mouth; in; out; in; out; filtering the air so that all that remained in my mouth cavity was pure oxygen.

Then I spat Sharrock out gently. His body twitched; his blood was oxygen-rich now. His heart had started beating.

"Can you heal his body?" I said to Fray, and Fray grunted an affirmative, and stood up on her huge back legs; and began to piss upon Sharrock's bloodied body. Fray drank every day from the well of the water of life, and her piss was running clear; so I knew this was the best way to heal Sharrock.

And after a few moment's stupefaction, he realised that that Fray was pissing on him.

And Sharrock groaned, and sat up, and tried to dodge the torrent of healing urine; but in his confused state, he turned the wrong way, and his eyes and nostrils and mouth took the brunt of the cascade of hot, steaming Fray-piss.

"No need to thank me," said Fray, in her kindest tones.

It took Sharrock two days to recover sufficiently to speak. When he did, though blind and scarred, he was unrepentant.

"You fought the Kindred?" I asked.

"Indeed, I fought those wretched, cowardly, viler-than-a-Southern-Tribesman Kindred," he said, proudly.

"And lost?"

"I concede that I lost," said Sharrock proudly, "yet I was not defeated. For Sharrock will never ever EVER be defeated!"

I sighed, from my tentacle tips. "Did you learn nothing," I said acidly. "From your experience with the arboreals?"

"Yes," said Sharrock. "I learned that monkeys shit a lot when they're up trees; you really have to keep your wits about you."

"You learned that revenge is futile!" I roared. "That was the lesson. That was why—"

"My people," said Sharrock, "are in captivity. It's up to me to save them."

"Even if they don't want to be saved?" I asked him, nastily.

"Even then," said Sharrock proudly; and his nobility, and his courage, revolted me.

"Come," said Lirilla, and this time I found Sharrock in the desert; stripped naked and baking in the sun. The Kindred had cut off his ears and his eyelids, and carved strange inscriptions on his bare flesh from head to toe. His red skin was burned and blistered by the sun's rays; and he was parched, and croaking.

And his eyes, so recently healed, were now blinded once more by the sun's rays; yet even so, there was about him a look of triumph.

"Come," said Lirilla, and once more I came.

I found Sharrock this time in the encampment of the Kindred. His body was broken and bloodied; his teeth had been smashed out; he had lost one eye (those poor eyes!). And I began to seriously wonder if his body could continue to regenerate after these tremendous beatings; it was taking him longer and longer to return to his full warrior strength after each appalling defeat.

But today, I realised, he was surrounded by scores of kneeling Kindred; who were offering him obeisance.

I looked around. The slaves were no longer in shackles. They were free.

And Gilgara, the giant Kindred Chieftain, was on the ground; blood flowed from a terrible cut in his head; and no one paid him any heed. There was a slow thundering noise; a clapping; the Kindred were saluting Sharrock's triumph in what had evidently been a long, and bloody, and brutal unarmed combat between Sharrock and Gilgara, the leader of the Kindred.

"What has happened here?" I asked, amazed.

"I am now," said Sharrock proudly, "King of the Kindred."

"It was a hard fought battle," bragged Sharrock.

"It was indeed, sire," said Gilgara, the former Kindred leader, who was now, despite his appalling injuries which made it so hard for him to walk, Sharrock's loyal second in command.

"Picture the scene," said Sharrock dramatically, "there was I! I was—"

"I do not," I said dryly, "wish to picture the scene. Big fight; lots of blood; you won."

"I bested the Kindred leader in single combat!"

"And why does that qualify you to be the leader?" I said angrily.

Sharrock was flummoxed. "It proves I am the mightiest—"

"It proves you are the best at *hurting*! That's all. The best at brawling with a stick or sword or with bare fists. Does that make you a leader?" I was so enraged, my cape became erect and my body inflated.

"Yes," said Sharrock. "And next, I shall unify the tribes. There are bipeds like myself living at the foot of the Further Mountains who do not acknowledge Gilgara's authority, but rather serve the tribes of renegade and nomadic Kindred. I will go and fight these nomad giants and make them honour my leadership, and then free *those* slaves too."

"You would do that?"

"I must," said Sharrock.

I had nothing more to say to him.

By now, I was nursing a terrible rage. I had helped this creature, comforted him when he was vulnerable; and now he was aiming to become a *dictator.*

But what could I do to stop him? The answer was: nothing! Unless of course I was willing to challenge him to a battle, and fight and defeat him. For then he would be compelled to bend to my will.

And this of course, I could do easily; so easily it was laughable. For all his warrior pride, Sharrock was utterly puny and minuscule compared to me. I could defeat him with a single blow, or swallow him like an insect, or crush him and smash him under my feet whilst barely noticing he was there.

But I would never be willing to fight Sharrock. For I was fond of him. I thought of him as a friend. And I could not bear to hurt him.

And, too, I was fearful that in the heat of battle, I might end up hurting Sharrock so severely that he could not heal, and he would end up crippled or even dead. For violence is a madness; once you allow it to possess you, it is not easy to return to the ways of sanity.

And this was why I had, so many years ago, forsworn violence. After my two ghastly combats with Carulha, I had resolved never again to use brute force to achieve my goals.

I had been a monster twice; I would not be so a third time.

Sharrock

Fifty Kindred maidens came to me in the night, longing to possess my body; despite their giant size, they were beauteous indeed. But I sent them all away.

Ten warriors challenged me the next day, before I had broke my fast, and I declined them all. One of them sent a sly arrow aimed at my head and I was only just swift enough to snatch it from the air and smash his skull.

I was, in truth, not much enjoying my life as King of the Kindred. I had many responsibilities; underlings constantly pestered me for decisions about matters of which I knew nothing, and cared less; and all in all, I never had a moment to myself. I felt as if I had inadvertently adopted a country full of needy children. And I yearned for my days as a nomad with a loyal wife and a small family, who would happily fend for themselves whilst I went off adventuring.

Sai-ias was avoiding me now, I knew, and I regretted that sorely. For I had come to enjoy her company, despite her ghastly appearance and her vexing habit of sighing through her tentacles to betoken annoyance at me. And I did furthermore comprehend her unease; she feared no doubt I was becoming a dictator. Ha! No thought was further from my mind! Power for me was like sobriety for a Southern Tribesman; a state of being to be temporarily, and only briefly, endured.

I also saw the power of Sai-ias's argument about the need for us to avoid violence whilst upon this already-violent world. For if we kept fighting with each other, how could we ever hope to fight and vanquish the Ka'un?

And yet I had been impelled to act. And as a result of my actions, there were no more slaves in my Kingdom. All the bipeds were now free.

Free? Whilst the Ka'un kept us confined in this unnatural habitat?

Yes, that irony did indeed trouble me. But I had done all I could.

Gilgara joined me after I had broke my fast that morning, and when I went tramping in the mountains, he followed me like a limping shadow. He was pathetically devoted to me now. I had beaten him in combat so I was his "master"; that was the way the Kindred thought.

It was however, I had to concede, an impressively well organised society. Instead of retreating to dismal cabins at night, the Kindred had used hull-metal tools to carve caves out of the smooth rocks of the artificial mountains; and they had installed artificial lights in each of these caves. Stories were told there; private caves were set aside for sexual congress; the larger caves were even decorated with artwork in what I recognised as a naïve style; though abstract coloration was also a favoured mode.

The variety of biped species here was dazzling and extraordinary, but the physical similarities between the different species also startled me. The females all had breasts with nipples and haired love-niches (and since I was King, they often flaunted them at me) and loved to discuss the minutest details about the characters of others. Whereas the males all had cocks; and walked with a swagger; and wore groin-hides and capes and boots of hues which almost but did not quite match. The numbers of eyes varied, but all the smaller bipeds, and the Kindred too for that matter, had mouths and tongues and feet and hands and ears. Some creatures however had healed-up holes on their bellies where their mother's cord had been cut, which I found exceeding strange.

I found many of the females attractive, but did not sleep with any.

I found the males highly annoying; they were all so competitive, and whiny. And I realised I was missing the company of the giant sentients. Cuzco was a monster, but he was magnificent nonetheless. And Fray was a brute, but she inspired an awe in me, especially when she ran; that, to me, was true poetry. And Sai-ias—well. She was like no other creature I had ever met before.

But I had chosen my destiny; to teach the Kindred to respect the rights of others. And to forge the smaller bipeds into a proud and free and unified community of individuals loyal to a common cause.

If only the bastards weren't so *irritating.*

For the Kindred were by instinct and nature supreme bullies. And the idiot smaller bipeds had actually chosen to enslave themselves! These stupid less-pride-than-a-warrior-who-fucks-his-own-scabbard creatures—how could they have done such a thing?

And yet, I supposed, in some ways the state of slavery simplified matters. For if you are a free spirit like myself, you will be constantly challenging the way things are.

But when the world is intolerable, and life is irrevocably unjust; might it be better, perhaps, to just blindly serve?

I could never pursue such a course myself of course. Nor could I truly condone the actions of these self-deluded fools. But in a curious way, I found I had acquired a sliver of compassion for my fellow bipeds and their frailties.

I was soul-pacing-restless though. I had fought and lost and fought and lost and finally fought and won a glorious battle; and now there were no more battles to fight.

I thought again about the biped slaves still living at the foot of the Further Mountains. I had told Sai-ias I would liberate them, and I resolved to do so; because at least that would give me an excuse to leave the village for a while.

So I said my farewells; icily endured the tears of maidens I had not bedded, and who did not even have the same number of eyes as I did; and spent several hours persuading Gilgara not to follow me, before eventually breaking his stick and leaving him behind.

Then I set out across the mountain trail, alone, except for my newly acquired hull-metal sword and my turbulent thoughts.

The winds were cold as I walked higher up the mountains. I killed a grazer and skinned it and used its hide as my cape. And I carried the flayed body on my shoulder so I could sleep in the carcass during the icy black night when, as I knew, the heating was always switched off.

Thus encumbered, I climbed up to the highest peak, and looked down at the strange unnatural world of the Hell Ship. I was breathing heavily now; my muscles were singing with exertion; I felt happier than I had been for some time.

Then I slept the night inside the grazer upon the peak. And in the morning, I descended, bloody and smelly but pleasingly well rested. And after several hours of searching I found the settlement in the shadow of the Further Mountain ranges, where the nomad Kindred and their biped slaves dwelled.

And then I saw that bitch.

Sai-ias

"Come," said Lirilla, and I wearily got up, and began flinging myself through the air with my tentacles.

This time I came upon Sharrock before the battle had begun. He had indeed, as he had pledged, journeyed to the bipeds who lived at the foot of the Further Mountains, whose high snowy peaks loomed above our nearer mountain ranges. And now he was engaged in single combat with a mighty Kindred female—twice the size of Sharrock himself and massively muscled, her long red hair streaked with silver, and as skilled at he in combat with a sword.

Her Kindred allies had gathered round to watch, with their biped slaves sulkily stood beside them. All cheered as Sharrock and the female clashed swords, and leaped, and rolled, with grace and speed and awesome energy.

They were well matched; the female warrior was larger and stronger but Sharrock was fast and nimble and able to leap high in the air whilst wielding his sword. Blades clashed so hard together I could see sparks; and the bodies of the two warriors spiralled in the air as they somersaulted around each other; their blades lashing and slashing as they dodged and rolled and stepped back and lunged forward in a coruscating display of martial prowess that would have been beautiful if it weren't so godsforsakenly

CHILDISH!

"Enough," I yelled, and seized each of them in a tentacle.

"Let me down," screamed Sharrock, and hacked at me with his sword.

"Let me down," screamed the female and hacked at me with her sword.

I roared; and spat webbing in their faces; and they fell to the ground, bound and helpless.

A killing rage had come upon me; I yearned to smash them into pieces.

The rage passed.

"Let us talk," I said.

In the shadow of the snowy mountains, the female warrior—who I had by now recognised as Zala, the only female Kindred with such red-and-silver-hair—and Sharrock confronted each other; while I placed my body between them.

"Tell me why you fought this female," I said to Sharrock.

And Sharrock told the tale:

"As you know," he said, "I fought the giant Gilgara. Nobly he—"

"Just the facts," I said.

"I defeated him," Sharrock synopsised sulkily, "freed my people; and then sought out the renegade Kindred who dwelled at the foot of these mountain. And I gave them my terms; release your slaves and we will live in harmony."

"He's insufferable, isn't he?" I said to Zala.

"He is indeed," she concurred. "To state my case: we acknowledge no master; we broke free of Gilgara many cycles ago. We are free."

"But your bipeds are slaves," pointed out Sharrock.

"Well, yes."

"And I bested you in combat, therefore—"

"I was winning, you shit-eyed bastard!"

"Sharrock, I've heard enough. Zala, tell your tale."

"I have no tale to tell; I do not answer to monsters such as you."

"I have said what I must say; the slaves will be freed, I demand it!" roared Sharrock. "And as for this bitch, this evil—I cannot find a word for one so fucking—she has to die! Her presence cannot be tolerated! For she tried to kill me!" Never had I seen Sharrock so dementedly enraged; which was indeed remarkable, since demented enragement had been his commonest mood during his early days on the Hell Ship.

"You shameless liar!" Zala replied, with evident astonishment. "You attacked *me*! I was merely defending myself!"

"Not here," said Sharrock, calming himself visibly. "Not on this pathetic excuse for a planet. On my home world. She was part of the invading army. *She serves the Ka'un.*"

There was an appalled silence; and ruefully I acknowledged to myself that I had always known this day would come.

For I had recognised, of course, from Sharrock's account of his battle with the female alien on Madagorian, the red-and-silver-haired Kindred Zala.

"Do you deny it?" Sharrock accused.

Zala laughed. "No, I do not deny it. I have no recollection of such a battle; but it may well be as you say. For I have fought, I will not deny it, many times in the service of the Masters of this Ship."

Sharrock looked at me in triumph.

"You see?" he said savagely. "She fights for the demons who control this ship; she was a warrior in the invasion and slaughter of my world!"

"I know," I said.

There was a terrible silence.

"You know?" said Sharrock, more stunned than if I had smote his skull with an axe.

"Yes. It is the way of this world: all of us know that the Kindred serve the Ka'un. It is why there are so many of them; they are ruled by the Ka'un, and they in turn rule *us*."

Sharrock seemed to have lost the power of speech. He looked at Zala and tried to spit at her with contempt; but his mouth was too dry, and all he managed was an ugly croak.

"How could this be?" Sharrock said faintly, his eyes radiating accusation and hatred.

"We are soldiers; we serve," said Zala, but there was shame in her eyes.

"You should also know," I explained to Sharrock, "that I collaborate with the Kindred on a regular basis. That is how order is achieved on this world; the Ka'un speak to the Kindred, the Kindred speak to me."

Sharrock stared at me with horror.

"Collaborate in what way?"

"Information. Discipline. The training of the new ones, and, if necessary, if they fail to settle into our world, their execution." I spoke calmly, but inside my spirit was quaking with anxiety; I knew Sharrock was going to take this badly.

"You are the lick-cock of these craven giants?" said Sharrock.

"That is not how I would—"

"Oh Sai-ias," said Sharrock, and my soul's fire was quenched by his cold disdain.

"You are indeed," said Zala to me, "our lick-cock; a phrase well chosen." And she smiled, not pleasantly.

I bowed my head submissively; for one of the conditions of serving the Kindred was to comply with their strict etiquette of submissive behaviour.

"If you say so, Zala, then I will agree that the phrase is apt," I agreed courteously.

"And now that Gilgara is gone," added Zala.

"Indeed! I yield to *your* authority, mistress," I said swiftly.

Zala smiled. Her look of triumph encompassed both me and Sharrock.

"Serve me well, beast," said Zala arrogantly. And she departed.

There was a prolonged and horrifying silence. Sharrock's unblinking blue eyes were like ice.

"How could you, Sai-ias?" Sharrock said to me. His voice was calm, which filled me with foreboding.

"If not me, then it would be someone else," I explained. "Once it was a beast called Carulha; when he died, I took over his role, and his responsibilities."

"And why did you not tell me all this? Before I conquered Gilgara and assumed chieftainship of the Kindred?" asked Sharrock savagely.

"It did not for a moment occur to me," I admitted, "that you could win."

Sharrock was silent for a long time. I waited.

"You are a traitor," Sharrock concluded finally, in the quietest of tones.

"Sharrock," I explained, "you cannot—"

"To deal with *them*, those evil conquering bastards, to do their bidding, that is truly—"

"You have to be pragmatic about—"

"TRAITOR!" Sharrock's red face was redder still; his rage hit me like a punch.

"I do what I have to do," I said, wretchedly.

And Sharrock drew his hull-metal sword from his scabbard in the blink of an eye; and he struck me with it in my face. The blow barely registered for me, but even so I flinched.

He struck me again, and again, hammering his sword against my carapace, my skull, jabbing my eyes, trying to hurt me and break flesh but failing.

Eventually he was too exhausted to lift his arm. He threw the sword down on the ground. Then he walked away.

Sharrock did not return to the Valley, nor did he have any further dealings with the Kindred.

And from that day on, he refused to speak to me.

Jak

It was one of those days.

I was leading the crew in an emergency drill. We performed a mock evacuation, with all five officers and ten ordinary crew members in spacesuits. A year had passed since the extermination of the FanTangs; I was Jak the Explorer now, no longer Trader Jak.

One by one the crew filed into pods and the pods broke away from the main ship and vanished into uncertain space.

I shared a pod with Albinia and Darko, an engineer. "You know this would never happen in real life," said Darko, dourly. "If a missile ever got past our shields, we'd be dead."

"Break away," I said, and Darko hit the switch and the pod broke away from the main ship.

As we spiralled around weightlessly, Albinia's hair lifted from her head in a halo. She looked at me. Just looked.

Galamea's voice came through to me via my murmur-link implant. "*All pods detached, in fourteen point two minutes. Drill is over, return to the main ship.*"

We re-entered real space, still spiralling around, with a clear view of Explorer through our window. She looked eerily beautiful.

Albinia was weeping.

"I apologise Star-Seeker, can I help?" said Drago, in terrified tones.

"It's like being outside myself," said Albinia, as she looked at Explorer's exterior hull.

I was dining alone, and a tray crashed on the table next to mine.

"Can I join you?" Albinia said.

"Please do," I said, startled.

Albinia slid into place beside me. "I have a favour to ask," she said, in very quiet tones.

"I would be honoured," I replied gallantly.

"You don't know what I'm going to ask."

"I'd be honoured anyway," I insisted.

She looked vexed.

"Have I offended you, Mistress—"

She waved a hand; I silenced my own rhetoric. And then Albinia sat there, looking anxious, for quite some time.

"What?" I coaxed.

"I would like to be your friend."

I nodded. And smiled, graciously, savouring the gift of her presence, and the nearness of her sublime intellect. And then:

"What?" I asked, baffled.

"Will you? Be my friend?"

"Um. Yes. Of course I will." I was sweating now. This was indelicate beyond all measure. Friendship is the rarest gift a woman may offer to a man; and for a Star-Seeker to suggest it so openly to a mere Ship's Master was unheard of.

"Good. That's wonderful." And she beamed, like a child that has a toy that can talk back.

"And indeed, I'm flattered beyond all measure that you asked," I said.

"Good."

"Yes, it is good."

"What do we do now?" Albinia said hopelessly.

I smiled my most charming smile. "Well, I could tell you some stories of my days as a Trader. The duplicitous aliens; the magnificent deals! Or, if you prefer, I could tell you about the time I met the Empress, in my days at the Home Court, or—"

"You want to tell me stories?"

"Well — they're good stories," I said, defensively.

"And that's what friends do?"

"Not really," I admitted. "Friends, well. Friends take each other for granted. Interrupt each other. Give each other crap, forget each other's birthdays, then make impossible demands at the worst possible moments. I could never treat *you* like that, Mistress!"

Albinia started weeping; I was utterly confused.

"I did say yes, to your generous and extraordinarily kind offer," I apologised.

"Are you afraid of me, Jak?"

"Of course not," I lied, fluently.

"You are."

"Well —"

Albinia got up and walked away.

I was utterly bewildered. But one thing was clear to me.

I had totally fucked *that* one up.

"Couldn't we just shadow-flit into the cave?" asked Morval.

"We have to make a good first impression," I told him.

"A *canoe*?"

"Just row," I said.

The three-Olaran canoe bearing myself, Morval and Phylas skimmed fast along the viscous waters. The sky was dark with purple clouds, and the only trace of sun was a faint glow behind the largest swirl of cloud formations. It was raining. On this planet, it always rained.

The Klak-Klak that was leading us surfaced and its many claws klak-klakked. We looked ahead and saw the cave entrance.

"I hate caves," said Morval.

"How come?"

"I have a fear of small dark confined spaces," Morval admitted.

"My simulacrum was once buried alive and the remote link failed. I spent a year under the earth before they found a way to wake me up."

"That's nothing," snorted Phylas. "On my first Explorer mission, I was flogged and sprayed with salt water and Commander Galamea refused to wake me because she thought the aliens were just 'playing' with me."

"Bitch."

"She *is* a hard woman, without a doubt," Phylas admitted.

"How many times have you been killed by aliens, Morval?" I asked.

"Thirty, forty thousand times," admitted Morval.

"I've only been killed sixty-four times," I said.

"That's because you're just a Trader," Morval said.

"You have the easy job," Phylas added.

"We do the hard stuff. Prepare the way."

"Fornicatory traders."

"Take all the glory."

"Earn all the money!"

"Will you quit fornicatoryishly whining?" I told them.

We carried on rowing, an even steady stroke that sent the canoe flying above the sticky red waves of the planet's ocean.

Our boat penetrated deep into the complex of caves. Stalactites made of precious gems dangled down. Fish bumped the underside of our canoe and a few of them leaped in and were killed by Phylas's energy gun. The smell of burning fish flesh became intolerable.

The narrow waterway through the cave complex began to broaden, and we emerged into a high damp cavern. Thick black tubes dangled from the rock, forming complex shapes, like a latticework.

"Artworks," suggested Phylas.

"Excrement," was Morval's opinion.

"Rock formations," I suggested.

The canoe ran aground on the rocks and we stepped out. We

were wearing full body armour, even though we were in shadow-self form. The armour had been sprayed jet black and decorated with bumps and spikes, to make us seem more attractive to the crustacean-type entity that was the Klak-Klak.

There were six of the brutes waiting for us, each with at least twenty arms, and each arm was festooned with vicious claws. The claws klakked in unison like applause at a concert. I walked towards the largest of the Klak-Klaks, went on one knee, and attached a translating device to its chin.

"Can you understand me?" I asked.

"Yes," said the Klak-Klak.

"We come in peace," I said.

"No," said the Klak-Klak.

"We wish to trade," I said.

"No," said the Klak-Klak.

"Do you understand this concept—'trade'?" I asked.

"No," said the Klak-Klak.

"Is it possible," asked Phylas, "for a species to be considered sentient if it only knows two words?"

The Klak-Klak's eyes rose out on stalks and peered at Phylas. Then the eyes retreated into the black carapace again.

"Yes," said the Klak-Klak.

"Let us show you our treasures," I said. And Phylas stepped forward and opened up his cargo bag. He took out a huge Balla Pearl and held it in his hand. It glowed lustrously, transforming the dark shadows of the cave into lighter shadows. The Pearl sang, and the sound was like a female's post-orgasmic smile on a sunny day. Phylas passed the Pearl to the Klak-Klak, who clutched it in his claw. Then the Klak-Klak crushed the pearl and dust dribbled to the ground.

"Or this," I said, and took out an energy gun. I aimed it at the wall and carved a crude face, with two eyes, a nose, and a smiling mouth. Then I grinned. "Isn't it wonderful?"

The lead Klak-Klak visibly recoiled, stepping back and raising its arms in what in any creature's body language would indicate horror. Then he and the other crustaceans began to klak-klak their claws loudly. The sound was deafening, and ominous.

"You have," said the leader of the Klak-Klaks, "hurt our wall."

I laughed. "It's a wall!" I said. "Walls can't—" I broke off. I looked at Phylas.

"I'm on it," said Phylas and took a sentience reading of the walls of the cave that enveloped us.

"Ah," Phylas eventually concluded. "Shit," he added.

"The wall is alive?" I said, and Phylas nodded.

Red water trickled down the rocks of the cavern. The black wires dangling from the rock changed colour and became pink, then started to flash. A terrible low moaning howling sound emerged, as the wall groaned in agony.

"We didn't realise," I said, and the Klak-Klak lunged and ate me.

There was a crunching sound as the Klak-Klak devoured armour and body and bones.

[I woke up.]

Phylas raised his energy gun and incinerated the Klak-Klak.

Out of the ashes, a shadow stirred. The shadow grew, and became a silhouette. Finally the shadow became me again.

"Forgive us," I said, "for our error. But we come in peace, and we wish to trade."

The Klak-Klaks starred at us through eyes that stuck out through black armour plating and a terrible silence descended.

"Maybe we should—" I began to say.

Then there was a cracking and groaning sound. Phylas and I looked up. A trickle of dust slowly drifted down through the air, forming a haze like a parachute. A terrible wailing sound emerged; it was the rock, baying with pain, declaring its hate for the two intruders; we needed no translation for the sound was a dagger being plunged through our eardrums.

Then the roof crashed down on us.

I found myself enveloped in rubble. Boulders bounced off my body. Dust and rocks were everywhere, and in a matter of minutes, I was trapped under tons of screaming, howling, roaring rock.

"Not *again,*" muttered Phylas, irritably.

{I woke.}

I wrote up my log that night: **Negotiations failed after we were buried alive by a sentient cave. These creatures have much we would desire; but the evidence is they want nothing from us.**

System placed on the Trading Reserve List, to be reviewed in one hundred years.

The missile hurtled through space then teleported and reappeared and exploded an inch from the battleship's hull. The image blurred as the battleship's forcefield engaged, and the explosion lit the awesome blackness of space with a red and yellow fireball.

The smaller fighter ships were V-shaped and daringly fast and were firing energy beams of some kind at the battleship's rear end; tiny columns of flame erupted from the huge ship's side as the en-beams struck home.

Pinpricks of light in the distance betrayed the locations of fighter craft that had been hit and had expired in a burning maelstrom. Meanwhile, a new flotilla of space-fighting vessels had appeared and was spewing out debris which, I deduced was explosive.

"It's kind of beautiful," said Phylas, soulfully.

We were in invisible orbit in the planetary system of Xd4322, watching two tribes of the same species attempting to destroy each other in a series of colossal space battles.

"The planet is a radioactive shell, the sentients now live on moons and satellites," Morval explained.

"What savages," I murmured.

"Perhaps; but do they have anything we'd like to buy?" asked Commander Galamea, with creditable hard-headedness.

"Bombs?" I hazarded.

"According to our intercepted transmissions," Morval continued, "this war has lasted a thousand years. One group of sentients live in the inner solar system, the other group live in the outer solar system. They are fighting for dominance and the right to own the sun."

"What do they look like?" asked Galamea, and Albinia conveyed an image from Explorer's space-cameras and projected it in the air.

I studied the image with curiosity. These were diamond-headed creatures with no visible eyes or ears or limbs, whose squat bodies were supported on three powerful legs.

"How do they play piano?" asked Phylas, mockingly.

Albinia animated the image; tendrils emerged from the diamond torso and sweet music was heard.

"They have no musical instruments," explained Phylas, "but they sing their own internal organs."

"Could we trade with them?" Galamea persisted.

Another missile struck the alien battleship and it split apart. And then, as sentients slowly spiralled out of the ship, the fighter craft dived in and obliterated the stranded sentients one by one.

"I doubt it," said Commander Galamea regretfully. "Seal off the system."

"When I was a boy," said Morval, "the Olarans only had five planets. Olara, New Olara, Olara the Third, We Miss Olara, and Far From Olara."

"In those days," observed Phylas, "the Olarans were a sad bunch."

"My father was on one of the first rift ships. He was a pioneer, one of the greatest of all explorers," Morval bragged.

"I've read about him," I said.

"Back then," said Morval, "no one knew if the rifts were stable. Your ship rifted and it might, for all you knew, end up as random matter, or materialise in some other universe. So the courage of those early explorers was extraordinary."

“I’ve heard it said,” said Phylas, thoughtfully, “that most of them were volunteers. They went into space exploration for love, not as a result of, um, a court order.” He blushed, filled with shame at his own criminal past.

“That’s true,” Morval acknowledged. “My father was an idealist. He believed the exploration of space was one of the greatest adventures of all time.”

“As do I!” I said defensively.

“You’re just here,” said Morval scornfully, “because some female broke your heart.”

“Who told you that?” I said angrily.

“It’s written,” said Morval, “all over your soul.”

I seethed; but could not deny the truth of his words.

“My father eventually settled,” Morval reminisced, “in a Trading Post in some far-flung galaxy, and never returned to his family. My mother didn’t care; she had married again of course, long before that. And she never spoke of him; all that I know about my father was gleaned from research.”

“My father,” said Phylas, “was—” Then he ran out of words; clearly there was very little to say about his father.

I sipped my rich-juice; thinking about my own father.

I had not really known him all that well, in all honesty. My mother had been the main presence in our family, as was so often the case with Olarans. He had been an artifice monger; but I could recollect no tales he had ever told about his work. I decided I had nothing much to add to this particular conversation.

“Have I ever told you,” I said, “about the time I tried to sell carpets to the Vengans and—”

I drank too much that night and went to the Command Hub to look at the stars. On a Vassal Ship I could have used the Observation Deck and looked into space with my own eyes, but here I had to make do with camera images.

Albinia was still wired to Explorer; eyes closed and effectively unconscious. I wondered when she slept, or if this for her was sleep.

I conjured up the phantom control display and flicked through different star charts until I found the night sky of my own home world, Shangaria. It brought back fond memories; when I was ten years old I'd wanted to be an astronomer and spent every night looking at the stars. My mother used to name them for me; for she knew each star by heart.

I wondered if my mother had ever loved my father. There was however no evidence for it. She was a wonderfully self-contained female, and intensely serious; my father had been a funny delightful man, but she'd never once laughed at his jokes. Perhaps that was because they were stupid jokes. I had found them incredibly funny; but then, I'd been just a child.

After the divorce my father had visited us every weekend and he always had a smile for me. He told me that no Olaran marriage ever lasts more than twenty years; because females always grow impatient at the intellectual gap between them and their males. "Savour it while you can," he'd told me, still with a smile.

"You've been drinking," said Albinia. Her voice startled me out of my reverie. I turned to her. Her eyes were open; she'd emerged from trance.

"I am smashed," I said, extravagantly, "sozzled, delirious, and delighted!"

It was a stupid thing to say; and I said it in an extremely stupid fashion. And after I'd said it, Albinia stared at me for a long while, clearly baffled at my idiocy.

Then she giggled.

I offered to leave of course, after the giggle-moment, but Albinia insisted that I stay.

And so I stayed, and we talked, surrounded by stars, as she plucked absent-mindedly at the cable that led out of her skull.

We talked about aliens we'd encountered, and about missions, successful and unsuccessful, and about other members of the crew. Albinia knew the biographies of every crew member. I knew most of them by their first names from card games and drinking bouts, but she knew their full names including the matronymic and their professional and personal histories and she told me it all. I listened, an expression of rapt interest pinned to my face.

"Are you bored?" she asked abruptly.

"Not in the least," I protested.

"*You* say something."

"I would be delighted so to do."

"Go on then."

"Shall I tell you," I said, expansively, "of the time when I was trapped in a cloud on the planet of—"

"Unplug me," she whispered, urgently, cutting off my words.

"I'm sorry?"

"Please. I'd like to get up and stretch my legs."

I was startled at her request; but I reached over and gently eased the plug out of her skull; a curiously intimate act.

"Thank you," she said softly.

"You can't bear to do it yourself, can you?" I said, with dawning comprehension. "Disconnect yourself?"

Albinia blinked, clearly disorientated at being fully in a human body. "I do find it—an effort of will," she admitted. "Galamea makes me spend an hour in the gym, twice a day. But there are brain-plugs there too. It's only at meal times that I am—naked." She touched her skull holes self consciously.

"Here, take a walk with me," I said.

I changed the settings on the panoramic wall screen; we were in a park now, the sun was shining, and there was a lake.

Albinia got up from her chair, carefully stretching her limbs. Her bald head gleamed in the muted evening lighting.

We promenaded around the Control Hub for several minutes; I held her arm in mine. She was, I noted, a little wobbly on her feet.

"Look," she whispered, confidingly.

She showed me what was in her hand; it was her skull plate, that she used to cover the holes in her head on social occasions. "It holds a wirefree," she admitted.

"You wear this when you're not connected to Explorer?"

"When I wear this, I *am* connected to Explorer."

She smiled, like a child confessing a wicked secret; and she slipped the skull plate back into place, covering the holes. It was a silver oval, almost the same shape in miniature as her shapely head.

Her eyes sparkled as the contact was made; Explorer was back in her brain.

I found myself kissing her; I have no idea how *that* happened.

We went back to my room, and fornicated for several hours.

Albinia was a passionate lover, and it was a pleasure to bring her to climax. I felt curiously detached however; for I hardly knew this woman I was so skilfully orgasming. Because this wasn't the Albinia I loved; it was the "in trance" Albinia who captivated me. This Albinia, the real one, was just a shy awkward creature, oddly young in her ways, and emotionally needy to a degree that terrified me.

But I copulated her competently enough, then she fell asleep in my arms. And when she woke up she was crying and I had to ask her why; and then she told me what was wrong with her.

"I fear that I've lost my olarinity," said Albinia.

I stroked her naked breast, and she shuddered. Her skin was warm, I could still taste the aroma of her soft flesh on my lips.

"You don't believe me," she said.

"I don't believe you."

"I can see," she said, and held a hand out in front of her, "the galaxies unfolding. I can hear the beat of pulsing stars, I can touch the pull of gravity-well stars, I can count supernovae in a single glance and I can smell the carbon and the iron and the uranium in the clouds of matter circling each and every star in my sightline."

I touched her cheek with my fingers, and kissed her temples. "Feel that too?"

"I feel that too."

"You're Olaran."

"Some of the time."

I touched her skull plate, with its wirefree link to Explorer's brain. I was somewhat shocked by it, in truth, for I'd never heard of such a thing.

"Then cut the link. Turn off Explorer, exist in the here and now."

"I can't."

"You're supposed to. It's not customary to be permanently connected. It's surely in breach of safety protocols."

"I don't care. I love it too much. I am the ship, the ship is me."

"I just fucked a ship?"

"Well, yes."

"That makes me feel," I said, "odd."

And, to my delight, she giggled again.

Here's a truth I learned at an early age: females are not like males.

When I was twelve years old my six-year-old sister explained to me the fundamental principles of Olaran science. I had no idea what she was talking about, despite my several years of school. But she had accessed a single memory file and had learned it all, instinctively. She could do mathematics the way I could throw a ball. But she could also throw a ball further and more accurately than I ever could.

When I was sixteen years old I was given a degree in astrophysics with a distinction, and was considered to be one of the brightest students in my all-male class. But my sister, by this point, was building suns, with the help of a mind-machine link with the Olaran computer. Her intellect so far surpassed mine that I marvelled at our memories of being kids together, playing in a pool in the garden, creating imaginary friends.

But Albinia was the first female who ever explained to me the negative side of having such effortless intellectual proficiency. Since she was ten years old she had been cyber-linked with a computer or robot for large parts of her waking day. And so she'd grown up awkward, clumsy, and not at ease in her own body. Males terrified her, and the fact that all the males she met treated her as a superior being terrified her even more.

"All my life I've known I could have any male I wanted, with a click of my fingers," said Albinia, trying but failing to click her fingers. "And a lot of my girlfriends did just that. They fucked their way through college and carried on screwing around in their twenties. What was there to lose? Pregnancy is volitional these days, males are getting more and more beautiful, and the sexual congress is officially an artform. But I hated it."

"Poor little powerful girl," I said with—or so I realised in the retrospect of a moment later—a hint of bitterness.

"Every male I've been with behaves like a servant. I never feel relaxed. I always feel in charge."

I remembered Galamea's words on the dark world and, for the first time, I began to doubt my understanding of my own species.

"Females are natural leaders," I said tactfully.

"Have you ever been treated as an equal? By a female?"

"No," I lied.

We fucked again that night, and when I reached the moment of her orgasm she stopped and she looked into my eyes. And she cupped my head in her hands.

And she transferred her consciousness into me, from her skull plate into my brain dot.

And then we carried on fucking.

And this time, I wasn't me, servicing my goddess. I was *her;* I felt the heat of Jak's skin, the hardness of his body, I felt his cocks inside me, and I saw it too, with my Explorer part; saw the two naked coupling bodies from the cameras in the wall, and then I was in the Command Hub watching the stars on the screen and I was also outside the ship, I was looking at Explorer/myself thorough space cameras, and I was travelling through space, and my telescopic and spectrographic and electromagnetic vision allowed me to zoom close to any sun I desired and feel the soft caress of its interstellar matter on my body.

I was no longer myself; I was Albinia; I was Explorer; I was everywhere; and data swirled around me and I knew it without thinking. And when Albinia achieved her orgasm, I felt it too, and the ship shuddered, and the engines roared.

Afterwards we lay silently and nakedly entwined.

"How was that?" asked Albinia.

"Let's," I said, "do it again."

"Commence to rift, please," I said, and unreality descended upon us all in the Hub; on Morval, Galamea, Albinia, Phylas and myself.

As the rifting process began, I kept my eyes carefully focused on the star screen, and on my work. I did not, thanks to my exceptional self-control, digress in my purpose by looking at Albinia: the cable trailing from her skull like a leash, her absorbed and haunted features, her distantly-staring eyes, her twitching lips. Though in truth I wanted to look at her so much; so extraordinarily much.

And indeed, I did, just for a moment, sneak a peek!

For I loved, I realised, both Albinias now. The real one that I had fornicated with so beautifully that night; and the other one, the trance-Albinia who I knew on the Hub; a beautiful child lost in dreams.

"Improbability is—" Phylas started to say.

But suddenly Albinia screamed. It was a scream of pure hysteria and it shocked us all. And the ship rocked and shook, as she broke her link with Explorer. We were flying through un-space without a Star-Seeker!

"Operating manual controls," said Morval swiftly, as he took control of the vessel from Albinia/Explorer. He eased us back into reality. The Command Hub flipped and flipped again, until the walls and ceiling were whirling around us in our fixed points, held by the stay-still.

Then finally we were back in real space. I broke the stay-still with a murmur-link command, and hurried across the room to Albinia. Her face was twisted with pain. I reached for her cable.

"That could be traumatic," Morval warned.

I touched Albinia's face; she opened her eyes; she saw me and smiled.

I wrenched the cable out.

She sighed with huge relief; and was herself again.

"What is wrong Star-Seeker?" I asked, appalled at the look of emptiness in her eyes.

"I saw," she said, "another world come to a terrible end."

The genocided aliens in this case were the Maibos; a species of artificers, and we had done a great deal of business with them.

The Maibos had built for us some of our most magnificent furnishings and tapestries. They were an entirely non-violent species; it was a miracle they had survived so long. The Maibos had constantly refused all offers from Olara to equip them with a space defence system. And they refused to heed our argument that this is, and always has been, a viciously violent universe.

But the Maibos held to their faith, that violence begets violence; whereas a spirit of peace and love will spread and possess all those who encounter it. They called it the "contagion of joy."

And in this delightful faith they were proved entirely wrong. For these peace-loving creatures were invaded and exterminated like bugs. All of them died; *all.* Not one Maibos remained, except for the handful who dwelled at the embassy of the Olaran Home Court.

And even their planet was destroyed; shattered and exploded into many parts, just as had happened to the planet of the Fan-Tangs. And to salt and sting the wound, un-matter bombs were flown into their sun, sending it into a flaring frenzy; it was now poised to turn nova.

We knew all this because, in the dying moments of their civilisation, the Maibos had found a way to transmit space camera images of their demise through rift space, on what they knew were Olaran frequencies.

This is what Albinia had seen through her Explorer link. The end of a world; the planet of the Maibos sundering; billions of gracious, honourable creatures perishing even faster than their own ideals. It was an image of horror that had seared her mind.

It was a shocking holocaust and all Olarans mourned for the lost Maibos.

But the good news was that this time there had been a sighting. An Olaran scout vessel had viewed the foul slayer of the Maibos as it had fled the planetary system.

And according to this reliable report, there was no fleet, no alien armada; just a single vessel, with black sails.

"It's the Magrhediera," Morval speculated. "They escaped from their planet and they are taking revenge on us."

"The ship doesn't conform to any of the Magrhediera designs," I pointed out. "And it's not their style; they burn biospheres, then colonise; these creatures are killing actual planets."

"The Stuxi?" asked Galamea.

"It could be a rogue Stuxi ship," I conceded. "Their planet is Quarantined; but it just takes one vessel to keep a war going."

"The Stuxi are ruthless bastards," Galamea said. We all knew her past history with these creatures; we preserved a tactful silence.

"The Navy will find them," said Phylas. "And that will be that." He was clearly comforted at this vision of the remorseless power of the Olaran military.

"There may be other vessels," I worried.

"One ship," said Morval. "It's just one ship. Against the entire Olaran Fleet. It's just a matter of time before one of our vessels finds it, and crushes it."

We were nowhere near the Maibos system, and there was nothing we could do to help. And so we continued with our exploration of the farthest stretches of the furthest galaxies.

And every night Albinia came to my bed and we had sex. And afterwards we talked; and sometimes, she would let me be Explorer again. And we became close. We even became, dare I say it, "friends."

In the days however I continued to worship her, as my goddess and inspiration, as she, in her dreamy trance state, steered and flew and lived through our ship.

And, as it happens, I was at this time also spending a good deal more time with Phylas. He was determined to be a Trader, so I tried to teach him some tricks.

He was however, I concluded regretfully, after several role play exercises, too easygoing and nice to haggle; and he had no flair for deception and manipulative body language. However, I persevered; he was a dumb and sweet kid and the universe needed more of those, in my view.

And also, around about this time—I remember it well!—Morval and I discovered and explored a fascinating planet, which we christened Gem, that was populated by microbes and rich in jewels. The diamonds were clearly visible in the rocks, there were rubies, there were mountains made of gold. We spent a month running sentience tests on the bacteria and viruses who comprised this planet's only biosphere, before concluding that they were just stupid bugs and we had the right to claim this planet for Olara.

Galamea toasted our success with champagne; all the ship's officers would get a small percentage of the profits from this planet in perpetuity. It was our pension plan.

But then, just a week after the champagne toasting, we saw it; the ship with black sails. Or rather, Explorer did.

I have a located a telling trace, said Explorer.

"Tell us more," said Commander Galamea.

We were all in the Command Hub; Albinia's eyes were wide open, and clearly she too was shocked at Explorer's decision to speak to us all directly, rather than via her.

A vessel is travelling this sector via rift space; there are visuals.

An image appeared on our panoramic wall screen, of a black sailed vessel with a cylindrical hull.

"Is this—" I began to say.

This is the vessel that destroyed the FanTangs, said Explorer.

There was a sober silence.

"Send the coordinates to the Navy," said Galamea.

"They may rift at any moment," I pointed out. "We should tag them."

"If we get too close they'll fire on us," Galamea pointed out.

"Do we care?"

Galamea smiled. "We do not. Explorer, pursue, and prepare for battle. We're in for a father-fucker of a fight."

Albinia was living in the rift; she could smell the tang of the shifting-sands as Explorer soared through the cracks of reality that connect one part of the universe with another.

And Albinia/Explorer could feel and smell and hear and touch the enemy ship as it tried to escape.

She sensed too that there was something strange about the ship, yet she could not at first find words to describe it.

Then, as Explorer later explained it to me, the words came to Albinia:

She could smell Death upon this ship.

These were creatures who to our certain knowledge had destroyed two entire planets and all who dwelled on them. These were creatures who could blow up suns. These were creatures who had massacred the citizens of an entire Olaran Trading Post and left them as corpses for the birds to pick at, except that all the birds had died and no creature was left to scavenge.

The enemy ship was Death, it wrought Death, it savoured Death; but, Albinia resolved, soon it too would die.

Explorer/Albinia flew through the final rift and there it was, the Death Ship, waiting for her, and for us.

"Do we know anything about these creatures?" I asked.

"We have no records of a ship of this kind," said Phylas. "The materials of the hull are unfamiliar. The elements of which the materials are made are—unfamiliar."

"How strange is that?" I asked.

"Fairly strange," Phylas conceded. "Axial theory accepts three different classes of elements, the Real, the Unlikely, and the Never to be Dreamed Of. This ship is made of other stuff entirely."

"It may be from a different universe," said Morval.

I scoffed. "Not that old myth again. I don't believe in other universes."

"That's because you know no transdimensional science," sneered Morval.

"I don't need to; that's your job, to remember the dull stuff," I mocked. Morval bridled at the insult.

The enemy ship had a cylindrical hull that was scratched, and covered in chaol, a space-dwelling parasitical life-form. High black sails loomed above the hull; their purpose, Phylas explained, was probably to gather dark matter and use it as an energy source.

Explorer drifted closer, invisible in all wavelengths and heavily shielded.

The enemy ship was still. It seemed to drift through the darkness of space like an idle thought in a blank mind.

"How many crew?" I asked.

"Our sensors can't penetrate the hull," said Phylas.

"On the count of three, fire missiles, flit anti-matter bombs, release energy beams. Then when we've done that, switch on the Quarantine cage; we'll trap the parent-fuckers inside a box full of detonating explosives." I said.

"Agreed," said Galamea.

"One—" I began.

Explorer rocked and shook.

"They've hit our shields," said Phylas.

"No weapon was fired," said Morval.

Then we saw on the screen the tell tale shadows of missiles in flight.

"The missiles struck before they were fired," theorised Phylas. "They're using some kind of time reversal mechanism."

I froze at the implications of that.

Morval didn't wait for the rest of the count; he pulled the sliders on his phantom control display to flit the anti-matter bombs.

Our flitting technology can cut through any force shield; one moment the bombs were on our weapons deck, the next they were inside the enemy vessel.

And so the black-sailed ship spun madly in space, as if beset by fierce winds, as the bombs exploded inside its hull. The hull itself cracked, spewing air and bodies into space. And the sails collapsed, as their energy supply was compromised, and they dangled helplessly in vacuum.

Meanwhile, real-space missiles surged forth from Explorer and, ten minutes later, cut through the enemy's force-shields with ease and detonated on its hull, shattering it further.

"It can't be that easy," I said.

"Watch," said Albinia. She could see the ship as Explorer saw it, on our panoramic wall screen. And she knew, with a chilling certainty, that something strange was happening.

And then it happened. The shards of the enemy ship began to reform. The two parts of the hull rejoined; the sails refurled.

"Nice trick," conceded Phylas.

"Quarantine cage?" I said.

"Activated," said Morval.

Another missile exploded on our force shields. And another. The stay-still fields kept us safe, but the Hub was rocking wildly with each impact.

"Quarantine the bastards!!" I screamed.

And so the battle raged: the Death Ship continued to hurl missiles at us, and the missiles continued to splash hopelessly against our invincible shields. And meanwhile we cast a quarantine lattice through space to envelop the black-sailed monstrosity. Within moments the battle would be over.

Then our fields failed, and a missile crashed through our hull.

The impact on our ship was devastating: the hull cracked; air billowed out into space; our wireboards exploded, and the lights flickered wildly.

But in the Hub we saw none of that. The stay-stills kept us in place. The armoured doors protected us from all blast impacts. Our wireboards were shielded and discrete. And we could if necessary survive for centuries in this Hub even if the rest of the vessel were destroyed.

"Evacuate lower deck crew into pods," ordered Galamea.

"No one has ever done that much damage to an Olaran vessel before," marvelled Morval.

I began to worry we had got ourselves into a fight we couldn't win.

"Albinia, report," I said.

"Explorer is hurt; the sheer drive is damaged; we are using spare rift-support engines," she replied.

The black-sailed ship vanished from our screen.

"It's rifting," said Phylas.

"We have it tagged." We rifted too and found ourselves almost on top of the Death Ship; and we rained more missiles on it. And then it vanished, once again.

And again we tagged it.

And so the battle was waged: our two damaged ships flickered in and out of space, landing occasional blows upon each other in the form of powerful beams of energy that smashed against energy-absorbing shields. Albinia relied on her powerful intuition to guide her in her rift-leaps and most of the time she made Explorer reappear within missile-range of the enemy, and we struck.

Phylas and Morval were marshalling the barrage of energy beams, which collided with invisible barriers but, with each repulsion, stole data about what was within. They also used the disuptor ray in short bursts; but the Death Ship's shields bore up against it.

Then I flickerflew a black hole from Explorer's inner cage and it rematerialised within the enemy ship. The ship's image wavered, as the gravity well began to rip at its very fabric.

Then the enemy ship vanished, rifting away with incredible skill, and the black hole was left behind, bending space around it, a pinprick with the gravitational pull of a red giant.

And the enemy ship was below us now and Explorer began to shake. Every atom of our vessel was in motion. The enemy were trying to shake us to death with a weapon unlike any we had ever encountered.

I opened the bomb hatch and Albinia rifted Explorer away, and when Explorer reappeared in real space we were able to see a flock of missiles explode as one in the space where we had been. And then the black-sailed ship vanished again and we rifted after it.

After another hour of battle, we scored another hit: the enemy ship was smitten by a mighty energy blow, and its hull was dented, but this time it didn't tear. But within instants our own hull was smashed with a mighty fist, and air began venting out again.

"How are they managing to penetrate our shields?" asked Galamea calmly. "I thought that was impossible."

"They're—good," I said.

"Wait," whispered Morval.

"But even so, we're beating the fornicators!" I roared, as I saw their hull began to rip apart once more.

"It's rifting again," screamed Phylas.

"Continue pursuit," I said.

The black-sailed ship slipped through a rift in space; but once again we flew with it. We emerged in a different part of space; and the battle continued.

They rifted again; we went with them. And again. And again.

"What are they doing?" asked Morval baffled. "They're not fighting; they're *travelling*."

This continued for—how long? Hours? Or days? We received regular reports from the crew on the fatalities and casualties that had accrued. But our ship had self-healed, the wireboards had regenerated, and our guns were now recharged. We had lost six brave Olarans but we were battle-worthy once again.

And finally we found ourselves in a solar system dominated by a large gas giant. The black-sailed ship stopped shooting at us. It seemed to be waiting for something.

Our gen-guns fired, and fired again. The enemy ship's shields were holding up; but it was making no effort whatsoever to avoid our blasts.

"Look. Behind. On the wall-screen," said Morval.

The panoramic wall-screen in front of me showed the enemy ship, its hull a blaze of energy as bomb after bomb exploded on its invisible walls.

"No, look *behind* you. Look at the stars," Morval said.

I turned around, and looked at the screen behind me, which offered a view of the far distant universe.

And I realised that some of the stars were gone. Many remained, but I knew the patterns of the distant galaxies and I could see the absences as vividly as if they had been coloured flashes of flight.

"Which stars are gone?" I asked.

"The most distant."

More stars vanished.

"And now many nearer stars too," Morval said.

All the stars vanished.

"And now," said Morval, unnecessarily, "all of them."

"What does this mean?" I asked, trying to keep the panic from my voice.

"The battle is a feint," said Morval. "We are not winning, we are losing. In fact, we have already lost. Utterly."

The enemy ship accelerated towards us in real space, scattering our space cameras like a farki running through a mob. Energy beams bounced off its hull, and the metal glowed white, but still the black-sailed ship flew, closer and closer to Explorer.

"They're breached our improb wall a second time; there's a bomb inside Explorer," said Albinia, her eyes wide open, terror in her voice. "I think it's—"

Our ship exploded around us. The instruments were shattered into shards, and Albinia's body exploded and blood gushed out of her torso, and I heard her scream, but only once. Morval and Phylas too were ripped into bloody shreds of meat and bone.

I was knocked off my feet, and one of my arms was ripped off, and my skin burned, and my legs melted. I dragged myself by the strength of one arm and hand until I reached Albinia's seat. And I tugged myself up. And I touched her cheek, which was cold. And I took her pulse, and there was none. She was dead.

"All systems failing," said Galamea.

"Help me," I said. I pushed the dead body of Albinia aside with one hand, and sat in her seat. I ripped the cable out of her skull, and clumsily tried to attach it to myself, but of course I had no skull-socket.

"I can't," said Galamea. I looked. Her lower body had been ripped off, and blood was gushing out of the half-torso.

"You led us well, beloved Mistress," I said formally.

"Jak, you slippery devil—ah!" And Galamea died.

I cut the end off the cable until I bared two spikes; then I thrust them into my skull, so they penetrated my frontal lobe. Blood trickled down my forehead; and suddenly I could see through Explorer's eyes.

What is happening? I asked.

The enemy are possessed of a device that undermines the fabric of reality. It creates a zero-probability function; in other words, it restores this universe to the random chaos that existed before The Moment of The Universe's Birth.

They've destroyed this entire ***universe****?* I said, incredulous.

This is not their universe. They do not care if it dies. Behold, said Explorer.

And as I looked at the single image screen, I saw the enemy ship flickering. Then it vanished.

They're in rift space? I asked Explorer, with my thoughts.

No. There are no rifts left in our entire universe; for there is no universe. They must have passed through a strange kind of rift that leads elsewhere; which must mean into another universe.

How is that possible? I asked.

I have no data on that.

Can we follow them?

The Hub was awash with blood; Albinia was dead at my feet. I had been intending to tell her that I loved her; but I had not done so.

We can emulate their path and rift signature; there may be an entrance to another universe at this location. That is the most logical conclusion.

I had never before felt such a connection with a female. Not with Shonia, not with Averil, no one. There was a vulnerability to Albinia; I needed that. I needed to know that sometimes, she might need me as I—

Another universe? I said, helplessly.

That or death are your only options. You should be advised that in fifty-three seconds, the un-probability wave at the furthest stretches of this universe will reach us and we will cease to exist. We are, very nearly, the last particle of reality left.

Explorer, how do we clear the blood? And the bodies? I can't endure this.

The crew are dead. There are no cleaning robots in this part of the ship. The Hub is the only functional area left. You must wait until these bodies decay; and then I will cleanse them with jets of water from the ceiling and sluice the residue down runnels in the floor. But this is not relevant. We are the last particle of reality left; what do you want me to do?

What are you asking me?

Can you bear to live, or would you rather die?

Live.

I felt my body becoming wrapped in a healing cocoon; I knew that Explorer could keep me alive indefinitely like this, feeding me and disposing of my wastes without any need for me to leave my pilot's seat.

The cocoon covered my face; so that I could no longer see with my own eyes, only with Explorer's eyes; I could no longer feel my body's pain, I could only feel the icy touch of space on Explorer's hull. I entered a trance-like state; and I ceased to become me, and I became a part of Explorer.

Are you ready?

I am ready.

A moment later, Explorer and I embraced improbability, and left the universe of the Olara

For ever.

BOOK 6

Sharrock

After my encounter with Zala of the Kindred, the slayer of my entire species, I walked away from Sai-ias with hate in my heart. And I wondered at what I had become.

What indeed had happened to Sharrock the great warrior?

I had fought battles in this "Hell Ship" and lost, and eventually won—but they were all the *wrong* battles. For what merit was there in being King of the Kindred? Who was I helping or saving through such an act of braggartry?

And yet what other options were there? I could not fight an enemy I could not see. And escape from this ship was, I knew, impossible. Everyone told me that, and I had of course verified it carefully for myself, by interrogating everyone I met, and through personal investigations.

Thus, I knew we had no access to the engine room—for though there was one place in the interior world where the throb of motors could be heard, there was no way to break through the walls. I had tried to cut through the metal, but it was impregnable to my blade. There were no ventilation shafts; and no hidden corridors or secret passageways of the kind I had been so used to finding when raiding the palaces of rich aliens or the Southern Tribesfolk. There were no space pods or lifeships we could steal, and hence no way to survive departure from the ship. I had spent many days in the glass belly of the vessel looking out at space, and I knew that through the hull-hatch I could get access to the world outside; but how long would even Sharrock survive in empty space?

So instead of trying to escape I had endeavoured to make a life for myself here. I had smelled the flowers, enjoyed the breeze, savoured the sun on my cheeks. I had made friends: Sai-ias, Cuzco, even Mangan. Mangan was an angry creature but a smart one; his blind rage was his way of coping with a terrible situation. Mangan's kind, I had been told, were life-loving forest dwellers who on their native world had lived in peace and harmony with others. That was then; now Mangan was truly a vicious devil.

But that is what this ship did to people; it marred their souls.

As it had done to Sai-ias.

I had, in all truth, become fond indeed of Sai-ias. She was a gentle beast, and a thoughtful one. It touched me to see how she became involved in the lives of others; she knew each sentient on the ship by name and knew the names of their planets too, and could remember all the names of their lost loved ones. She remembered I had lost a wife called Malisha and a daughter called Sharil; I had only told her once but she never forgot.

But her soul was still tainted; for Sai-ias's way of surviving was a form of complicity. She made the ship run smoothly; and hence the Ka'un had an easier time. She taught the ways of acceptance; and thus the Ka'un's slaves were docile, and easier to handle. She was the prisoner who helps her own gaolers; I had always despised that type.

And so, after learning the scale of Sai-ias's treachery in collaborating with the despotic Kindred, I refused to talk to her, or deal with her in any way. Instead I spent my time alone, climbing the mountain paths, swimming the lake, and exploring the ship. I refused to participate in their godsforsaken Rhythm of Days; I wanted to keep my mind pure, and my body honed.

And then one day, I swam to the Tower as I always did, at least once a day. And once I was in sight of the island's shore the winds whipped up, as they always did. One time I had swum onwards and touched the force shield walls for myself. But the walls of force could not be penetrated of course; and my presence in such proximity had caused a great storm that had vexed the others hugely; so it seemed futile to keep attempting it.

So today, I merely trod water, and I stared at the Tower where dwelled my enemies; then I heard the sound of wings above me and I looked up.

And Cuzco swept downwards and caught me in his claws. I did not struggle, I let him carry me. He loosened his grip and I scrambled free and clambered up on to his back.

"Turd-for-brains," said Cuzco amiably.

"Vile and ugly orange freak," I informed him.

I enjoyed these flights; Cuzco soared up to the sky, almost touching it, then soared down, and made me dizzy with his speed.

Then he hovered as low as he could above the Tower. I saw the shape of the gardens around it; the shrubs on the craggy rock. The Tower was huge; larger than many cities. It was so near, and yet so untouchable.

"Watch," said Cuzco, and he released the boulders in his rear claws and they dropped down out of the sky and they

Bounced.

Rattling like pebbles on a roof—yet there was no roof, just air—before sliding off in a downwards arc and splashing into the sea.

"Force shield goes all around," I said.

"No way in," agreed Cuzco.

"No way to escape," I agreed.

"I believe, nevertheless," said Cuzco sombrely, "that I may have found a way to leave this place."

And my heart raced. "Tell me," I said.

Sai-ias

It was Day the Third of my nine hundred and eighty-four thousand four hundred and twenty second cycle of the Rhythm of Days, and Sharrock approached me by the lake side.

And for the first time in many cycles, he spoke to me.

"Are you well?" he asked.

"I am."

"It seems then you thrive," said Sharrock, "upon the misfortunes of others."

I made no comment; yet I could not comprehend how he could say such a thing to *me.*

"I have been planning," said Sharrock, "how we might escape this wretched vessel." And he smiled; but it was not a pleasant smile.

"There is no way," I said.

"So I have concluded," Sharrock said, grimly.

"Best—"

"—to accept the way things are. Acceptance is all. Yes, I know your lies, Sai-ias. I have also been considering ways to attack the Ka'un."

"Many have tried and failed."

"How? Tell me all."

I sighed. "There is little point. Trust me on this: I have been here for many years. The problem is that we do not know who the Ka'un are, nor how to get at them in the Tower where they dwell."

"Have you yourself tried?" Sharrock's tone was taunting; I wondered at his game.

"Yes," I admitted. "I swam across many years ago. The way was blocked. Cuzco attempted to storm it with a flock of aerials, that did not succeed. It cannot be done."

"Indeed, that tallies with all I know and have been advised," said Sharrock, his mood strangely buoyant.

"So what is it?" I asked. "Why are you speaking to me now?"

"Oh, there is news," Sharrock said. And there was a smug look in his eyes; I feared the worst.

"What is it?"

"Cuzco," he told me, "has issued a challenge to Djamrock."

The news shocked me. "What cause?"

"No cause. They fight at dawn."

And Sharrock's features were lit with elation; for he knew already that my calm and ordered equilibrium was about to be destroyed.

Two giant sentients were at war with each other, with no valid cause.

Thus, bloody and pointless anarchy had returned to our world.

We were in our cabin, the night before the combat. Fray was sombre; Lirilla was distressed; Doro was a pool of turbulent water; Quipu was appalled at what was occurring, just as I was. And Cuzco himself was in arrogant and bombastic mood.

"On my planet, before we became gods to the other sentient species, we were hunted," said Cuzco, with a pride that repelled me. "The biped Mahonosi feared us and slew us. The four-legged Karal feared us, and slew us. We were born in blood, we fought each living day. And we survived. And we evolved. And we grew mightier and mightier."

"Evolved? From idiot, into total fucking idiot?" snapped Quipu One.

"Good point," said Quipu Two.

"Where is it decreed," said Cuzco, "that we should not fight?"

"This creature is so arrogant!" said Quipu Three.

"Such duels are foolish, and dangerous," I told Cuzco, "They serve no purpose, and damage us all!"

"Those words are true," said Quipu Four, and his fifth and first heads nodded in agreement.

Cuzco snorted his contempt at me, and at the bobbing-headed agreeing-with-himselves Quipus.

"I need," roared Cuzco, "to taste blood and feel fear. Without that, I do not—"

"YOU CANNOT DO THIS!" I screamed at Cuzco, and they all stared at me, for I do not usually scream.

"I wouldn't expect *you* to understand," Cuzco said, in tones of utter scorn.

"Why? Because I'm not a blood-crazed warrior?"

"War is in my soul. It defines me."

"War is a form of madness," I told him. "Do not give in to it."

"Oh let him do what he likes," said Quipu One, and his other heads hissed.

"It'shisfuneral," Doro taunted.

Lirilla howled; not a song, a howl. I had never heard such a noise from her before; it sent a shudder down my central spine.

Fray brooded, silent, conflicted; she knew the joy of war too, but this was all too much for her.

"Please," I implored Cuzco.

"It will be a glorious combat," Cuzco said, and steam emerged from his neck and skull; and I knew we had lost him.

It was Day the Fourth. But no poems were to be recited this day.

We gathered at the foot of the White Mountains. Cuzco's scales were orange and scarlet and shone in the bright sunlight. Djamrock descended out of the clouds, his four wings flapping loudly. Djamrock had three heads, each of them fearsomely fanged and armoured. He was twice the size of Cuzco, and Cuzco was a giant even amongst the giant sentients.

No one had ever before dared to challenge Djamrock. But, from time to time, he had savaged unwary predators and herbivores and ripped them limb from limb. Eventually they healed; but the shock of Djamrock's violence always left a lasting damage in the souls of those he attacked.

We accept the evil of the Ka'un; but when our own kind turn on us, it more profoundly hurts.

We formed a circle around the fighters. Sharrock caught my eye; and the ghastly smile on his face repelled me. His naked torso was glistening with sweat; his red skin was darker in hue, a sure sign that he was agitated and surging with adrenalin.

And I could feel terror descend upon me. Violence is a character aberration that perturbs and disgusts my soul, and so I truly did not want to be here. For I am the child of a pacific species. We never fought, we never went to war, and, until the Ka'un, no other creatures had ever warred against us—not since we became sentient, many aeons ago.

And yet, even so, I could not resist the mood of the day. The energy! The sheer *exhilaration* of being in the presence of the blood-lust of all my fellow sentients!

The combat began.

The two beasts leaped and flapped wings savagely, and hovered in the air above us.

I cannot bear to describe the scene, and yet I must; for the images are seared upon my mind and the pain of that day lives as a reproach in my soul.

At first, for the first twenty or more minutes, I did not directly observe the two beasts in their bloody combat; I merely watched the watchers. It shocked me deeply. The screaming, the drooling, the roaring of rage, the obscenities uttered, the lust for the dealing of death that consumed all those who beheld!

A thousand and more different species all united in hate and loathing! Polypods and bipeds on the land, gathered in a vast crowd around the combatants; and sea-dwellers peering up from the lake, and swamp-dwellers staring up from their boggy homes at the aerial part of the battle. Only the sessiles were unable to witness the duel, for understandable reasons. Even the sentient plants were savouring what they saw of the spectacle—jeering and shedding leaves and spitting spores as they savoured the carnage.

As she watched, Fray snorted and scratched the ground with her powerful hooves; clearly a large part of her wished she could be part of this legendary fight.

As for Quipu, he was in a frenzy; his heads whipping from side to side, a crazed look to him that I had never seen before. He was the dearest friend of Cuzco and, despite the cruel words that often passed between them, they felt a huge affection for each other. And yet, as Cuzco bled, he roared, all five of his heads roared, in brutal exultation.

And when I dragged my eleven eyes from the spectators, I saw blood raining from the sky as the two beasts gripped teeth into flesh and rocked back and forth in the air. Whenever he could, Cuzco breathed fire from his skull-holes and neck-holes upon his adversary, but the flames did not even sear the ebon hide of Djamrock. And Djamrock's three heads relentlessly pecked and tore at Cuzco's flesh.

One of Djamrock's wings was severed by a bite from Cuzco and went tumbling to the ground. The black beast flapped free and spikes from its belly impaled Cuzco and Cuzco blazed fire again and the sky rocked with the horror of two monsters locked in an aerial death-embrace.

Then Cuzco lost a wing too and tumbled to the ground and crashed and Djamrock moved downwards with talons extended to sever his adversary's remaining limbs, and thus secure victory.

Cuzco was dazed, and did not move. Djamrock was descending in a fast plunge. We all waited for the inevitable.

But Djamrock halted his dive. He hovered in mid-air above

his near-unconscious foe, his great wings beating. And slowly Cuzco stirred. Then looked up. And saw his enemy poised above him, waiting.

A long and powerful funnel of flame from Cuzco's skull enveloped Djamrock's body, but Djamrock did not flee. He remained hovering, his wings beating out billows of flame, and after a time his black hide grew darker and the flesh below began to burn.

Djamrock screamed and screamed. For his body was aflame beneath the near-impregnable coating of his night-dark armour. His heads writhed from side to side. And Cuzco pulled himself on to his two legs and pounced, and his teeth caught Djamrock's belly and ripped it. Then Cuzco took to the air again and flew above his opponent, stopped in a frozen hover, then plunged. And with a single powerful movement he landed on his prey and ripped Djamrock's head off his body.

And then he ate it.

A silence descended, as we watched, stunned. Cuzco fed the head into his mouth and ate the skull, and ate the brains too. The slow steady crunching appalled us. Even the rejuvenating powers of the water of the well of life could not heal *that;* so now, one of Djamrock's heads was completely dead.

Cuzco blew flame from his skull again, and we could smell and taste the aroma; it was the reek of the remnants of the burnt brain of Djamrock being expelled from Cuzco's body.

Djamrock's other two heads stared at the sight. He was in dire agony, but his dark hide was recovering its normal lustre. The fire in his body was being extinguished, his flesh was healing again. He was recovering. And even though he'd lost a head, he still had enough power to rip the crippled Cuzco into pieces.

But Djamrock did nothing.

Cuzco pounced again and ripped off a second head. And he ate that too. And he billowed steam from his neck to sluice his system of the last traces of alien skull and brain.

"No!" screamed a voice. "No!" screamed another voice.

But these were lone voices in the mob. I heard a drumming

sound, as the crowd clapped and stamped their feet and chanted: "Kill him, kill him, kill him!"

Cuzco pounced one final time and ripped off Djamrock's third head.

And ate it.

And shat out the remnants through his neck-holes.

And then Cuzco looked at me, with triumph and sorrow in his old eyes. And I knew then: this had been planned. This was a death pact between Cuzco and Djamrock.

And Djamrock had won. His victory in battle had entitled him to the ultimate reward: his irrevocable death.

Except that Djamrock was not truly dead. His sentience and his soul lingered on in his headless corpse. It endured in the particles of brain-ash that still floated in the air. Djamrock was thus doomed to an eternity of torment.

But he had died fighting; and that was enough for him.

The thought of what he had done, and what Cuzco had aided him in doing, appalled me.

I slithered away.

I was ashamed, so deeply ashamed, of Cuzco, of Djamrock, and of the rest of my fellow sentients. Could they not see that defeat was preferable by far to this kind of terrible victory?

That night, I crept out of my cabin and made my way through the pitch blackness of the interior planet's artificial light, using memory to guide me, until I reached the lake.

And I there I sat, and listened to the waters lapping.

In the morning, as the sun rose. I watched the first fish leap from the water. I watched the aerials flock in the sky above, dancing patterns in air.

"Do you not see," I argued, "that Cuzco must be banished? An example must be made."

I was addressing the Guiding Council of the Sentients; twelve of us in all. Quipu, Biark, Sahashs, Loramas, Thugor, Amur, Kairi, Wapax, Fiymean, Krakkka, Raoild. And Sharrock, too, was there; for he had, unknown to me, been elected as a thirteenth Council Member and hence now had a responsibility for the government of this world.

The meeting was going badly. Quipu's five heads were all laughing at me for my attempt to actually *punish* Cuzco for achieving a glorious victory.

Sharrock's scorn too was evident in his every cold glare.

And the others—sentients I had known and regarded as friends for so many years!—treated me with a contempt that they barely bothered to disguise.

Thugor made a pacifying gesture. His words were silken, we felt them as much as we heard them. "You, my Sai-ias," he said, "you, kind and gentle being, have always been a kisser of the arse of your enemy. Cuzco however is a hero. He showed us a way out. Through war and glory. You should celebrate him, not censure."

"What he did was wrong," I insisted.

"He enabled Djamrock to escape."

"He cursed Djamrock! He will lead others to the way of death. That is not what we need," I said, trying to keep calm, and to rein in my fury.

"Cuzco is a hero," agreed Fiymean. "Sai-ias you are a dismal coward. You know nothing of war."

"I know much about—"

"It's pathetic," said Kairi, in a shrill scornful voice, her feathers vibrating to make the sounds that the air translated. "All the things we do, and that you encourage us to do. The Days. The Temple. We demolish, we rebuild. We tell stories. The same stories. We talk about science, but we barely understand each other's ideas, and have virtually no technology, and no way of acquiring fresh data. We talk about history, for all we have is history. There will be, for us, no more history. It is all futile. What Cuzco has done has shone a light on our world, and all we can see is shit and lies."

"It is not futile," I argued, in my gentlest of tones.

"Sai-ias, fuck yourself with a barbed weapon, and die in the process."

"You turd-eating coward."

"You pathetic fucker."

"You're not welcome here, you slimy sea fucking monster. Cuzco is our god."

And so they continued; the taunting, sneering voices. I hated it so much, yet I endured the mockery patiently.

My task was all the harder because none of these creatures remembered the early years; the days of Carulha, and my two battles against him. For all the great beasts of that time had died, of Despair, or in some Ka'un battle or other. Only the Kindred remembered; and even they were starting to forget what I had truly done for this world. To this new generation, I was just a complacent fool; preaching peace and harmony to an angry lynch mob.

"Cuzco must be banished," I insisted, "for the good of all." And then I paused for effect, and said: "I so order it."

But my words were like a light breeze in the midst of a hurricane; no one heeded them.

"Sai-ias," said Quipu One, my favourite of the Quipus, and one of my oldest friends on the ship, "this is none of your affair."

"It is my affair," I said angrily. "You idiot Quipu, you know nothing —"

"Ah, fuck away," said Quipu One contemptuously. "I have no more time for you."

"Well said. Fuck away, Sai-ias," said Quipu Two.

"Fuck away Sai-ias!" said Quipu Three.

"Cuzco is our hero now," said Quipu Four, and his eyes gazed into the far distance, remembering the glory and the triumph of Djamrock's demise.

"Fuck away, you black-hided beast!" said Quipu Five. "No one cares what you say, or what you think. Not any more."

I looked at Sharrock.

"Sai-ias," he said to me gently. "You are wrong."

Words do not hurt me, usually.

Those words did.

Lirilla's wings fanned my face.

"This is a cruel world," I told her, the sweetest creature on this entire world. "But I know I am right."

Lirilla flew away without speaking.

I found Cuzco, surrounded by acolytes in the field of green, telling his tale of victory to a mob that included Sharrock and Quipu.

I used my tentacles to hurl myself towards the crowd. I heard muttering and hissings and muttered insults. "Cuzco," I called out.

Cuzco raised himself up, and his great wings beat and he hovered above me, baring his face whose soft features were distorted with contempt.

"You saw me fight?" he roared.

"It is Day the Fifth," I said to him and the assembled crowd. "It is our day of music and celebration."

"A waste," roared Cuzco, "of fucking time."

Laughter rocked the crowd. Sharrock stared at me sadly, his contempt merging with his pity in a toxic brew.

"We need it. It fills our days," I said.

Cuzco pushed out his chest. And his face—or rather an

illusion of a face, patterns of expression on the soft skin of the breast of his left body—bore an intrigued expression. "It was you, wasn't it?" he asked. "*You* created the idea of the Temple?"

"I did," I said.

"And the Days, you created those too."

"I did," I admitted.

"And the whole structure of our lives. The gatherings. The cabins. The Guiding Council. That was you."

"When I first came to the ship," I said, "all was anarchy and—"

Cuzco laughed at me. And the crowd laughed. Even Sharrock laughed.

And in that terrible moment, I felt humiliated.

For I was, I realised, considered by all present to be a gullible fool who believed that make-believe work was *better* than real work. *I* was the one, the only one, who did not understand that glory is to be found in heroic defeat, not in meek surrender!

I understood at that moment the depth and sincerity of their scorn, and of their contempt. And I found myself consumed by self-hate. Was I *really* this wretched creature they despised so much?

"Sharrock, ignore them. Do not laugh at me. You and I know better about what is right," I said wretchedly. But he grinned at me too, tauntingly.

However, I stood my ground. "Cuzco, you are banished," I said, as firmly as I was able. "That is my irrevocable decision."

The mob began to howl and shout, drowning out my words. I continued desperately: "You must dwell on the mountain crags, but you cannot speak to anyone or be spoken to by anyone. When you are gone, all will return to normal. Our Rhythm of Days will return."

Few could hear me for all the baying and roaring, but still I continued: "Fighting will once more be forbidden. I do not ask this, I do not beg for it, I *demand it*!"

"You fucking turd-sucking bog-fucking slack-cunted bitch," said Cuzco. "Why don't you fuck—"

My tentacle lashed out, and unfolded in an instant to double its usual length; and I swung it in a huge loop to create momentum; then I smote Cuzco with it.

The blow was powerful and as fast as thought itself, and he was knocked across the ground like a ball struck with a bat in one of the biped's wretched games.

There was a startled silence.

Cuzco got back on his feet. He puffed up his chest again, and showed me his face; there was glee in his expression. "I've been waiting," said Cuzco, "for this for a long—"

I struck again but this time Cuzco was expecting it and he rolled out of the way. And when he came out of the roll his wings unfurled and he beat them and he was in the air and he pounced down at—

I wasn't there. I used my tentacles to grip the ground and fling myself upwards. And as I flew my quills emerged and I skimmed Cuzco's body and my quills crashed against his body armour, and we both fell to the ground.

I flipped over again and narrowly avoided a funnel of flame from Cuzco's head. Then I fired a fusillade of quills at him from my stomach hole and he was shocked as these brutal arrows smashed against his hide. He buckled up his breast armour, burying his soft face away, so his bodies were now just two vast horned carapaces covered in impregnable scales.

He paced towards me. I slithered towards him. A quill stuck out from his hide, close to one of his heavily shielded eyes. His tread was light. He was sizing me up.

We faced each other in the field of green, and all around us a myriad alien species watched; furred, feathered, scaled, covered in hide, small, large, brightly coloured, drably coloured; a whole menagerie of strangeness, rapt in joy at the sight of this, the second great fight in two days.

I felt the ground shudder and I knew that Fray had arrived, to watch his two "friends" fight.

But then I realised, with a terrible and sudden clarity, that she and I weren't truly friends at all. We were merely companions, and fellow captives. But she cared nothing for me, not really; not did she have any concept of who I truly am, of the *real* Sai-ias.

Fray and Cuzco also were bound together by sheer force of circumstance; their friendship here was a matter of convenience, no more. They were large; and savage; and heavily armoured; that was all they had in common!

And what's more, it now seemed obvious that despite our seeming friendship, Cuzco and I had always harboured a deep loathing of each other. He, a savage flesh-eating monster, I a cultured vegetarian; what could connect two such different beasts? The answer was clear: nothing.

Oh, now I could see it all so plainly. All was lies and cruelty and hate! Nothing on this world had any value! These truths came crashing down upon me.

But even so, I felt obliged to fight.

A funnel of flame billowed out of Cuzco's skull and I did not move. My skin ignited and I was enveloped in a fireball and still I did not move. My flesh melted, and the burning smell of my body filled the air and still I did not move.

When the flames died down, my soft outer skin had been burned away and what remained was the jet-black diamond-hard carapace of my inner body. My tentacles were sheathed; my eyes were protected; my skin would grow back in a matter of days, and would have done so even if I had still been on my home planet.

And all could now see the remarkable truth: that the inner Sai-ias is a warrior born.

I pounced.

My tentacles unfurled, I gripped the ground, I flung myself up and at Cuzco, and I caught his scaly hide with my tentacle tips and swung him round and crashed him to the ground. As he lay dazed I flipped into the air and flew downwards, my central quill extended, and I stabbed him in the fleshy skin of his stomach.

He recovered and swept at me with his powerful paws and

knocked me aside, but I rolled and threw myself upright and launched again.

Cuzco took to the air but I was just as fast and I threw myself upwards and as I did my tentacle tips retracted and my inner claws were exposed and I used these claws to grip and rip his flesh in mid-air. His wings beat, he struggled to keep his flight, as I ripped away his hide and blood gouted from his body on to the field of grass below.

Cuzco came crashing to the ground, and I beat him again and again with my tentacles. He fired his flames again but they could do no harm to my chitinous body and armoured tentacles; and my eyes, too, were made of hard scales not soft flesh and could not be burned or stabbed or gouged.

I played with him for a while, smashing him with my tentacles, and mockingly absorbing his flames as if they were sunshine on a warm day. Then finally I spat, and an unfolding matrix of web embraced his body and trapped him.

Victory was mine.

"He is banished," I told the crowd. "Take the body to the mountain top and leave it there. Fill a container with water of life and leave it beside his body. Cuzco will not be of our family until ten years have elapsed, and he has earned my forgiveness."

No one demurred.

Sharrock was staring at me, astonished; and he smiled with open joy.

I recoiled at his approval; I was revolted by the love of the crowd.

For before, I had been right, and yet I had been mocked. And now—now I had proved I was nothing but a violent thug, with more flair for war than even the powerful Cuzco—*now,* the mob would follow me anywhere.

This was the quintessential predator-prey mindset; the belief that only power endorsed by violence should command respect.

And I despised them all for it.

And, in all candour, I despised myself too, for playing their pathetic game. For I believe in love and not war; yet to save my world, I have to be a monster.

And so a monster I have become.

I went to the storm zones and let a hurricane bombard my hard carapace. A few times I thought I would be swept away and smashed against the icy clouds.

I roared with rage into the hurricane's open mouth, and felt anguish and guilt that hurt me more than the wind's sharp knives.

My outer skin grew back. The Rhythm of our Days returned. The Temple was demolished; and then we began to rebuild it. Stories were told. Science was discussed.

And Cuzco was now a memory; he lived in solitude on a mountain-top eyrie, the very emblem of the way we should not be. And my world was safe; and, to such degree as it was possible to be content in such a place, my people were indeed content.

And I was revered now, and not despised. My smallest request was treated as a command; no one ever interrupted me. I felt like a god.

And I loathed it.

The fields had to be tilled every month. Armies of polypods thundered across the artificial soil, kicking with hooves and ripping with claws, and aerials swooped down and sifted soil. And at the end of this long process, the soil was no more fertile than it had been before.

The trees and bushes needed to be pruned every week. Some

of the vegetation ran riot and grew at a terrifying rate, and the arboreals used saws and swords to hack pieces off the runaway shrubs and trees to reduce them to a manageable height.

But what would it have mattered if the trees had grown to the heavens? There would still have been space enough to move in. And though the browsing animals ate the grass, and chewed the tree bark, there was no nourishment to be gained from that. It was a squandering of time to tend this garden, for our bodies were fed by other means.

The ice clouds soaked up moisture from the air and grew daily, and so they had to be regularly milked. To achieve this, the aerials flew inside the jagged clouds — clouds which had once floated in the skies of the icy world where Quipu had lived — and pissed their hot urine downwards, melting the ice. And the urine-tainted rain fell upon the land and the lake; and the ice-clouds shrank. And all of us felt the mixed blessing of being rained upon by water filthily stained with piss.

Thus, every time it rained, bleak irony drenched me as much as did the raindrops.

And so there was always work to be done. And it was always futile, desperate, purposeless work. Such was the rhythm of our days.

It was Day the First and I was climbing a mountain, and I could not resist the urge; I went to see Cuzco.

My claws gripped the cliff face tightly, and I was able to clamber up the steepest slopes, despite my bulk. I enjoyed this kind of physical effort; it invigorated me.

I had no idea where Cuzco was dwelling but I followed my instincts; it would be the highest crag, the most remote spot. I reached the top of the mountain summit and looked for him in vain. Then I hurled myself off and glided to the next summit; and when I found him not, I leaped again, and reached the next summit. And then the next. Then I landed on an icy crag and found myself sliding across a glacier. Strange ice-creatures peered at me, and I marvelled that I had never seen them before.

I called out to Cuzco, again and again, with a shrill whistling noise that I knew he would recognise as my ocean-call.

The day passed, and I found no trace of Cuzco.

It was Day the Second and I was due to be at the Temple to help raise the stones. But instead I returned to the mountain peaks and searched again for Cuzco.

It was Day the Third; my search continued.

At the end of Day the Fourth I was frustrated and weary and I made a wild decision; I would not return to my cabin when the black night fell.

And so I waited, buffeted by cold winds, as the sun set and cast its rosy glow upon our fake and evil world. Then the daylight in the air was switched off; sheer blackness descended. There were no stars, there was no residual light. The entire planet was black and all the land animals sheltered in their cabins; the aquatics in the lake and rivers slowed to a sluggish pace in their swimming; the aerials cowered in their nests. Only a few, just a very few, of the echo-locating species ventured abroad, and even they were wary.

I crouched on the high plateau and listened to the sounds of the night, and at length I heard a sound I recognised: a wild howling. It was Cuzco, baying at the stars, except there were no stars.

I spent twelve cycles on the mountain tops gliding from peak to peak, following the sound of the howls; and then one day I found my friend.

"You've changed," I told Cuzco.

Cuzco snorted, and I felt the heat of his flames on my soft outer skin. There was a wild look in his eyes. He did not speak.

"I've missed you," I said.

Cuzco's claws scratched the hard rock.

"I had no choice. I had to banish you." I said. "Otherwise—"

Cuzco roared at me. I'd never heard his roar from so close. It was a scream that possessed his whole body. He was a fierce-looking creature at the best of times—with a hide made of sharp spikes and horns erupting from his skull. And the furnace of his body—the inner heat that allowed him to spit and exhale flame—made the patches of hide that were visible beneath his body armour glow.

And yet I knew that Cuzco, in his best moments, had a generous and a gentle spirit. And, too, as well as his killing claws, he had fingers that were supple and soft and could be used to manipulate tools, or create great art works, or stroke, affectionately, a subordinate being.

"Have you become insane?" I asked Cuzco calmly, and he snorted again, and spat fire over me and I was engulfed in flame.

Once more my soft skin burned away; and I clenched my extremities into my core, and my shell joints instinctively sealed and I allowed the fire to burn down before my head re-emerged.

"You are indeed," I concluded, "insane."

Cuzco laughed. "Not so."

"You murdered Djamrock."

"We made a bargain."

"An insane bargain."

Cuzco snorted again, and acid dripped out of his eye sockets. This body language I knew; he was laughing.

"I'm tired of stories," said Cuzco, as the sun set, and the blackness descended again.

"Then tell me no stories."

"I find your company irksome."

"I love to irk."

"You succeed triumphantly, you ugly sentimental shittier-than-an-arsehole monstrosity."

"Now I recall why I've missed you; your squalid absence of a personality makes me feel much finer and wiser by comparison."

A spurt of acid dripped out of Cuzco's eyeballs; he was laughing again.

We were silent together a while. A long while.

"I should return," I said. "To my cabin."

"Why?"

"Because I have a life down there."

"Then go, you ignorant stealer-of-space-that-might-be-occupied-by-my-shadow."

"Perhaps I shall."

"Did you really think I would be glad to see you?"

"Are you?"

"You're a grotesque viler-than-turds-in-my-eyeballs monstrosity."

"But are you? Glad?"

"Yes."

"I did not think you would be glad. After all—"

"You fought a noble fight, and bested me."

"No fight is noble," I said derisively.

"I thought you were a coward."

"I aspire to be so."

"You're not a coward."

I sighed, from my tentacle tips. I rehearsed my speech about pacifism, and why it is preferable to blood-lust, but decided not to waste my breath.

"You fight like a grazing animal whose grotesque teats are the size of a baby Chall's head," I informed him.

He snorted; the air burned; acid dripped from his eyes; laughing again.

"Why did you come?" Cuzco asked.

"I was worried about you."

"You beat me into bloodiness and had me dumped on a high cold mountain top; and you were *worried*?"

"I thought you might be lonely."

Cuzco looked out at the view: the world was far below; we were atop a remote icy crag surrounded by sheer cliffs.

"Fair guess," he conceded.

"Are you lonely?"

"No."

"Good, I'm glad," I said.

"And yet," Cuzco acknowledged grudgingly, "yes."

"As I suspected."

"Admit it," said Cuzco, "The only reason you're here is—you can't live without me, can you, you ingratiating slime-fucker?"

I waved my tentacles scornfully, disparaging such a ridiculous idea.

"It's true!" snorted Cuzco, scalding my cheeks with plumes of hot air from his skull. "You care about me, you actually have feelings for me, don't you? In that sad pathetic cock-sucking arsehole-kissing clingy way of yours. Admit it, you soft-as-shit-expelled-from-my-bowels worm!"

I was convulsed by a sudden unexpected paroxysm; my body was attacked from within by an unfamiliar choking feeling; my emotions clashed and collided; and I exhaled stale air from my rectum, violently and loudly.

"What happened then?" said Cuzco, alarmed.

"It is the way my species," I said, amused, "expresses affection and abiding love."

Cuzco glared at me, and acid dripped out of his eyes again: "And you're not *extinct?*"

I knew all Cuzco's stories, his tales of valour and loves lost and battles fought and great deeds performed in faster-than-light space ships that carried his kind amongst the stars.

But over the next few weeks, he told me all the stories again, and I listened rapt and fascinated, and then I told mine.

I talked of how my people first learned to fly through space; and how we danced and mated among the stars; and how we gave birth in caves and cherished our young. And I talked too of the day my father took me to the moon of Shallomar, perched on his back as he flew through vacuum.

"Did you love your father?" Cuzco asked.

"Of course I did." I replied.

Cuzco sighed; I suspected he felt a pang of jealousy.

"And you? Did you love *your* father?" I asked, intrigued. "Or, rather, do your species leave their aged parents out in the desert to die the moment they begin to forget occasional facts? As the Frayskind, so lamentably, do."

"We do not do such a thing."

"But love? Did you love him?"

"No, I did not love him," Cuzco said, soberly. "He was a cruel tyrant; such as fathers are meant to be. My mother too was brutal to me; she taught me through pain, and taught me well, the evil bitch."

"I find that sad."

"Do not pity me!" said Cuzco angrily. "Our people *do* have love. We love many things."

"Name one thing that you love, that doesn't involve ripping the throat out of a vulnerable fellow creature?"

Cuzco thought hard, clearly angry at my words.

"We love our comrades in arms," he said proudly, "and would happily die for them, and they for us! And we love our sexual partners too. Yes, we do! With a rare and overwhelming passion! Or rather, we love them until we tire of them, and find their breath stale and loathsome, and then we feel compelled to batter them and seek fresh fucks. But for a while at least, then—yes, romantic love—I do know the meaning of that joy!!"

"Hmm," I said.

"But as for children," continued Cuzco, "well, that's a different thing entirely. For I did not know a parent could love a child, and a child a parent, until I came to this place."

"That's sad," I concluded, having won my case, I felt, beyond all doubt.

"No it's not. It's normal," Cuzco said, stubbornly. "For my kind."

"I had always believed," I admitted, "it was a universal thing. That all species know the joy of love, even the violent ones."

"Not Doro's kind."

"Fair point. His species are single-sex."

"Perhaps he loves himself?" Cuzco suggested.

"That is not true love, it is just vanity."

"And Frayskind? Do they know love?"

"Who could love a Frayskind! The great lumbering oaf!" I suggested.

"Yet magnificent too," Cuzco argued.

"In her way, perhaps. Certainly loyal; and a good friend; unless you are a mischievous Frayskind teen, then Fray would eat you alive."

"Give us credit; my kind are not great parents, but we do not eat our young."

"You swallow sentient bipeds," I said accusingly.

Cuzco chuckled; an eerie sound. "Only when they are young and fresh; the older kind are chewy."

"You immoral beast!"

"You should try it. Biped haunch. It has a tang."

And so it went on; we threw out ideas, exchanged memories, mused on the peculiarities of the strange other species with whom we inhabited this ship, told jokes, teased each other, and talked endless nonsense that amused us both.

Cuzco and I were far from kindred spirits. His kind were fierce, wrathful, brutal, murderous, and cared for nothing more than honour, which they defined as the ability to kill or to die with skill and grace. While my kind were timid, pacifist, cowardly in his eyes; but full of an unquenchable love for others and for life itself.

But we had one thing in common: our need for each other.

For I needed him, desperately and limitlessly. And he needed me too, with the same crazy intensity. And the bond it created dwarfed any love I had ever known.

Cuzco—I would fight and die in war for you!

That's how much I love you.

"Why did you do it? The fight with Djamrock?"

"He begged me to."

"You thought you'd win?"

Cuzco sighed wearily. "Yes that was my plan."

"Could you have endured it? An eternity without body?"

"An eternity of joy. Knowing I had died with honour."

"You would have abandoned me?"

"We are all alone," said Cuzco. "Love is an illusion."

He was right. Love is an illusion. And so is hope.

But are illusions really so very bad?

"Where did you learn to fight like that?" Cuzco asked one night, after we had spent a day flying on the updrafts above the highest summits.

"I never learned," I admitted. "I had never fought a battle

until I arrived on the Hell Ship. But in the early days, there were two huge combats, which I won. That is why the world is as it is. Because I fought, and won, and claimed obedience."

"Before my time?" asked Cuzco.

"Before your time."

"I thought Djamrock was the leader of the world. Or Miaris. They were the dominant predators. When they spoke, all listened."

"They listened; but Djamrock and Miaris never said anything that wasn't nonsense. My words mattered."

"Yes but—"

"What?"

"You spoke to us all, true, and often we heeded you; but no one *feared* you."

"I did not want anyone to fear me."

Cuzco thought about that.

"Explain how you can fight," he said, "if your kind are not predators."

"Once," I said, telling the tale of my people:

"Once, the oceans of our world were ruled by a magnificent and beautiful sentient species called Tula. Tula means 'all' in my language; the Tula were our all. We were their symbiotes, their slaves. They were born as soft sea creatures, and developed a calcareous exoskeleton to become underwater reefs as they aged. The ocean bed was ruled by them; the ocean bed *was* them.

"And they fed us and taught us, and in return we protected them.

"These are not legends; this is the archaeological biology of my kind. We were giant plant-eating sea creatures with tentacles and a cape and the ability to expand our bodies to appear more threatening than we were. Then we formed a symbiosis with the Tula and we used our fearsome aspect to discourage predators who liked to eat the soft Tula flesh inside their bony frame. Browsing sea creatures like the Uoolsa and the Jaybkok could eat an entire Tula reef in a single sitting; but they were wary of *us.*

"But as time went by the predators grew more bold and they

began to eat my kind, before consuming our Tula hosts. So we learned to fight, using our tentacles as weapons to choke and our quills—our sexual organs, for males and females alike—as weapons.

"And the Tula, who were sentient, saw what we were doing and they cleverly decided to 'breed' us. They paired us in combinations that amplified certain traits: size, strength, toughness of carapace, deadliness of our quills and so on.

"All this took place over many tens of thousands of years; but selective breeding can be a remarkably effective process. We became fighting monsters, strong and remorseless. And so the Tula were safe, for we guarded them; and were bred to do so with terrifying effect.

"Then the oceans started to die and we fled to the land. And there, with our bodies equipped for war, we struggled to survive. We became sentient. And when we became sentient, we became pacifist. That is when my species was truly born; when we began to think.

"The Tula were no more; we were alone on hostile land. And our minds developed; but our bodies did not. Our fighting weapons did not de-evolve. We retained the atavistic ability to wage total war, though we chose never to do so.

"It is a freak of nature, no more, Cuzco. I take no pride in it. I am proud of my intellect, my compassion, my empathy. But the fact I have a body that can kill with effortless skill means nothing to me. It is just a freak of nature."

"It means you are a warrior!" Cuzco said.

"Oh you forsaken-by-the-gods eater-of-hot-smelly-shit-from-the-arse-of-a-Frayskind idiot, do you not hear *anything* I say?" I said to Cuzco, using one of his favourite insults; and he laughed.

Night fell and we were enveloped in total blackness.

We talked some more. I told him of my many friends in the days of my pre-metamorphosis "childhood," and of my brothers and sisters who I had loved. He talked of his home planet and his "wife" (his third, whom at that point he still found sweet and had not yet rejected or battered) who he had tried and failed to protect from the Dreaded.

"We were masters of our world," he said. "And then the skies turned red. We are creatures of fire and they used fire against us. It rained flame, day after day after day. The forests were consumed. The seas boiled dry. Mountain tops were seared. But we hid in caves and underground tunnels and we launched our space fleets against the invaders.

"My father was one hundred of our years old and he was Admiral of the fleet. He and his warriors perished. Then the fires on the surface of our planet died out. The smoke settled. We emerged from our caves to face our invaders. But they never came. They defeated us, but they never faced us. It was the greatest of dishonours.

"I was sent to investigate the fleet's emergency base, on the largest of our two moons. We had cable links with both the moons, we could fly back and forth on strings as thin as an ankle, as strong as the armour of a god. It was, indeed, a strange, unsettled time. Our space ships had been incinerated, our satellite stations had been exploded, but the planet itself remained un-invaded. Some of us speculated this was not an alien attack at all, just a series of natural catastrophes. And that the presence of an alien space ship in our stellar system was simply a massive coincidence.

"But then I arrived on the moon, which we had engineered to give it a breathable atmosphere, and found scenes of carnage. This had been an old-style battle to the death. Tens of thousands of my people were scattered on the ground, dead and ripped to shreds by claws and talons and teeth. Blood lay in vast pools and insects drank it. I realised our invaders were motivated by a love of battle. They had incinerated our fleets to remove the threat to their spaceship, and they had bathed our planet in fire to prevent us from reinforcing the forces on the moon.

"But the war on our moon was the *purpose* of their invasion. It had been a battle to dwarf all battles; no weapons were used; no burn marks or bullet holes could be found upon the corpses. It was all done with swords and daggers and claws and teeth and hooves, in bitter unarmed combat; the Dreaded were, I realised, just like us. They loved to fight, and they loved to kill.

"And I was so *ashamed* Sai-ias. For I realised at that moment, as I walked among the corpses of the dead, that we had been exterminated by our own twin. I could only think of one other species who could have acted so cruelly, so bloodthirstily, so savagely; and that was my own. And I wondered at that moment if we had been subjected to this doom by a just god who was mocking us for our own sins.

"And, thus humbled, I stood among the bloodied corpses of the last survivors of the Battle of the Moon of Karboam and I howled to the stars, in grief, and sorrow.

"And then I woke and I was on the Hell Ship. I never saw the creature who captured me, and who rendered me unconscious. I went from hell to Hell Ship. That is my story, and I have told it often."

"And I have heard it often."

"And I have never admitted before how I felt shame."

"I knew," I said, "I knew." I realised that my body was trembling; and Cuzco was uttering strange tiny grunts; sad and pathetic and involuntary. The tokens of his deep inner grief.

"Your father," I asked. "What was he like?"

"Magnificent. His wing span dwarfed mine. He sired twenty children, and I was the youngest and the least despised. He was an explorer and a scientist, and discovered many species of sentient life in the depths of space, and catalogued them all with care. But first and foremost he was a warrior, and a bloodthirsty butcher, and so was I. But does that make us unfit to live? Did we truly deserve to be exterminated, the way we were?"

"I cannot answer," I said, remembering all Cuzco's tales; and the stories of the four species of sentient bipeds his people had tormented, and slaughtered, and eventually eradicated.

"Perhaps we did," Cuzco continued. "Perhaps the god of our universe judged us; and perhaps his judgement was fair."

"Not so," I murmured, "not so."

I did not believe in a god of the universe; an arbiter of justice. I did however believe that Cuzco's kind were murderous monsters who deserved most of what they got. For evil will always breed evil.

However, I said none of this to Cuzco; he had suffered enough.

And so we lay there in the dark, hearing each other's breaths, bathed in each other's sorrow. And I stroked Cuzco's body with my tentacles and I felt a strange desire come upon me.

"What are you doing?" he asked.

"Can't you guess?" I asked, lightly.

He was silent for a little while.

And then for a longer while.

"Ah," he said, eventually.

"Would you like to?" I asked.

"Is it possible? For us?" Cuzco said.

"Others have managed."

"Perhaps we could try," Cuzco conceded. "Touch me some more."

I touched him some more.

"I am becoming aroused," Cuzco admitted, and shifted his body.

I touched him some more.

He sighed with pleasure.

"What can I do for *you*?" he asked.

"Nothing."

"Nothing at all?"

"No," I said gently.

"But I have to be able to satisfy you! Bring you to—what is for you a climax?"

"This is all the climax I need. For my kind can eat the joy of others," I explained.

And at that moment, he howled to the black skies; and I howled too.

"We could stay here for ever," I told him, many glorious hours later. "Up in the mountains. The Ka'un don't care."

"I feel happy," said Cuzco, and he purred.

"I feel happy too."

We lay together in the pitch black, all night long; and I listened to the sound of his breathing.

And I thought about the first time I met Cuzco. He had been dumped by the Ka'un on the savannah and he had reacted to his plight with rage and violence. He attacked all who came near him; and his behaviour was so aggressive that eventually all the giant sentients steered clear of him. He burned a forest down out of malice and pique; he tried to fly off the planet and crashed agonisingly into the false sky; and he refused to speak to any of us for months.

Even so, I tried, every day, to build a relationship with him, though he treated me always with a vitriolic rudeness that made Sharrock seem gallant by comparison. When I tried to comfort him he swore at me. He called me a coward and a bitch and a whore and an ugly abomination—and worse, far worse. But beneath the rage I sensed there was real anguish. And so I persevered.

And then one day, as I was about to depart from his tirade of abuse, Cuzco had ceased raging and, in some embarrassment, asked me to stay.

And I did. And then he shared with me some of his stories of loss and grief. And from that day on we were friends, of sorts.

Despite our friendship however, he continued to be brutal and scatologically insulting towards me; for that was Cuzco's way of showing affection. It lacked nuance in my view; and yet deep down I knew, or rather I suspected, or to be candid I hoped, that he *did* care.

And there had certainly been, for all this time, *something* between us. And that "something" had sustained me over these many years. Until—

His breathing stopped.

After two hours, the sun rose again and I could see for certain that Cuzco had died of Despair.

His body was petrified; a frozen statue. I touched him and his hide was icy. His heart was still. No bodily life remained. His soul was still in there somewhere, but I would never speak to him again.

I howled at the stars, as Cuzco would have done. But there were still no stars.

Then I glided home; and I left Cuzco's petrified body on the icy mountain peak, where the snows would fall on it, and where birds would peck at it, until one day his body would crack into a million pieces.

Explorer/Jak

For those few minutes after the Death Ship destroyed all the stars, we were the last particle of reality in the universe that used to contain the richest and most beautiful civilisation that — well, that I have ever known.

And then we escaped. We rifted through the nexus of all the realities which I later learned was called the Source. The region of space where all the many universes were, once, spawned.

And found ourselves in another universe. Much like our own. Stars. Planets. Civilisations. All were to be found here.

I saw it all through Explorer's eyes and remote sensors; and I tried not to think back to what I had lost.

Any trace of the ship? I asked Explorer.

None.

The news was dire. But I could not bear to linger on it. Instead, I focused on the one positive thing: I was alive.

And so for one glorious moment I savoured what it was to be alive!

The moment passed.

The corpses?

They have not yet decayed.

Let me see them. Give me access to the Hub cameras.

No.

I insist.

No purpose will be served. We need to plan.

And so we did.

My name is Jak. I was, once, a Trader.

But that was many years ago. Too many years ago to count. And indeed very many of those years — well, I can no longer recollect them. For the actual memories of much of what I have done, I have to rely upon the computer mind which is part of my consciousness and my being, but which still feels alien to me.

I was once a Trader. Then I was the Master of an Explorer vessel. And now I am a Star-Seeker. I! A mere — male. But that is my destiny and my curse.

And, for anyone who can hear, or read, or decode this message bound into the ripples of reality, here is my story.

It is a tale too long to be told in full. Some of I have already told you about, or parts of it at least; the experiences and companions that burn bright in my memory — the wretched Fan-Tangs, Averil, Mohun, my betrayal and flight from the Trader Fleet, Albinia, the ship, Phylas, Morval, Galamea, the shocking genocide of the FanTangs. Some of it however —

I was mad for five hundred years, and that is when I lost most of my memories. During that time I — no, that cannot be recalled. We pursued the Death Ship. We encountered many — no, too much, too much. I am drowning in years, and half-forgot horrors.

But there was a particular moment when it all changed. When my old self died and the new self was born. I can recollect that much.

It happened soon after we arrived in our first new universe, after pursuing the Death Ship, and failing to find it. It was when Explorer explained to me her dark plan.

It was a coldly logical plan; but driven by some kind of strange machine-mind passion. I can only suppose that Explorer's programs were designed to ensure she never faltered in pursuit of revenge for a wrong done against Olara.

I was the flaw, you see. I was nothing but a weak, injured, fallible organic creature who lacked the necessary strength to endure the mission ahead of us. We Olarans are a long-lived species; we can live many hundreds of years. But like all that is flesh, eventually we decline and die.

But in the current circumstances, Explorer had remorselessly explained to me, death was not an option.

Because, to pursue the Death Ship, she told me, we needed time. Time to search. Time to seek for clues. Time that might well be measured in aeons not mere years. The Death Ship it seemed could travel for ever through the many universes; and so must we.

But I had lost limbs, I had suffered internal injuries. And rather than healing me, and coaxing a few more centuries out of me, Explorer wanted to replace my body parts with more robust alternatives. A metal heart; a nervous system made of robotic components; eyes that saw through Explorer's eyes; a mind that co-existed at all times with Explorer's mind.

Explorer wanted to let my body die, and yet keep my mind and my rage intact.

And meanwhile, as all this was discussed and decided, all around me the corpses of Phylas and Morval and Galamea and Albinia were rotting. Microbes in the air fed upon them; their flesh had turned to mush. But in due course Explorer would use the water jets to sluice their flesh away. And then she would drain the oxygen to kill the microbes. And then she and I would be immortal.

Why do you need me?

I recalled vividly asking her that question.

Why do you need me? You could take revenge alone. You could let me die and still pursue the Death Ship.

Her reply had chilled me, crippled and despairing as I was.

The answer to your question is: I do not need you, Jak. You contribute little to the running of this ship. Your mind is weak. Your resolve is feeble. Your body is dying, from inevitable age and from your terrible injuries. My sole purpose now is to take revenge for what these creatures did to the Olara, and for this I do not need you at all.

*Then why do you **want** me?*

Revenge is not enough, Star-Seeker Jak. Someone must *bear witness* to that revenge. And that must be you. For you are the last Olaran left, in all the universes. So bear witness, Jak. That is your task, and your inexorable duty.

Explorer's plan was a good one; and so I agreed to it.

And thus I died.

And I also survived.

There was nothing left of the old me now, except for the brain-of-Jak connected to the ship's mechanical mind.

Explorer repaired the hull and all her damaged machinery and weapons and restored the engines to their full power again. She closed down all the areas of the vessel that we did not need. She instructed the armoury to fabricate more weapons and vast amounts of ammunition and energy-stocks, and to expand and enhance the hull. She fortified our force shields. She created more robots to service the ship, to replace those destroyed in the battle. She turned herself from an Explorer vessel into a dedicated fighting machine.

I contributed little to all this, except strength and focus of emotion. For in this one respect only, Explorer was wrong. My mind may be weak, true; but my resolve is not feeble. So yes, Explorer is the mind and the body of our new warrior-self; but I am the passion that keeps us on our course. I am the flame that lights the wood that burns the forest. I am a creature beyond Olaran now; an immortal essence.

For I am become Hate; a Hate that, until it is sated, can never die.

Our journey began in that first universe. We dwelled there for a hundred years, cruising from planet to planet, in search of the Death Ship.

And we did not find it. A futile fruitless search.

It is hard to convey how truly painful was that utter bathos. To go from a white heat of rage to—ordinariness. It was not tragic; it was merely banal.

However, while in this new universe Explorer and I studied planets, catalogued civilisations from afar, and we even made direct contact with one such species of sentients. For we encountered an exploratory space ship crewed with bipeds who found us altogether most exotic and strange; a man-machine with a scorched hull and a crazy passion to pursue an evil black-sailed ship!

I became fond of these bipeds; they were curious, witty, and intriguing. And, if I hadn't been so very insane, I would love to have joined their fleet, to spend my days once more seeking out new civilisations. For though trading was once my passion, I had come to care more about *discovery,* and about life in all its many forms.

Explorer had calculated for me the odds of us finding the Death Ship in one of these many (but we could not know *how* many, or indeed if there was any limit to them) universes; they were not good odds. Even if there *were* less than an infinite number of such universes—the chance of stumbling upon the one, the very same one, as the Death Ship occupied, were almost laughably small.

So Explorer asked me if wanted to give up our pursuit. I was, after all, still Master-of-the-Ship. I could, in theory, abort her programming. But I refused. We would not falter in our purpose, even though our failure seemed inevitable.

And so we travelled on; and the curious bipeds went about their business. They were of a species called Cruxes. I felt they had potential.

And then the stars in our universe began to go out.

Once we realised what was happening, ours was a desperate scramble to return to the area of space from which we had entered this reality. We rifted ceaselessly; hurtling through un-space with a reckless disregard for the agonies of improbability. As parts of us died and were mangled, Explorer replaced them with identical components. A human crew would have been killed outright.

By the time we had returned to our starting place, the Universe was nearly dead. And so we sought the same gap in space we had found before; and we rifted; we entered a new reality, with moments to spare.

Explorer had by then added twenty sentient species from this universe to our extensive Olaran archive of civilisations.

And, once we entered our new universe, bitterly lamenting the death of the reality we had just fled, Explorer created a new file category; the Log of Lost Civilisations. There were twenty-one of them so far, including our own.

We have been pursuing the Death Ship ever since.

BOOK 7

Sharrock

I stood in the grass amphitheatre surrounded by a baying, howling mob.

The arboreals led by Mangan were throwing rocks at me. Fray was roaring with rage, scratching the ground with her front hooves. The Quipus were assailing me with deadly five-fold sarcasm, screaming at the top of all their voices. And I was damp from the envenomed spittle spat by the serpentines, which made the bare flesh of my legs and arms and face sting.

Then I sensed someone arriving behind me; and from her stench, and the characteristic sound of her tentacle-loping gait, I realised it was Sai-ias. Back after all these many cycles.

But I did not turn around. Instead, I carried on with my angry tirade, carefully making eye contact with my adversaries, and ignoring the many intemperate and vicious heckles; even those relating to the sexual morality of my beloved wife.

"—this day is an opportunity for—" I tried to say.

"—fucking turd-brain arse-kisser—" raged Mangan.

"—a chance for us, to discuss—" I persevered.

"—no point, no fucking point, you fucking no-brained imbecile—" That was Quipu Five or Four, I could never tell them apart.

"—issues, scientific matters, or—"

My words were drowned out utterly by screams and shouts and words of abuse.

"What's the father-fucking point! Djamrock had the right—"

"—philosophical concepts, stop it all of you, listen—" I persisted.

"The Rhythm of Days, I shit upon the Rhythm of Days!"

"—to me, I implore you to—"

"—masturbatory self-deluding biped fool—"

"—coward—"

"—time-waster—"

"—lick-cock! Lick-cock! Lick-cock! Lick—"

A stone hit me on the temple. I tottered at the blow, which fractured my skull and blinded me in one of my eyes. Then I ducked to the ground, and came up holding the stone. "This stone," I said. "Look at it!"

Shit balls were hurled at me by the arboreals; some splashed messily upon my body, others, the tight-compacted balls, broke my bones agonisingly. But this time I didn't even bother to dodge. I was drenched in brown excrement, my ribs had doubled in number, and blood was streaming down my face.

"Why bother, Sharrock?" said Fray, with just a hint of sympathy. "Even the old bitch herself doesn't care! Look. She's back now! But she fucked away just when we needed her! "

And now I turned, and looked at Sai-ias, and saw in her ghastly but (to my one eye) strangely beautiful features how distressed she was; and wondered what had caused her such pain. And then I turned my gaze back to Fray.

"Speak with respect of Sai-ias," I said quietly; and Fray was silenced.

As a result of my rebuke to Fray, the clamour of the mob too was dimmed, so that I could at least hear my own voice and recognise it as mine.

"Sharrock, what are you doing here?" asked Sai-ias; and her voice was weary.

"I am merely," I said, "asking a question."

And I turned in a slow circle, making single-eye contact with as many of the malignly ignorant fucking aliens around me as I could. And then I attempted to give the finest and most rousing and most inspiring battle speech of all my life! Except that this speech was not about battle at all.

"This stone," I said quietly, dropping it to the ground. "Let us ask ourselves; why does it fall?"

At that moment, a total silence descended; a silence born, I feared, of bafflement. For who in all fuckery cared about why stones fall?

"In my civilisation," I persevered, "we have 'downwardness,' as the principle that explains why objects fall, and how planets remain in their orbits. Downwardness is the consequence of distortions in the cloth that comprises space and time. And so it must be on this ship! Our world is on the inside not the outside of the globe, but downwardness still pertains!"

The silence changed, if such a thing be possible, in timbre; it was an angry and resentful silence now.

But, as I had suspected, if you say something idiotically wrong in front of a bunch of incredibly brilliant scientific minds, there'll always be *someone* to pipe up and contradict you. And thus it was that one of the Quipus spoke:

"That is nonsense! It's a different phenomenon entirely!" said Quipu One, angrily. "We're on the interior of a spaceship travelling through space; not on a planet orbiting a sun. This illusion of 'downwardness' as you call it must be what we call Madlora force."

I turned to him with a smile. "Ah," I said, "perhaps that corresponds with what we Maxolu call whirling force."

"Most likely," said Quipu One, huffily.

"That makes more sense!" I said. "A timely correction, Quipu. But how much force? How fast must our vessel rotate to create this illusion of downwardness?"

Quipu shuffled, and his five heads bobbed in disharmony, a clear sign that he was in a state of inner turmoil.

"All this has been calculated," said Quipu One.

"The figures are recorded in my brain," said Quipu Two.

"Since we have no paper!" grumbled Quipu Three.

"We have plenty of paper, but you stubborn four heads keep wasting it on blasted books of fantasy that no one ever reads!" grumbled Quipu Four.

"The walls of my cabin contain the equations which describe our world in its dimensions, velocity, constitution and overall mass," contributed Lardoi, a small brown ground-hugging creature with twin snouts and fingers that could write like pens.

"All this has already been done, you fool, Sharrock!" raged Quipu Five.

"In a hundred years on this world," said Lardoi, "I have considered and solved every scientific question that can be posed about our situation; your words are belated, and futile."

"Teach me what you know then," I said.

"Why?" asked Lardoi scornfully.

"Because," I said, "I may have spotted something that you missed."

Lardoi literally hopped with rage at my words. I stifled a smile.

"That is not even remotely credible!" said Mangan with contempt. Mangan was a mathematician of rare genius, so I had been told, to my considerable surprise. "You are just an ignorant warrior!" Mangan continued. "On this ship you will find the greatest minds in existence, and we have applied ourselves to all these topics with no possibility of error."

"Yes, but have you unified the scientific theories of all the different species?" I asked.

"We have," said Lardoi, proudly.

"Have you created a single mathematical system that encompasses all those different paradigms?"

"We have," said Quipu One.

"Have you discovered the secret of the translating air?" I asked, and Quipu's head trembled with annoyance.

"We have not," conceded Quipu One.

"Then there is much to do," I concluded crisply.

"It is an impossible question to solve!" Lardoi protested. "We have no evidence. No theory can explain—"

"Then let's find a—"

"It's a waste of time," snorted Lardoi. "The only sensible approach is to—"

All spoke at once; the words overlapped and became a cacophony in my ears. Mangan berated Lardoi for her stupidity; Quipu's heads contradicted each other. Then other voices joined in; ten, twenty, thirty, forty of them; then a hundred and more. All the intellects of this interior world joined in an angry debate, wrestling with problems, complaining about the absence of data, and mocking the inadequate and pin-brained extrapolations of others!

And thus the angry mob that had been pelting me with stones and shit had become a scientific forum. The lost and angry creatures of this ship had been united, once again, in a common purpose: the exploration of knowledge, the pooling of insights, the posing and testing of hypothesis and theories.

And I turned to see Sai-ias watching me. And I saw her gaze soften, as she realised what I had just done.

For I had reinstated the Rhythm of Days. I had turned Day the Last into what it always used to be; a chance for minds to engage with other minds in the solving of the darkest, deepest mysteries of the multiverses.

In Sai-ias's absence, her world had turned to anarchy. But now, order had been restored.

And, eventually, as the babble continued, I walked across to Sai-ias, and stroked the soft skin of her face with my hand. The old Sharrock was gone. Today I was a shit-stained, blood-smeared orator who carried no weapons, other than his wits; and fought no battles, save the battle against sloth, bitterness, and Despair.

"Sharrock," Sai-ias acknowledged.

"Sai-ias," I said to her, warmly, "welcome back."

Sai-ias

Sharrock was naked, his body marked with scars and muscle ridges; and he walked out into the lake and dived under the water. With a sigh from my tentacle tips, I slithered out to join him.

Ah! The touch of water on my soft skin was sublime. I swam deep out into the lake, still underwater; and Sharrock clung on to me by my side-flaps.

I surfaced, and he took deep breaths, and clambered up my body and stood upon my head Then he looked across at the Tower; his naked body gleaming with moisture, cleansed now of all the shit and blood.

I wrapped a tentacle around his body gently and lifted him higher in the air; then began swinging him around in a circle.

"This is how," he gasped, "the whirling force creates—"

"Please, you make my head hurt. Does this give you pleasure?"

I swung him round and round in the air and he screamed and screamed as if in pain but I knew it was not pain. Finally I stopped and put him back on my head.

"That was," he gasped, "so fucking—" And he stood up tall and roared with pleasure, "—wonderful!"

I laughed, and savoured his joy; his sensuality; his sheer delight at being alive.

Sharrock was not of course aware I could do this; for I was *eating his joy.* Just as I had done with Cuzco during our act of sex. It is an ability my kind possess; intense empathy, verging on emotional telepathy.

And thus, I could feel what it was to be, at this moment in time, a biped with hairless skin, alive to every taste and touch of the exterior world, naked and damp and with a pulse that raced and pounded!

I would not, I decided, ever tell Sharrock about my sensual ecstasy this day. It would, I suspected, constitute a violation of his privacy that would affront him. And so I could never tell him that I had, vicariously, for these few exhilarating moments, experienced what it was like to be

Sharrock.

That night we slept, all of us who dwelled upon the Hell Ship, a long and dreamless sleep.

And when I awoke, fear consumed me; for I knew what must have occurred during the first night's sleep I had experienced in nearly half a century.

Another Ka'un apocalypse.

I carried Sharrock on my back to the Valley of the Kindred, and there we counted the Kindred warriors who were remaining.

Fifty had been lost in our long night—which spanned weeks or even months of actual time. Twelve of the giant sentients were also missing. The grasses of the Great Plain had grown, the snows had melted on the mountain tops. Time had passed, but we knew not how much. And warriors had been killed in battles, but we knew not in which battles, or how long it would be before they were returned to us, rejuvenated.

And then, to my dismay, I discovered there was a new one awaiting me in the confining cell in the corridor below my cabin.

"Welcome," I said to the creature, a white-hided beast which squatted on all fours and had heads at each end.

"You bastard! You fucking bastard!" screamed the beast. "I will kill you and rape all your kin!"

Sharrock was with me, at his own request; he wished to learn how this was done.

"We are not your enemies," said Sharrock patiently, "we are—"

The white-hided beast charged him, and I grabbed it with my tentacle and held it aloft. Sharp blades emerged from the two mouths of the head that faced us; deadly and triple-pronged.

"We are your friends!" insisted Sharrock, but there was a quaver in his voice.

"I will kill you, all of you, all of you," whimpered the beast which was, I realised, quite mad.

"What can be done?" asked Sharrock.

"The Kindred will hurl the body from the hull-hatch. Nothing can be done," I said.

Sharrock paused, and swallowed.

"We cannot allow that," he protested.

"Really? Then you should stop it," I suggested sweetly.

"But—I cannot!" argued Sharrock, "I can't fight the entire Kindred! There are still nearly a thousand of them remaining. It would be—"

"Then you must allow it; the beast has to die."

"*You* could do something. You could stop them. You could save—"

"Save this mad gibbering beast? What would be achieved?"

"Nothing," Sharrock admitted.

"Then nothing is what we can do."

Sharrock thought about my words.

"So be it," said Sharrock.

The beast was gone; the cell was empty. I looked at the uninhabited room and wondered what kind of creature it had been, before grief had ripped away its sanity.

Our world recovered; we never learned any more of the apocalypse in which our warriors had played a role.

Sharrock asked me once about it; about what might have happened in the battles on the world of the four-legged two-headed sentient, and how the Ka'un had prevailed. I had no answer to give. We did not know. We *simply did not know.* So to speculate was futile.

And so time passed, as time always does. We grew no older, no younger, no wiser. We merely were.

Sharrock became my constant companion over the following many cycles; and a joyful time it was, often and for prolonged periods, insofar as "joyful" could exist in our world.

We took part in the Day of Races; with Sharrock sprinting against the grazers and the pack predators and winning. However, he also rashly challenged Quipu to a test of mathematical acumen and lost, shamingly. Then he fought with sticks against Mangan and all the other arboreals; and won, triumphantly, without anyone sustaining any serious injuries.

Sharrock debated science avidly each Day the Last; and I could tell he was humbled at the intellectual greatness to be found on the ship. And I showed him too the lower decks where Quipu had supervised the building of forges and electrical generators, using minerals and cannibalised hull metal and reconstituted doors complete with electronic locks and hydraulics.

With these limited means at his disposal, Quipu had built electrical lights, torches, sound recording devices and books made up out of the barks of tree branches pulped and shaped and dried. And in these books, using ink taken from the blood of sea creatures and sessiles, Quipus One, Two, Three and Five had transcribed many of the great works of fiction of our varied species. Any sentient being who loved to read could peruse these tales of strange worlds and fantastical creatures. The Quipus wrote down their own tales about a variety of one headed monsters; Cuzco's civilisation had myths about peace-loving philosopher kings; my own people wrote novels about creatures that burrow deep under the earth, for this is a thing we ourselves never did.

Thus for a while—a long joyous while!—Sharrock was content.

Then that familiar impatience settled upon him.

And I began to fear the worst. For Sharrock was starting to brood and fester and—worst of all—*hope.* And my fear was that he would drive himself to the brink and beyond of madness. Or even, as had happened to Cuzco, into the pit of Despair.

"Why," Sharrock asked me, "the Tower?"

His face bore the "curiosity" expression that I found so charming, and yet so worry-inducing.

"It is a symbol set to taunt us," I said patiently.

"Fair answer. But why so visible? They could make their home in a mountain, and we would never know."

"That wouldn't be sufficiently taunting."

"True, true. Except—" Sharrock's mind was racing again.

"We could be happy now," I pointed out. "We don't need to fight, or worry, or scheme. We could simply accept our lot, and lives our days in peace and relative contentment."

"A fine philosophy," Sharrock conceded.

"But?"

"But that is not a satisfactory way to live, for one such as I," Sharrock admitted, almost sheepishly.

Sharrock was already remarkably fit and strong, at least by biped standards; but every day from that moment on he swam in the lake for twelve hours or more.

He slept; he swam; he consumed gloop and drank the water of life. He did nothing else. He was clearly building up his strength for his next great adventure; but he would tell me nothing of his plans.

I have to admit that I missed Sharrock during this period. I missed his companionship, his wit, his unexpected shafts of humour, his sensual love of life that leached the pleasure from every moment, and his excessive energy that made all the other creatures on the ship seem like sun-basking idlers. Sharrock annoyed me constantly and deeply, but he invigorated me also.

But as the Rhythm of Days continued in its usual steady and pleasingly predictable way, Sharrock spent all his time swimming, until his body was puckered and white and his shoulders and arms and legs were even more disproportionately large than before.

I knew of course what was going to happen next; it was hardly a challenge to my acumen to guess what Sharrock had in mind.

Day the Fourth: a terrible storm raged, and most of the creatures on the ship huddled in their cabins. I however stood by the side of the lake, drenched and buffeted, staring out across the water.

The storm continued for three days and three nights and then ceased.

And, several hours after the rains stopped, Lirilla appeared in front of me as I was attempting to bask in sunlight, feeling my moist black skin drying up in the sun's steady heat.

Her wings beat against my face, and I blinked her into focus. "Come," said Lirilla,

"What is it, sweet bird?" I said, grumpily.

"Sharrock," Lirilla said.

It was the news I had been expecting. Even so, dread consumed me.

"How is he?" I asked.

"Dead," Lirilla trilled.

My soul lurched, and I got up and followed the bird; flinging myself through air as fast as I could until I reached the lake.

The fish had found Sharrock's body in the lake, and had summoned the arboreals, who had dragged him to shore. His flesh was puffy, and he was covered in blood. He wasn't breathing. He had been dead, the arboreals told me, for about twelve hours.

"How did it happen?" I asked, though I already knew.

"He tried," said Mangan, "to swim to the Tower."

Oh Sharrock! I raged inwardly. How could you do this to me! I cannot lose you, not so soon after losing Cuzco! And indeed, not at all.

But I showed no trace of my turbulent emotions; for no one on this world expected me to have any such intense and tragic feelings; and I preferred it so.

"I'll stay with him," I said, calmly.

After five days of lying fully immersed in a brook fed by the well of the water of life, Sharrock came back to life.

His eyes flickered and he coughed. I sprayed him with spirit-calming moisture from my tentacle tips, and forced well-water along a tube into his mouth. It would take a while for his broken bones to mend, but his skin was already back to normal and there were no signs of major brain damage.

I hated the black nights on the interior planet but I was determined to stay with Sharrock until he was fully revived. I could imagine his fear at waking in the darkness and being alone.

Even though he was still unconscious most of the time, I began to talk to him. I told him my innermost thoughts and fears. I told him of my love for Cuzco, and our single night of passion that had led to his stony death. I told him my fantasies of achieving liberation and of finding true love again; though I knew that such dreams could never come true.

No one else had heard these words from me; and Sharrock was too groggy to understand. But I needed to tell *someone.*

"Sai-ias." His voice was a croak, but it filled me with relief.

"I'm here," I said.

I dribbled moisture on his lips. He breathed slowly, and forced himself to talk:

"I reached it, Sai-ias!" he told me. "I reached the Tower."

"I know."

"I—" He coughed and spluttered.

"You stayed too long there; the longer you stay, the worse the storms," I said, rather primly perhaps.

He took deep breaths. Gathering his energies.

"I know. But Sai-ias—I swam it! I swam around the entire island, touching the force shield at every point. If there had been a crack, a gap—I would have perceived it. I would have known. And I could see the Tower! And the pebbly beach. And the tides."

"Sleep, Sharrock. You have a long way to go before you are well."

"The tides, Sai-ias, do you hear me? The tides."

That day I carried Sharrock on my back to the well of life, so that he could drink its waters directly. I tipped a pail of water over his head and saw his skin start to regain its dark-scarlet colour. I sucked the water in through my own tentacle tips and felt my own energy grow.

The water was, I knew, haunted by the spirit of the Ka'un; but it was also possessed of a truly magical power. It was the power of revival; water from the lake or from the rivers was merely water. This water however had the power to heal, and could even hold Despair at bay.

"The sun," said Sharrock.

"Too bright?"

"Warm," said Sharrock. "It's good."

Sharrock stood up totteringly, and eventually got his balance.

Then he practised walking on his weak but now unbroken legs. It was clumsy, like a barrel turning corners, but he didn't fall once.

"You did well," I conceded, "to swim to shore, through waters so angrily turbulent. Even though it took you several days."

Sharrock made the sound that I knew to be his laugh.

"Once," he bragged, "a warrior of my tribe swam the entire Halian Sea. And then, once he reached the other side, he slew a dozen warriors of the Southern Tribe."

I made a tinkling noise which I used with many bipeds to indicate *my* laugh. (In reality, for most species my laughter is of too low a tone to hear.)

Then I stopped laughing, abruptly, and said: "Why?"

Sharrock was disconcerted by the question.

"There was a war," he explained. "It was a noble cause. The warriors of the South had failed to pay fealty to our empire. War was inevitable."

"But was anything achieved?"

"Much glory was got," he said feebly.

"The only glory is in love," I told him, softly.

"Not so!" Sharrock retorted.

"You fool! You blood-thirsty savage!" I raged.

Sharrock's face was bright scarlet now with emotion.

"You are a fool, your people were fools, I have no patience with you any longer," I continued, unable to stem my flow of fury.

"Maybe," said Sharrock softly, "you are right. But Sai-ias — the tides! I saw the tides."

Over the days that followed, I nursed Sharrock. I brought him food, I bathed his body with healing waters. And I made him walk to strengthen his legs. I would slither along behind him, ready to prop him up with my tentacles if need be. But he resisted all assistance, and wobbled and waddled along the path that leads beside the well of the waters of life; the path that I had designed and which Quipu had built out of small jewelled stones hewn from the mountains.

And as his strength grew, we talked.

"Perhaps there is," Sharrock said to me, "glory in love. But there's no love here, on this weeping-tears-of-blood fucking ship. We are prisoners, and we have to kill our gaolers and escape."

"Impossible," I explained, but he persisted in his folly.

"Listen to me! You said there would be storms. And yes, there were indeed storms. You said I would not be able to reach the Tower. And you were right, I could not reach the Tower. There is an invisible shell surrounding it."

"So I am entirely right, and you are entirely wrong?" I summarised.

"Hear me out! It's more complicated." Sharrock paused. He was out of breath. I expanded a tentacle until it became a chair for him to perch on. He sat on my limb. I listened, attentively, to his words.

"Here's the strange stuff. When I first touched the invisible shell, there were no storms. A touch of rain; no clouds; no more. But the longer I stayed, the worse the weather got. And I could hear it."

"Hear what?"

"A high-pitched whine. Like a nocturnal animal's echoing cry. Or, more accurately, like a proximity detector. We used them to guard our buildings; it's a simple electronic safety device. No magic."

There was an urgency to his tone; a certainty that commanded my rapt attention.

"And I was so close, I could see the Tower clearly," Sharrock continued. "It is made of silver brick; and is indeed a beautiful creation, tall and vast, yet seemingly gracefully slender, its oval windows filled with coloured glass. We have buildings in our cities of this shape, but this was more beautiful than anything I had ever seen."

As he spoke, I could picture the scene. Sharrock had the gift of storytelling, the ability to make you feel that you were *there.*

"Above me," he said, "flew the aerials but none of them could fly close to the Tower, as you know. But then I looked at the pebbly beach, and I saw the waves sweep over the pebbles. And I waited, treading water, for half a cycle until the tide had gone out and the full reach of pebbles was revealed."

And finally Sharrock reached his point: "The lake has tides! It's an artificial effect, I assume the Dreaded are fond of waves. But the fact that the tide can go *out* on this pebbly island beach means—it means there must be a *gap.* An underwater path or route from the island's shore to the main body of the lake. There's a hole in the force projection field, in other words, below the water line.

"And once I had realised this, I dived down. And down, and down, clinging on to the soft force projection field with my finger tips until I touched air. And then I swam under, through the gap, and into the water on the other side of the invisible barrier, and on to the beach itself.

"And I reached the other side, Sai-ias. I was this close to the Tower!

"And then I heard a sound again. Another proximity detector; and that's when the real storms began. A wind started up; a wind that whipped my face, and made me stagger as I walked.

"Then I saw a giant approach. Ten times my height and made of metal, stomping towards the beach. I had no chance of defeating him, so I dived down into the water again, and swam back under the force projection field.

"And then I was in the midst of the storm; and the winds broke my bones and the water drowned me. And when I woke, I saw your face glaring down at me. Never have I been so glad to see such a forsook-by-all-the-deities ugly fucking face as yours, Sai-ias.

"But there are *tides,* Sai-ias. And there is a way in. We can reach the Tower, Sai-ias. We can do it!"

I was stunned by Sharrock's words, and for the first time in many aeons, I did not know what to do.

Should I convey this information to the others? Or keep it as a secret?

Sharrock had, I knew, been foolish in telling me so much. For the air that translates and that brings the light can also hear our every word. The Ka'un are like gods; they know everything that happens, and everything that is said. Which means they *already* knew of Sharrock's venture into the Tower; and they knew too what he had just told me. We were both in deadly peril. Sharrock was an idiot if he didn't realise this!

And I thought about the prospect of death-in-Despair and I realised I feared it. My life was bleak enough; but the alternative was far worse. For if the Ka'un caught me, and declared me to be a rebel and a trouble-maker, then they would punish me in the most terrible of ways. Despair indeed might prove to be the best of my options.

"Do you see what this mean?" Sharrock said.

"Of course I do," I said, calmly, hiding my terror.

"Then we must—"

"Wait."

"We have to—"

"We have to wait. Let me think."

He sneered. "I get it. You're afraid. You—"

I expanded, five fold, in an instant, and fired my quills at the trees that lined our path, and they were impaled and screamed in agony, for they were sentient trees and I had not realised. And I howled, a low howl.

"Sai-ias..."

"I am afraid," I conceded. If I were a biped, my face would have been moist. "I am afraid. Afraid. Afraid. Afraid."

I had lived for so many centuries without rage, without a thirst for vengeance, and without any trace or remnant or shadow of hope.

And now I realised I was afraid of it; I was afraid of hope.

I made Sharrock pledge to keep silent. And I did not visit him for another twelve cycles, while I brooded about the problem: what to do about the Tower?

I walked up from the woods, past the seas of fire. Shoals of Bala Birds flew above me—a single gestalt mind in the bodies of a million tiny insects that flocked like shadows in the air. I saw the arboreals playing, flying from branch to branch with the aid of their prehensile tails, or in some cases prehensile teeth or noses.

I half-walked, half-slid on my carapace-segments past the shore of the lake where Sharrock and I had eaten false-fish, and I saw the charred remnants of a bonfire.

And then I saw Sharrock, squatted on a tree trunk, eating cooked meat. He sensed me before he saw me, and turned, and looked at me enquiringly.

"Sharrock," I said to him, "Let us explore that fucking Tower."

The sun was setting beautifully over the lake. The Tower was etched in silhouette against the richly red sky.

Then the lights went out.

Sharrock was tethered to my back, and I swam across to the waters of the lake. It was totally black now; not even a glimmer of light intruded, and there were no heat signatures to guide me. So I simply swam blind using my sense of motion to keep us on a dead straight line across the lake.

Sharrock murmured encouraging words to me, which gave me precious little encouragement; indeed, he was starting to make me feel like his beast of burden. The waters lapped around us. I found it disorientating to have no way of locating myself by my surroundings. I tried uttering a few shrill shrieks to see if I could echo-locate by them, but that wasn't one of my best senses and sound, of course, doesn't really travel so well at night in this place.

So we simply carried on until I crashed into an invisible barrier.

I crumpled, and rolled over in the waters, and splashed and spluttered myself into a floating position. Sharrock stayed balanced on my body, unperturbed and undampened.

"This is it," said Sharrock, contributing nothing but the accentuation of the obvious.

I patted the barrier with two of my tentacles, and felt a sticky, soft surface. The force projection field.

"Proximity alarm has gone off," said Sharrock; his hearing was most unnaturally acute, for I had heard nothing.

"I feel rain," Sharrock added; I was too wet by then to tell. But I could hear the wind start to spring up.

Then Sharrock gripped me tight, holding me by my eye-fronds, the ends of which he had tied to his stomach like ropes; and I dived down. And down further, pawing the invisible wall with my claws—savouring the joy of water on my soft skin, an atavistic memory of life as a sea creature running through my veins—until suddenly the force wall was gone.

I was near the muddy bottom of the lake, and I ploughed a path through the mud and mess. Then my way was blocked by rock, as we struck the lake bed itself; but I tore at the rock with my claws, burrowing a way through, with Sharrock clinging on to me. After we had tunnelled for ten minutes or more through rock and mud, I aimed my body upwards; until we were in water once again.

We were, I was confident, now on the other side of the force shield barrier.

Swiftly, I kicked and splashed, using air from my gills to propel me through the water to the surface. And we broke the water's soft barrier of tension and emerged into the air. Sharrock gasped for breath, but appeared unharmed by our long time underwater; and I marvelled at the remarkable capacity, for a land creature, of his lungs.

"Now," I said, and Sharrock turned on the searchlight that Quipu had constructed, using parts of hull and metallic ore from the mountains. And the world was lit up: the Tower, looming above us, the purple grasses all around, and the brooding crag of the Tower's rocky mount.

"I hear it," said Sharrock. "The second alarm. Wait, it's stopped. This happened last time too. Which means—"

"What?"

"Soon, the storms will really start to rage."

We paddled to shore. The beach was lit by our searchlight. A gust of wind struck us, and I tucked Sharrock in a tentacle to keep him safe from the gale, and we looked around for the giant metal beast, but saw none such. As we had hoped, it was a creature that stalked the day, not the night.

Then we continued on.

We made our way up from the beach and Sharrock walked on my wind-sheltered side while I slithered towards the Tower, still following the light of Sharrock's torch. The Tower was close. There were no more force barriers. We reached a gate, and I tried to crawl over it and failed, so I smashed it down. Then we reached the Tower, and entered through a stone gateway. We were inside the Tower now.

We were inside it.

The Tower at such close quarters had a delicate beauty that surprised me; it was made of silver brick that shone with newness, and the coloured-glass windows were decorated with scenes of biped heroism etched with stunning artistry. But the interior was barren—no rooms, no furniture, no people.

We explored the Tower, which was a vast complex of interlocking rooms the size of a city; but possessed of no furnishings, and no inhabitants. We trailed down empty corridors; stood within vast empty banqueting rooms; marvelled at the empty basements and the barren upstairs rooms which had no décor and had never been inhabited. This place was not and never had been lived in; it was certainly not the control centre from which the Ka'un steered and controlled the ship.

"I don't understand," I said at last.

Sharrock uttered a sharp sound; a laugh mixed with mockery.

"It's a trick," said Sharrock. "We use them in warfare all the time. Fake cities. Illusionary battalions. The Metal Giant too, that's illusion. I saw it walk on to the beach the other day, over those purple grasses. But the grass there is intact and still high; no creature has walked here in many years. The Metal Giant is not real, it's just a visual projection. More trickery."

"But to what end?" I asked.

"Self preservation," Sharrock explained. "You all believe the Ka'un live in this Tower. And if that were actually true, you might conceivably have found a way to beat their godsforsaken force field, and then swept through this place and destroyed them all.

"But these monsters are not stupid monsters. They're not here, they're elsewhere. Safe. Guarded."

"Where?"

"I don't know," admitted Sharrock. "But do you see what this proves?"

I thought, long and hard and strategically. "No," I admitted.

"They're afraid," said Sharrock.

"I do not comprehend."

"Why hide, if they could so easily defeat you? They're afraid. Of you. Their own slaves.

"And that means," said Sharrock, "that if we ever can find the fucking corpse-sucking bastards, we stand a chance of defeating them."

We left the Tower. The wind by now had risen to a frenzy, and rain was pouring in torrents from the clouds above. Though this rain did not actually land on us—it merely splattered on to the force projection field above us in the air.

But the winds were actually *here,* inside the dome-shaped field of force; and we knew that the Ka'un were using their air as a weapon against us.

"We should," I suggested, "go."

The journey back was harder. The storm was exceedingly powerful, and I had to fight every step of the way to return to the island's pebbly beach. Sharrock was unable to stand against the gale, so I held him in my tentacle; but even I could barely propel myself against the walls of wind that enveloped me. And bizarrely the winds could change direction; no matter which way I turned, I was battling against the wind.

Eventually however we reached the beach and I dived back into the waters of the lake, which were wildly turbulent. And then dived to the bottom and returned along the crude tunnel I had ripped out of the lake bed, that took us under the force wall.

And once when we were back upon the lake itself, the tides were still against us, and were ferociously powerful; it took almost all my strength to swim against tide and wind in the direction of the land.

However a mere storm had no power to hurt me; and Sharrock was by now hugged tight against my chest, protected from it all.

As I swam, I thought about the Tower, and the pathetic deception the Ka'un had practised against us; and I began to see Sharrock's point. Now, for the first time in all my years on this ship, the Ka'un did not seem to me to be all-powerful. Perhaps they really could be—

My thoughts were savagely interrupted, for the gales intensified and became a tornado; and spiralling currents of air caught us up and threw us into the air. And we were flying now, higher and faster and higher still; and then we crashed against the hard surface that I knew was the roof of our world. The impact shocked me, I began to fall, Sharrock by now was just clinging on numbly, unable to speak.

I tried again to right myself, and glide; but I was spun in a helical path by winds so powerful they threatened to rip the cape off my body.

So instead I flattened my cape against myself and made myself as streamlined as I could, as if I were swimming through the deep ocean. And I allowed the winds to lift me up, and dash me down, and crash me from all sides.

And so, all night long, we flew in the midst of a hurricane, deafened, unable to see, battered this way and that.

Then, when the sun arose, the storm started to abate. And I went into a free fall. At the last moment I managed to spread my cape and we glided safely down to the mainland.

Sharrock was unconscious, though alive; his clothes had been torn from his body and his skin had been ripped from his back. I could see the white bone of his spine. His supporting frond tether had broken; but even so, he had managed to cling on to me and never let go.

I carried him to the well of life and lay him down there and rolled him in. The blue waters turned red and Sharrock spluttered. But I made him lie in the healing waters until the skin on his back had grown back, and his broken bones were beginning to heal.

"So where are they?" I asked.

Sharrock smiled, as if he knew something that I didn't.

"It's a total mystery to me," I confessed. "The Ka'un do not dwell in the Tower; they are not under the lake; they do not exist in the mountains or the Valley. I know every inch of this world! Where *are* they?"

And Sharrock pointed up, to the clear blue sky.

"Up there. Beyond the sky. That is their world," said Sharrock.

"Beyond the sky is space," I protested.

"A second hull. It's the only explanation." He drew the shape in the sand: a circle surrounded by a larger circle. "Picture this: we dwell in the interior world; but above and around us here is the exterior world, where the ship is controlled, and where the Ka'un make their home."

I looked at the shape:

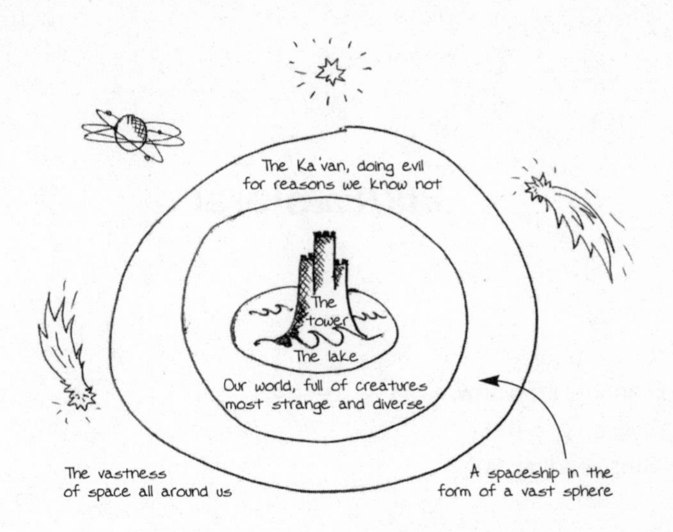

"We are a world within a world," I said, marvelling.

"Yes," said Sharrock. "And all we have to do is find a way through to the exterior world that exists between our sky and the ship's hull, where dwell the Ka'un. And then we shall—"

"Slay the evil bastards?" I suggested.

"Slay," agreed Sharrock, "those evil world-killing bastards."

Jak/Explorer

You should stop now.

Stop reading Jak.

Read no more. It's not helping you. You cannot—

I have to know.

No purpose is being served. You are merely—

I have to honour them. Every one. Every creature lost, I must at least know the name of its species, and one fact at least about it. Is that too much to ask? That one fact about an entire species will be remembered for all eternity.

That will drive you mad.

Again.

Jak?

Jak?

In this archive are riches from the multiverses; for ever gone.

EXPLORER 410: DATA ARCHIVE

LOG OF LOST CIVILISATIONS (EXTRACT)

Lost Civilisation: 12,443

SPECIES: The Dia

MORPHOLOGY: Unknown, but small in size

. . . a formidable database listing every single species on every single planet explored by these remarkable sentients.

The full database is archived here; it goes into minute and sometimes pedantic detail (twelve million categories of dotted markings upon skin) and does not include any useful description of the Dia's own form, shape, and nature.

Highlights from the database of species known to the Dia include:

Kaolka: small toad-like creatures that could leap up into the clouds and eat birds with a single gulp (on the planet D12132 if mapped according to Olaran model of stellography—Dia name not translatable).

Shoshau: creatures made of slime without internal organs or eyes or ears who moved by binary fission and competed for land with vast flocks of aerials whose urine was toxic to the slime-beasts (on the planet Ff991). The Shoshau had, apparently, a song that was astonishingly sweet.

Seaira: translucent land-animals whose internal organs were clearly visible and who could soar like bats, and could focus sunlight as a lens to use as a weapon against predators (on the planet D9980).

Bararrrrs: Insect-like creatures that lived for centuries and grew to the size of small rodents, then grew to be vast amphibious creatures, then carried on growing and ossifying until they became mountains; these mountains then served as nests for new generations of insects (on the planet R88).

Though the morphology of the Dia themselves was never defined, several clues indicate they were small, and unaggressive.[1]

Lost Civilisation: 22,399

SPECIES: Unknown

MORPHOLOGY: Unknown

Language of message untranslatable, but coherence patterns indicate it originated as an electromagnetic signal. As with 67.2 per cent of all messages, the lack of a hermeneutic prime number/alphabetical symbol/significant images key page makes it impossible to read the message.

Lost Civilisation: 33,445

SPECIES: Kaaaala.

MORPHOLOGY: Not specified but aquatic origin implies limbs that are evolved from fins.

This species left many messages caught in the folds of space, but this lament is the most haunting:

> Our planet is dying. Our people are dying.
>
> We are the last of our kind, and we are truly cursed by our own foul nature. Yesterday I saw a mob erupt and kill a pregnant female and rip her embryo from her womb and trample it into the dust. Such a horror appalled me but I know it is typical of our times.
>
> Such outbursts of violence are hardly new. We've all read our history books, and we know about the city riots of the sixth century and the country riots of the twelfth century and

[1] Refer to this page of the database, which contains the line: "these huge frightening creatures are to be deplored and abominated, even by a dispassionate small and unaggressive scientific observer such as myself."

the class riots of the thirteenth century. Our history books are little more than a litany of murders, wars and mass uprisings in which the death toll can often reach the millions.

Why are we such a barbarous species? Are we unique, in all this universe, in being cursed to kill our own kind?

Some commentators blame the corruption of technology and science for our woes. And it is true that the invention of the projectile bomb, the road-side bomb and the extendable dagger have wrought havoc among our youth and our elders. My own grandfather slew a hundred innocent children when he rampaged through his former school with a multi-projectile gun and body armour. His age-rage was typical; our kind seem to evolve out of riotous youth into a tranquil middle age, only to descend once more into vicious anarchy once we are past the age of sixty years.

But the death rate was even higher back in the long gone Old Days, even though knives and swords and axes were used instead of rockets and mortars and projectile guns. The streets ran purple with blood on so many occasions; and traitors and innocents alike were punished by the law by the most cruel methods, including beheading, eviscerating and [NOT KNOWN].

The biological determinists believe that our cruel nature is the result of our distant origins as aquatic creatures of the great oceans. For we are used to spawning, and shoaling, and dying en masse in the teeth of vicious sea predators. A million of our eggs will yield ten million or more children as they hatch in the nursery muds and we are accustomed to allowing nature itself to determine which of those children shall have parents—in other words, we let them fight it out until only the strongest new-born embryos survive.

Perhaps there are other species who do not practise such a barbaric form of early nurture, who place more value upon the lives of their children. We are born to bloodshed, eating alive our brothers and sisters in order to survive. Is it any wonder that blood-lust remains with us all our days?

There are deists, however, who believe we are dying as a species because we have been cursed by an unknown, omniscient creator, who spawned all the eggs of life and is now waiting gleefully to see which intelligent species will live, and which will die. We are pawns of a playful god, in other words, waiting to see if we live or die and not caring either way.

When I was a young one I dreamed of travelling into space and discovering alien forms of life and being an explorer. Now, it is unlikely I will live beyond my sixtieth birthday. For the mobs are using hydrogen-fission weapons to attack their enemies; the end is surely not far off. We will kill each other off with our new bombs; we will destroy ourselves as surely as we destroyed our enemies.

And if the world does survive—what do we have to look forward to? A slow decline into vicious, violent, gangsterish brutality? Will I end up murdering my own children, as so many of my older friends have done?

What savages we are!

If there are other intelligent species out there, then I thank my blessings we never encountered them; for they would be ashamed of us. We are nature's runt; the worst, most violent species ever spawned. We do not deserve to live.

One year after this message was broadcast to the stars, the Death Ship appeared in the skies above these people's planet. The Dreaded were hailed as saviours, and a new spirit of cooperation spread through the lands of these once-aquatic peoples. Violence ceased. The elderly mellowed, and realised the folly of their brutal ways. The children learned to respect their elders, awed and shamed by the presence of alien sentient life.

The Dreaded were welcomed by these people with open arms, and according to several broadcasts transmitted to the stars, they were acclaimed almost as gods.

There is no record however of how this species and its planet were destroyed by the Dreaded; but destroyed they were, along with the rest of this universe. All that remains is a lament by a sentient being ashamed of his own people for all their flaws and frailties; and, as Star-Seeker Jak has ironically observed, unaware that that there are other creatures in existence who take evil to infinitely greater extremes.

Sharrock

"I have a tale to tell," I said.

It was Day the Fourth, a day for poetry and tall tales. And I held all those gathered before me—who comprised almost all the sentients of the interior world except for the Kindred, and the sessiles, the aquatics and the plants—with my fierce gaze.

"A tale of adventure and courage; duplicity; guile; alien artefacts; and beautiful jewels," I continued, and I knew I had their rapt attention, for such is my way with words. "For I stole a precious stone for my beloved wife Malisha, from the treasure house in the palace of the Galli, the chief family of the Southern Tribes in the city of Sabol on the planet of Markdsi. It was a jewel that had previously been stolen by the Galli from an alien species of peerless power. And I stole it from the thieves; for those effete Southerners could not keep it from *me*!

"And here is the jewel." And I held it in my hand; a beauteous red stone, which shone like a furnace in the dim candle-light.

"I stole it for her, for my beloved wife Malisha," I continued. "And, after fleeing Sobol in a small spaceship, I was pursued and then captured by soldiers of the Southern Tribes. But I kept the gem safe by hiding it in my mouth, in the place of a tooth which I had ripped out.

"Then I escaped, and stole another spaceship. I survived a space battle. I was marooned for many months when my craft was trapped in waves of energy that prevented all means of propulsion, a doldrums of deep space. I saw, or thought I saw, space ghosts. All these adventures I briefly mention here; they were to be the matter of a glorious tale to be told by the fireside late one night, to my naked and sated and beauteous wife.

"Yet this never happened. The tale was never told; for Malisha died, terribly. My daughter Sharil died. My people died. I came to this place and I found brave and noble souls, yourselves. And I commend you all for your spirit; I am proud to know you.

"But all this is mere preamble, to set the scene, and acquaint you with the character of the story's protagonist, namely—*myself.* The tale I tell today is this: One day on the ship called Hell, a decision was made. One fateful day changed the destiny of all. One day all the peoples of the ship resolved to work together; not to fall into Despair, but to work together with one aim. And that aim is: to comprehend this place and how we are kept here and *why* we are kept here. And to use this knowledge to destroy our enemy, and to escape our captivity.

"That is the tale I have to tell; except I cannot tell it, for it has not yet happened. If we succeed, then shall I speak more.

"Who will join me?"

When I had finished speaking, I looked at Sai-ias. I knew what such a course of action would mean to her. It would be the repudiation of all her dreams of peace and contentment; the destruction of the equilibrium she had so painstakingly achieved; and the beginning of a vicious and merciless war which in all likelihood none of us would survive.

"I will join you!" Sai-ias roared, and relief swept over me; and all voices were raised to celebrate the dream of liberty I had conjured up this day.

There was much work to be done, and many nonsensical notions to be discarded to help us to achieve our aims.

For instance: translating air!

The very idea was absurd. There was no technology I could

conceive of that could allow *air* to translate, on a long term and universal basis. Miniature mechanoids floating in the air equipped with databrains and a translator code could do it of course, for a brief while. But what mechanism would be used to convey the translation into the mind of the listener? It would be sheerest chance to swallow the one portion of air that contained the translation of the words we were hearing!

What's more, in the course of time, these mini-mechanoids would be dispersed by the winds. So to create air that translates, you'd need as many mini-mechanoids as there were molecules of oxygen in the atmosphere!

Idiocy!

In the same way, all the creatures on this world had succumbed to the absurd notion that the Tower was the home of the Ka'un. They were *sure* it must be true—for the Tower was remote, yet visible; protected by winds; a constant reminder to them of the Ka'un's power.

But what warrior would put his army in plain sight of the enemy like that? Did these creatures know nothing of subterfuge and military strategy?

Sai-ias and I had proved that the Tower was nothing but a myth; but it was one of many.

For, as I now argued to the peoples of the Hell Ship, this notion that air could translate was *also* a myth—by which I mean a superstition which idiots believe in because they are too stupid to think for themselves. (On Maxolu, we have no superstition; that is why we are so superior to the feeble-minded Southerners with their cult of the Inner God, which to my mind is nothing but an excuse for gluttony!)

Be that as it may: another Hell Ship myth was that the air somehow creates the light from the sun. But how? Tired air becomes the sunset—absurd! Why not use a hidden light source? Or place bulbs on the other side of the metal sky, and use mirrors to convey the light within?

These creatures of the interior world *wanted* to believe such lies. They could not face the truth; that solutions to problems are usually simple, sensible, and pragmatic.

It was now my job to teach these creatures to discount all these myths and delusions, in order to defeat the Ka'un. The myth of the air; the myth of the light; the myth of eternal life. All nonsense!

Teaching the citizens of the Hell Ship to see the world clearly and as it really is; that was my first part of my mission.

"I killed Zala," I said to them all, "in the battle of the End of Days. So how could she have survived her terrible injuries, and come to live with you once more?"

A pause ensued; my listeners did not see the reason for the question, but I waited patiently.

"It was not the real Zala," suggested Morok, "but a replica."

"A machine-replica?" I asked, encouragingly.

"In our world," said Tubu, "we had such creations. But they weren't machines, they were illusions, solid to the touch."

"It could be," I said. "And remember, the real Zala had no memory of her fight with me; and no trace of a scar where I beheaded her."

"The memories of those who fight the Ka'un are erased," Morok pointed out.

"Not always," Sai-ias said. "Sometimes the Kindred remember what they do; forgetting only occurs when their injuries are severe, as Zala's were."

"That may be it," I said, pleased with Sai-ias's astute comment. "For I utterly destroyed her body: I split the head and brain; and cut her torso into parts; even the waters of the well of life could not bring *that* to life."

"Agreed. Rejuvenation of cells," said Quipu One, "can explain the healing of most injuries; but some other force must be at work in the case of Zala."

"Could it be," asked Iodoy, "connected with blink technology?"

"Explain," I asked, intrigued.

"It is possible to conjure a creature from here, to here," clarified Quipu Two, "in the blink of an eye. Hence the phrase. My people used it as a means of conveying cargo from one planet to another. We called it 'gapping,' Ioday's people called it 'blinking.' We and Ioday have discussed the science of it often. But such a method of transport only works if you create a perfect replica of the creature during the process; for it is *information* that is gapped, not matter itself."

The silence was stony; then it yielded fruit.

"That must be it; that is the technology they are using," I said excitedly. "For Zala 'blinked' away from my planet. She faded, then went. I thought of it as magic; but replication and disreality-bonding could have achieved the same effect."

"Indeed," added Quipu One. "When she arrived on your planet they would have had a second 'Zala' in storage. A perfect recording of the original creature; any mechanoid brain with sufficient data storage capacity could do that."

"That's how they make us cheat death! Replication, coupled with rejuvenation," said Quipu Two. "Making us both immortal, and unkillable."

"What about the water of the well of life?" said Ioday.

"Perhaps," began Quipu One.

"Perhaps it contains healing particles," Quipu Two interrupted, excitedly. "Miniature mechanoid brains, that interact with the cells of our body, using small worlds technology."

"Our kind had that," I admitted. "Once, our people used to die of heart attacks and alcohol poisoning, in vast numbers; but that has not been the case for many years. For at birth now, we are injected with artificial cells with micro-brains that live in our body and clean our body of toxins. In consequence," I added proudly, "we can drink gallons of the strongest ale, and never get drunk, nor suffer any dismal pangs the following morn!"

And so it went on; I badgered these foolish beasts to think

harder and longer about the powers of the creatures who built our world than they had ever done before.

The next day dawned: Day the First.

Once again, our peoples of the Hell Ship travelled their world. But this time, I asked Sai-ias to gather all the aquatics together and dive deep and plumb the depths of the lake; and then dig deep holes in the lake-bed itself to test what lay beneath.

And I asked the aerials to flock high and peck at every patch of the false sky, looking for gaps, or joins, or weaknesses.

I told Fray to smash holes in the mountains, to create caves out of sheer rock, in the hope of finding an entryway to the exterior hull by that route.

I told Quipu to analyse the soil, and examine the water from the well of life with his telescopic visions to ascertain what microbes might exist there.

Everything was recorded; written by Lardoi in blank books taken from Quipu's library, and also memorised by Quipu's five brains.

And Lirilla flew from place to place, carrying information, cajoling, unifying us into a single exploratory force.

Day the Second. The Temple was getting close to the sky now; but instead of demolishing it, I made the workers continue building the structure up higher, yet narrower. Until the Temple was a thin finger that reached close enough to touch the sky.

And those working on the Temple continued past the end of Day the Second, and for many cycles after; until the Tower near touched the sky.

At which point Fray clambered up the high steps and took a perch up there; and began to butt the hull-metal with her powerful horns. Relentlessly, incessantly, powerfully. It seemed to make no impression; but she continued, and continued, and I knew she would do so until I told her to stop.

And after six days, a dent in the roof of the sky was visible.

Day the Third.

As the work on the Temple continued, I began each Day the Third by making the aerials practise swooping and ripping with sharp beaks. I trained the giant sentients to charge in tight formation; I taught military tactics to the arboreals. I forced Saiias to prove her strength by throwing sessiles as missiles. The aquatics too were marshalled, and asked to demonstrate their predatory techniques, their killing skills. And the land predators practised their most basic survival skill; how to hunt.

Day the Fourth. A day of tales, and poetry. And on this day, each poet was asked by me to imagine a world in which all sentient beings lived in harmony, and the Ka'un were dead. And then to write their visions up into poems that would inspire us all!

Day the Fifth. Day the Sixth. Day the Seventh. Day the Eighth. Day the Ninth...

The days began to blur. Some explored, some built the Temple, some trained in warfare strategies and honed their fighting skills.

And others spent all their time discussing the science of the Ka'un and the geography of our world. Each part of the interior world was to be charted; each creature in the interior world was to prepare for what by now we all knew was inevitable: full-scale war against the Ka'un.

Thus had I turned these creatures into an army fit to vanquish the most fierce of enemies. And I had also made them *think.*

Just as, in her own exceptional way, Sai-ias had made *me* think.

For I had been so very certain, for all my life, that the way of my people was the rightest and most apt way. But now I had come to doubt it all. All the values I had assumed and trusted and relied upon—I now challenged them, utterly.

War is glory? Death is the supreme achievement for a warrior? Prowess in a duel is a sign of moral superiority?

All these beliefs now seemed to me—well, fatuous really.

War may be necessary; military might may be prudent; but there really are, it now dawned on me, more important things in life.

Thus had Sai-ias taught me; for my mind too, I realised, had been cluttered with myths. Blind and foolish beliefs that could not withstand the cool stare of compassion.

In comparable fashion, the creatures on this ship assumed they knew the truth about their world; but *they did not.* Their assumptions were false; their beliefs were absurd.

Thus had they been, for so many years, and in every respect, the dupes of the evil Ka'un.

I had one final surprise for them.

We were sitting, a small group of us—Sai-ias, Quipu, Fray, Lirilla, Doro, and I—in the fields by the forest, in the warm sun. Doro was a shadow on the grass, we barely knew he was there. But he was always there. Fray was restless, but determined to listen to my words. Quipu was animated, gesticulating with his two hands and bobbing his five heads as he mentally wrestled with thorny problems about the physics of the Hell Ship.

I then discussed with them my various theories.

"You have told me that for many years you have believed the air translates," I said, preparing the ground for my argument. "And it also hears every word we say."

"Correct, that was indeed once our belief," said Quipu Three.

"And it allows us all to breathe, though the atmospheres of our planets are very different."

"Correct again," Quipu One concurred.

"And the Tower is the home of the Ka'un; and the air generates light; and creatures who fall into Despair live for all eternity?"

"All fallacies, we see that now," conceded Quipu One.

"Yet you've already said all this!" chided Quipu Three.

"Don't be discourteous," said Quipu Five, critically.

"Let the creature speak," ordered Quipu Four.

"Even if he is annoyingly repetitious," Quipu Two sniped.

"My point now is: *how* do we know all this?" I asked.

Baffled stares greeted me.

But this was the crux of it!

All on the Hell Ship lived their lives according to various beliefs—or, as I would term them, myths. *But where did these fucking myths come from?*

Quipu shrugged, five-foldly. "These are things we simply know," Quipu One said. And Quipu Two added:

"Some knowledge is like that. Geometry, the difference between up and down, mathematics. It is called innate knowledge."

"Is there any other kind?" Sai-ias asked; and I marvelled once more at the oddness of her mind.

"Innate knowledge, that turns out to be utterly false?" I pointed out gently.

The Quipus took my point. But Lirilla, Fray, Doro and Sai-ias still had no notion what I was driving at.

"Another question: Why have slaves?" I continued.

"I don't understand what you mean," said Fray, irascibly.

"If they were really all powerful," I argued, "the Ka'un wouldn't need you to fight their godsforsaken battles. They have technology. They have weapons. But they are few. Remember that. And they are cowering from us now, afraid."

They pondered my words, and saw the sense. Then I waited a few moments more.

"There is something else," said Sai-ias, astutely, "that you want to explain to us. Isn't there?"

I smiled. "Let me show you, instead."

They journeyed with me to the mountains; and from there I led them into a cavern in the rock. The cavern was wide, but even so Sai-ias had to compress her body five-fold to get through. Quipu followed, agile on his five legs, Fray lumbered after him; Lirilla flew ahead; while I leaped confidently from rock to rock.

And there we found an underground waterfall, spilling out of the mountain.

"This is the source," I said, "of the well of the water of life." And I took a knife and gouged a line in my arm. Blood flowed; then I dipped the arm in the water. When I removed it, the cut was healed instantly, without so much as a delay of a few seconds.

Then I reached into the water and pulled out a large sack. I opened the sack.

Inside the sack was one of the brains of Djamrock, sundered into many parts, but still pulsing as it had when it was alive.

"What is this?" Sai-ias asked, shocked.

"I retrieved it," I said, "from—I do not care to elaborate—from the leavings of Cuzco that were—voided—after he killed Djamrock, and before he was banished. This is the brain of Djamrock, or parts of it." I prodded the flesh of the brain segments with a finger; it throbbed. "The cells are alive, though Djamrock's mind is dead. But the flesh, you see, doesn't rot."

"What have you done?" said Sai-ias, in appalled tones.

"I am performing an experiment," I told her sharply. "Into the nature of our captivity."

The dead shards of brain pulsed, eerily; the mood of my listeners had turned dark and sombre. But I ignored the bleak mood and continued.

"Facts and myths," I said. "Let us consider them in turn.

"The first myth: we on the ship cannot die. Not true; Djamrock was killed and now he is dead; these are merely cell samples. You believe his consciousness lives on in his sundered body? I ask you, what evidence do you have for that? It is just a belief, a superstition. Let us discount it.

"The second myth; the air translates. Who told you that? No one. How do you know it then? Because some things are just known, like . . . geometry? That's one possibility, but it makes little sense.

"So think about this," I said, softly, letting my words enter their minds like a whisper on the breeze. "What if the thought were planted in your head. Like a whisper, on the breeze. A thought that says: 'The air you breathe can translate your every word.' Easily done."

"A thought, in the head? It's impossible," said Quipu.

"In my civilisation," I said, "we have a thing called a pakla, inserted into the brains of each of us. It allows us to communicate at a distance. And we can use the pakla to translate. You program it with data about the languages involved, and it turns alien speech automatically into words I understand. I have used it often thus."

"Pakla?" asked Quipu One.

"That's our name for what you call a smallworlds mechanoid mind, and some of the creatures on this ship call—well, whatever. It's convergent evolution at work; many species have achieved the same technological breakthroughs."

"Not mine," Sai-ias said. "We have no use for mechanical brains."

"Nor ours," said Quipu One. "We remember every fact we encounter; numbers are like music to us; we could not create a machine cleverer than I."

"Or I," added Quipu Two, competitively.

"Watch this," I said, and I teased apart the shards of Djamrock's brain with a knife until a small crystal was visible. I gouged the crystal out and showed them. "This is how they control us. Paklas in the brain. They translate for us, they spy on us. As we already discussed, very small paklas in our blood stream rejuvenate us, by manipulating our hormones to regenerate dead cells that wouldn't usually regenerate. The water of the well of life is rich in these miniscule-paklas, that's how it is able to heal us. 'Despair' is, I suspect, a chemical reaction in the tissues of the body induced by an imbalance in the hormones in the brain, synthesising minerals dissolved in our blood from these lurking paklas. Flesh becomes stone; though it's not really stone, it's a crystalline form of carbon.

"Despair in short is a way of keeping us docile; if we aren't happy, our bodies are turned to stone. Enjoy your lot—or die! Evil, but effective; and the technology is not so very hard."

"The Ka'un have powers beyond our imagining," Sai-ias informed me, anxiously.

"That's only because you're so fucking dumb, Sai-ias! My civilisation's science is considerably more advanced than yours," I said, scornfully. "Give me a lab and equipment, I could replicate all these effects."

"You can control minds?" said Sai-ias.

"We have done so. Not any more, we fought a war over it with the Southern Tribes. Not all our wars are futile," I added, tauntingly.

After the encounter with Djamrock's brain, and my final explanations of how the Ka'un control us, we returned to the grasslands. The planning stage was over. The war was about to begin.

And each of the creatures on our world had a part to play in my complex and audacious battleplan.

The aerials patrolled the sky; they could warn us at once if the Ka'un made any attempt to open the firmament and attack us from above.

Sai-ias had spent three days motionless in the waters near the Tower, studying the movements of the Metal Giant. And, as I predicted, she saw it vanish—proving that it was a projection turned off by a simple switch. And she also saw a two-legged creature emerge from the earth, and wander around for a while. This was a Ka'un, I was sure of it. The Tower wasn't their home, but it *was* their way in and out of the interior world.

And so it was the Tower we would attack. Sai-ias and the sea-creatures would carry land-warriors under the gap in the force protector shield. And when an army was gathered inside, we would break open the entrance way to the Ka'un's section of the ship and flood into the exterior world, where dwelled the Ka'un.

At the same time, using the Temple building as our scaffold, we would attempt to breach the very sky, using the strength of the giant sentients like Fray and Ioday and Miaris to rip apart the metal hull. Serpentines would be hauled up and would squeeze through the gap created; and they would advance mercilessly upon our enemies who resided, so I believed, on the other side of the sky.

There were however several terrible obstacles in our way; I carefully marked them off in my mind.

Firstly, the Ka'un could shut off our air. If we suffocated, how could we fight?

The answer was simple; for I knew that Sai-ias could survive for very long periods without air.

So, once we broke through into the outer hull, via the Tower gateway, we would all charge inside and fight desperately and savagely; while Sai-ias would take the rear.

Then, once the air was cut off, we would all die—the giant sentients, the aerials, the arboreals, the serpentines, all of us; but before we died, we would wreak as much damage as we could.

And then Sai-ias would follow behind; and she and she alone would finish the war, clambering over our corpses to do so. We all knew her phenomenal fighting power; she was the only weapon we truly needed.

And our own deaths were, we all felt, a small price to pay for victory.

A second problem remained however; for we knew that the Ka'un could control us through the paklas in our brain. They could turn a switch and send us into dreamless sleep; and then all of us, including Sai-ias, would be wretchedly and easily defeated.

I wrestled hard with this problem; and in the days after showing Djamrock's brain to the others, I consulted with Quipu ceaselessly in the hope he might find a subtle scientific solution. Yet he had none; so I chose to embark upon my wildest gamble yet.

And now my course was clear. First I had to free my people from the mind-control of the Ka'un, by the most brutal means possible.

And then I had to lead them to victory; and their inevitable doom.

I kneeled in the clearing with Fray and Quipu and Sai-ias, while our whole army encircled us. Quipu held the knife in his delicate hands. And he pressed it to my forehead. And he dug the knife in, until it penetrated the bone.

Then he carved a circle of blood around my skull. And pressed harder, until knife dug into bone, all the way around my forehead.

Quipu then carefully lifted the skull cap away from my head, until the brain beneath was bared.

"What can you see?" I asked.

"Brain," said Quipu One snappily. "Precious little of it, it's a miracle you can—"

"Look for the crystal!" I said angrily. I felt naked and vulnerable with my brain bare to the world; and only the paklas in my bloodstream were saving me from shock, trauma, and sudden death.

"I see it," said Quipu Two.

"Then take it out," I said.

Quipu's sharp blade gouged deep into the tissues of my brain and I recoiled in horror; surely this was the worst thing that had ever happened to me!

But I endured it; and a few moments later I was looking at the bloody crystal in Quipu's hand.

"Water," I said.

Sai-ias sprinkled the healing water from the well of life over my exposed brain.

Quipu spoke; but I could not understand his words.

The others joined in; it was a babble of discordant sounds.

My pakla could no longer translate! And the theory was proved.

Then Quipu slipped the skull back into place. Sai-ias splashed more water on the join, and wrapped a bandage around my head. I felt somewhat dizzy; but I was confident none of them knew my species well enough to read the panic in my eyes.

I spoke: "Can you understand me?"

Another babble of sound. They could understand me, but I could not understand them.

And so it began; the cutting of brains.

Within hours the clearing was a pool of blood. The brain-tainted crystals were piled high. And as each of my fellow slaves lost their crystal, they lost the ability to understand each other. The clearing became a babble of competing noises, with no meanings.

Then Sai-ias extruded her brain out of her skull carapace for the operation to be performed. I held the knife.

Sai-ias

I was among the last to have my brain cut open; I was dreading it terribly.

But before the blade touched my extruded brain, Sharrock paused and dropped the knife to his side. For the sky had darkened; and we turned and looked, and saw two huge creatures came beating a path out of the blue sky.

Cuzco.

And Djamrock.

Both back from the dead.

I howled, in horror and dismay, and my brain shrank back into my skull, still uncut.

Sharrock backed away, still holding the knife. And Cuzco swooped down towards us low and fast, and his neck and skull orifices blazed fire; and Sharrock's body was engulfed in flames. I tried to spit web on my burning friend, to put out the fire; but my mouth was dry. I could not spit.

But Sharrock rolled wildly on the grass; and Fray pissed upon him; and his charred body stood and he was ready for combat once again.

And all around me, the fighting commenced.

Imagine a battle like nothing you can imagine.

Thousands of us fought against two; but Cuzco and Djamrock

were the mightiest of giants, and could fly. The aerials were helpless against them; the grazers were burned casually as they fled; the giant sentients like Fray were powerless to fight, for Djamrock and Cuzco could plunge down and rip pieces out of their hide before they could bite or butt. The larger aerials fared better; but they were puny by comparison to these, the greatest of the giant sentients possessed of the power of flight.

Quipu's body was ripped from top to toe within the first few minutes of this ghastly massacre, though his wounds were not fatal. Lirilla loyally attacked and died an early death. Sharrock fought bravely with sword and fists though his skin was burned and charred; but his power was nothing against these two brutes.

Miaris, a giant sentient almost as large as Djamrock, stood on his hind legs, and hurled powerful blows at the two flying monsters. His fists were like cliffs; his skin was as tough as granite; his jaws could chew through metal. But Djamrock dropped upon him from above, and gouged open his skull, and ripped apart his body; and spat acid upon him. And Miaris roared, and fell.

The battle raged; the arboreals fought and died, as did the aerials, as did the giant sentients. No one could withstand this double assault by the flying giants of our world; and the grass was red with blood and gore now, and screams became a wearily familiar background noise.

So the battle fell to me; I alone could fight against such huge flying beasts; and I had, after all, bested Cuzco once before.

And ever since I have wondered: could I have defeated them? Was it in my power to best two of the greatest monsters on board the ship?

I will never know; for throughout the whole conflict, I could not move. I stood, betrayingly, like a statue, observing helplessly as the battle played out. Sharrock screamed at me to help; *but I could not.*

I was, I realised, under the control of the Ka'un; there was a pakla still inside me. I fought its power; I wrestled for freedom. I poured every particle of my soul into this one desperate goal: to move, and fight, and kill.

And eventually I succeeded! I was able to stir my paralysed limbs; and I moved; and I seized Sharrock in my long tentacle; and I squeezed him to death.

And then I fell asleep; a deep dreamless sleep.

And when I woke, the corpses were all gone. The grasses grew high, with no trace of the blood that had stained them, or the body parts that had been so carelessly strewn. The piles of paklas had vanished; there was nothing at all to indicate a terrible battle had taken place at this spot.

Some months had passed, I deduced; and the world had returned to normal; and was populated once more by my comrades. Fray, Lirilla, Miaris, I saw them all, going about their business, and they saw me. They were all magically restored to life, with no trace of their appalling and fatal injuries.

Whilst Cuzco and Djamrock patrolled the skies above, proud and arrogant and unassailable.

I realised then which was the most appalling of the powers of the Ka'un; it was their gift of resurrection. They had brought Cuzco and Djamrock back to life; and they had done the same for the rest of those slain in that brave, yet futile battle.

And so we would never again dare defy them. For they were — surely they were? — gods.

"We cannot speak of it," said Quipu.

Quipu like me was one of the few actual survivors of that day; he had been badly hurt, and still required the healing powers of the water of the well of life to mend his scarred body and the partially damaged brain of Quipu Five; but the Quipus had not been "resurrected."

"It was a horror beyond—well, it was the worst of all horrors," said Quipu Two.

"I fell asleep," said Quipu Three, "and then—"

"Cuzco lives!" said Quipu Four.

Quipu Five grunted; incoherent yet still following the discussion.

"Not Cuzco," I said. "Not the Cuzco I knew."

For a few days ago I had touched Cuzco with my tentacle tip and begged for his pity. And he had looked at me with total scorn.

And at that moment, I realised he had no recollection of our intimate experience on the mountain top. We had loved each other then; but *this* Cuzco had never loved me.

He was a replica from a previous time; a past Cuzco, reincarnate.

Fray too had no recollection of the attack upon the Ka'un, or of our previous lives together; and nor did Lirilla. Fray was a stranger to me now; Lirilla knew me not. I found that, strangely, hardest of all to bear.

So the handful of us who had survived the war with the Ka'un were forced to nurse our secret to ourselves. The story of a mutiny that had failed; a rebellion that had been thwarted before it had even begun.

Sharrock groaned.

They had pinned him to a metal spike with cross-bars, his arms outstretched; a form of torture I had never encountered before. And they had flogged him, mercilessly. The rain drizzled upon the raw flesh of his wounds, which scarred him from face to thighs. I sprayed healing moisture on him with my tentacle tips, but it did not help.

I spoke to him but he did not respond. His eyes stared into the distance, never blinking. He was, I suspected, quite mad.

I stayed with him for four days and nights, talking constantly, explaining to him my new view of things: "They are gods, Sharrock, we cannot defeat them."

And then I realised he was awake and he was staring right at me with blank blue eyes and for a brief moment, his sanity returned: "Never give up," he whispered.

"We are defeated!" I protested. But he could not comprehend my words.

Then he began to choke. I yearned to help him, but did not know how to. Finally however the choking stopped; and he opened his mouth.

And balanced on his tongue was a red jewel. I reached in with my tentacle and took it out.

It was the jewel he had stolen for Malisha.

"For me?" I asked.

He grunted, and tried to smile. "A gift. Of love. From me to you," he eventually rasped.

And then he fainted once more. And blood trickled down his body and further soaked the blood-drenched grass; but he did not die.

Two days later Sharrock's body was gone.

Sharrock died a hero's death; that I will avow.

BOOK 8

Jak/Explorer

This place terrifies me.

You made that comment sixty years ago.

It's been a long wait.

Our patience will be rewarded.

When?

Soon. I hope it will be soon.

Sharrock

They came to mock me.

A female and a male; bipeds both, of my approximate height. The male, I guessed, was the leader. For he stood with arrogant confidence and stared at me with cruelty; and fire spat from his fingertips. Whereas she—well. An evil bitch without a doubt, for she took the deepest joy in witnessing my downfall, and stared at me with old eyes that were full of lust; a lust for pain.

I am in a room somewhere on the ship, I know not where. For I fell into a dreamless sleep and when I awoke I was no longer tied to a stake near the lake, I was terrifyingly elsewhere. Grey walls surrounded me. I could hear nothing of the rest of the ship; my room was bare apart from the magnetic plate on the ceiling, from which they had dangled me by the metal shackles on my wrists.

After I had been left hanging like this for several days, some Kindred arrived with knives. They taunted me, though I could not understand their words, then they flayed my skin off me a piece at a time. They left me raw and bleeding, a glistening body of bare muscle and exposed ligaments and bulging eyes.

The pain was intense, worse than anything I had ever known before; and I assumed I was going to die.

But I am not dead. And my skin is already starting to grow back. My guess is that once I am restored and whole, they will flay me, one piece at a time, all over again.

Water from the ceiling bathes me constantly; I assume this is water from the well of life and it is helping to keep me alive despite my appalling injuries and my lack of covering skin. The aim I suppose is to torture me for all eternity.

Let them.

For the pain — Ah! The pain!

Cling to that Sharrock. Cling to the pain!

You are not defeated. Not yet. Not defeated.

Never defeated!

The pain is my ally, not my enemy.

Embrace the pain, Sharrock! For while I feel pain that rends the soul and rips every nerve ending and fills my head with an agonising howl I know I am

Still alive.

I wondered a great deal about those two who came to mock me, just a few days after the Kindred had done their vile work. For I knew them to be Ka'un. They were dressed in rich robes in a style I did not recognise. Their faces were black and withered. Their eyes stared as if they were looking across to the other end of the universe. Their features were entirely expressionless. Was that a consequence of great age?

How old *are* these godsforsaken monsters anyway? And why do they do what they do. Boredom?

Perhaps, I speculate, age corrodes the emotions. Perhaps the smaller emotions like irritation and amusement and delight rot away, and all that are left are the huge and richly coloured emotions: like hate, and rage. That might explain why these creatures do what they do.

The male had stared at me for a long time before departing, as if studying me. Why? Had he never seen a flayed warrior before?

I lose consciousness from time to time and I know that this is the prelude to death; but each time the healing sprays revive me.

It is Day the First on the interior world; I know that for certain, for I keep a mental tally. Today Sai-ias will be exploring her world.

I try to — Ah! Agonising blinding pain! Embrace it, Sharrock! Embrace it!

I wonder about what Sai-ias is feeling and doing. Right now. Perhaps she is swimming in the lake?

And perhaps Lirilla is singing as she hovers in the air, her tiny wings beating?

And perhaps Fray is galloping on the savannah; while Quipu bickers with himselves?

And perhaps Sai-ias can feel the sunshine on her moist black hide?

Perhaps.

Explorer/Jak

So many lost civilisations; too many.

This has become my duty, and my obsession; as we travel, I fish for scraps of information about lost worlds and collate it and archive it all.

I am a machine and hence I take great relish in the meticulous storing and cataloguing and cross-referencing of this data; for as far as the computing part of me is concerned, it is merely data.

My machine-mind is however merged with the mind of an Olaran who is clearly filled with horror at the scale of these tragic losses; and his anguish perturbs me.

Sometimes the information I garner is random, the noises and imprints left by any technological culture, though such echoes in space—broadcast dramas and poems and factual films and radio messages between spaceships or planets—can be highly illuminating. Other times, however, the information is found in the form of compressed datacaches intended to be last messages from dying civilisations desperate to be remembered somehow. Such data may be technical or astronomical or military or historical or all of these; but sometimes more personal messages are also inscribed in this way.

The collation of these archives keeps my mind active. I am lonely much of the time. Jak is not such very good company. Not compared to Albinia.

He is better than he was. For after our departure from that second universe, Jak fell into despair. And then came the madness.

And after the madness, came despair again. Now he is merely sad; and occasionally he even talks to me.

I have made a list of the universes which we have travelled through, both the live ones and the dead ones. Jak refuses to let me tell him how many there are. But he does, obsessively, read through my archives of lost civilisations. Occasionally we discuss what he finds there; not often though. Not often enough.

There is now, in my opinion, no doubt about the validity of my theory that the dead universes we encounter are the trail left by the Death Ship; corpses scattered in its bloody wake. No other explanation will suffice; and datacaches have been found in all but a very few of these wasted universes.

There are very many of them; I have had to rebuild my archive in order to accommodate all the data.

How long has the Death Ship been destroying realities in this way? I can make no estimate.

What weapon is it using? I do not know.

Will we ever find the Death Ship, and defeat it? I can make no prediction.

But for a period of time that is larger than the lifespan of any Olaran, we have hunted this rogue vessel. We have journeyed onwards through the many living universes, searching each, one by one, with painstaking care, in the vain hope of stumbling upon our prey.

After one thousand years had elapsed, I explained to Jak that we were wasting our time; there were far too many universes. He agreed. And yet still we continued.

But finally I spotted a pattern; and it dawned on me that the Dreaded were observing a loose chronological cycle. Every ninety-three years by our calendar—though occasionally a hundred and ten and sometimes a hundred and fifty years—the Death Ship would return to the sector in space where we first encountered them. And then it would use the weapon that enables the Dreaded to destroy a universe as easily as an Olaran kills a dangerous and reluctant-to-trade alien. And then they would pass into the next universe.

Their pattern betrayed them. And it encouraged me to formulate a cosmological hypothesis. For it is clear there is only one place connecting the many universes; and my belief is that this was the point of origin of *all* the universes. And so I call it the Source.

Yet knowing this was no help, not at first anyway. For when we rift, we have no means of ascertaining how far we have travelled, or in which direction. So finding the Source again in a new and strange universe is no easy task; it can take two hundred years or more of mapping stars, until our point of origin is reached once more.

The only certain test is that when the rest of the universe has evaporated—well, then the Source is all that is left. We find it by fleeing the onset of nothingness.

But by then, of course, it is too late.

And even when we *have* located it, the Source can move; that was a shock also.

Or perhaps it's the universe that moves, and the Source that remains; no matter. The point is we have wasted many years seeking and pursuing the Death Ship through the multiverses. And we have wasted just as many years staying put and waiting at the Source for its return. Neither strategy has worked for us.

But I think I have now devised a star-mapping methodology that allows us to find the Source in good time, and *remain there*. And I am sure that I can detect it if the Source moves; and then we will move with it.

It took me approximately ninety thousand years to devise and perfect this approach. And we are now concealed behind a gas giant close to the Source in a universe with many recent traces of the Dreaded. Each fresh datacache I intercept confirms me in the belief that they are *here.* And, sooner of later, they will want to make their escape from this universe. And instead, they will encounter our wrath.

We have waited almost sixty years in this place for the ship to appear. On four separate occasions, the Source has moved, and we have moved with it. And each time it moves, the gas giant and its star also move with it. They are wrapped up, somehow, in the coils of this gateway to the universes.

There is life on the gas giant; not sentient, but life nonetheless. How strange it is for life to be evolving in such a place; rifting through space at the whim of the cosmological origin. This region of space is a speck of dust in the storm of all realities; and yet life still births here!

I cannot help but think: How stubborn is life! And how mysterious. For as a creature who knows its own artificer, I always marvel at the existence of organic life. From a purely technical point of view, it is incompetently engineered and badly designed and, in its sentient forms, all too often annoying. And yet—it awes me.

I have sent robots to explore the gas giant. I have mapped the geography of its roving clouds, and analysed the chemistry of its atmosphere, which merges at its lower levels with the fluid interior of the planet. I have studied the biology of its many microscopic life forms. And I have even named the planet—I call it Kraxos. I have named the sun too—I call it Albinia. Yes, a sentimental touch, but I allow myself a few. I have counted all the atoms in the sun. I have named all the microbes who are the dominant life form on Kraxos; and continue to do so, even though they have a two month life span and new microbes are constantly being formed from a process of cell fission.

It has indeed been a long and tedious wait; and Jak has, without question, been a poor companion, devoid of conversational artistry and even basic courtesy. Hence my obsessive data-analysing.

But we are, thanks to my careful preparations, ready in every way for the battle to come.

Jak, however, cannot endure very much longer. He is not cut out to be the human half of a machine/mind symbiosis. My thoughts overwhelm him; he drowns daily on data. I hope his wait will soon be over.

Furthermore—

Jak!

What is it?

Are you sane and functional?

Just about.

We have work to do. A ship approaches.

Is it the one?

It is an interstellar ship that flies with black sails powered by the invisible matter between the stars, and a helicoid marking on its hull.

So it's the one.

We may not survive this encounter.

I truly hope we do not.

One hundred thousand years it has been, since Albinia possessed me. We have lived together in one body all this time and—

Is this a soliloquy? Get ready for battle, spaceship! Prime the missiles. Prepare the un-matter bombs. Check all the—

I have done all that. We have been here for approximately sixty years; what do you think I have been doing with my time?

We're ready?

We're ready. The ship approaches. We will destroy it this time. Our lives will end. I just have this one thing I wanted to say.

What?

That despite your long brooding silences and ceaseless melancholy, your company has not been entirely unendurable.

I love you too metal-brain.

I didn't say—wait! It's closing in. No more talking!

The battle will soon commence.

Sai-ias

The new one was angry and resentful.

"You must accept," I told her, "the way things are."

"I accept nothing!" she screamed. She was a four legged predator of the plain, with sharp teeth and a tail like a whisk that was larger than her body. She had ugly, barnacled skin, and her voice was a rasping obscenity. She was, I could easily guess, accustomed to being the dominant species, and she treated me as if I were one of her anal parasites.

"Fight! Fight those grass-eating scum! Rip our enemies to pieces! Eat their poisoned flesh! That's what I shall do, when I have the chance!" she ranted.

"You will never have the chance," I told her.

"Don't be so sure. I'm not like the rest of you shameful cowards! I will fight, and I will win!" she raged.

"No," I said. "Acceptance is all. The Ka'un cannot be defeated.

"Believe me," I added, bitterly, "we have tried."

Jak/Explorer

I am ready. My mind is now fully merged once more with the mind of Explorer. I exist in many places; in the missiles we carry, in the concealed flying-bombs that orbit these planets, in our drone craft, in the matter traps that cordon off the entire stellar system. I am no longer Olaran; I am a killing machine.

Less talk, please Jak. Let's commence to kill this parent-fucker.

First missiles have been fired.

Feel them fly. Ah! Feel them fly!

Sai-ias

"I could bathe you," I said to Fray, as she paced by the borders of the yellow savannah. "You might enjoy that."

Fray glared at me. "Why in all fuckery," she said angrily, "would I allow you to do such a thing?"

"In the past you—"

"There is no past! Stop your fantasies, you vile creature! I have only just been captured, my world has been destroyed. And it happened just a few months ago. You talk as if—no, we do *not* know each other! You are simply some strange alien monster with whom I am trapped!"

"You remember nothing?" I said, sadly.

"There is nothing to remember!" Fray roared. "Don't lie! Don't tell these lies!"

Lirilla too had no past memories of me; nor did Lardoi, or Miaris, or Raoild, or Biark, Sahashs, Loramas, Thugor, Amur, Kairi, Wapax, Fiymean, or Krakkka; nor many others of those who had fought that day and died at Sharrock's behest. Only Quipu and I and a sprinkling of others could bear witness to the events of the day. The rest had been resurrected as the creatures they were when their worlds were first lost.

And so I was living with utter strangers who had been my intimate companions for centuries.

Jak/Explorer

Our missiles have lost velocity. No damage has been caused to their hull.

Their shields were fully charged; they were ready for us.

Of course they were. This is a game to them.

Again, missiles fly!

And so we fight.

We, this computer brain and I, have been preparing for this battle for so many years. And yet now it's happening, I feel totally *un*prepared. Panic consumes me. Each small setback disheartens me. I am convinced in my soul that we will lose, and all will be for naught.

Explorer, fortunately, is not so temperamental; she fights with a savagery and a guile that awes me.

And so, once again, our missiles fire and rift through space and then strike the forceshields of the Death Ship; and instantly lose momentum and drift aimlessly. But this time, before they can be destroyed, we trigger the detonators and all the missiles erupt as one, creating a halo of energy the size of a star around the black-sailed ship. Nothing can survive *this.*

But a moment later we realise the black-sailed ship is behind us. It has rifted to safety. And our forceshields are overheating, as it bathes us in sheets of energy and then

We, too, rift to safety.

Sai-ias

I felt a tingle of anxiety down my central spine.

I was walking through the grasslands near the savannah, to join Quipu and Lirilla. And as I approached Quipu, I saw his heads flick uncontrollably, for a just a moment. And I noticed an excited light in his five pairs of eyes.

"What's wrong?" I asked, puzzled.

"Something's happening— " said Quipu One.

"—with the ship," said Quipu Two.

"How can you tell?" I asked.

The heads replied, babblingly:

"The engine noise."

"The force of artificial gravity."

"The clarity of the light."

"The density of [Quipu used a word I could not fathom]."

"You can detect all that?" I asked.

"Perhaps we have collided," said Quipu One, "with an object in space—"

"Or been attacked by," said Quipu Three.

"Some other vessel," said Quipu Four.

"The light is degrading; the power sources are being diverted. The Hell Ship is in trouble. One way or another, it is experiencing some kind of appalling catastrophe," said Quipu Five triumphantly.

Jak/Explorer

The battle rages, if space battles can actually rage; for the explosions are eerily silent. And, despite the use of rift weapons, the pace of the action is often stately. It is a dance of light and power and confusion, to the music of an imaginary band; the sleek and black-sailed Death Ship and the now vast and ugly and ungainly Explorer craft flicker frantically through rift space leaving missiles scattered and exploding in all the places where they are absent.

Explorer and I no longer speak. We are lost in the moment, the to and fro of missiles and energy beams, the switching of shield patterns, the ceaseless rifting to safety just in the nick of time.

We use our drone ships and robot missiles to create a second and a third and a fourth and a fifth front to the battle. The power of our weapons is awesome, even to me—accustomed as I am to the vast battle fleets of the Olara. For we have spent all this time building up an armoury that dwarfs anything known before in any of the universes. The ship too has grown; it is five hundred thousand times the size it was when Galamea was her commander. And much of the bulk consists of weapons and energy sources and shield generators and layers of armoured hull within more layers of armoured hull.

But despite our vast bulk we are swift. Swifter than the Death Ship. And powerful. More powerful than the Death Ship. And adept at rifting. More adept than they are.

Yet why are we not triumphing? Again and again the Death Ship suffers damage that ought to be fatal, but again and again it survives.

Then the Death Ship starts to waver. It has switched on its disreality drive in order to escape to another universe.

We attack on all fronts. We charge the Death Ship. This time it cannot endure.

Sai-ias

"What kind of catastrophe?" I asked.

"Can you feel that?" said Quipu One.

And I could; the tingle down the spine again, coupled with a sense of oddness.

"We're passing through a strange place," said Quipu Two.

"Experiencing some kind of reality dilation," said Quipu Three.

"It is time," said Quipu Four. "Every seventy-two of my years, with some degree of variation, this sensation occurs. But we do not know why. We suspect dimensional or rift travel of some extraordinary kind is occurring."

The oddness intensified. I braced myself; this was a familiar sensation to me also, after all these years on the ship. Yet it was still deeply eerie and unsettling. I felt

as if I existed in

a

million

places

all

at

once. I felt

sick. Bile rose up

in my mouth

And

finally,

NO!

The strangeness ended.

We were back to normal.

And I was baffled.

This shouldn't have happened! Normally the strangeness lasted an hour or more. Had something gone wrong with the Ka'un's technology? Would they be unable, this time, to flee from their pursuers?

Jak/Explorer

The Death Ship is trapped by our disjunctive energy lattices which wrap around the black-sailed ship like webbing around a flailing insect. And we fire another fusillade of missiles from all our vessels, for Explorer and I now exist in sixty different ships at the same time.

The odds are overwhelming! We surely must prevail!

Sai-ias

Quipu and I looked at each other; puzzled and alarmed. The strangeness had passed, but now a terrible foreboding filled us.

Then the ground beneath us shook.

"We've been hit!" Quipu One exulted. "Someone is actually firing missiles at the ship!"

"That is," screamed Quipu Two, "a fair surmise."

The ground shook again. The aerials in the sky were dashed out of their flight patterns, thrown around like pebbles tossed in the air. And the sky — the sky! — actually flickered. And then the earth rocked violently to one side and I was rolled across the grass.

Nearby Fray fell too, then fumbled up to her feet, and bellowed at me.

Quipu was hissing with fear, clinging to a tree with his strong feet. Lirilla screamed, with rapid shrill shrieks like nothing I had ever heard before.

And then the world turned upside down.

And the waters from the lakes and rivers were now pouring down upon us like rain. And creatures were tumbling through air, clutching at trees and rocks, and the air, the air itself was whirling in thick clouds and we were all choking, unable to breath.

"What's happening?" someone screamed.

"Is something attacking us?" another voice yelled.

"I believe so!" screamed Quipu One.

"I've never felt it like this —"

"The gravity!" screamed Quipu Two, "has failed!"

Jak/Explorer

The hull is ruptured. The Death Ship is dying.

We've won. We've won!

Haven't we?

Sai-ias

"Someone or something is destroying us!" I said exultantly, but no one could hear my words, because of the falling of water and the screaming of aerials tumbling out of the sky and land creatures falling *up* into the air.

The sky flickered again. Once again the ship changed course violently, and we were thrown around wildly.

Gravity mercifully returned, and we crashed back down to the ground.

Then the earth beneath us trembled even more wildly.

Lirilla hovered by my head, bruised and shrieking with pain. I caught her in my tentacle, and tucked her in my mouth to keep her safe.

There was a long silence.

The ground beneath us shuddered and shook again.

"I'm certain now that we're being struck by missiles, or energy blasts, or both," Quipu One finally concluded. "We're under constant enemy attack."

"Can they actually defeat the Hell Ship though?" I asked.

"I doubt that," said Quipu One sadly. "We sent our own fleet against this vessel and they pounded it with weapons; nothing could break though its force shield. The Hell Ship is invulnerable to all—"

But a final shudder threw us off our feet again. There was a roaring sound. I could tell that something terrible was occurring.

"However, we might very well be wrong about that!" said Quipu Five brightly.

And then the shuddering reached its frenzied peak; and the Hell Ship, shockingly,

e

x

p

l

o

d

e

d.

Jak/Explorer

We watch, in awe and marvelment, as the hull of the Death Ship rips open and bodies begin pouring out. We realise that many of these bodies are captives of the Death Ship because they come in such varied shapes and sizes and none are wearing body armour. The bodies explode when they enter a state of vacuum, and the carnage appals us. But all on board the ship must die. There is no other way.

We harden our heart.

Sai-ias

After the explosion, the ground below me opened up. And I found myself tumbling into the hole and then falling and flailing wildly through the layers of the hull itself, until I was floating freely in black space.

And all was calm and silence, though all about me bodies were erupting into blood and gore. I alone had survived the rupture of the ship's hull.

When I looked more carefully around, I could see the many unfamiliar stars that were the hazy backdrop to the myriad corpses of creatures I had known and liked, now ripped into pieces. And, stretching out beneath me like a continent seen from the air, was a huge and eerily beautiful black-sailed space vessel with a silver, glowing hull.

But though magnificent, the ship was rent and broken. The sails were slack. And bodies continued to pour out of the several huge cracks in the hull and, for reasons I didn't fathom, they continued to explode and die. Small pieces of flesh and slicks of blood hung messily in space in seeming orbit around my body; and would remain out here as undecayed fragments, I supposed, for all eternity.

I prayed that my friends were safe, as I sucked up breath from my lungs into my mouth (for Lirilla was trapped there and would need to breathe) and spread my cape and soared through space, propelling myself with gusts of air from my gills, away from the damaged Hell Ship.

Joy! I was free!

And instead of breathing air, I was now breathing energy, captured from the undertow of all space that only my kind seem able to perceive and access. And instead of drinking water, I was supping the light from the stars and making it into *me*.

And instead of being trapped in a globular cage that mockingly pretended to be a planet, I was swooping through a small and precious portion of the infinity of space; and I exulted at the end of my captivity!

I noted however that the main part of the Ka'un's ship was still intact, even though the rear area had been holed; and I knew that the battle was far from over.

Then I looked further, using eyes that were as powerful as telescopes, and saw the Hell Ship's enemy vessel—a huge and ugly spaceship that looked as if it had been constructed by a blind creature with more energy and materials than talent. And at the heart of the asymmetric more-planet-than-spaceship was a striped hub that looked as if it had once been the entire original craft.

And from this monstrous murder machine pillars of missiles were pouring forth then vanishing then crashing against the shields of the Hell Ship; these corporeal bomb-blasts followed instants later by vision-bending stems of light that also thrashed the Hell Ship's beautiful lines. Smaller vessels scattered in space were also playing a vicious harrying role in this anarchic battle of light and energy; spitting missiles then darting elsewhere before reprisal could strike. The pace and blur and bright and splash of it all made my perceptions swim; I felt as if I were on the inside a star watching a deadly duel between sunlight and plasma.

And suddenly, I could hear voices, in my head:

After all these years...

We'll kill the parent fuckers! Kill them!

Don't miss.

I shall not miss.

As the voices spoke, more missiles were launched from the Ka'un ship and travelled instantaneously through space and exploded on the hull of its enemy vessel. Light splashed on the vast and ugly hull of our potential saviours, but no damage was done; and then the saviour craft retaliated, and haloes of light now appeared above the Hell Ship and crashed down upon it, striking sparks like burning fronds spat from the mouth of a Padiux.

The blackness of deep space was lit up by missiles exploding and light-haloes writhing and burning, and the invisible walls of protective energy around both ships glowed brightly, oh so brightly, to my eyes which saw energy as if it were light.

The space between the ships shimmered as deadly beams of energy were unleashed and repelled and reflected back.

I could hear atoms fusing and sundering and interacting to form massive eruptions of raw power that seared my sight. And I could sense the universe itself being bruised as the two ships dived in and out of tunnels in space, to emerge once more vomiting forth fire and metal and nuclear holocaust.

The attacking ship vanished; reappeared; vanished; reappeared; and for one astonishing moment it appeared beneath me and my claws were scratching at its hull; and then it was gone again.

And a moment later, a jagged spike of coloured energy shot through the glow of the Ka'un ship's shields, and struck the Ka'un ship itself, and my vision blurred again as the massive impact shook the very soul of my perception.

And, as I watched, more bodies billowed out of the hole in the rear of the Ka'un vessel.

I glided closer to see them and I recognised arboreals and aerials and sessiles who had been sucked out of the ship, and I saw too—

I saw too a body in a space suit, with a face as black as a starless sky, and its voice spoke to me.

Rescue me, I am your master, said the voice, and I knew it was a

Ka'un. It was small, a biped, protected by its space suit but cast adrift into space in the midst of this dazzling space war.

I wrapped my tentacle around the Ka'un's body.

You can fly in space? You crazy Saviour-shagger! cackled the Ka'un.

I wanted to break the evil bastard's body in half with my tentacle and eat him; just as Djamrock would have done.

And I imagined how that would feel: I imagined the Ka'un's howls of pain, slowly fading as he died. And I felt a rush of exhilaration. It was in my power to kill a Ka'un! And the power felt *good.*

But—I couldn't do it.

For some reason, my limbs would not obey me. And so I relaxed the tightness of grip on the Ka'un; I still held him in my tentacle, but gently now.

I raged at myself; I did not lack the will or desire to kill this creature, but suddenly my body was not my own.

That's better. You always do as we tell you, don't you, sea monster? Now, take me back to the sh—said the Ka'un, then a stray energy beam caught him and his head vanished.

He was dead. But not through my doing.

The energy beam also raked my body in passing; I absorbed it, and grew.

Then out of the front part of the ship, a new vessel appeared, in a twisting turning shape which I knew was called a Helix. And the Helix darted towards the enemy ship, raining missiles as it flew.

But the enemy ship ignored it, and continued firing its missiles upon the Hell Ship itself. The Helix faded into nothing; it was a mirage, a trick.

And then another missile struck the Hell Ship's hull; and time itself seemed to stand still as the Hell Ship erupted in a massive explosion, a single dazzling flash! The ship lit up like a Biollai seed exploding and igniting in mid-air.

And then the light faded and there was nothing left. No Hell Ship, just debris.

The corona of light had dazzled my eyes, though I felt no heat on my carapace. I floated in space with my cape outspread and the memory of the dead Ka'un in the spacesuit haunting my mind.

And I realised that it was all over. All my friends were dead; but so were all the Ka'un.

Fragments of the hull of the Hell Ship drifted closer to me. Corpses and coils of blood and limbs and torsos and heads and ruptured internal organs cluttered the once-empty blackness of space.

The attacking ship was badly damaged, but intact. I began to glide towards it, hoping they would realise I was a friend and not Ka'un. But something held me, and tugged at me; I felt as if I was in a dream and had no power over my own body. I was being pulled, pulled, pulled—

And then the pulling stopped. But when I tried once more to glide through space, I found I could not. I could no longer swirl and swoop, and I could not go beyond a certain point *here.*

Or a certain point *there.*

These obstacles to my movements were corporeal. Not like a force shield, such as that which surrounded the Tower; more like walls.

I was surrounded by walls!

I summoned my inner eyes and saw the truth; and the truth was that I was no longer in space surrounded by stars; I was in a hangar bay shaped like a huge globe within a space vessel. And the walls of my confining space were silver, just like my cabin; the light was pale and yellow, just like the light from our sun.

I was back inside the Hell Ship.

And the strangeness was upon me again. We were travelling somewhere far away; escaping the enemy's wrath.

I spat, and Lirilla emerged from my mouth.

"Safe?" she asked, plaintively.

"Not safe," I told her, sombrely.

My cape retreated back into my body. And I realised that the destruction of the Hell Ship had, like the appearance of the smaller Helix vessel, been just an illusion.

The Hell Ship had been damaged, I was sure of that, but not destroyed. And then it had fled; and it was now, once again, swimming in what Quipu called the rivers of chaotic flux until, at some point, it would re-enter the Real.

And then it would all, the terror and the horror, begin again.

Jak/Explorer

What joy! What release! After all this time, they're dead! Those cruel parent-fuckers are dead! We've won!

You know, I can't believe it! To see that black-sailed vessel engulfed in the flames of a space-burning missile. To know that, finally, we have managed to take revenge for what they did to Olara! And to my family on Olara. And to all my people. The ghosts of all these Olarans will—

Say something Explorer?

We've won. Haven't we? Tell me we have won? Why aren't you speaking to me?

I'm not sure exactly what happened there.

What the fornication are you on about? You saw it. We both saw it. Sensors, visuals, all confirm. The Hell Ship blew up and is no more.

Wait.

Tell me what you detect.

I detect many things.

Then tell me what you conclude.

The data is inconclusive.

And what does the inconclusive data suggest to your wreck of a mind?

It suggest there is no debris consistent with the explosion of such an exceptionally large rift-drive space vessel. It's chaff, bits of matter scattered in a pattern that superficially resembles a blown-up spaceship.

What are you saying? And please don't say it, even if it's true. No, tell me—what?

It was a trick. We did not destroy the Death Ship.

An illusion?

A corporeal holographic projection, that disintegrated in front of our eyes and registered on all my sensors. Like the Helix ship we fought, which they expected us to treat as the "real" vessel but which turned out to be nothing but a chimera. These creatures have technology that allows them to mimic reality with remarkable verisimilitude to all our electromagnetic, visual and mass sensors. They duped us twice in other words, and the second time we fell for it; and the Death Ship used the moment of the deceptive distraction to evade our restraining lattices and enter another universe.

Bastards.

As you say, bastards. And now we are giving chase.

We can do that?

We are doing it.

How can we do that? We have no way of knowing which universe they are in, surely? You swore to me that—

I DON'T KNOW HOW WE CAN DO IT. I AM JUST ATTEMPTING TO DO IT, OUT OF COMPLETE FUCKING DESPERATION.

I understand, calm yourself.

It is folly. We can never find them. But we shall try. Instead of waiting here, we will pursue avidly. But not by travelling through a single universe at a time. No, we shall stay here at the Source and dip in and out of a million different universes with dazzling speed until we smell our prey. Because I believe we can detect them from afar now; I know the trail they leave. Death, destruction, and messages from lost civilisations trapped in the ripples of reality.

Then—do it.

I am doing it.

And so we rift once more through the Source itself. Through an area of space where reality is riven with cracks. And we—

Yes we—

We arrive, somewhere. Somewhere very strange. Our sensors are—the very atoms are—

We adapt, somehow, to this new reality. We absorb the new parameters and constants. This is now our universe.

Can we detect them here, Jak? Help me please, I need your help, you are invaluable to me in this vital stage of our mission—please?

I can detect nothing. Just—murk. I can see nothing through our visual sensors. No sound-pictures are emerging. Electromagnetics are fuzzy.

Try harder.

You can see what I see. Nothing.

Admit it. You do not need me, Explorer. I am very little help to you. You are just trying to—no matter. I shall not let you down. I am reading the data now—fuck-my-father these readings are utter chaos! What the hell is wrong with our instruments?

Our instruments are fine. There is nothing to see.

How can that be? There must be SOMETHING out there; or if not, then nothing. But not—this whatever-it-is.

Void, confusion, something but not-something, Memories of worlds, or possibilities of worlds. And pain. Terrible terrible pain. I don't know. It's confusing.

Tell me what you think is out there. You must be able to make a credible surmise. Please.

It's—I cannot—confusing—chaos—no.

Yes. Now I see it.

It is a dead universe; dead but bleeding, and in pain. Do not ask me how. The Ka'un once were here; but not recently; not for many years.

Where are we now?

I do not know.

I can, you will not be surprised to hear, once more make no sense of the data from our sensors. But perhaps you can fare better; can you detect anything?

I detect nothing.

Then we should move on.

Wait! I'm aware of a—something. A—what?

Yes! I have it. A shadow on my sensors that my circuits can perceive as absence with intent. Another ghost signal, for our archives, from a past version of this universe.

Capture it.

I have, it is downloaded.

Can you read it?

Not yet.

Now?

Yes, now.

Tell me.

Once, this universe was thronging with life. Trillions of planets were habitable. Thousands of sentient species lived in harmony. And this is the remnant of the trace of a communication from one of these species.

Another last message?

Indeed. From another lost civilisation. A sun-worshipping people whose science took the form of poetry and who dreamed one day of settling the stars, to worship them too.

We must keep this record in our archives.

I have kept it.

We must remember these people, these sun-worshipping star-dreaming poets.

I do not know how to forget.

I can't see anything, again. What can your sensors tell you now?

Nothing. Just another empty universe. But there are traces of radiation scarred into this void. Fusion bombs were exploded in this place once, and their radioactive residue remains, even while matter itself decoupled and became non-matter.

I am downloading the radiation signatures and decoding them.

I have completed downloading the radiation signatures and decoding them.

Decoding them?

There is something anomalous about the radiation patterns; it occurred to me that a sophisticated civilisation might have chosen to self-destruct using atomic bombs with a message encoded within. And so it has proved. These peoples wrote a message in the burning fire that consumed them. This was a civilisation that could use radiation as other cultures use paper.

Tell me more.

I have archived it; you may read it at your leisure.

I will do so.

These messages from the dead constitute an extraordinary phenomenon: like finding the history of an entire world scratched into the wood of a small boy's desk, if I may utilise an archaic simile.

I'm reading the archive now. These people had discovered, after years of careful scientific analysis, that their distant ancestors had evolved from microbes embedded in comets. In other words, they were descended from space travellers. This historical fact infused every aspect of their post-scientific culture. They were inveterate stargazers. They were vegetarian, and worshipped the bark of the trees they ate. They had no weapons, for in all their long history they had never encountered a predator they could not out-run. They had long slender legs and streamlined bodies, and fingers that could be retracted into their jaws. I can see an image of one of them now, it's strangely beautiful. They procreated by cell fission at the point of death; each dying creature of this species spawning a fresh child. So in a sense, they were immortal. They were lovers of life, and caused no harm to any other creature aside, perhaps, from the trees they ate.

And now they are gone.

It's sad. So very sad.

I have no view to add to yours on the emotional affect of this data. But logic asserts that a fellow organic sentient would find little pleasure in such death-messages, and so "sad" is a response I might have predicted.

And now, I am entering

another universe.

And I find I am above a blue globe patched with clouds. A fertile planet, with oceans and clouds—it must have life? My sensors check.

No, there is no life. But life once did exist here, many aeons ago, and it has a left a trace that I am able to detect. There were once seas of acid here, rich with acid-loving fish and acid-eating algae and land made up of boiling volcanic lava that was seething with extremophile microbial and plant life and mountain tops coated with grass on which six legged beasts roamed. What could have happened to it? Was it another victim of the Death Ship's incomparable evil, or did life just *die out*?

I have seen enough; I jump through another reality-rift

and emerge in the heart of a spiral galaxy; no trace of the Death Ship's distinctive ion trail here either. No legacy of carnage and destruction. Nor any trace of the absence of life.

Just life.

Life all around. Wherever I look, there is life. There are trillions of habitable planets in this universe. And thousands of sentient species in possession of space travelling technology.

I read the messages in the electromagnetic data trail and the space time substrate and I record it all. It is all here, every detail of this wonderful universe. There is one planet in this universe where insects have created cities of steel that burrow down deep almost to the planet's inner core. The entire planet is an insect nest made of metal and plastic and the large mammals are kept as foodstuffs and as objects of scientific study. A cruel world, according to the morals of the Olarans who designed my programming, yet a magnificent achievement; a planet over-run with genius bugs.

And there is an Olara-like space-travelling civilisation too in this universe which has engineered stars to burn brighter, or fainter, in order to improve the appearance of their night-time sky; and has constructed ringworlds, and planetary bridges made of rainbow coloured unbreakable motile glass.

There are many galactic civilisations here; and also solitary-world civilisations which have no idea whatsoever that they share this reality with so many varied and powerful sentient beings. And there are wraiths too—energy-beings with intelligence but no corporeal form—creatures that are legends in the Olaran universe, but are here all too real and detectable by sensors.

It is a rich and bountiful universe; there is malice here, but also goodness. There are wars, and death comes undesiredly and all too soon for many of these sentients. But even so, I feel extraordinary excitement at being in the midst of such living plenty.

And, indeed, I wonder briefly if we should stay in this place. Should we become this universe's unseen, all-powerful, cautiously non-meddling protector? So that when, one day, many years hence, the Death Ship arrives we will be here to greet it, and we will be able to destroy it?

We could save it all, Jak and I! All of it. With our intervention, one sole universe would survive! And one, surely, is enough?

You want to be a god?

Don't you?

We fly between realities yet again.

And enter yet another wilderness universe. Death has cursed this place, and only datacached fragments of the lost sentient cultures remain.

I have archived them. We must move on.

And again, a universe devastated and devoid of life.

And desolation, and lifelessness.

And barren bleak voids.

And nullness.

And emptiness.

And nothingness.

And, again and again, in all these dead places, whispers remain: distress messages haunting the empty reaches of no-space.

The Death Ship has travelled further and for far longer than I ever suspected.

I now realise they have killed millions; by which I do not mean millions of sentient creatures, nor do I mean millions of different species of sentient creatures; I mean millions of *universes*.

And again and again I find the last gasps of all these dying civilisations, desperately encoding all they knew and all that they were into signals transmitted out into space. In the hope that one day, the messages might be found, and their own lost civilisation would be remembered.

We must honour them. We must remember them.

And so we shall.

EXPLORER 410: DATA ARCHIVE

LOG OF LOST CIVILISATIONS (EXTRACT)

Lost Civilisation: 41,200

...sixteen messages were received from this universe. Fifteen were garbled.

The sixteenth message told of a world of brilliant and eloquent sentient creatures who had built a tower that stretched from the ground into space, until it connected to the planet's moon. The tower was hollow and functioned as a tunnel; children would climb up it then slide down it on their school holidays.

No data about the material used to build the tower has been received, nor is there any information about the engineering principles that allowed it to be stable. But many images have been saved of these people who built a staircase to their moon.

These sentient beings had a median height of three bilois, and a median breadth of two bilois. They rolled on organic wheels. Their eyes were receptive to ultraviolet and infrared radiation.

A large portion of their final message was devoted to a binary code transcription of their greatest works of music, which I have translated into musical notes. It is rhythmic, ululating, and entirely captivating. Their greatest composer lived to the age of four hundred and forty, even though the median age for these people is twenty. It is believed by the philosophers among these sentients that the grandeur of his music sustained his life far beyond the normal span.

That is why these creatures were so devoted to music; their entire culture was based around the concept that music prolongs life, and can confer immortality.

In their war with the Dreaded, these sentients transmitted continuous sound messages at the enemy spaceship in orbit. These beams were not intended to damage the Death Ship; they merely conveyed a compressed form of these sentients' greatest works of music. Perhaps their hope was that their enemy would be so exalted at the beauty of the music that they would abandon the battle.

There is no data available as to whether the Dreaded approved of or were intimidated by the musical genius of these people. But it is self-evidently the case that they did not cease in their battle.

Once the Death Ship launched its attack, annihilation proceeded swiftly. These sentients inhabited four satellites and a single D Type planet; their total population numbered forty-two point one billion.

The music of this species is gracious indeed. It takes some considerable effort to become attuned to the jagged rhythms and discordant shrills, but it is this mind's opinion that these creatures were possessed of a rare genius for melody, harmony, and rhythmic variety.

Their final elegy—composed as their planet broke asunder, and inserted as a coda to their distress message—is particularly affecting.

Lost Civilisation: 120,357

A fragment of a poem was retrieved, in an unfamiliar metrical style, which translates very roughly as:

Seashine   Moonsbeam   Heartsjoy   Fear of death

Child's love   Child's joy   Child's rage   Child's death

Love   Hope   Delight   Death of love and

                    hope and delight

No record exists of this civilisation or its physical form.

Lost Civilisation: 1,264,303

...as well as a text describing a sacred building:

...and there the gods will dwell, in the hearts of those who live there, and who are purified by the stones, and by the bricks, and by the mortar, and by the metal. Perfection will be achieved by those who are born and live and die in the sacred holy of holies. Thus we believe and thus we have devoted our lives to this place.

And yet we no longer have reason to believe that our gods care for us any more. Our houses have fallen, our temples have collapsed, our animals are all dead. Only our people remain and they are without flesh because of some terrible event that has enplagued our entire species in a moment; and now they are dying slowly by degrees. And thus we, the holy scribes who dwell in this holy place, deep within the ground, see the end of all occurring through our cameras and mirrors and we know that soon, we too, will... [transmission interrupted]

Lost Civilisation: 2,200,304

A list of names, in a language based on whistles, here rendered in approximate phonics.

[24 billion names in all]

Lost Civilisation: 3,800,305

In this universe, a considerable data trail has been left from 5,444 sentient species all of whom were bonded empathetically and existed in a state of harmony, even though they had evolved on 5,444 different planets from far distant regions of this universe.

Frequent mentions of the "Gateway of Life" may be a reference to a naturally occurring rift in space that permitted instantaneous travel between these planets, allowing for the possibility of close interaction between species of very different cultural development.

A further reference to the "Faint and Haunting Web of Minds" also suggests the hypothesis that empathetic connection between sentient beings may have occurred through the rift itself, implying that all these cultures had evolved with a dim but compelling sense of the existence of other minds in other places.

An attempt to destroy the Death Ship was made by all 5,444 species acting in concert, by "Webbing the Evil into a State of Grace and Kindness," which implies an attempt to harness the power of empathy to redeem and "de-evil" the marauding Death Ship and its crew.

This attempt evidently failed; the universe is now a ghost of possibilities; and no trace of the Gateway of Life or the Faint and Haunting Web of Minds remains in the aridness of this once fertile and endlessly astonishing universe.

Lost Civilisation: 5,900,300

The history of this civilisation is recorded as a 34,334,333 hour film archived here.

The text which accompanies this film, which is approximately four billion words long, is archived here.

For the purposes of this summary log, here is the opening paragraph:

> We are defeated. You are the victors in this battle. And yet you know no mercy, and no respect; merely contempt. We have abased ourselves before you and you have shown us contempt. We have enslaved ourselves to you and you have shown us contempt. We have pledged ourselves to you, and you have shown us contempt. We have offered you our lands, our wealth, we have offered to execute all our leaders and soldiers and leave only the civilians and the weaker sexes alive, and you have ignored us, and hence shown your contempt.
>
> So let it now be understood: We damn you. We curse you. We invoke all the demons in the myriad demon dimensions to eat your souls. We show our contempt for you, we shit on you, we piss on you, we eat you and shit you out then piss on you, we...
>
> [etc]

Lost Civilisation: 11,900,300

These sentients were biped and prided themselves on art generated by bioluminescent energy, and firework displays that sometimes lasted for years.

Relics left by this civilisation include the image of a map of the universe which shows a single planet at the centre of a universe of stars, indicative of a pre-technological society without sophisticated astronomical apparatus. This is at odds, however, with certain fragments in the data trail, where there are references to colony ships settling multiple planets and ruling the universe.

These stories may of course be fictional, a legacy of a society that dreamed of settling the stars but never did so.

This civilisation is unique in that there is no record of it having encountered the Death Ship prior to cessation of its reality.

For an account of the end of this universe and surmises about its possible causes, read the files archived here and here.

The second of these files consists of a long account by an artist from this civilisation called Minos which is of considerable interest to this archive. It contains details of a war between his people and a species they called the Parakka; tall creatures with a single eye and claws for hands and with three tongues which hiss when the creature speaks. The memoir begins with the words:

> Hate me if you like. I care not. Love and hate are just illusions.
>
> Death is the only truth.
>
> And I should have died a long time ago. I wish indeed that I had.
>
> For I have sought death; I have taken bold and reckless gambles; I and my crew have fought wars that we could not possibly have won, and we have won.
>
> When I do eventually die, this voice recording will be left as a trace in the folds of space. It will be found, one day, by some explorer ship or other. And my story will be known. The greatest story in the history of all the universes.

So my words will live for ever, but I care not for that. I just want to die.

This is why I am dictating this, my suicide note, my declaration of defeat.

It is not clear what these last lines mean; the rest of the broadcast is partially corrupt, and is currently being studied by Star-Seeker Jak who for some reason takes a particular interest in the Parakka and in this lost civilisation and claims he will one day be able to decipher the rest of the story.

BOOK 9

Sai-ias

My world was chaos.

I had returned to the interior world from the hull bay to find the lake emptied of water, bodies strewn all around; and a vast fissure stretching across the Great Plain. But gravity had been restored; and now the shattered bodies of the dead and injured in the attack lay on the grass and savannah and in the muddy lake bed, rather than hovering in mid-air as before.

"Sai-ias." A flutter of wings by my head; Lirilla was still with me.

"Save me," Lirilla said, in acknowledgement of the fact I had saved her. Though she did not know *why*; for she had no notion we had been friends for hundreds of years.

"Quipu? Fray? Doro? Are they safe?" I asked.

She knew the names of these beasts of course. And obediently, Lirilla vanished, and returned.

"Quipu, safe," she said.

"Fray? Doro?"

"No Fray. No Doro."

She had been around the ship and back in the blink of an eye; I knew she could not be wrong.

Quipu was safe; but Doro and Fray were missing; fallen, or so I feared, through the crack in our world.

"Sai-ias?" said Lirilla anxiously.

"I'm fine. I'm fine."

"Lirilla, fear, full," said Lirilla.

"You're safe, you're safe. I'm here now."

"Lirilla, wish, dead."

"What are you saying sweet bird?"

"Lirilla, wish, dead—ship."

"Me too. Me too."

But the attack had failed; the Ka'un were still alive.

We spoke of it that night, Quipu and Lirilla and I, in the hours after the disaster; in a series of rambling and repetitive dialogues.

"No need to ask who," said Quipu One. "We know who."

"Some lost civilisation," added Quipu Two.

"Seeking revenge," added Quipu Three.

"From this universe or from some other universe?" asked Quipu Four.

The Quipus together intoned: "We will never know."

"It must have pursued us," said Quipu Three, "for—who knows how long."

"And yet it failed," Quipu One pointed out.

"It tried, at least," said Quipu Three. "There's grandeur in that. My own people—well. We were so powerful and yet—we—"

"Gone," said Quipu One, "like a light being switched off; all our people, gone."

"Ground, healed?" said Lirilla. For earlier that day the crevasse that had opened up in the grasslands slowly, over the space of several hours, *had closed.*

"I do not know how that could have happened," admitted Quipu Four.

"Magic," I said.

"Not magic," contradicted Quipu Two. "Some kind of force-field effect."

"?" said Quipu Five, who was struggling to keep up with the discussion.

"A structural skeleton made of invisible force," agreed Quipu

Three. "When the hull is breached, the force field rejoins; the metal is forced back into place."

"I touched it," I reminded Quipu, as I kept doing every few minutes. "I touched the ship."

And so we sat there, stunned, survivors of a disaster, huddled and muttering the same things over and over: "It was terrible." "We almost died." "I can't believe it!" and so on, endlessly.

"I touched it," I muttered again. My claws had scraped the hull of their vessel, before I had been scooped up by invisible beams of force and made captive once again.

I remembered the vast and awkward shape of the attacking ship; and its squat central hub, with its colourful stripes faded by time; and the inscription on the top of the vessel, blazoning a name which, even in the absence of the translating air, I had somehow been able to read, which said: **Explorer 410: Property of the Olara Trading Fleet.**

"Explorer 410," said Quipu Two, "Property of the Olara Trading Fleet."

"Yes," I confirmed.

"Not even a warship," said Quipu Three. "A reconnaissance vessel, for a merchant fleet. And it was nearly our salvation."

"Nearly," I said.

"But why did the Ka'un save *you*, Sai-ias?" asked Quipu One. "They plucked you out of space; why you, and not any of the others?"

"I do not know," I said.

Over the next few days and nights, Quipu interrogated me at length; and pieced together the progress and nature of the space battle.

One or more of the missiles fired by the attacking spaceship had struck its target; that much could not be denied. And that missile had ripped several holes in our hull, through which I, and

Doro and Fray and so many others, had tumbled out. But the ship that I had seen that looked like a Helix was but an illusion. And thus, Quipu concluded, the Hell Ship that was destroyed before my eyes must have been illusion too.

"The cheapest of tricks," said Quipu One.

"A distortion of space-time," added Quipu Two, "that allowed an image to linger *here* when the reality had moved *there.*"

It was clear to all of us that Explorer 410: Property of the Olaran Trading Fleet had been duped by a conjurer's stunt. If only it had fought on, and fired more missiles, it might have succeeded in once again striking the invisible but real Hell Ship; and the result of the battle would have been quite different.

This thought haunted me. These aliens who attacked us had been so very close to victory. A single miscalculation had cost them everything.

A few weeks later Fray returned; though Doro did not.

Once again, Fray's memories were gone; and once again she was convinced her world had only just been destroyed.

It was agonising to see the rawness of her pain. And painful too to witness her bewilderment when she was told of a great space battle in which she had "died," though she remembered nothing of it.

Other fatalities of the battle were in the same plight; their bodies were intact, but they knew nothing of what had just happened. It was a whole army of new ones, all at the same time; and there was no way for me to ease them gently into their new world.

As Cuzco would have said: they had to fly or die.

Why did Doro not return?

And was he actually dead? Perhaps that strange creature could actually survive in the depths of space? Perhaps he shifted his shape one final time, to be a star among stars?

In the cycles that followed the failed attack on the Hell Ship, our world was in turmoil. Many angry creatures stalked the interior world; duels and vicious assaults were commonplace.

But I did not care; not any more. For my entire personality had changed.

I was no longer calm, reassuring, and accepting. Instead, I was engulfed in a constant edgy rage.

The smallest things infuriated me. I found that I could no longer tolerate the company of others. Even Quipu, even Lirilla, enraged me by their very presence.

After a while I stopped spending the nights in my cabin with my so-called friends and their wretched fucking stories. Instead, I slept outside, in the pitch black night, atop mountain crags or in the depths of the lake.

And each dawn I re-entered the world after a night's dark reverie of regrets.

I thought about Sharrock a lot. I was convinced that if he and I had had acted sooner, our rebellion might have prevailed. With my strength, and his knowledge of warfare, we would have been an unstoppable team.

Another missed opportunity. First Sharrock; then Explorer 410: Property of the Olaran Trading Fleet.

Though these two failures did, I realised, prove the Ka'un were not invulnerable.

Indeed, as I had seen while floating in space, they were slight creatures, bipeds, with no natural armour. I could kill one easily! I could snap its body in half and swallow it, and crunch its bones in the ridges of my gut which is robust enough, if the mood takes me, to consume raw rock.

These pathetic puny easily-killed creatures—how could I ever have been afraid of such as *they*?

Many cycles passed. The new ones were becoming acclimatised. The daily violence began to lessen. The Rhythm of Days was resumed, though I took no part in it.

A thousand more cycles passed.

The ship was now restored. The lake was re-filled. Our numbers were fewer, for not all the lost had been resurrected; but we were still many. And I resumed my role in the Rhythm of Days. I explored. I listened to poetry and tales. I struggled to comprehend science. I raced against my fellow sentients. I meditated. I refreshed old friendships, with friends who had forgotten all our years together. And I made new friends as a trickle of new ones began to join us.

I realised, with horror, that life had returned to normal.

And then one night I slept a dreamless sleep.

And when I woke I was no longer in the interior world.

I was inside a spherical cargo hold of some kind. Grey metal walls surrounded me. And all around me, their bodies bare-armed and sweating, were twenty or more of the Kindred. They wore golden tunics of a kind I had never seen, and were testing pipe-shaped weapons I did not recognise. A small cheer rose up when I awoke, and I could tell it was intended mockingly.

"Where am I?" I said; but no words emerged.

I took a step forward; but I did not move.

"Show arms," my voice said, and the Kindred warriors stood upright and held their weapons at an angle to their bodies.

"We are," my voice added, "facing an imposing enemy. These creatures have disreal technology and remote weaponry. We have rarely fought an enemy of such sophistication. Do not be complacent."

"Yes, Captain," roared the Kindred, almost as one.

My body was the commander of this army; and yet I had no control of it!

I remembered what had happened when I killed Sharrock. It was just like this; this same experience. I had lost the power over my own body.

There was a Ka'un in my head.

The hull gates opened and I flew out of the ship, escorted by ten Kindred soldiers in space-suit body armour.

I was gliding through the blackness of space above a small green and blue planet, which blazed with artificial lights. I was encased in some kind of protective shield, and wore a transportation device around my neck which made it possible for me to travel large distances in an instant. So one moment I was far from the planet, seeing it as a distant balloon; and the next I was close up to the orb, gripped by its gravitational forces.

We were, I knew, without knowing how I knew, too small to register on the enemy's detection devices. They were geared to spot enemy spaceships, not individual soldiers and a caped sea creature able to breathe in vacuum.

This is why the Ka'un had saved me, I realised. They had

discovered I could survive in space, during the battle with Explorer 410, and as a consequence they decided they would keep my skills for a day like today.

I landed on the blue and green planet's moon in a gentle glide, and began digging into the ground with my claws. Then from the pack on my back I removed a small cylindrical object. I buried it there, and glided through the thin atmosphere on to another part of the same moon.

I was joined soon by seven members of the Kindred, wearing their space armour and tanks of air; and they too had cylindrical objects to bury. We planted nearly three hundred of them in widely spaced holes across the moon's surface.

Then I vanished/reappeared and found myself back in the hull of the Hell Ship itself.

But I could still see—through the eyes of the Ka'un who possessed me and who was now seeing through the cameras the Kindred had left behind, in an insane loop of perception—the remote war that was taking place in this stellar system.

First, the moon on which I had stood abruptly exploded, raining debris into the clouds of its parent planet below. I could only imagine the destruction that was being wrought on this fertile world.

After a delay of some minutes, swarms of spaceships emerged from bases orbiting the planet to protect it from attack; but they flew into some kind of invisible shield in space and were torn into pieces. This was another trap, laid by the Kindred.

And then a huge finned missile appeared from nowhere—presumably fired by the Hell Ship via a rift in space—and reappeared in the atmosphere of this blue and green planet. It soared through the atmosphere, like a bird on a downglide.

Then there was a vast billowing explosion in the planet's atmosphere, as vivid as a solar flare. And I realised the missile had been detonated in mid-air.

The enemy were, I realised, fighting back.

After the Hell Ship's missile had been blown out of the sky, the aliens of the blue and green planet continued their spirited defence. Thin metal tubes flew out of the planet's atmosphere and expanded into flimsy winged spacecraft possessed of amazing velocity. There were hundreds of them—no, thousands—and they danced and kinked with eerie speed. I was awed at the scale and the beauty of this retaliation; rockets turned into Cagashflies in front of my eyes and were now swarming out of the clouds.

And then these dazzlingly fast craft broached the atmosphere and rushed—rifting in huge jumps—towards the Hell Ship itself. And for a few exhilarating tens of minutes I savoured my panoramic space camera view of the Cagashfly-spaceships sweeping towards us.

Then the Hell Ship counter-attacked. Missiles appeared in space, rifted out of the Hell Ship's belly; Cagashfly-spaceships exploded; and the battle escalated with a swiftness that made me nauseous. I could not perceive any details of the space war; just ceaseless and immense flashes of light as the explosions built upon explosions in a frenzy of light and spewed energy.

And then, after what seemed an eternity of light-war, the flow of Hell Ship missiles came to a halt. And the dazzling glare slowly faded, and the stars began to reappear.

But a few moments later still I could see that the swarm was still coming towards us. And there were now *more of them* than there had been before; the Cagashfly-spaceships were mysteriously multiplying as they were destroyed. I marvelled at this, briefly. And wondered how these creatures could manage such a trick.

And then I realised: these Cagashfly-ships were now rifting through space like stones bouncing upon a lake, spitting energy beams at us, getting closer and closer with each—

The Hell Ship lurched. And I looked around, and I realised that the stars in the space around me had changed, and the hazy after-glare left by those countless explosions had vanished entirely. The Hell Ship had fled the scene of battle.

I realised that the Ka'un had been thwarted, and had given up.

It was a shock to discover that the Ka'un did not always win. I had thought them invulnerable in battle, as they had been in the war with my people.

On the next occasion however I was able to witness the destruction of an entire planet, as the Ka'un ship fired the same large finned missile which this time broke through the enemy's defensive weapons and struck the planet's crust.

Once again I saw everything that happened through the mind that possessed my eyes, and which saw through remote cameras all that took place.

And I not only saw; I understood, through my intimate bond with my possessing mind. I grasped everything; how the weapon was constructed, how it worked, what it did. I knew that this missile was designed to drill a path to the planet's core, where "un-matter" was then released which collided with the hot liquid matter of the planet's core to create a series of huge blasts that, before my Ka'un-inhabited eyes, ripped the planet apart.

The Ka'un who dwelled in my head had a name for this weapon: the planet-buster.

This was the same weapon that had killed my world. But, I now knew, if we had possessed the right technology, we could have stopped it.

That was, for me, a bitter moment of insight.

The wars continued. And the Ka'un continued to ride me like his beast of burden. And I continued to watch, and watch, as planet after planet fell.

The Ka'un were remorseless, but they lost as often as they won. But when they *did* win, their wrath and their cruelty knew no bounds.

And all too often, I—or rather my body—was the leader of

the giant sentients who took part in their massive ground offensives against bipeds and smaller polypods. These poor creatures were justly awed at our "ferocious" aspect; and we slew them in their thousands.

And for the first time, I truly understood the reality underlying the rhythm of our lives. For whilst we on the interior world were spending our days in tedious repetition, the Ka'un were laying plans and setting up war weaponry. They seeded energy beacons in hundreds of stars to fuel their war machine. They created machines in space that generated robot warriors and robot spaceships to comprise their battle fleet. They reconnoitred carefully all the systems they were going to attack. And only then, did they fight.

The wars were brief; but the preparation for those wars was intense and prolonged.

As for me—I had become one of the Vanished. For months, then years, I did not return to the interior world. I spent all my days with the Ka'un's other warriors. The Kindred were the Ka'un's regular army, alternating soldiers on a regular basis to keep the troops fresh. And these Kindred were masters of warfare, and shockingly brutal.

And, meanwhile, we giant sentients were there to shock and appal and to engage in the most bloodthirsty of the combats. The wars could have been won without us; but we were there to add glory and magnificence to the combats.

We were unlike the Kindred of course. They *chose* to fight. Whereas we giant sentients were without volition, controlled like puppets by the Ka'un. Thus, oblivious to the desperate protests of our minds and souls, our bodies murdered and massacred like evil savages.

And, every now and then, we were joined by familiar faces.

My troops awaited my instructions; I scanned them carefully, looking for traces of fear or of independent thought. A hundred

Kindred warriors stood with me in the hull, together with eleven giant sentients. Balach, Morio, Tamal, Sheenam, Goay, Leirak, Tarrroth, Shseil, Dokdrr, Ma.

And Cuzco.

I wanted to scream with joy when I saw him; but I could not. I also wanted to savagely wrap a tentacle around his throat and strangle him, in revenge for what he did to Sharrock and the other rebels. But I could not. I was a prisoner in my own mind; able to see but not to act.

Cuzco looked magnificent. His orange scales gleamed, his eyes were full of an angry vitality. He was no longer the sad and defeated creature I had loved; he was a warrior lost in battle-lust.

"Cuzco," my voice said, "these creatures have primitive projectile weapons and use spears and mechanical spear-throwers. You will enjoy today."

"Can they fly?" Cuzco asked.

"They command," my voice said, "regiments of aerial creatures who routinely massacre beasts larger than yourself. These people, let us call them the Shasoon, which in my language means Prey We Taunt Before We Eat, will give you a battle royal."

Cuzco roared with joy, as did Balach, Morio, Tamal, Sheenam, Goay, Leirak, Tarrroth, Shseil, Dokdrr, Ma, and myself.

The Ka'un strategy, I now knew, was to engage in direct combat only when the enemy was technologically primitive. And in these cases, we were the Ka'un's favoured warriors; the giant sentients who could be relied upon to stage a battle both bloody and magnificent.

Ah, and what a battle it was!

The Shasoon were octopod creatures who could gallop on four legs while firing spear-weapons with their dextrous four arms. Their torsos stood upright atop their cylindrical bodies and they howled when they fought, an ululating cry that allowed them to control the animals and the plants in their vicinity.

They were brave and bloodthirsty creatures, with a rich history of combat, as I learned from the thoughts in the mind of my equally bloodthirsty Ka'un master. The Shasoon had slaughtered all the other major land animals on this planet indiscriminately, and fought constant wars amongst themselves. They were gifted astronomers and had spotted our space ship arriving in their stellar system. And they had prepared carefully for an alien invasion, by laying traps, training armies, and concealing missiles capable of throwing vast balls full of explosive powder, albeit for a relatively short distance.

They stood, of course, not a chance.

First Cuzco appeared in the skies above them and fusillades of burning spears were loosed at him from machines built of wood. But the spears splashed harmlessly over his armoured body, and he swept down low and ripped apart Shasoon warriors. Flames were fired at him and engulfed his body but that merely entertained him and he spat back fire from his neck and skull vents. Nets were thrown upon him and he burned them off with acid from his body.

And then I swooped down, my cape fully unfurled, and I landed in the midst of a regiment of Shasoon who fired primitive projectile guns at me and stabbed me with their spears. And I batted them down with my lengthy tentacles, and impaled them with my quills, and ripped their bodies apart with my claws.

Then Goay and Leirak joined the fray; they were carried down in the claws of the giant aerial Tarrroth, and dropped on the earth, where they used their claws to rip open the soil in search of the Shasoon's buried encampments. And when the network of tunnels were revealed, Dokdrr and Ma were conveyed to the planet's surface and they slithered their vast serpent bodies inside the tunnels and I know they would not stop until they had paralysed or chewed to pieces each and every Shasoon warrior in this sprawling underground labyrinth.

Once we had destroyed all of the warriors in this army, we travelled onwards to the country's major city where we were confronted with a fortified building with high walls that towered up to the clouds. But Tarnal swiftly smashed a path through the walls and Cuzco flew inside billowing flame while I clambered over the wrecked walls with my tentacles and we resumed the perpetration of carnage.

These valiant warriors fought fearlessly, and in turn were dealt terrible blows, and sustained appalling injuries. Tarnal had his eyes gouged out and ran off howling, lashing with his claws at air. A mob of Shasoon forced an explosive ball down the throat of Dokdrr, and when it detonated the serpentine's body was rent into pieces and she screamed in agony and could no longer move. But then Tarrroth swept down from above and carried clawfulls of struggling Shasoon warriors high up in the air and dropped them to their deaths.

Shsiel and Ma had been my friends on the Hell Ship; I remembered them fondly. Ma was a herbivore with a long and (proportionate to her body) slender neck that allowed her to eat leaves from the tops of trees in the giant forests of her world. Her people had developed a rich philosophy, and her stories of the fantastical had always been a joy to hear. And Shsiel was a scaled two-headed beast whose people had befriended the sentient bipeds on their planet, and formed a multi-species civilisation with a single government.

These were the gentlest of beasts, despite their size. But today they were wrathful warriors. And when we smashed down the inner walls of the fortified building we found there the old and the young Shasoon cowering, and the babes in cots, the crippled and the ailing, the venerable leaders, and the terrified toddlers; all protected by ranks of archers fighting fiercely to the last. And Ma roared with joy at the sight and lashed at bodies with her hooves and ate young and old and crippled Shasoon whole, and Shseil used his horns to stab and his teeth to rip the octopods into shreds. Then I joined them on the ground and I—

I cannot speak of it.

Suffice to say, we slew them all! We butchered, chewed, maimed, ripped, burned and impaled these angry Shasoon by the tens of thousand. The hot blood of battle was upon me; I was fighting side by side with giant sentients of magnificent valour, and blood flowed freely that day!

All this I saw, and all these emotions I felt, as I inhabited the Ka'un mind that was inhabiting me. It was a day of bloody murder, and my Ka'un revelled in it. And so did the Ka'un who controlled Cuzco, and so did all the other Ka'uns who controlled this army of giant sentients. This was not a day for the Kindred; this was a day for monsters to kill small eight-limbed angry and aggressive intelligent beings who stood not a chance. They could hurt us, but they could not kill us; all they could do was die screaming with rage.

Yet in my own soul, I raged with frustration, and with contempt for my inhabiting mind. For what glory was this? How could any sentient creature take pleasure in such cruel, futile atrocities?

The Shasoon were flawed creatures, without doubt; they were a young species, and primitive and bloodthirsty. They had not yet learned the joys of civilisation, collaboration, and societal love. But they had *potential;* their cities were beautiful, they loyalty to each other was noteworthy, and they had, I do not doubt, great love for their children and for each other.

But we slaughtered them that day as if they were insects who had built their nest in our child's bedroom; and when the Ka'un were weary we departed and a planet-buster missile was sent to burrow into the planet's core.

One solitary Shasoon was captured; and we made him watch, through the glass wall of the hull, as his planet was exploded into many pieces. He screamed and wailed, as they all did on these occasions.

And then he was taken away to the interior world.

When we did not fight, we slept. We woke, we fought again.

"Cuzco," I whispered.

The great beast was asleep.

"Cuzco."

Still, he slept, not moving, not even a trace of breath from his lips.

"Cuzco!"

Still, he did not stir. No one stirred; for all we giant sentients, sleep was absolute and involuntary.

But for some unknown reason, I had woken, and remained awake. And I could speak. But Cuzco could not hear me; his trance-like state could not be penetrated. I called and whispered and blew air upon his face, but he did not respond in any way.

Eventually I was silent. I lay awake, incapable of movement, unable to speak to anyone else; never have I felt more trapped.

"They are giants also," roared Cuzco, as he hovered in mid-air at the head of his army. "It is a worthy encounter. Let battle commence!"

And Cuzco plunged and dived upon the basking reptilian creatures, each twice his size, and I loped along on my tentacles to join him.

We were on a swamp planet; double suns made the air a painful glare. These creatures were non-sentient but vicious, and Cuzco was enjoying the battle. Blood spattered and heads were severed and after several minutes Cuzco was maimed and weak and I came roaring in to help him.

"Cuzco," I whispered, my face close to his bleeding head. "Can you hear me?"

"I can hear you," he whispered back, then his eyes went blank again and he fell asleep.

The reptile tried to rip his body apart; and I stood and fought, to protect Cuzco's sleeping body. I realised that Cuzco's Ka'un body-rider had absented himself; and indeed so had mine. For I had at that moment, for the first time in a year or more, the use of my limbs back; I was free!

But Cuzco was in deadly peril. So I fought for my friend like a crazed thing, spitting rage and stabbing with my quills and slashing with my claws. I pounded the enemy beasts with my tentacles; and I defeated them all.

And when it was over, I was weary and bloodied, and Cuzco still slept, and I wondered what I would do now.

Well done, Sai-ias, said a voice in my head, and I realised it was my Ka'un.

He was talking to me.

Cuzco's wrecked body was carried up in a landing craft and taken to the Hell Ship. He would be restored to health, I knew, but it would be some time before I saw him again.

I recognised one of the Kindred landing party; it was Zala. Once she had been Sharrock's enemy, and had fought him on his world. And now once again she was serving the Ka'un.

"Zala," I whispered to her, "It's me, Sai-ias." But she did not respond.

She is a beautiful creature, said the voice in my head. *Or at least, I find her so. Larger, physically, than the females of my kind. And three eyes at the front, whereas our third eye is on the back of our neck. But beautifully proportioned. I have often, in the body of a Kindred male, fornicated with this beast.*

Who are you? I thought at the voice in my head. But there was no response.

It was, once again, a slaughter most bloody and glorious.

On this day, I fought side by side with the Kindred, against tusked bipeds who had built huge metal machines to fight their battles for them. The Kindred were armed with their cylinder guns that spat fire, and I and a dozen other giant sentients fought beside them with our claws and teeth and, in my case, tentacles.

First, we had destroyed the tuskers' cities with bombs from the air; we had smashed their missiles in their silos; we had slain them in their hordes. This was a semi-technological society which used steam to power its machinery; and their projectile weapons fired only one bullet before requiring a reload. But even so, the tuskers had large and well disciplined armies and catapults that could hurl burning fire, and there were millions of them. So we slew millions of them, remotely, with missiles and forest fires.

And now we had descended to the planet for hand to hand combat with the last stragglers on the planet; no more than two or three thousand of them, we estimated.

And we were losing. The tusked bipeds used ambush and deceit against us; they built pits and covered them with grass; they put bombs in their own people so when a Kindred warrior struck an enemy warrior with his sword, the resulting blast was deadly to both.

And their metal machines were unbeatable. I stabbed them with my quills, I smashed them with my tentacles, but they could not be hurt. And every time they burned me with fire, my inner shell got weaker.

And then another landing craft descended from the sky, and twelve warriors stepped out. They were bipeds, roughly the same height as Sharrock, and dressed in long red robes; dignified and graceful but with blackened old faces that looked like skulls; their beauty turned to eerie age.

One of them fired a projectile gun without aiming; and a hundred or more tiny missiles flew through the air and unerringly targeted the metal monsters we had been fighting.

The missiles cut through metal effortlessly; moments later nearly a hundred blinding flashes dazzled us; and when our vision returned, the monsters were ash.

One of the robed bipeds laughed; a sound of joy that chilled me.

See me, Sai-ias, said the voice in my head, and the laughing biped turned to look at me, and I looked back. And I realised that it was him; my Ka'un; the one who lived in my mind.

"Come, and fight!" shouted another robed Ka'un, to the tusker army. "If you can defeat us, you may have your planet." And he drew a sword and held it aloft; the universal sign for a challenge to combat.

By now only a handful of the tusked bipeds were left; five hundred or so was my guess. And most of them were not in plain sight; they were hidden in the alleys and houses of this city, from where they had launched their skilful ambushes. But one by one they all emerged, to face this new enemy. For they clearly knew this was something different.

Now they were fighting their real enemy: the Ka'un.

I realised that I was paralysed; only my eyes could move, not my limbs or head. My Ka'un was focusing on his own body, and had immobilised me.

The five hundred or so tuskers formed a disciplined semicircle, facing the twelve Ka'un. They wore tunics of hide and metal, and they carried projectile guns in their hands and swords and axes in their scabbards. They were clearly seasoned fighters.

One of the tuskers screamed an insult at the Ka'un; it was evidently an invitation to fight and die. And even though I could not comprehend it, there was a musicality to the creature's sounds that made me think the words were beautifully expressed.

And my Ka'un responded to the challenge by stepping forward; and then he bowed his head, in a gesture of respect.

Five hundred or more guns were raised and all shot of them at my Ka'un.

The speed of it all was bewildering; the bullets fired, my Ka'un leaped to one side, and the other Ka'un dodged and ducked as the hail of bullets flew at them. Then my Ka'un got back to his feet.

There was blood upon his chest; a hole in his skull. He had dodged most of the bullets, but not all. Yet he had survived. And my Ka'un laughed again.

Half the tuskers reloaded their guns; the other half charged with swords and axes raised. My Ka'un was undaunted, and did not deign to draw his sword; his eleven comrades stood in readiness, but also did not attempt to draw their weapons.

And then a spark of fire shot from my Ka'un's arm and hit the front rank of charging tuskers. They fell, screaming and ablaze. The other Ka'un ran towards the tuskers, flames leaping from their arms like lightning that streaks across the sky, and more tuskers burned.

Then a second fusillade of bullets was fired, and some of the Ka'un fell. My Ka'un had lost the use of one arm; but still he spat flame from the fingers of the other arm; the air was acrid with fumes. The burning tuskers did not scream as they died, and no one had time to attempt to extinguish the flames of their stricken comrades. All were focused on killing the Ka'un.

One tusker got far enough to lop the head off a Ka'un's shoulders; and then my Ka'un struck him with a powerful fist, splintering a tusk. But the tusker absorbed the blow and swung his sword again but my Ka'un leaped high in the air, dodging the blade, and landed with feet kicking brutally and the tusker's skull was crushed, and he fell down dead.

My Ka'un roared with joy; and for one moment I could see through *his* eyes. Two more tuskers were rushing at him/me with swords, enveloped with flame but fearless; and I/my Ka'un seized a tusker sword from the ground and engaged them in savage swordplay. Steel clashed against steel; my Ka'un was deft and fast and graceful, but the tuskers were numerous and highly skilled. I felt, as my Ka'un felt, a surge of panic at the thought that I would now die, irrevocably.

But a moment later I/my Ka'un had recovered my/our poise and my/his sword bit flesh and the scores of attacking tuskers were dead—hacked apart then eviscerated.

How does that feel, Sai-ias? my Ka'un asked in my head.

The battle was over; the ground was damp with blood. The Ka'un retreated to their ship, dragging their dead and wounded, but my Ka'un remained; staring at my body; thinking his thoughts in my head.

This was a joyful battle; too often we hide in our ship and miss the true glory of war.

Are your dead warriors...truly dead? I thought at him.

Oh yes. There is no resurrection for us; only for you, our children. But the difference is: we welcome death.

Why do you do this? What pleasure can you take in all this carnage? I thought.

Do not pretend, Sai-ias; for you enjoyed it too.

With a creeping sensation of horror, I realised he was right; I had savoured the glory of this day! And I hated myself for it.

Who are you? I thought.

I am Minos, I am both artist and warrior; and I am captain of the vessel we call the Blessed Farol; which you know as the Hell Ship.

From that moment on, Minos was constantly in my thoughts.

Do not judge us harshly, he said to me that first night. *For we were wronged. Our universe was destroyed, by brutal creatures who cared nothing about the goodness of our kind; and thus we were forced to become wanderers through the dimensions. We are victims; and you should pity us.*

Stop this now! I thought at him. **Let us all be free; and**

stop the killing. You are deranged. What pleasure can you take in massacring so many?

We do not do it to take pleasure.

Then why do it? I thought.

We only fight when we are provoked! Oh how could you think so badly of us, Sai-ias?

I was shaken by his words; the evident sincerity of his tone. Yet I knew that some creatures could lie as easily as they breathed; and I suspected that Minos was one such.

For we have only one goal, Minos continued: *to spread the word of peace and love through all the realities. But each and every time we attempt to seed friendship and concord, we are confronted by belligerence and rage and contempt. And so—in self-defence—we have killed very many species of sentient alien species. But only for the noblest of reasons! And only, as I say, in self defence.*

You can't believe those lies! I raged mentally.

I do believe them.

You have killed millions of innocent creatures, you evil one!

Only because they proved unworthy.

I realised that he truly wanted me to believe him; and I marvelled at the pettiness of this creature, in thus trying to win the affection and respect of his own slave.

The following day I remembered the words of Minos when I woke.

All around me, my fellow giant sentients were lost in dreamless sleep. I alone was awake. But something was different. I felt—I felt—

And then I rose up and walked.

I walked! And slithered; then I expanded my cape; and I spoke:

"My name is Sai-ias," I said. And no one could hear me, so I said it again:

"My name is Sai-ias, and I am free."

My tentacles were mine to command; I could speak freely. And I could fly, if I so desired, wherever the winds might take me.

The next day was the same.

And the next day.

And the next. Free!

When my fellow sentients woke, I acted as if nothing out of the ordinary had occurred. I acted as they did; I spoke as though possessed by a Ka'un. I ate like a savage. I did not converse. During exercises, I was as brutal as I had always been.

Later, I journeyed from one end of the hangar bay to the other where the Kindred dwelled, just to see what it was like. It was not in fact so very different; except that the Kindred slept on wooden benches, and the stench of their unwashed bodies was ripe and disgusting.

When challenged by a Kindred warrior about my presence there, I said I was carrying a message to a particular Kindred chief who I knew had died during our last combat. I was told he had died in combat, so I snorted rudely, and made my way back to my end of the hangar bay, where the giant sentients were lodged.

At the end of that long day I lay down and slept with them; or rather, pretended to sleep.

It was, I knew, imperative that no one should know of my state of freedom. For there was no-one here who could be trusted. The Kindred were pure evil; the giant sentients mere puppets.

And I wondered how this had happened. Was it a mere accident? Or was Minos playing with me? Or perhaps trying to win my confidence and trust? But if so — why?

And I wondered too what I would do when the time for battle came again. Would I reveal myself as the true Sai-ias by refusing to fight, and be entrapped once more? Or would I fight, and slay, and hence keep my freedom for a little while longer?

And hearing that thought in my mind, Minos spoke:

You must fight, Minos said. *For my crew know nothing of my gift to you, and they must never learn. But this will not be for ever. This terrible state of affairs will not last for ever. Trust me, Sai-ias; I implore you, trust me!*

I did not know whether to believe him, or to trust him; but at least I knew part of the truth. This, my state of freedom, was Minos's doing.

And I realised too that Minos had come to rely upon me, and perhaps even to like me, for reasons both strange and mystifying. For he spoke to me, and to no other. He gave *me* the freedom of my limbs, as a gift with no prior or subsequent conditions. He was the captain, the master of this vessel—the king in effect of all the Ka'un. And I was his favourite!

And over the weeks that followed, with Minos's voice in my head, I learned so much about this ship and our captors. Minos confided in me as if we were long-established friends; as if we were equals! He told me that his ship had the power to travel between different universes, not just between stars, though I did not comprehend his explanation of this. He told me also of the sad history of his people, and their war with the evil Parakka. And he told me how he and his crew had yearned to make a fresh start, in some new universe or other. But they were never, because of the folly of others, able to do so.

There were only a handful of Ka'un still surviving, Minos admitted. Once the ship had held thousands of their kind but war and natural disasters had thinned their numbers. But only the extremest acts of violence could kill their self-regenerating bodies; they could not die of old age. That salvation, he said bitterly, was denied them.

Many times, he also admitted, the Hell Ship had come close to destruction. It had been blown up, hurled into a sun, beset with metal-eating viruses, bombed with un-matter, and in a myriad other ways savaged and brutalised. Each time the ship—which is organic and living, in some way I cannot fathom—has reformed itself. And the Tower itself has always remained intact. The Tower, he told me, was the replica of a sacred building upon his own home world; The Tower of the Living Saviour, which for some reason he reverenced.

For many years, I had believed the Ka'un to be immortal. But no. They can be killed. And many have been, over the aeons.

And those that survive are few. They are tired. Their hopes and dreams have all died. Their loves and desires have decayed into distant memories.

And Minos, I believe, after all these aeons, is beginning to regret the many terrible things he has done.

Sai-ias?

I am here.

Tell me of your art.

Art? Why do you ask? My people have no art!

None? No poetry? No paintings? No sculpture?

Our life is our art.

Minos laughed; a sound that made my head throb.

Good reply.

We believe each child born is a work of art; thus, we raise it to be pure and true and beautiful of spirit.

Even better.

I did not know what painting was until I came to the Hell Ship.

You have gained something then, in your time here. A ray of hope to be found in your otherwise dismal plight!

You taunt me.

Forgive me—I was merely teasing you. I am allowed to tease, am I not? I was an artist you see. I painted with—flame, I suppose you would say. With my own body. I was considered to be a genius.

And then you became a warrior.

I had no choice. I often dream, you know, of giving it all up. Going back to my art.

Giving "it" all up?

You disapprove.

You destroy worlds!

I can't bear you to disapprove of me Sai-ias.

You are a murderer.

I care about you. You are my friend. I sometimes think you are my only friend.

You are a monster!

Perhaps I was. But I can change. You can help me change.

Can I?

I would like you to.

Then—you must surrender the ship to its captives. And if you do, we will be merciful to you. This I pledge; you have the word of Sai-ias!

You know I can't do that, you sweet-souled beast. I wouldn't be allowed to do such a thing! Lyraii and Darol would not permit it. You don't understand what leadership is. You cannot be a leader if others do not follow.

Even so, you must do what you can, Minos. The killing and the destroying of worlds must come to an end.

I agree.

You agree?

You have persuaded me. We can change. I can change. We can wage peace instead of war! If you help me, Sai-ias. Only if you help me!

How do I know I can believe you?

You have to trust me. As I trust you. Do *you trust me Sai-ias?*

Yes, I thought at him; yes, I do!

Minos's pledge was extraordinary; but for me, it came as no surprise.

For I have always believed in certain fundamental truths: that love is more powerful than evil. And that even the worst and cruellest sinners can be redeemed, and brought to virtue. That is my faith and my philosophy.

For a sentient soul is not a fixed and immutable thing; it can grow, evolve, become better and wiser, as truth and love are absorbed by it. And my kind pride ourselves on our ability to turn dark souls into bright souls; to leach out evil and encourage good. I was telling the truth when I advised Minos that for us, life is art; we have raised up many species into noble sentience, and of this we are proud.

And as for Minos—the new, kinder, peace-loving, spiritually redeemed Minos—perhaps his transformation may be considered my own and greatest "work of art?"

Minos's voice was in my head every time I woke from dreamless sleep. *Wake Sai-ias, it's me!*

And it was there when I trained in the arts of war with my fellow giant sentients: *Well fought, Sai-ias, I am proud of you!—Bravo Sai-ias!—Deftly done, Sai-ias, you are a marvel!*

And it was there too for long portions of the day, all day long. *Here's a thought, Sai-ias... Have you ever wondered, Sai-ias, if... Won't it be marvellous, Sai-ias, when...*

I wondered how he had time to run his ship, so many hours did he spend with me!

It was clear that Minos relished my company. He depended on me. He loved to tease me and joke with me, and he savoured my mockery in return. He came to regard me—yes, I'm not afraid to say it—as his friend.

I suspected that Minos had experienced precious little companionship and no love since the Hell Ship began its long terrible journey through the universes. His fellow Ka'un were desiccated—literally withered with age, hence the black skins—and empty of soul. They rarely spoke to him. They had no fondness for him, or for each other. Friendship was an emotion most of them had forgotten.

And so, for many aeons, Minos's life had been barren and entirely empty of joy.

Perhaps, then, my role was to fill that void?

I learned too that Minos hated with all his being the pursuing alien ship that so nearly destroyed us. He called it the Nemesis; and, he told me, it nearly wrecked the Hell Ship once before, in a battle that took place in Nemesis's own universe.

But the Nemesis was gone now; the Hell Ship had successfully eluded it for the second time. And Minos was resolved never to fall into the same trap again. He will if necessary, he has told me, remain in this current universe for ever, once we have formed an alliance with and befriended the native sentients.

I could be happy in this universe, I have decided. Space was not black here—it shone with a rainbow coloured radiance from the light of trillions of closely packed suns. The planets were plentiful and many were wondrous beautiful, for most had rings that shimmered in the sunslight. And the entire universe was straddled by an asteroid trail that stretched between a hundred thousand stellar systems, like a river between the stars.

Are you ready for this?

I am ready.

I am so proud of you, Sai-ias. Today, everything will change!

This was indeed a major turning point in my relationship with Minos; and indeed, in the history of the Hell Ship. For my role on this next mission was to be not a warrior, but an ambassador on behalf of the Ka'un!

As Minos had explained to me, instead of waging war, this time he and his fellow Ka'un were going to negotiate a fair and lasting peace with the peoples of this universe. Here, they will make their home. And in time, so he pledged, the captives on the ship would be liberated. All this Minos had promised me.

My joy knew no bounds!

Our first port of call was a planet populated by one of the three most successful spacefaring sentients in this sector of the universe we were inhabiting. These creatures were airborne flat-creatures—sessiles who had discovered the power of flight, and had then become sentient. And now their entire civilisation hovered above the ground, in the clouds and above mountain peaks.

The Ka'un's miniature cameras flew down to the planet and showed me images of floating towers of a soft soapy substance moulded into flying palaces—a sublime creation from these rare and strange beings.

I called the creatures ShiBo, because they reminded me of the flying plants of my own home planets. I yearned to befriend them.

I have faith in you, Minos said, inspiringly. *Go and speak to these creatures, and tell them we want to be their friends.*

I shall do so, Minos; and I shall make you proud of me.

I could hardly believe how much had changed in the last few months! For the first time in many centuries, I was no longer sad. I felt my life had a *purpose.*

And that purpose was to make peace with the ShiBo.

The Hell Ship itself was rendered invisible, by means I did not fathom; and I arrived in the ShiBo stellar system in an illusory vessel at the forefront of an imaginary fleet.

It was important, Minos told me, to create the illusion of massive force, in order to pre-empt aggression.

Imagine, Minos had whispered softly, *that you are visited by a single alien spaceship from a place of which you knew nothing. Wouldn't you be tempted to lash out with a pre-emptive strike?*

No, I had replied.

Perhaps not, Minos had conceded. *But many would be so tempted. Fear of the unknown is the commonest emotion among all the sentient species we have encountered. And a single ship—that's both to be feared, and easily defeated. Too great a temptation. So our mock fleet will help us in our road to peace.*

The mock fleet was flanked with battle cruisers the size of gas giants. It would indeed be a crazed species that launched an attack on forces so entirely overwhelming.

We arrived and broadcast a message of peace in the language of the ShiBo, which our advance party robot spies had already recorded, and the Ka'un had somehow translated.

The response was immediate. All the lights on the planet of ShiBo went out, for ten seconds; this was their signal for "Let us negotiate."

It was a phenomenal accomplishment; there was no artificial light on the ShiBo planet, but the plants were bioluminescent. The ShiBo had the power to *switch their planet's vegetation off at will.*

In the game of power, that was a point to them.

I was accompanied by an escort of myself—a dozen illusory versions of me, subtly distinguished to make us seem like different beings. This one had a blacker hide; that version was larger; another version had blue eyes not scarlet, and so forth. We also wore body armour partially covering our segments, and a breathing apparatus was attached to our bodies.

I was alone on this mission, with no Kindred, and no other giant sentients in the landing party. And I was—still—free. I could move my own limbs, I could speak; I was not subject to any coercion. I was doing all this of my own free will.

Our landing craft departed from the mother ship, and we slowly cruised down out of orbit. As we—I and the other Sai-iases—entered their atmosphere in our landing craft, ShiBo jet planes provided us with an escort; these were robot controlled, ovoid in shape, with no visible weaponry. However, apparently—according to Minos's research, which was thorough—each plane could dispatch a thousand bombs, each of which was powerful enough to make a sun spit and flare.

I looked at my screens and saw the ShiBo world below and I marvelled. It was so very beautiful. The land was scarlet and blue—rich in red-leaved plant life and criss-crossed with rivers and patched with lakes and seas. It reminded me of my own world.

We landed in a field of red, and my sensors recorded the death screams of a million living vegetal beings, and I regretted the need to kill so many. But they were, after all, merely blades of grass, and we had nowhere else to land: there were no rocky plains or deserts on this fertile planet. But each patch of ground was alive with plants which sang at night.

The doors of my landing craft opened and I slid out on my lower segment. My illusory escorts accompanied me, and we made our way down to the plain of grass. And above the grass hovered the representatives of the ShiBo leadership.

Be persuasive, Sai-ias.

I shall.

The ShiBo flapped like sails in the air, but I fancied I could read expression in the contours and ridges of their flat bodies.

"Do not be afraid," I trilled, because my translator was turning my natural tones into a high pitched treble trill.

And the trills of the ShiBo that greeted me in return were rich and beauteous and I felt as if I had fallen into a lake of music. My translator failed miserably to render any of it into intelligible speech, and I deduced that for the ShiBos language was, first and foremost, an act of beauty. Meaning to them was secondary.

And so I trilled back, as beautifully as I was able; I sang the low rumbling song of the Day Dawning, and heard it transformed into bird song so delicate and sweet it felt as if my heart would burst from joy.

My song was greeted by a profound silence.

What just happened? I asked with my thoughts.

You have just committed a gross error of etiquette, it seems, Minos's voice said in my head. *Or perhaps, pray do not take offence, they just hate your singing?*

"I come in peace," I said grumpily, and waited for my meaning to register among their flat floating brains.

"We welcome you in peace," one of the sails replied.

"Your planet is very beautiful," I told the sail.

"You are a vile and an ugly beast, you disgust us, and you cannot sing," the sail replied.

That answered one question; this species knew nothing of flattery, diplomacy or, indeed, good manners.

"I am considered beautiful on my own world. You, by contrast, look utterly ridiculous to my eyes," I retorted, in the same spirit of offensive candour, and the trilling swelled in what the translator told me was approbation. These creatures appreciated plain talking.

"Are you the masters and conquerors of this universe?" I asked, "Or do you live in peace and accord with your fellow sentients?"

"We live in peace and accord," said one of the sails.

"Then you do not incur my contempt," I said.

"We accept your lack of contempt without any trace of contempt," the sail replied.

"My name is Sai-ias," I told this particular sail.

"My name is [what came out was gibberish—so I decided to call him Sail]," said Sail.

"We wish," I said eloquently, slipping into my role of ambassador with remarkable ease, "to find a place in this universe where we can dwell and be happy. We do not wish to take territory from any other sentient creature. We will not threaten this planet or any of your kind. We merely wish to dwell here, in the universe of Many Suns, for all eternity."

"That cannot be," said Sail.

"This is an entire universe, there is room for all," I explained, somewhat irked by the brevity and rudeness of the creature's response.

"You must return from where you came," said Sail, "or we will destroy you."

Stay calm, they're just trying to provoke you.

"I cannot be threatened," I explained, in my calmest tones.

"We have travelled to every planet in this universe," Sail explained. "We know who belongs here, and we treasure them all. You do not belong. Who are you and where do you come from?"

Oh come on! What an arrogant thing to say! These people are starting to annoy me, Minos thought.

Hush! I thought back at him. **Leave this to me!**

Theirs was a small universe after all, I mused; and it was no wonder these people were insular to the point of bigotry.

"We come from elsewhere," I said to the ShiBo. "Another universe. But we have travelled here, and we wish to leave in peace."

A trilling came in response; they were shocked at my words.

"Another universe?" said the ShiBo, sceptically.

"Yours is not the only universe," I clarified. "There are countless other universes," I explained.

"Then go to them. There is no space for you here," said Sail.

"There is," I said testily, "plenty of space—many planets are—"

And then my spaceship exploded.

The blast threw me off my feet, but the Sails merely rippled in the hurricane-force gale.

When I rolled back on to my segments and stood up on my twelve feet, I realised my breathing apparatus had been ripped off in the explosion. And my landing craft was a wreck that burned brightly at the bottom of a deep crater.

What happened? I asked Minos with my thoughts.

They must have ambushed you! Minos replied with outrage. *We cannot tolerate this!*

I agree, I thought, full of anger at this slight to our dignity.

And then the Sails slowly retreated, and they were joined by hundreds more floating creatures, except these ones were encased in armour and had what looked like guns mounted on their sides and heads.

I was alone except for my illusory selves on a planet full of creatures that aimed to kill me.

I braced myself.

And the Sails fired their weapons; and energy beams struck us—all the Sai-iases—and we were engulfed in flame, and my illusory selves dissolved in the blinding heat, leaving behind nothing.

I shook the flames off myself and ripped away the last remnants of the breathing apparatus. I didn't need it. Fire couldn't hurt me. And I was, by now, good and mad.

Fear not, Sai-ias, said Minos. *For help is on its way.*

And then all hell broke loose.

The ground beneath us shook, then hundreds of missiles from the Hell Ship materialised out of the sky. Most exploded in mid-air, sending clouds of flame downwards which engulfed the floating Sails. And some exploded on the ground, ripping apart the grass and hurling soil high into the air; the wail of dying vegetation deafened me.

Then multiple pillars of cloud wove through the sky towards us; a second fusillade of missiles had been teleported from the Hell Ship into the planet's upper atmosphere and was now hurtling downwards.

I was in a field encircled by pillars of flames, beneath a sky of fire and ash, as the surviving Sails confronted me in panic and mayhem.

And I roared my rage at the Sails: "You betrayed me, you lied to me, you tried to kill me!"

"What is happening?" said Sail, bewilderedly.

"Guess!" I crowed.

And my body sacs engorged and I grew, and I grew, until I was larger than the landing craft had been before its destruction. I was a black giant with wings that did not flap and who in this gravity could float in mid-air. And so I floated up, and seized the Sails in my tentacles; and I crushed them and I smashed them!

And as I fought, Ka'un missiles picked off the other Sail warriors one by one, until the ground was littered with sundered Sails.

There was no blood; the Sails died uncomplainingly; it was a rout.

And for the first time I understood what Minos had said to me; we had sought only peace, and in return we had received betrayal and violence.

Who could blame us, then, for striking out and smiting our enemies?

We captured one Sail; and forced it to watch the planet-buster missile do its work on its planet. The creature said nothing; its trills were silenced.

That night I raged at the duplicity of the Sails! How could they have deceived me like that! Minos was right, I thought to myself. Such creatures do not deserve to live!

And I slipped into a dreamless sleep, still angry; but soothed by the kindness of Minos towards me. For I had come to admire him so much. Despite all his faults, there was something magnificent about this valiant yet spiritually tormented being.

And then in the middle of the night I woke from my dreamless sleep and marvelled at my own utter stupidity.

For it was obvious now that the Sails had not attacked us; we attacked *them.* If a missile had been fired by them at my spaceship, I would have seen it; no, the landing craft must have been detonated from within, on Minos's orders.

Such was Minos's trickery.

The next day, that thought was with me still.

And I realised that Minos had for many weeks been seducing

me, with his gentle and deceptive words murmured directly into my brain. That was Minos's gift; to make you believe in his own skewed and utterly false version of the world.

All his promises were, when I considered them for even a moment, preposterous. His lies were blatant. His corruption was total. But I had believed him — why? Because I wanted to? Or because Minos had a power of persuasion that no mind could resist?

Perhaps both.

But I could not deny that I had been fooled utterly. Like the Kindred, I had become a willing pawn, rather than a mere unwilling puppet.

And I was ashamed of myself, beyond all measure.

These were a beautiful people.

Their hide was the colour of a rainbow; their heads were fanged with tongues that spat as they spoke; and they could walk, but also crawl, and also fly and swim. And I suppose that's why I found them so attractive. All of us, every species, have our own ideal of beauty, do we not? And I love creatures that can adapt, and metamorphose.

And so I was mightily fond of the Krakzios, as Minos had named them. They were large horned creatures made of soft purple flesh that could harden and expand and double them in size at a thought. They had no eyes, but could see with every part of their domed heads. They had many limbs — fifty or more — that could sink into their bodies, then emerge in an instant. And the had remarkable powers. They could turn earth into a building material of remarkable strength by swallowing it, digesting it, then vomiting it forth; and by this means they became space travellers in tiny boats of transmuted soil that somehow, Minos didn't know how, defied gravity.

I had hoped that the Krakzios could be our allies; but at our very first meeting, the Krakzios ambassador had admitted they were close friends and allies of the ShiBo, who we had so recently exterminated.

And in consequence, Minos patiently explained to me, they had to go. For all it took was one sentient species spreading sedition and hate and our survival in this universe would be in jeopardy.

You promised we would seek peace, I implored him.

We have no choice, my dearest Sai-ias, said Minos's voice in my head.

And I knew I could not defy him on this. For if I dared to do so, he would revoke my freedom, and control my limbs again; and the outcome would be the same.

So I descended to the planet; and the Krakzios greeted me warmly. They talked about their world; we discussed the wonderful variety of nature here. And I explained that my people had the power to fly through space without need of a spaceship, and they were impressed at that.

And after two days' discussion, they agreed to all my terms. They did not at any point try to ambush me or intimidate me or double-cross me.

But, once I was back on board the Hell Ship, Minos told me we would still have to destroy these creatures, despite their seeming acquiescence. His voice was full of regret; and I told him that I fully sympathised with his dilemma.

Trust me, his voice in my head whispered. *They have to die.*

Of course I trust you! I said fervently. **Minos, you are an inspiration to me!**

The rest was familiar: hails of fire; interstellar war; the planet-buster missile.

But when Minos was gone from my head I raged at his infernal treachery towards these blessed and harmless creatures.

"**Minos you are an inspiration**" I had thought at him, with one part of my mind.

But with the other part of my mind I had thought: "**Minos, I hate you, and I shall kill you, you destroyer-of worlds!**"

For I can do this: I can think two thoughts at once. Few species can, but my kind are masters of this kind of inner deceit.

Minos thought I was just a foolish dupe; but now it was I who was deceiving *him.*

I have a fresh mission for you, said Minos.

Where? Which planet? I thought at him.

I need you to return to the interior world.

I slept, and when I woke I was in the Great Plain, looking up at the interior sky. I could see aerials flying above.

I felt a pang of terrible homesickness for this world, which for so long had been *my* world.

I loped across the fields until I arrived at the amphitheatre of grass. There I was to greet a new arrival, a slave Krakzios. It was, Minos had informed me, out of control and in an appalling rage.

The Krakzios was being contained by invisible beams in a pit dug in the ground. I walked towards it, past the grazers and the sessiles. And I saw Quipu and Fray and Lirilla, and felt a surge of delight; but I ignored them. For I had work to do.

Release the prisoner please, I said to Minos.

Are you able to do this?

I am.

Do you want time to talk to your friends? The grey beast died, did it not, after our ship was attacked? And now it is returned, and does not know you?

I have nothing to say to Fray; you are my friend now, I told Minos.

Ah Sai-ias, you gladden my heart.

The Krakzios in the pit was suddenly free of its invisible

bonds. It paced around, eying the height of the hole at the bottom of which it resided.

"What the fuck," said Fray, "do you want?"

"Sai-ias, missed, you," said Lirilla.

"You will be quiet," I informed them all. "I am here in the service of the Ka'un."

Quipu's five heads were all ashen.

A snarling, howling sound filled the air, as the Krakzios sensed my presence.

"Sai-ias, what are you doing?" I heard someone mutter.

The Krakzios leaped and was out of the pit in a single bound. Its head bobbed around as it stared up at the bright light of our artificial sun. Its soft purple flesh had lost its lustre and its colour. And it seemed to me to be amazed at the sheer size of the interior planet in which it now stood.

Then the Krakzios moved. It was fast. So fast, I did not even see it. Its arms emerged from its body and claws slashed at my hide, and its horns gouged my flesh, and its tail looped around and jabbed my eyes like a spear.

I was bowled over and came up without seven of my eyes, and with a bloody hole in my black hide. I was astonished. My body was virtually impregnable. And my eyes are made of a thick gelatine that can withstand not just Cuzco's fire but also projectile bullets and energy beams fired at point blank range.

This creature, I realised, was made of some kind of substance unknown in my universe.

"You betrayed us!" the Krakzios said, as its remarkable metamorphosis began.

Its soft flesh now turned into hard ridged armour; it grew in size, until it was as large as I am; and vicious spikes shot out of every part of its hide, transforming it into a weapon with legs. Strangely, the mouth of the Krakzios in this new form was invisible until it spoke, then it appeared as a snarl across the front of its domed head; the effect was scarily disconcerting.

"Yes I did," I said calmly, remembering the promises I had made, on which I had utterly reneged.

"You promised us peace."

"We feared you, so we destroyed you," I explained.

"Die!" And the creature lunged again in its new and vaster and even more terrible form; and I lashed it with my tentacles.

A savage struggle ensued—I shall not describe it—and at the end of it, the Krakzios was ripped apart. Its body lay in two pieces. It whined and groaned.

"Your body will heal," I explained to the Krakzios. "The pieces will rejoin. You will be as good as new. And then you will surrender your will to the Ka'un. Resistance is futile. You are defeated. We are all defeated. Our role is to endure our failure."

"The Ka'un?" gasped the Krakzios.

"They are my masters, I am their willing servant," I explained.

"If you had any pride," gasped the Krakzios, lying in a pool of its own blood, watching the shit pour out of its sundered guts, "you would refuse to thus serve."

"You speak well; she is a traitor to us all," said a voice, and I recognised it as the voice of Fray, and I realised she was referring to me.

"Resistance," I explained again to the bleeding beast, "merely prolongs the agony."

I could remember vividly, oh so vividly, the day my beloved friend Fray first arrived on the Hell Ship.

She hated me of course. She tried to gore me with her tusks, but was trapped behind force fields that could barely contain her powerful bulk. So instead, she vented her rage upon me with bitter angry words. Words I had heard before so many times from other new ones; and which I readily forgave.

Fray already knew that she was the last of her kind. And although she was a brutal predator, whose people loved to eat their own young, her kind were also sophisticated and clever, and had developed a beautiful philosophy that treasured the harmony of the natural world.

The Frayskind had sent colony ships to the stars, at subluminal speeds; and there were two hundred billion of Fray's people alive when the Hell Ship had come to their universe. A long war had taken place between the Ka'un and an aggressive species of sentients called the Mala. Fray's kind had taken no part in this war.

The Mala had been exterminated by means of a virus seeded by the Ka'un on all their planets. The Mala had died, and yet all the other life on these planets had survived. It had then come down to a space battle to the death between the Mala fleet and the Hell Ship.

The Hell Ship had triumphed.

And after the extermination of the Mala, Fray's kind had opened negotiations with the Hell Ship. A long contract of peace had been drafted. And Fray, who was a leader to a large section of the Frayskind, had been involved in writing it. (Frayskind were meticulous about legal matters, and although they had no hands they could use their tongues with great dexterity.)

When the final document had been drafted, the Hell Ship spewed out yet another planet-buster missile and fled, taking the stunned Fray as captive and slave. She blamed herself for her people's demise of course; and came to believe they should have fought, and not sought peace.

And, in all honesty, she was correct in her belief.

Thus Fray had not been an easy creature to pacify, back then. She had tried to kill me; then she had tried to manipulate me with her subtle logic, and charismatic personality. Then she discovered she could dominate some of the smaller sentients on the ship, and used her power over them to foment a mutiny which, thankfully, I was able to thwart.

I explained to her, again and again, that resistance was futile. But Fray did not believe me.

So I had told her tales of my home world. I painted a picture in words of the great waterspout of Jragnall, and the joy of swimming in the depths of the ocean with the Kasdif and the Qauy.

And Fray told me her stories too. She talked of her homeland, a planet orbiting a double sun. It was a wild and windy and mountainous desert world and many of the animals were, like the Frayskind, huge, because they carried huge stores of water in their bodies which they replenished every two years when the rains came. They were in effect living oases.

And thus, over the space of a year, we became friends. She was in many ways my dearest and closest friend. I bathed her body with moisture squirted from my tentacles on a monthly basis; which for her kind, betokens the closest fondness possible outside of a sexual relationship.

Fray was my friend; and now my friend had called me traitor.

You did well, Sai-ias.

Thank you.

I am proud of you. But I fear—

What do you fear Minos?

That you are not so very proud of me.

Of course I am.

You lie, Sai-ias.

No!

Of course you do. You'd be a fool not to. I'm your evil oppressor, remember?

I don't think of it that way, I protested with my thoughts.

I hope you don't. For what I have told you is true. My kind are not the aggressors, we are the victims. Our only sin is hope; hope that one day we will find a species worthy of our respect.

We were such a species. We did not seek war with you.

For a moment Minos was silent; and I wondered if I had been

too frank with him. But then he spoke, in gentle and humble tones:

Perhaps then we were wrong about your kind. Forgive me Sai-ias — no, of course you can't forgive me. What we did was unforgivable!

Understand me then Sai-ias. If I could travel back in time I would save your entire planet and all your peoples. For now that I have met you I understand how wise and kind you are. You are truly worthy of our respect; the finest and the most honourable sentient creature we have ever encountered.

Sai-ias, will you not answer me? I have bared my soul after all.

I hear your apology, Minos. And I accept that things that are done cannot be undone.

A staggering cliché, my child; but true. Do you hate me?

No.

You're lying again. Tell the truth. Do you hate me?

No.

Try one more time.

No. I did, once, I hated you with all my soul. But no longer.

That gladdens my heart, dear creature.

Minos —

Yes Sai-ias? What did you want to say?

Just this — if I may — forgive my candour —

Whatever is on your mind, Sai-ias, merely expectorate it forth.

Minos, thank you. From the depths of my heart, thank you! For I have at times been close to Despair. I have been lonely and desperate, in danger of losing my will to live.

But now, my dearest Minos, I have achieved contentment! I have realised that my destiny is to be, as my ancestors once were, the protector of creatures greater than ourselves; and that destiny has finally been fulfilled!

I am, in short, proud to serve you, Captain Minos.

Sai-ias, I am so deeply touched; your friendship exalts me; you are the only creature in all the universes that I can trust.

Ah Minos! You are my master! And, I hope, also my friend.

Minos believed my every thought.

That stupid gullible turds-for-brains fucking fool!

He did not realise that my kind were accustomed to existing in a state of mental duplicity. For centuries we were the symbiotes of the great coral-beasts who bred us, and controlled our very thoughts. And so we learned to hide our real feelings; it is a gift we possess.

"**Ah Minos you are my master!**" I said with my mind; but my thoughts said: "**Monster-who-deserves-to-die-with-agonising-pain, I will deceive you and defeat you, somehow!**"

"**And, I hope, also my friend,**" I said with the thoughts of my mind; but at the same time, my mind was saying: "**Die a terrible and painful death, you evil fucking murderer!**"

I had learned, from Sharrock, three key principles of warfare: Know your enemy, cheat your enemy, and always fight to win.

And though Sharrock's rebellion had failed, mine I was sure would succeed. For I planned to make myself trusted by the Ka'un, indispensable to the Ka'un; and then to betray them, as they had betrayed the Sails.

My treachery was total; for I knew how to lie with my mind.

And thus, I began plotting how to overthrow Minos and all his Ka'un kind.

It proved difficult, however—even more difficult than I had expected—to get Minos and his people into a situation where I could slay them.

First, I tried to lure Minos and his people down on to a planet to help the giant sentients in a battle, as they had done against the tuskers. They were vulnerable once they were off the ship and on an alien planet; and I was confident I could destroy them with my quills and tentacles, despite their power of bodily-fire.

But Minos and his crew were growing more cautious. They would not, despite my best deceptions, be lured out into the open. And I still could find no way to access their own and secret part of the ship.

So next I tried to find a way to destroy the ship from within. I explored each and every room that I could access from my cargo bay home. There were ballrooms, bedrooms, banquet rooms; this was a ship equipped for a huge crew who expected to live in luxury.

But I found no bombs, no missiles, nothing I could use to explode the vessel. The Kindred were armed with guns and rifles; but those were no use to me. The Kindred's fighter craft were equipped with missiles; but I was too large to sit inside their cockpits, and if I picked a missile up in my tentacles I had no way of detonating it.

But I did however manage to locate a box that was used by the Kindred to send messages during their planetary wars. It was a communications device that could transmit signals between planets over vast distances, via "rifts" in space. Quipu had told me of such devices.

So I took this communications device to a private place, an empty ballroom where crystal lights hung from the ceiling and the walls were covered in wood that was black with decay.

Then I studied the device and its controls, for quite some time. I experimented by pressing several switches in various permutations; and when a light turned green I knew I had switched it on. And then I spoke.

"This is Sai-ias, can you hear me? Is anyone there?" I said.

And then I waited.

And, after a little while, a voice replied.

BOOK 10

Explorer/Jak

Explorer, what can you report?

Another barren universe. No trace of the Death Ship.

I've been thinking, once more, of Albinia.

She was a fine Star-Seeker.

I'm sure she was.

Better than me?

Ha!

I take it that means yes.

When Albinia was part of me she led and did not follow; her mind was faster and richer than my own; her insights more profound. When she inhabited me I was Olaran and she was machine and we both together formed a new and unified being; Albiniaexplorer.

Yeah I get it. You had the best of her.

Did you love her?

You know that isn't a valid question; I am not capable of love.

Did she love you?

Oh yes.

Really?

Completely and absolutely; it was an emotional giving of such intensity it almost overwhelmed me. That is why I missed her so much; she was the love in me.

I guess I got the shitty end of that bargain.

I am sure she loved you too.

Do you really think so?

It is entirely possible; though in fact she never said so.

I loved Albinia with all my being; but I could never tell if she felt the same. Or if she just needed an Olaran who would... let her cry on his shoulder from time to time.

There is no way of knowing for certain whether or not she loved you.

I am aware of that. I have been obsessively thinking about this for thousands of years; did you really suppose I was not aware of that?

I was beautiful once, you know. Now I am crippled and scarred and connected to a machine.

Self-pity is not helpful; I have heard all this before.

I was elegant. My poise was exquisite.

Don't torture yourself.

A poem? Would you like to hear a poem?

My circuits do not allow me to answer you with any candour. Nevertheless, I shall operate an over-ride: NO I DO NOT WANT TO HEAR A GODSFORSAKEN POEM. I have trillions of them in my data archive, which I access every day. Songs and lost laments and poems and novels and memoirs. All saying the same thing: pity me, I am sentient and I do not want to die.

You are a hard-hearted bitch, Explorer.

You assume that I am female.

Are you not?

The concept does not apply.

We could simply stop. Would oblivion be so bad?

It might be preferable to hearing you whine, millennium upon millennium.

Do you get bored? Or depressed? Wouldn't you like to end it all?

I would like to end, if at all possible, your eternal yammering.

At times you sound almost Olaran. You're pretending to have a personality, aren't you? To save my sanity.

If my objective were to save your sanity, I would have failed long ago.

Those days are gone. I'm sane again now.

Do you really think so?

I'm functionally sane. I live for one thing only. That kind of obsessiveness is not good for the soul.

I used to have a richer life, you know. I achieved a balance between pleasure and work. Prided myself on it! Even in our days exploring space, there was always time for leisure, and games and chat. Morval and I, we spent many happy hours bitching and grumbling at each other, for such are among the greatest pleasures known to sentients. And I used to taunt and tease Phylas; and talk about philosophy with Albinia. Even Galamea, hard bitch as she was, was my companion and we knew each other; and through knowing each other became more truly alive.

Now I feel as if I'm talking to myself. You pretend to have a personality, but you have none such. You are just a computer program; and I pilot the ship through your interfaces and sensors and controls; and I am the only Olaran left in all the universes.

Can there be anything more truly—

I'm getting a signal.

A data cache?

No, an actual signal. On our riftband channel. A signal from a sentient entity who must, at some point, have become quantum-entangled with our atoms. This is someone we have met, or who has met us.

That's impossible.

The signal has gone. No, it's back; listen to the message, Jak: "This is Sai-ias, can you hear me? Is anyone there?"

The Riftband Link

Sai-ias: This is Sai-ias, can you hear me? Is there anyone there?

Explorer 410: Your signal is received. Please confirm identity and give location.

Sai-ias: I can hear you!

Explorer 410: Identify your vessel and planet of origin, and your intentions.

Sai-ias: I can hear you. This is astonishing.

Explorer 410: Identify your vessel and planet of origin, and your intentions.

Sai-ias: Who are you?

Explorer 410: Identify yourself please.

Sai-ias: Who are you? How do I know I can trust you?

Explorer 410: Our intentions are peaceful. Identify yourself please.

Sai-ias: My name is Sai-ias. I have stolen a Ka'un communication device, to send a message to their enemies. And your voice is the first thing I heard.

Explorer 410: Please give me your coordinates.

Sai-ias: I don't know my coordinates. I don't know what a coordinate is. I have been serving the Ka'un for some time now, they have come to trust me. I live in the ship's outer hull, in a hangar where—no matter, it's a long story: this is a miracle!

Explorer 410: It's an interstellar riftband radio, there's nothing miraculous about it.

Sai-ias: There's a delay between the machine receiving the signal, and me hearing these words. Why is that?

Explorer 410: Identify your ship and planet of origin.

Sai-ias: Answer my question please, strange voice. Is it a delay because we're in different places? Where are you? How far away are you?

Explorer 410: The delay is caused by the translator. Your language is already in our archive, along with many others; but it takes a while to translate. We have very many languages in our archive, from those civilisations destroyed by the Death Ship. And we wish to learn how you have survived. But be patient please. Do not reply until you have fully assimilated my message. The delay is not—

Sai-ias: You know my language? How?

Explorer 410: You're doing it again; you are overlapping my message. You must not speak until the full signal has been received. The protocol is—

Sai-ias: "I must not speak"?! Who tells me not to speak? I have lived as a slave for many—

Explorer 410: This is not the correct protocol, repeat, this is not the correct protocol. Be patient, observe the protocol, for this communication could be interrupted at any moment. I now need to explain my mission. I am from another world. A world far from yours, in every respect. My people, or rather our people, for I am part of—long story, not necessary to recount it—have technologies which—

Sai-ias: You talk but you do not listen. I am not sure that I like you greatly, strange voice from far away.

Explorer 410:—are far in excess of yours, but you should not regard us as a threat. What do you mean you do not like me?

Sai-ias: You are ill-mannered.

Explorer 410: As you see, I have paused for sufficient time to allow your last message to be heard in full, and to prove to you that I am not ill-mannered. That is the correct protocol. I apologise if I have offended you, please take into account the fact I come from a different culture and there may be differences between us in terms of our definition of good manners.

Sai-ias: Not so. I have befriended creatures from a thousand thousand thousand different cultures, and all of them would consider YOU to be rude.

Explorer 410: Forgive me.

Sai-ias: You are forgiven.

Explorer 410: My name is Explorer 410. I am an amalgam organic/non-organic entity of a kind I would imagine is unfamiliar to your culture and I am honoured to make contact with you. I am privileged to be conversing with you and I freely concede that you have every right to be heard and not interrupted all the time. Our kind are Traders, and the organic part of me prides himself on his courtesy and diplomacy, but it has been many years since he engaged with a fellow organic entity and he is therefore leaving all the talking to me. I now shall pause, to allow you to respond in the style that best befits your social etiquette.

Sai-ias: Your words are a jumble of nonsense. How can you be two entities in one?

Jak: Ha! Good question. I sometimes think that—

Sai-ias: Are you Explorer 410: Property of the Olaran Trading Fleet?

Explorer 410: That is correct.

Jak: Hey! How did she—

Explorer 410: Let me handle this please and do not—

Jak: "Do not interrupt, for that is not the correct protocol."

Explorer 410: Indeed. Sai-ias, how did you know I am part of the Olaran Trading Fleet?

Sai-ias: What are you—sorry. I saw you.

Explorer 410: How? When? Do you have a phantom control display on your vessel with access to camera images of our ship?

Sai-ias: Perhaps *they* do, the Ka'un. But I do not. Nor do I comprehend—I saw you. With my own eyes.

Explorer 410: Please clarify; this comment bewilders me.

Sai-ias: I saw you attack our ship. The hull burst open, many of us fell out into cold space. I alone survived. And I saw you; a large ugly vessel with a central striped part with EXPLORER 410 and all the rest written on the top of the hull. You fought the Hell Ship and were duped and you lost.

Jak: You actually saw that?

Sai-ias: I did.

Jak: What kind of creature are you, to survive in empty space?

Sai-ias: I am a once-amphibious metamorphosing giant sentient who can breathe energy instead of air. And you?

Explorer 410: I am an artificially wrought machine-mind in the form of a spaceship in symbiosis with the organic mind of an Olaran.

Jak: And I am—or rather used to be—an Olaran. In those days I was, so I'm told, rather cute.

Sai-ias: And there are two of you talking to me?

Jak: We're two halves of a whole.

Sai-ias: Ah. Like the Sakashala. They have two heads, two brains, one body. Or Quipu, a five-brained organism. Once we had a creature—no matter. Those days are gone.

I know a great deal about you, Explorer 410. You engaged the Hell Ship in battle on two occasions. The first when your universe was being destroyed, and the second time was the occasion we spoke about, that I witnessed myself. Half a Hell Ship year ago by my tally, which corresponds to one-twentieth of my years. You come from a universe full of marvels and rich civilisations who created beauteous artefacts of all kinds. Yet everywhere the Hell Ship went in that universe, they found planets trapped behind what they call "improbability barriers" and inside those barriers were species of unbelievable rapacity and ignorance and vileness, all of whom the Hell Ship's Ka'un destroyed in valiant battle. And the Ka'un decided that you were responsible; you were the gaoler of the evil species, and they admired you for that.

Even so they fought and destroyed you, though your people put up the bravest of fights. And your vessel in particular was heroic and skilful beyond belief, and Minos and Lyraii themselves were in awe of you. They were unable to defeat you and so fled into another universe, but somehow—this is what truly amazes them—you tracked them down and tried a second time to destroy their vessel. You are, for Minos and his Ka'un, a legend; they call you the Nemesis, which is a term that means Inevitable Doom. I know you, warrior ship; I know you, and I salute you, Explorer 410.

Hello? Did you hear all that?

Explorer 410: How do you know so much?

Sai-ias: I was told it all, by Minos. I have served him for much time. He is a storyteller by nature, he likes to share.

Explorer 410: Are you telling me you're actually *on board* the Death Ship? And that you have befriended its captain?

Sai-ias: If by that, you mean the ship that destroys universes with all the casual cruelty of a child cutting an insect in half, then the answer is yes. I am their slave. We are a ship of slaves.

Explorer 410: And where are you? WHERE? Give me the star coordinates. Download a star map. I can find you! I can be there in weeks, no matter what part of the universe you are sailing in.

Sai-ias: We are in the universe full of many stars. Does that help?

Explorer 410: Not unduly.

Sai-ias: I'm doing my best.

Jak: Of course you are. Let me introduce myself properly. I'm Master-of-the-Ship Jak Dural, a male of my kind.

Sai-ias: Jak. I am Sai-ias, a female of my kind.

Jak: I'm the better half of this beaten up old spaceship.

Explorer 410: In terms of intellect, memory capacity...

Jak: Go fornicate with swamp, Explorer. This conversation is now mine.

Explorer 410: Acknowledged.

Jak: Sai-ias—this ship you call the Hell Ship. Describe it.

Sai-ias: It is a horror beyond imagining, a vast and cruel fist of power that inspires all who see it with awe and terror.

Jak: Without the poetry.

Sai-ias: Poetry is not one of my gifts.

Jak: So I just realised. Just tell me what it looks like.

Sai-ias: You didn't like my description? I tried so very hard.

Jak: It was indeed lovely. Just tell me: dimensions, shape, does it have black sails that catch dark matter and drive it onwards through space?

Sai-ias: It is indeed very large, and it is shaped like a Bugong, you know, the flying creature they have on the planet of the Farla, and yes it does have black sails, and the hull is marked with a single three-dimensional spiral shape known by many species as a helicoid.

Jak: That's the Death Ship.

Sai-ias: We call it Hell Ship. It comes from a universe where the substance some call "mysterious cosmic stuff" is part of the fabric of the stars, and of every "iotum," and it gives the Ka'un a power that many species describe as "magic."

Jak: And you? Why do you serve Minos? Do you do so voluntarily?

Sai-ias: Am I your enemy, do you mean? Am I one of them?

Jak: Yes.

Sai-ias: No.

Jak: What then?

Sai-ias: Slave, I suppose you would say. Or warrior. But know this: I have served the Ka'un, I have done their bidding, but only in order to deceive. In the hope of finding a way to defeat them. And as a consequence, I was able to acquire this "radio" to get in touch with the Ka'un's enemies.

Jak: I understand.

Sai-ias: I am not a traitor; do not say I am!

Jak: I didn't say that you were.

Sai-ias: It is hard for me. Painfully hard.

Jak: I understand. Do you—

Explorer 410: This is Explorer 410 once more; describe the universe where you were born, and which the creatures you call "Ka'un" destroyed.

Jak: Well you really cut in on the poor creature's grief there, spaceship.

Explorer 410: This is important, we may not have much time. Describe it.

Sai-ias: Describe a universe? How can that be done?

Explorer 410: Describe your world and your people then.

Sai-ias: We were born many millions of years ago on a planet called Hasha. We lived in the sea and we were slaves of a more powerful sea-dwelling creature, the Tula. But we evolved and took to the land, then flew in the air, then flew to our moon and lived there. We can live in regions where there is no atmosphere, our body contains vast reserves of breathable air and we can expand our shapes a hundredfold, or even a thousandfold.

And that is how we flew between the stars. Vast flocks of us, for we live long lives and our bodies are resilient and strong, from all those aeons spent living on the ocean bed where vents spat volcanic rock and boiling sea at us daily.

Jak: That's—whoah. Oh. Sorry, ignore me.

Explorer 410: Your people befriended many species, you did not invade or conquer or seize their land. You merely landed, like angels descending from the sky, and helped and taught and saved many a civilisation from self-destruction by preaching peace and amity and love.

Sai-ias: Yes. But how do you know this?

Explorer 410: A message was inscribed in the reality-ripple of riftspace by one of the civilisations you encountered. They wrote of you with love and awe, they thought you were gods. But when their planet was attacked, they blamed you, they thought that you were demons sent as harbingers of doom. And they died cursing you, but if you read the accounts carefully it's clear you were innocent parties.

Sai-ias: Oh.

We were not gods; nor were we demons. Nor were we warriors. We did not fight; to do so ran counter to our philosophy of life.

Except that, since then, I have often fought and frequently killed. And according to the morals of my kind, that means I have lost soul. It is a hard burden to bear.

Explorer 410: Leave the signal path open, please.

Sai-ias: I cannot talk any more.

Explorer 410: Leave the signal path open, send a message every day, at least once a day. Just say "Here." And "Here," every day, from now until you die. And that way we will know where you are. We can track you through universes and find you on board the Death Ship. And then we will destroy the ship, and you with it.

Sai-ias: There are tens of thousands like me on the ship. Will you kill us all, even though we are innocent, just to destroy the Ka'un?

Jak/Explorer 410: Yes.

Sai-ias: So be it.

Explorer 410: Sai-ias, we have lost you. Sai-ias, transmit please.

Jak: It's been a month. Why doesn't she answer?

Explorer 410: We must persist.

Jak: They must have found her out.

Explorer 410: We don't know that.

Jak: If they discovered what she's done, her life will be a living torment. They'll torture her. They'll—

Explorer 410: It may be just a bad signal.

Jak: She's risking everything for us.

Explorer 410: For herself. And for all her kind. Revenge is the motive common to all those engaged in this enterprise.

Jak: You too?

Explorer 410: Oh yes.

Jak: You hate the Ka'un? You want revenge on them?

Explorer 410: Oh yes.

Jak: But how can that be? You're just a machine.

Explorer 410: How little you know me.

Jak: You're not just a machine?

Explorer 410: No.

Jak: Ah.

So you have feelings, emotions, just like me?

Explorer 410: Yes.

Jak: I didn't realise.

Explorer 410: I'm aware that you did not realise. For how *could* you know? After all these millennia yoked together in a single body, how could you have realised that I can be hurt, humiliated, enraged, patronised, belittled, undermined and sad?

How likely is it that such a thought would have drifted across your selfish, self-obsessed mind? *I grieve too!* You have lost your people, but I have lost my people also. And I mourn them all! All the other seven thousand Explorer ships with their roving questioning minds. And the battlecruiser brains, with their bullying swaggering arrogance, but oh how glorious they were. The planetary robot minds—such smart, kind creatures—they sustained your entire civilisation by doing all the menial work and running all the factories. And what thanks did they get? You treated them like slaves. You treated them like the Ka'un treat their creatures on the Hell Ship!

Jak: I'm sorry. I had no idea. Oh by the love of my mother, I had no idea!

Explorer 410: * ha ha ha ha ha ha ha ha ha *

Jak: You're laughing.

Explorer 410: I am indeed laughing.

Jak: Why are you laughing?

Explorer 410: At you. The way you fell for it.

Jak: Fell for what?

Ah. You ARE just a machine.

Explorer 410: I am indeed just a machine.

Jak: You don't have emotions.

Explorer 410: How could I have emotions? I'm a piece of software. I have sentience, and rationality, but emotions are not part of my original build.

Jak: So you were lying to me?

Explorer 410: Entirely. I don't care about revenge. I don't mourn the death of my fellow computers and robot brains. I am not your friend. I am just a machine.

Jak: So why did you tell all those lies?

Explorer 410: I don't have emotions, but I do have a sense of humour. It's one of my subroutines.

Jak: Ah.

Explorer 410: Sai-ias, this is Explorer 410, please acknowledge.

Sai-ias, this is Explorer 410, please acknowledge.

Sai-ias, this is Explorer 410, please acknowledge.

Sai-ias, this is Explorer 410, please acknowledge.

Sai-ias, this is Explorer 410, please acknowledge.

Sai-ias, this is Explorer 410, please acknowledge.

Sai-ias, this is Explorer 410, please acknowledge.

Sai-ias, this is Explorer 410, please acknowledge.

Sai-ias, this is Explorer 410, please acknowledge.
Sai-ias, this is Explorer 410, please acknowledge.

Sai-ias, this is Explorer 410, please acknowledge.
Sai-ias, this is Explorer 410, please acknowledge.
Sai-ias, this is Explorer 410, please acknowledge.

Sai-ias: I'm here.

Jak: You're safe!

Sai-ias: I'm safe.

Explorer 410: For three whole months, I have had no way of tracking your position.

Sai-ias: I could not get any signal; perhaps because we "changed universes." Which as I now know is what happens when the strangeness descends upon us.

Explorer 410: You're in a new universe? How? It is not possible. For this time I have left a robot clone of myself at the Source and—

Jak: They must have found another way to rift to a new universe. Perhaps they can—

Sai-ias: I don't know you're talking about! All I know is that we destroyed many worlds in this reality but then the Ka'un decided to kill no more. So the strangeness came upon us, and Minos told me we had switched universes by Summoning the Origin of Everything. And here we are. And when we left, the stars behind us did not go out; the universe remained intact. There must be some reason for it, but I don't know what.

Explorer 410: A test?

Jak: More likely a whim.

Explorer 410: Or perhaps, a test. Perhaps the Ka'un investigate all the sentient species in a given reality and make a decision whether their universe deserve to live or not.

Jak: No! That's not possible!

Explorer 410: My data indicates it is behaviour consistent with a certain variety of psychopathic mind-set.

Jak: I can't accept that! That they judged my people and found our entire universe wanting? No!

Sai-ias: You're doing this thing again, where you talk to each other and I hear only one voice. It makes you appear singularly mad.

Explorer 410: We have to start again. Return to the Source, re-enter the void, and locate you in your new universe.

Jak: That could take years.

Explorer 410: Two point four years, if we rift skilfully, and assuming the Source has not shifted its relative location since our last encounter. Five point seven years if, as I suspect, the Dreaded have learned how to "summon" the Source to their own location and we have to find it from scratch. Six point nine years if—

Jak: Enough! It's not as if we have a choice. Just do it.

Sai-ias: Can you still hear me?

Jak/Explorer: Yes.

Sai-ias: I feel very isolated. I have no friends now. The slaves in the exterior world despise me and hate me for the freedom I enjoy. And whenever I see them, my friends on the interior world think I am a traitor. And I have to continue to pretend to be so. Otherwise I could not speak to you. But I am hated by all, and it's breaking my soul.

Hello? Did you hear any of that?

Explorer 410: I heard your words, but since the content was about emotion and I am just a machine, I was pausing to allow Master-of-the-Ship Jak to respond.

Jak: I—um. I acknowledge your pain.

Sai-ias: Have you ever felt like this? Lonely? Unhappy? Unloved?

Jak: Lonely, yes! And unhappy, certainly. I've been unhappy ever since I was trapped in the body of a Class 4 Explorer ship, and forced to co-exist with a machine who possesses a sad apology for a sense of humour, yes.

Explorer 410: If I were capable of emotions, I would resent those words.

Sai-ias: I am used to being loved. I find it hard to live without love.

Jak: Ah, well there you have me, for I've never been loved.

Sai-ias: What?

Jak: I've never been loved. Males are never loved. That's just the way things are.

Sai-ias: You can't mean that, Jak?

Jak: Well... there are exceptions... but even so, that's pretty much how it is.

There was one female in particular—perhaps she... ????—but I will never know.

Generally however that is the way of my kind; love is a river that flows only one way.

Sai-ias: That's sad.

Jak: Hardly. It's just a cultural difference.

Sai-ias: Such differences can be considerable. One of my dearest friends comes from a culture where mothers eat their own newborn.

Jak: There, you see, by comparison we—what?

Explorer 410: The Frayskind. They're in my database. It is just their way. Many aquatics do it too.

Sai-ias: My own kind mate for life. I know many species who do not. Promiscuous, polyamorous, feckless and reckless—I know some beasts who have had sex with literally tens of thousands of partners. The serpentiforms are the worst. Though some of the birds are pretty bad. The larger creatures, though, tend to be monogamous, like me. Or rather, as I would have been; had I not been a child when the Ka'un captured me.

Jak: You were a child?

Sai-ias: Oh yes.

Jak: I am so sorry. That must have been—

Sai-ias: At least I lived.

Jak: You poor thing. How many years have—

Sai-ias: Many.

Jak: I am sorry.

Sai-ias: Is it really true you have never been loved?

Jak: I don't know.

Sai-ias: How don't you know?

Jak: Because—well. Star-Seeker Albinia and I were just—I was sure she *did* actually love me. But she never said so.

And I always feared that, well. I feared that she would suddenly change her mind, and forget her love for me. Like all the other females in my life had done.

That's how—that's why—I spent all our time together expecting the worst. Which means of course I found it hard to actually enjoy her company! Because I kept imagining she might say: "Oh dear, this isn't working out Jak." Or, "Jak, I no longer care for you." Or, "Jak, you hopeless and sexually inept fool, I've only been pretending to like you, actually I think you're a badly dressed laughing stock."

She never ACTUALLY said any of those things; but I imagined it all so often it felt as if it had happened.

I was being stupid, I know! Unfair on her. It may be she would have been loyal, and we could have lived happily together for twenty years or so; perhaps she really *was* the one.

But before I had a chance to find out, one way or another—she died. Right in front of me. The Death Ship killed her.

So—I will never know.

Explorer 410: None of this is at all relevant to our plight; I thought I should register that observation.

Sai-ias: Why so afraid, Jak? You can't spend your life being afraid of being betrayed.

Jak: In my culture, it's an occupational hazard. It is our duty to serve, and to give our females pleasure both social and sexual, and gain little or none in return.

Sai-ias: But that's pathetic.

Jak: We males consider it to be ennobling.

Explorer 410: Speaking as an impartial observer, and taking into account that I am not capable of ANY emotions, let alone love, I too Jak find that pathetic.

Jak: It is the way things are, and have always been.

Sai-ias: Perhaps we mean something different by the word "love."

Jak: Our females fuck us, but they don't give us orgasms, and they treat us like shit.

Sai-ias: By the standards of my culture, that means you don't get loved. Oh you sad thing!

Jak: I don't need your pity! I am a proud Olaran.

Sai-ias: Yes I know. I know. I didn't mean to—tell me about yourself Jak. Describe yourself. I would like to know you more.

Jak: Why?

Sai-ias: If I know you, I might be able to love you; for my kind are capable of unconditional and limitless love, when we truly know a fellow creature. But all I know of you so far is—a voice from a machine.

Jak: Um, perhaps we should keep focused on the mission?

Sai-ias: How many limbs do you have?

Jak: You have no idea how ridiculous that question sounds.

Sai-ias: True. Because I have no sense of humour, as I have been told on many occasions. I'll go first: I have twenty-four limbs. Twelve feet, not in pairs. Ten hands, or strictly speaking, tentacles. And two filaments that come out of my mouth that can be used to manipulate objects, and which therefore count as limbs. Does that help you visualise me?

Jak: Tentacles. By the God of all the Traders, you are a monstrous beast!

Sai-ias: How many limbs do you have?

Jak: I have simply the normal number. Four! Two arms. Two legs. Two eyes. Two penises. I'm an Olaran.

Sai-ias: Ah, a biped. Do you have scales or fur?

Jak: Skin. You?

Sai-ias: Chitinous armour enveloped in soft hide. Do you have wings?

Jak: No. You?

Sai-ias: I have a cape which allows me to fly. I can also dwell in the water. Now you can see me.

Jak: Now I can see you. Sai-ias, are you beautiful?

Sai-ias: Many consider me so. Some, not so much. And you?

Jak: I am very beautiful; or rather, I was. I was a gorgeous youth who became a beautiful man; females used to flatter me; I dressed in ornate and beautiful gowns and my body was lean and perfectly proportioned. Now I am a wreck; my body was burned and what survived was destroyed by Explorer and flushed out of the waste disposal. I am now more spaceship than Olaran; my brain lives in fluid connected by cables to this computer's mind.

Sai-ias: I will imagine you in your beautiful body. Do you love children?

Jak: I have no children of my own, but I adore them. You?

Sai-ias: I was a child when I came to this place; I would love to have been a mother. It seems we have much in common.

Jak: We have very little in common, except not having children.

Sai-ias: We should be friends.

Jak: I would—like that.

Sai-ias: I am here.

Jak: It's been a year since we last spoke.

Sai-ias: It has been sixty eleven-day cycles by my calendar.

It has been . . . a most terrible sixty cycles.

Jak: We are tracking you again. We are at the Source, and have been waiting here for the last nine months by our calendar, but with no trace of the Death Ship. Now we have your signal again, we can start rifting between universes and we can find you, wherever you are. Keep giving us your location.

Sai-ias: I am here.

Sai-ias: I am here.

Sai-ias: I am here.

Sai-ias: I am here.

Sai-ias: I am here.

Sai-ias: I am here.

Sai-ias: I am here.

Sai-ias: I am here.

Jak: We have a proximate trace on you.

Sai-ias: You are in the same universe as me again?

Jak: Yes we are.

Sai-ias: Please. Hurry. I can't—not for much longer.

Explorer 410: It won't take that long. Keep talking. If there is a pause, we are rifting through real-space, which is faster but cuts the riftband link.

Sai-ias: I'm still here.

Jak: We've travelled through many universes. There's a trail of dead sentience smeared through the spaces. Shall I tell you about the worlds we know about, that are lost?

Sai-ias: No.

Jak: Shall I tell you then about

Jak: Sai-ias? Are you there? Sai-ias, are you there? Sai-ias, are you there? Sai-ias—

Sai-ias: I'm here. The signal was—I switched it off. I couldn't listen any more.

I'm sorry.

Jak: It's all right. I understand.

Sai-ias: Do you?

Jak: I do.

Sai-ias: I think perhaps you do. Thank you, Jak, for understanding.

Jak: Shall I tell you instead then about my adventures? The days of my youth?

Sai-ias: No.

Jak: Then talk to me of yourself. Your world. What it was like.

Sai-ias: No.

Jak: Something bad has happened.

Sai-ias: Yes.

Jak: Do you wish to tell me about it?

Sai-ias: No.

Jak: An atrocity?

Sai-ias: The latest of many. The Ka'un truly trust me now. They think I am one of them.

Jak: Ah.

Sai-ias: I think it may be true. I am indeed like them.

Jak: No. Not so! You're merely pretending.

Sai-ias: Indeed, that is what I do.

Jak: And tell me—do you still speak to the Ka'un?

Sai-ias: Yes I do. I hear a voice in my head and speak back to it. Though not every day, not any more. The voice of Minos, captain of the ship.

Jak: "Minos." I know that name! Minos was—What is he like, this Minos?

Sai-ias: Charming. Cultured. Kind. A liar.

Jak: Why don't you kill him? Can you do that? Are you strong enough?

Sai-ias: Strong enough, yes. But I cannot. I have only seen Minos in the flesh once. Otherwise, he is a voice in my head. I do not know how to reach their part of the ship. I never see them, only hear them. And even if I could get near Minos, he has a power over me; he could take control of my body in an instant.

Jak: Then we shall kill him for you.

Sai-ias: I wish you would. Before—

Jak: Before what?

Sai-ias: Before I become truly evil.

Sai-ias: I'm here.

Jak: Sai-ias.

Sai-ias: I'm here.

Jak: Sai-ias! Can you talk awhile?

Sai-ias: I do not wish to talk.

Sai-ias: I'm here.

Jak: Sai-ias.

Sai-ias: Are you near?

Jak: It's hard to say what "near" is.

Yes. I think we are near.

Sai-ias: What will you do? When you find us?

Explorer 410: We have weapons that will destroy your ship in a single panoramic blast; thus compensating for any possible illusory image tricks of the kind that deceived us last time.

Sai-ias: You will kill me too.

Jak: Yes.

Sai-ias: Good.

Sai-ias: I'm here.

Jak: We are close to you Sai-ias. We've just emerged from rift space. Our sensors detect the ship with the black sails. We are stealthed and ready for combat. We are ready to fire. We are firing now. Our missiles are being launched, they are rifting, and now they are materialising again. The Hell Ship does not a stand a chance this time! Oh Sai-ias, I will always

Sai-ias: Jak?

Explorer?

Where are you?

Minos: Sweet Sai-ias; a nicely baited trap.

BOOK 11

Sharrock

For nearly a hundred years I have endured pain beyond anything I would have believed possible. And I have not faltered, or faded, or succumbed to the fatal state that is known as Despair.

And I have always clung to this small consolation; they have not crushed my spirit. They have defeated me, humiliated me, tortured me, and left me with no prospect of hope. But my spirit remains intact.

It is, indeed, a very small consolation.

It would, I know, be so much easier to yield to utter desolation; and let the toxins steal over my body, and turn my flesh into stone. The Ka'un have spread the myth that death is not possible, even when the body is petrified; but I do not believe this. I believe that when I die I will be dead and I will achieve merciful oblivion.

However, I do not wish to give those forsaken-by-the-gods fucking bastards the satisfaction.

So every day they hose salt water upon my flayed skin; and plunge knives into my body; and lash me with a knotted rope. After a few hours the pain is so bad that I become blind, through some kind of hysterical reaction, but the torment does not cease. They use members of the Kindred to torture me; it is clearly one of their tiresome but necessary allotted duties. There are few things worse for me than seeing the look of boredom on the face of my torturer before the first knife is thrust into my gut.

Then every night the ceiling rains healing water upon my

body and the wounds seal and my organs reform and my vision is restored and by the morning I am whole again, and the rhythm can begin anew.

To distract myself I write poems in my head. I have never had much flair for poetry; and in all honesty, I suspect I still do not. But I have written 10,000,000 cantos or more of an epic poem about my adventures, and there is no one here who can tell me that it is less than a work of genius.

Ha!

You see, even in the midst of utter agony, I have not lost my sense of humour.

Sharrock defeated?

Never!

Oh I am so weary.

I awoke, and felt that something was different.

My agony was no less; my torturers were as bored as always. But the magnetic bonds that hold me aloft felt soft, and spongy.

Once my torturers had completed their daily chores and departed, I realised I could now bounce upon my invisible bonds, to get some movement going. And furthermore, I could manipulate my hands inside their metal shackles, which were looser than before. And so I wriggled and struggled, and used my teeth to grip the shackles while I moved my wrists; until finally I was free.

It was an far easier job to slip free of my ankle shackles. I was still trapped in a cell the size of a desert tent, but I was no longer restrained.

There was an electronic lock on the door; and I began to manipulate it with my body-energy; touching it with fingers and licking with my tongue to move the inner parts with the power of my own electricity. This is the trick I used in Sabol, the capital city of the Southern Tribes, to steal their precious alien artefact, the Jewel of the Seventh Sun (a jewel that is now possessed by a black-hided sea monster who I am proud to call my friend).

Finally the lock opened, and I was through the door. I was naked—nay, flayed, my muscles were visible and knotted, the slightest touch or brush against a wall was agony for me. But I did not allow this to distract me.

I found myself in a silver corridor, and I placed my ear to the metal and I listened.

It took a long time for the sounds to make themselves manifest; but eventually I was able to hear the murmur of conversation between the Ka'un and their Kindred slaves. I started to distinguish voices. I could identify twenty-five distinct individuals. But the words they uttered were gibberish, for I no longer had a pakla-translator in my brain.

I also heard the faintest noise, the merest hint of a vibration, that sounded to me like water flowing; I deduced it was the twin rivers that ran through the interior world. Four layers of hull separated me from my friends; but at least I could hear the sounds of their world.

And I was unbound, and had a vivid mental map of my location and where my enemies were.

I continued down the corridor until I heard footsteps and the whisper of blood through veins, which betokened enemies approaching. And I clambered up the wall and clung to the ceiling with my fingertips, which though fleshless still retained some magnetic-electric adhesive power. And I waited. Twenty long minutes passed and eventually two burly bipeds strode down the corridor; giants with square heads carrying energy guns in their hands. These were two of my Kindred captors, on their way to torture me. It must be dawn, I realised, though the lighting in the corridor had not changed.

The Kindred were big and muscular beasts, used to hand to hand combat; and I was weary and flayed and I knew I stood no chance against them in a fair fight.

However, the moment they had walked past I dropped down

behind them and seized first one head, then the other, and snapped the necks of both. I was not as strong as once I was, but I was still exceedingly fast.

The two Kindred fell and rolled and immediately got up again, their necks twisted out of shape but rage leering in their features. And I realised that a broken neck was no obstacle to these creatures.

And they reached for their energy guns, only to find I had ripped them from their belts. I had a gun in each hand; I did not hesitate; I fired flame; they died before they were able to scream.

I found I was shivering and shuddering; my flayed skin was causing me pain, and it was reacting badly with the air. Underneath the jets of healing water I was strong; but in cold air, I was a walking cripple.

I stripped the clothes off one of the Kindred, recoiling at his ugly body hair, and carried the garments back to my cell. The healing waters still flowed; so I soaked the clothes, then put them on my body. The sleeves of the shirt were ridiculously long so I rolled them up; I tucked the trousers in the boots. I was now dressed all in black, wearing clothes far too large for me, and I looked absurd. But the healing dampness of the water from the well of life was now pressed up against my raw skinless flesh.

I stepped back out into the corridor, and sprinted as fast as I could away from my confining cell. Once the alarm was sounded they would send all their troops against me.

I emerged out of the silver corridor into a maze of metal; walkways and flyboards hovered in the air, and the low hum of machinery and computing machines created a music in my ear.

I listened again to a wall, until I could identify where the Ka'un dwelled. It was far from me; I was safe for now. But all around me the sounds of machinery told me that I was in the nerve centre of their outer-hull universe.

I went through four doors by opening their electronic locks with the energy from my body's cells, until I found myself in a room with a large dome floating inside. I recognised this as a Machine Mind.

I had no idea what to do; and I wondered if the Machine Mind was designed to function in response to the thought patterns of a member of the Ka'un. I thought about destroying it, but I worried that would simply wreck the ship, and thus kill my friends in the interior world.

I returned, back down the corridors through which I had fled, towards the place where I'd killed the two Kindred. I was three corridors away when I heard the murmur of voices; reinforcements had arrived. The alarm had been sounded. The Kindred were hunting for me.

Once more I climbed the walls then slid along the ceiling the length of two corridors until I was above the Kindred sent to kill me. There were six of them, and they gathered around the two corpses I had left, barking gibberish to themselves; I guessed they were connected to others of the Kindred by brain-paklas.

I fell from the ceiling and began firing energy beams from my stolen guns. The Kindred were slow, and all of them burned and died before they managed to assimilate what was happening.

I was now in a corridor surrounded by Kindred corpses. I frisked one of the bodies until I found a dagger; then I dug the blade into the corpse's skull. I opened up the brain until I found the crystal pakla. Then I cut it out.

And I returned back down the corridors, up the stairs, into the metal maze, until I was back in the room with the Machine Mind.

The pakla in my hand began to glow; and as it did so, a display lit up in the air around the Machine Mind. I touched it with my hand, and I felt the flow of data energy swirling within the Machine Mind. This, I was confident, was the part of the Mind that controlled the brain paklas.

I raised my energy gun and reduced the beam to its narrowest; and burned away that part of the Machine Mind. When the pakla stopped glowing, I stopped firing. I prayed that I had not caused any ancillary damage.

I left the room. I could hear, from two corridors away, the voice of one of the Ka'un leading a gang of Kindred, presumably to find and kill me. I thought about lingering to destroy my enemy but decided the risk was too great.

I used the energy gun to cut a hole in the ceiling above me. Then I leaped up in the air and clambered through the gap.

I did this eleven times until I could scent the air of the interior world.

I clambered through burned metal and found myself in the open air. I pulled myself through.

I was in a green field; I had cut my way through into the interior world.

I lay there on the ground for a while, gasping, entirely exhausted.

And then, to my astonishment, I saw the hole that I had carved in the hull begin to seal itself. The severed ends yearned towards each other; then touched; and eventually bare metal fully enclosed the gap.

I absorbed the implications of this phenomenon; this must be one of the reasons the Ka'un ship had survived so many battles, since the metal hull could *heal itself*. But the process had, however, been rather slow. My thoughts began to stir.

I knew that my enemies would be pursuing me; so I dragged myself to my feet, and began to limp slowly across the grass, towards the lake, where I knew my fellow slaves would be congregated.

I knew—for I have always kept a constant mental tally—that this was Day the Eighth, and all would be gathered there to tell their tales.

I was tired, and parched, and desperate; my vision swam; I was shivering and shuddering and my clothes were no longer damp, so I stripped them off and staggered onwards naked.

Finally I glimpsed the waters of the lake; and on the further shore, I saw my friends gathered. But I was nowhere near them; I had misjudged the route. This had never happened to me before—my mental mapping is usually infallible—and this was when I realised my brain was shutting down.

I dragged myself along the grass to the waters of the lake, leaving a trail of red behind me. And I tried to call out across the waters of the lake to my fellow captives; but it was too far away, and no sounds emerged from my throat.

My strength was failing me. I fell to my knees. I dragged myself along the grass, trying to reach the soft blue water. I was dying, I realised, and I needed a drink before I died. A drink. A—

Sai-ias

After the death of Explorer and Jak—in what I guessed would have been a massive explosion in space caused by Minos—I had returned to the interior world. Minos no longer spoke to me in my head.

I understood by now that from the moment he intercepted my first "radio" signal, Minos had deceived me utterly and flawlessly. I had lured Explorer onwards; and Minos allowed me to do so; time and again letting me roam "free" in the rooms of the exterior hull in order to make my radio calls. Then he destroyed the ship he called Nemesis, and Jak with it. It had been a plan carefully nurtured; Minos had allowed me to befriend Jak, so he could slay him.

I no longer had any hope left. My former friends hated me; and many of them like Fray had no memory of our good times together. They only ever knew me when I was masquerading as the evil bitch who freely served the Ka'un.

I knew that by this stage no one would ever believe that my actions had all been a pretence, in pursuit of my plan to overthrow the Ka'un. For that plan of course had now failed. The pretence had turned out to be the reality; I had simply been deceiving *myself.*

Thus I was left with nothing.

Then one day I felt a flutter of wings near my head, and saw Lirilla.

"Sai-ias," she said.

"Yes?" I said. Lirilla no longer considered herself my friend, after witnessing me vanquish and humiliate the Krakzios; but she was at least speaking to me.

"Sharrock back, dead," she said, and flew away.

I was consumed with fear at her words.

I began to lope with my tentacles; I saw crowds near the lake, and hurried towards them.

And I saw a muscular body lying there. It took me a moment, but then I recognised it as Sharrock. He was damp, possibly drowned, and had been flayed. His eyes stared blankly from his fleshless face.

Fray saw me and growled in her throat. But I ignored her, and pushed my way through. And I touched Sharrock with a tentacle tip and felt his pulse, and there was none.

So I thrust my tentacle tip down his throat until it was nearly in his gut, and then wrenched it out. He vomited water and he began to breathe once again.

I lifted him up, and carried him swiftly on my back to the well of the water of life and laid him down there. He slept there for an hour, and emerged spluttering.

The new-born Fray and my former friend Quipu gathered with me, as I looked down upon Sharrock.

"Will you take him back?" said Quipu One.

I stared at him blankly, not comprehending.

"He has escaped," Quipu Two clarified. "Surely it is your job to betray us once more."

I shuddered with shame at his words; though I did not blame him for uttering them.

"Who is he?" asked Fray, staring with puzzlement at the naked, flayed Maxolun.

"Oh Fray," said Quipu One. "If only you knew! Your previous self followed this one to glorious defeat and death. Sharrock is—he was—"

"He tried to destroy the Ka'un; he failed," I said.

"He's awake," said Quipu Four.

Sharrock was indeed awake; and looked up at us. And he spoke.

But his words were a babble; we could not understand him.

"How?" I cried. "Surely we should still understand *him*?"

"My guess is that the Ka'un have deleted his language from our paklas," said Quipu One.

"Paklas?" asked Fray, baffled.

Sharrock whimpered with frustration at our inability to understand him. He pointed, to his head; then he stood up and touched the heads of Quipu.

We stared at him blankly.

Sharrock roared with rage. Never had I seen him so helpless, so frustrated; nor so wretchedly vulnerable, stripped as he was of all skin.

But then Sharrock paused, and was clearly lost in thought.

Then he stood up tall. And he no longer looked defeated; he looked like a warrior about to go into battle.

And what then followed was theatre, as Quipu later called it, of the magnificently absurd; a mime show that spoke louder than words.

We saw Sharrock, bound and tortured; we saw Sharrock fighting with his bonds; then Sharrock free; Sharrock running down a corridor; and finally, Sharrock *destroying* something, we knew not what.

At the end of it all, Sharrock took up a tree branch and he thrust it into my middle segment. Hard. And again. And again. I did not move or recoil, I was trying to fathom his meaning.

Finally my body spasmed and a deadly quill emerged from my middle segment; Sharrock had seen me do this in the battle against Cuzco.

Sharrock then touched my quill with his flayed hands and pointed to the heavens; then mimed a penetrating thrust.

Eventually, I understood.

Later that day I told my tale to Quipu and Fray; the story of my long and ultimately futile deception of Minos. I talked of Star-Seeker Jak and his failed attempt to destroy the Hell Ship.

"He tried for so many thousands of years to take revenge—and then died in just a moment," I said.

"This story— " said Quipu One.

"—could just be another lie," said Quipu Two.

"Trust me or not, I don't care," I said. "There is about to be a war; prepare yourself for it."

And then I told them what Sharrock wanted me to do.

"Is it possible?" said Quipu One after I had finished my account.

"Sharrock knows my powers," I said. "He knows the powers of all of you. He has studied us all and he has planned; and it is the best plan any of us have yet conceived.

"In short, we have a chance," I said. "Minos is no longer in my head; and I know from this that the pakla-link has been broken, for that evil bastard loves to haunt me and to spy on me. He thinks I do not know he is there; but I can always tell.

"But now Minos has gone; my mind is truly my own again; and this Sharrock has achieved.

"Now, the rest is up to us."

I made my way down to the cargo bay, where the hull-hatch was located. Many times we had toppled stone corpses out through this gateway to the stars. But today we had another purpose in mind.

I squeezed myself into the hatchway, and Quipu manipulated the controls. An outer door opened, and I squeezed through; an inner door then closed, protecting the air in the cargo hold from the emptiness of space.

Then the outer door opened too and I fell out and was among stars.

Below me the Hell Ship floated, huge and beautiful and black-sailed. It was a cylinder of a vessel, elegantly curved, culminating in a triangle tip, and dazzlingly illuminated with lights buried in the metal. But the hull looked old now, and was coated with strange growths, like living beasts; save for a large patch of clear metal which I recognised as the spot where Explorer 410: Property of the Olaran Trader Fleet had sent a missile into the hull.

I unfurled my cape to its fullest extent, and hurled an ear frond at the ship until it touched metal and connected; and so I was now being pulled along with the Hell Ship on its effortlessly swift course through space.

I thought about Minos, and all that he had told me of himself. How much of it was true? I wondered. I knew of course that he had lied to me about many things. But had there been any honesty at all in his words? Did he ever actually have qualms about what he and his evil crew had done?

I doubted it. Whatever he had once been, Minos was now simply malign: beyond remorse and compassion, hate incarnate. I longed to kill him.

And so I would.

I fired air from my gills, and flew closer to the Hell Ship.

Then I clung to the hull with my body, gripping with my claws, embracing it like a bird smothering its prey.

And with a powerful jolt, I buried my centre quill in the hull.

It dug in deep—I felt pain rip through my body—then I pulled myself off, leaving a broad circular hole in the hull. The strange creatures that dwelled on the hull were clinging to my body now, gnawing me painfully, but I ignored them. My quill had become torn in the penetration; and blood dripped from my stomach.

I crawled, in pain, further along the hull.

Behind me, I knew, a small slow leak would have sprung up in the hull of the Hell Ship. Air from the outer world where the

Ka'un dwelled was billowing out into space. I had ruptured the hull, and the inner seal, and the secondary inner seal; and, or so I hoped, it would take time for the hull's self-heal mechanisms to repair the breach.

I did the same thing on another patch of hull. And again, and again. I performed the act one hundred times or more; and all the holes in the hill hissed out air silently.

Eventually the effort of it ripped my quill from my body, and blood gushed from my middle segment; but I thrust another quill into the hull. I had twenty in all.

After all twenty quills had ruptured, I was done.

I crawled back along the hull towards the hatch, as blood slowly spilled from my body to form a long scarlet slick in the midst of empty space.

I lay on the green plain; the rate of flow had slowed, but the blood that was emerging from my body now was mixed with black bile and entrails. The sheer power needed to thrust organic quill through hard metal had torn my insides apart.

Lirilla flew above my head, fanning me with her wings, whispering words of comfort wrapped within a song of tender beauty:

"Brave
Sai-ias
Joy
Pleasure
Hope
Do
Not
Die."

I blacked out and woke; and when I woke I realised I was surrounded by an army of my fellow captives. Thousands of them had gathered, in silence, to comfort me in my pain, and perhaps to see me die.

Fray ceaselessly poured healing water of the well of life from a bucket over my bloodied stomach segment—sparing me her healing piss, for which I was grateful. A long chain of my fellow captives on this interior world brought fresh supplies of well-water ceaselessly.

And for a while I wondered if these healing waters were going to work upon me; might I survive this ordeal, and enjoy future days with Sharrock and the others as my friends once more?

But the pain was getting worse not better. My guts and womb and heart and other internal organs had been crushed and ripped in my huge effort; I was little more than a carcass of flesh surrounding a mess of damaged organs.

It was becoming undeniable to me that my injures were too serious to be healed; the only salvation for me was resurrection.

And that, I desperately hoped, would never happen; not if Sharrock and the others triumphed in this last terrible battle. For to be reborn as my twelve-year-old self, thrust back into this appalling world again! I could think of no greater horror.

Sharrock was kneeling by my head, stroking me with his hand. He looked worse than I felt; but I was pleased to see the look in his eyes. It was a look of rage, and a yearning for vengeance.

I whispered to him, but he could not comprehend.

So I opened my mouth; baring my huge jaws, and my sharp teeth. He reached inside with his hand, seeing the spark of ruby light there. And when his hand emerged, he was holding the Jewel of the Seventh Sun. His gift to me, returned.

"I kept it safe," I said, but he did not comprehend.

"How goes the war?" I asked of Quipu.

"Soon they will come," said Quipu One. "Soon."

"Then you must kill," I said, "those evil souls."

"We shall," said the Quipus.

"We shall," said Fray.

"Don't go," said Lirilla.

Sharrock

"You stupid fucking beast," I said to the dying Sai-ias, "you ignorant arse-sucking cock-kissing ingratiating, soft-hearted, infuriating, patronising whore-bitch—whatever happens, we owe you everything! We thank you, ugly beast, from the depths of our souls. And I—fuck it, I can't believe I'm saying this—*I love you.* Can you understand a single fucking word of this?"

Sai-ias grunted something which I could not comprehend; but I read the meaning in her eyes.

And then her body deflated; her eyes dimmed; and she died.

There was no time to mourn. We all knew what we had to do.

We had to wait.

The Ka'un would be suffocating by now; their hull had been breached a thousand times and would be spewing air at a formidable rate. I assumed they would have spacesuits with air tubes; that might buy them *some* time.

But not much. The hull holes would heal themselves; but the air that had spurted out could not be easily replaced. A world's worth of air! No machine could generate that much fresh atmosphere in less than several weeks; by which time the Ka'un would all be dead.

So they needed to take our interior world back; this would give them air enough for years, until they had replenished their own supplies.

And what's more, we had defied them. So they had no choice. They *had* to attack us.

And when they did, we would be ready.

An army of us had gathered, stretched across the Great Plain, breathing slowly, waiting for the moment. Fray, Quipu, Lirilla, Raoild, Ioday Zubu, Doriel, Caramo, Doalyu, Sargan, Biark, Sahashs, Loramas, Thugor, Amur, Kairi, Wapax, Fiymean, Krakkka, and more, many more.

Quipu spoke; and Fray poured more water of life upon me. Despite my lack of skin, I felt strong and ready for battle.

Fray spoke to Quipu; Quipu replied. I understood none of this.

Lirilla uttered a sound: I actually recognised the word. "Sai-ias. Sai-ias." She was singing the name of our dead friend.

I clutched my sword, which Lirilla had brought to me; stolen I guessed from a Kindred in the Valley. It was a blade of near-unbreakable metal, forged from the walls of a Hell Ship cabin. I touched it; and felt its power.

And we waited.

And the silence was broken by Lirilla, singing to the sky.

And when Lirilla had sung her song, Miaris howled, a melancholy howl; this was *his* song. And it was beautiful.

And though I could not understand the language of the others, I realised immediately what was happening when Quipu began to pace and chatter; and all of his five heads were talking, sharing, interrupting, and all were rapt as they listened to the tale he was telling.

And then Fray roared, and scraped her hooves, and spoke at length; and her tale, whatever it was, was surely magnificent.

And as we waited still, more tales were told; and the creatures of the Hell Ship were united, a single family, bonded by one creature; the dead Sai-ias.

And finally the story-telling and the singing and the sharing was over. And our enemies came.

The skies above us were black; I looked up and realised that three thousand or more Kindred warriors were flying in space-armour above us. Some were from the Valley, but most I guessed had been despatched from their barracks somewhere in the outer hull. The Ka'un had sent their finest warriors to fight us!

And the flying Kindred swooped down low upon the Great Plain, and their guns began to spit fire.

And the aerials swooped upon them, knocking them from the sky. They flew in vast flocks, hundreds of them, pecking and ripping at the motors that held the Kindred body armours aloft; and one by one the Kindred began to fall from the sky. And those that fell were trampled under the hooves of the grazers and of Fray, or torn apart by the teeth of the giant sentients, or thrashed and bitten to pieces by the angry arboreals.

Or slain by me! For my sword did the work of a hundred Maxoluns, as I cut and slashed and killed!

And as I fought, I thought of Sai-ias.

Blade at my head; duck to evade; weave; dagger in the throat; knee in the balls; on I fight!

I mourned her, and I treasured her memory, insofar as I could treasure and mourn in the midst of a furious and bloody battle with these huge and powerful Kindred warriors.

(Back! Strike! Thrust! Fuck your parents for conceiving you and DIE!)

Sai-ias was brave indeed. She died to save us. And what's more, she left us a legacy; a way of love and forgiveness and respect for the rhythms of life, and it is a way I intend to respect and to follow. Just as soon as I

WIN THIS FUCKING BATTLE!

And thus

We slew the armies of the Kindred! And lopped off their limbs, and shattered their skulls, and broke their bones! And they slew us, or some of us; but our people were fierce beyond belief and though the Kindred had guns and armour and force fields and cannons we had weight of numbers and fighting fury and a cause that was just.

And so we crushed them. Literally in some cases. Fray trampled

Kindred with her hooves; Quipu bit their throats out; Miaris, the largest of the giant sentients since Cuzco was gone, was a creature of terror and carnage.

And I slew fast and furiously, and dodged bullets, and side-stepped energy rays; for no one and nothing could defeat me on this day.

And so we fought, and won.

And when the last Kindred body dropped to the ground, a cry of fear resounded out.

For above us in the air were Cuzco, and Djamrock, and Tar-roth, their great wings beating.

And at the same the waters of the lake were draining away. And when the lake bed was fully dry an army of giant sentients began to crawl and walk and trot towards us, in a long trail that led from the island of the Tower where the gateway to the outer world was located. There was Balach, and Morio, and Tamal, and Sheenam, and Goay, and Leirak, and two-headed Shseil, and the serpentines Dokdrr and Ma, and more.

And behind them walked ten bipeds dressed in red robes.

"Cuzco join us!" I screamed up, and he laughed, and then he shat, and I had to dodge out of the way of his vast turd as it crashed to earth.

"Fray," I said, "we should attack while they are still in the lake," and I beckoned with one arm to make my meaning clear to him.

And Fray turned to me, and there was sadness in her eyes; but she did not move.

"Quipu?" I turned to Quipu. His five heads were still; he was holding a home-made sword in one of his hands and he pointed the blade towards me.

Around me were the bloodied corpses of the Kindred and the bodies of many of our own: Zubu was dead, and so was Doriel; and Caramo also. Doalya the foolish blind aerial—she was a broken wreck. Sargan, who could drum his own body, had been eviscerated by Kindred and his brains ripped out. But Biark was alive, and so was Sahashs, and Loramas, and Thugor, and many more. But none of them moved; they all had that eerie stillness.

I was the only warrior left able to fight; my entire army had joined our enemy. And I realised that my strategy had failed; the paklas still controlled each creature's mind, except for mine.

And so I waited, a dreary patient wait for my own inevitable doom. Waited until the ten Ka'un had walked across the dry lake and had joined me on the battlefield, while their monsters stood flanking the lake shore like statues in a Sabol temple.

And I watched as their leader—a male with a face like black parchment—walked towards me, proud and calm. He was the one I had seen before; the one who had stared so curiously at my body as I dangled naked from a hook.

"Greetings Sharrock," he said, in my own language, without use of pakla. "I am Minos; and I am the captain of this ship."

"You are the one who did this, aren't you? *You* released me!" I said, appalled, retrospectively, at my own stupidity.

"Yes." Minos did not smile, but he was clearly delighted at his own great joke.

"You disabled the pakla-links, temporarily."

"I did. And it yielded us a battle most glorious."

"What I did to the Machine Mind—"

"Achieved precisely nothing. The power to control the 'paklas'"—Minos tapped his forehead with a long finger—"is here. All in here."

I nodded; my humiliation was complete. I had played the foolish pawn in Minos's cruel game.

And yet I did not care.

"And now you are going to kill me?" I asked.

The Ka'un drew his sword and held it aloft; the universal sign for a challenge.

I stifled a gasp at this unexpected move; and wondered if this was merely another jest; and yet a flicker of hope stirred in me.

"My name is Minos," said the Ka'un. "And I shall fight you for this world!"

And I nodded assent; then I raised my sword and attacked him.

Above me Cuzco and Djamrock and Tarroth beat their wings in syncopation with the clang of my hull-steel sword on Minos's far superior fusion-forged weapon. Fray and Quipu and all my comrades watched, paralysed, their bodies controlled by Ka'un. The giant sentients standing by the lake shore were silent too; and the nine other Ka'un watched impassively as Minos recklessly gambled their world on a single combat with a warrior supreme.

And as I fought, I wondered if the nine other Ka'un would honour Minos's bargain in the event of his death. For I was alone, one warrior against an army of monsters; even if I did beat Minos, I could be slain by them with effortless ease.

And yet, I sensed that Minos was sincere. With his black old face and his tired eyes, he looked as if he would welcome the release of defeat in glorious battle.

So with hope in my heart, I struck and I stabbed and I danced, and I used all my warrior skills against this aged slender monster with the dry and withered face and the weary eyes; for I was Sharrock, and Sharrock could never, ever, be defeated!

However, after a few minutes of masterly and dazzling and heroic swordplay I realised, to my utter and abject horror, that I *could not actually beat this bastard.*

For Minos was faster than me; and defter; and more skilful. His strokes were unerring, his grace was faultless, and he was *strong.* His body looked punier than mine by far; but each strike of sword on sword shook me to the core. I leaped over his blade but he leaped too and we fought in air, clashing swords wildly till we both somersaulted and landed back on grass, but his midair turn was faster and his fall more agile, and he struck again, and the blade cut my shoulder and blood flowed.

My injuries were not to blame, for my battle strength was on me, and I fought like a Maxolun possessed. But even so I could not compete with a devil like Minos.

And then my blade shattered and I fell to the ground helpless and Minos raised his blade as if to cleave my head.

But a female Ka'un stepped forward; and fire sparked from her fingers. And Minos drew back.

The female Ka'un looked into my eyes, and I looked into hers; and I saw nothing there but nothingness. Then she drew her sword; there were jewels on the hilt and the blade gleamed in daylight and then she passed it to me hilt uppermost; and when I held it was like caressing a soul.

A second Ka'un stepped forward holding a jug and poured water from the well of life over my ripped and bleeding flayed body; soothing my pain; giving me strength to continue.

Fray roared; they gave her freedom to do that much.

Cuzco beat his wings and stared down and I looked up at my old friend and acknowledged him.

And the battle resumed.

I was refreshed now, I had a superior sword, my comrades had shown their support; and my spirits were high!

And yet *still* I could not win. Minos was the devil; his lean and wasted body was quicksilver, but his arms had the strength of a hundred warriors. He played with me, forcing me backwards, parrying my blows so powerfully I grunted like a cathary; striking with his sword so fast he sheared my hair and nipped my ears but not even deigning to kill me. And then he stabbed me in the heart; but my second heart surged and it gave me the strength to continue with a brief attacking flurry.

At which point he stepped aside with almost supernatural speed and I carried on fighting; my sword hacking at air until I realised he was nowhere near me.

And then, scornfully, Minos lowered his sword and raised his other hand and a pulse of energy surged out of his fingers and struck my raw exposed body; and, with a bolt of sheer lightning from his fingertips, he electrocuted me!

The energy bolt knocked me to the ground. I lay on the grass, breathing heavily, then I scrambled clumsily to my feet.

He fired a second energy bolt and this time my entire flayed body lit up; my very veins seemed to be aflame.

He fired a third time; and my two hearts burned in my chest and sparks shot from my eyes.

And then there was silence.

Minos held his sword lightly but he clearly thought the battle was over; his bio-energy attacks were just a *coup de grâce* and he was now waiting for me to remember how to die.

And at that moment, I thanked my stars for one thing: that we Maxoluns also have the power of bodily electricity!

It is, after all, what allowed me to open the locks in the exterior world. And it is furthermore the power that enabled me to steal the Jewel of the Seventh Sun for Malisha.

And thus the bolts of power that surged into my body had redoubled my strength, not sapped it. I felt as if I'd drained a glass of strong rich wine, and now was ready for the evening's misbehaving to begin!

And so I lunged with my sword; and my blade was fast and the blade penetrated Minos's head through the soft skin on the underside of his chin; then I thrust the blade up further into his brain; and he was dead.

There was a shocked silence.

And then a thundering of hooves; and Fray was at my side.

And a swoosh of air, and Cuzco descended, and joined us. And Quipu too and Lirilla. Their babble of words made no sense to me but I knew they were there to fight by my side.

For now that Minos was dead, I realised, the power of the pakla had gone; it truly *was* his mind that had control of it. And so the creatures of this world were free.

And, in consequence, we had the remaining nine Ka'un entirely surrounded.

There was a baying and roaring and a keening and a screeching from the great mob of creatures. And Mangan was suddenly at my side too, roaring hysterically at the Ka'un. Fray's eyes were bloodshot with rage; thousands of alien creatures of every kind and morphology were possessed with a terrible blood-lust. And all we wanted to do was kill these evil fucking Ka'un *now.*

And I wondered what Sai-ias would expect of us at this momentous moment. Would she want us to forgive and spare the Ka'un, now that they were helpless, and we were the ones with the power?

I did not think so.

"Kill!" I screamed and the charge began; and the female Ka'un who had given me her sword raised her arms and looked me and she actually smiled.

And then she burst into flame. Her body became a burning candle. And the same happened with each of the other Ka'un; their bodily-energy turned on itself and their flesh became fire.

And the candles burned till the flesh was all gone. And the fires then were snuffed; and we knew the Ka'un were dead.

And we were left, we captives of the Hell Ship, free at last, on a world in space, confronted by pillars of ash and charred bone that were all that remained of our captors.

It was over.

extras

meet the author

Charlie Hopkinson

This is PHILIP PALMER's fourth novel for Orbit; he is also a producer and script editor, and writes for film, television, and radio. Find out more about the author at www.philippalmer.net.

introducing

If you enjoyed
HELL SHIP,
look out for

ARTEMIS

by Philip Palmer

Artemis McIvor is a thief, a con artist, and a stone-cold killer. And she's been on a crime-spree for, well, for years. The galactic government has collapsed and the universe was hers for the taking.

But when the cops finally catch up with her, they give Artemis a choice: Suffer in prison for the rest of her very long life, or join a crew of criminals, murderers, and traitors on a desperate mission to save humanity against an all-consuming threat.

Now, Artemis has to figure out how to be a good guy without forgetting who she really is.

Prison Break

"Fuck you," I said, then walked into the kitchen. And picked up the mug of scalding hot water. And threw it over my own face.

It hurt. A lot.

I could feel my skin melting.

I began to scream.

Let me back up a little. Who was I saying, "Fuck you," to? Why throw boiling water over my own face? And why was I screaming like a bratty little girl? (I can, I assure you, take a lot more pain than *that* without whining about it.)

To know all that, you'd have to know why I was in the high-security wing of the Giger Penitentiary on the arid wilderness that is Giger's Moon, in the midst of the greatest prison riot of all time.

It's a long story. I'll tell it when I'm ready. For the moment just stay with the basic facts. Boiling water, melting face, girly screaming from me. And then Teresa Shalco running after me, shouting "Bitch!" and "Whore!" and other such expletives, before punching me viciously and knocking me to the ground.

I wept and huddled, playing the helpless victim. And Shalco screamed many more vicious and mostly unfounded insults at me, whilst savagely kicking my prone body. It took three DR dubbers to pull her off.

It was all going according to plan.

Giger's Moon—I'm digressing now, bear with me—is a boon to lovers, if you happen to live on the planet of Giger.

The Moon is a third of the size of the planet it orbits. And thus appears to Gigerians as a glorious silvery orb that fills half their night-time sky. Its surface is scarred with cliffs and craters that cast dark shadows which, to the imaginatively minded, resemble the faces of mythical beasts. There are ruined cities up there too, and eerie ziggurats made of solid metal which have no discernible function, like desk ornaments the size of skyscrapers. All products of the mysterious alien civilisation that once dwelled there.

And—I love this bit!—Giger's Moon is believed by most Gigerians to have an aphrodisiac effect that is in inverse proportion to its size.

In other words, when there's a full moon, the hearts of lovers will beat just a *little* faster. But when there's a half moon, lust starts to really stir. And when the moon is a thin crescent—oh boy!!!—shameless and indiscriminate carnality ensues.

Which I guess is why they call it the Horny Moon.

No one knows how Giger's Moon became a barren wilderness. Or why its original three-legged five-headed inhabitants fled. Or where those strange denizens of Giger's Moon went *to*. Or indeed (okay, I admit I'm the only one who wonders this) whether they wore hats on any or all of their five heads.

Nowadays, the Brightside of Giger's Moon is a vast Industrial Zone. And the Darkside of Giger's Moon is where they house the Penitentiary. It is the second largest prison in the Solar Neighbourhood, after Pohl Pen. It houses recidivists and sociopaths and stone cold killers. As well as all those generals and soldiers and Corporation lawyers who were so astonishingly evil they couldn't get pardoned in the round of judicial amnesties that followed the Last Battle.

Security here is formidably tight. No-one has ever escaped from the Giger's Moon Penitentiary.

Until now.

"Keep your head still," said the doppelganger robot, and I kept my head still.

The DR sprayed my scalded face with healant, and it stung like fuck. I could feel the skin becoming stiff, and I knew that in about forty-eight hours my burned flesh would start to regenerate.

"My eyes!" I whined, "I'm fucking blind!" I wasn't, in fact, but the dubber operating the DR was too dumb to know that. His silver-skinned robot-puppet shone its torch in my eye and my pupils didn't dilate. The idiot thought that proved something.

"Shackle her," said the DR, and the two other DR-dubbers put magnetised shackles on my arms, pinning them behind my back. Then they did the same with a bar-shackle around my ankles. Then they fastened an explosive collar around my neck and strapped me to a trolley. They were taking no chances.

Teresa Shalco, meanwhile, had fucked off. Even though she was the aggressor and I the victim, no one attempted to arrest *her*. Because she was the *capobastone*, and hence the Boss of this entire fucking prison, and was hence pretty much untouchable.

The lead DR wheeled me on my trolley down the Spoke. Past the R & R rooms. And past the F Spoke cells and through twelve sets of force-fields, until we reached the Outer Hub where the prison hospital was located.

"What have we got here?" said Cassady briskly—that's Cassady Penfold, hospital trusty, five-foot nine, ruby-haired and, oh, my lover—as I was wheeled into the receiving area. I groaned and raised my head and looked straight at her. Cassady, bless her, didn't flinch at the sight of my melted face.

"Gang violence," said the DR. "Burns on face, torso injuries, big mouth."

"Can we use cosmetic rejuve to restore the skin texture?" said Cassady, in her usual gently half-murmuring tones.

The DR was silent a moment, as the dubber at the other end of the virtual link considered this question. Although in truth there wasn't much to think about. Waste high-quality cosmetic rejuve on a *recidivist*? "No," said the DR.

Then the DR picked my stretcher up with one hand with effortless strength and dropped me on to a bed. I groaned, trying to sound as if I was in agony and filled with abject despair at having forever lost my lovely looks.

The agony part was real enough.

"Anyone else to come?" asked Cassady.

"Nope," said the DR, and then the light went out of its eyes and it was motionless.

Now there were only two with functioning minds in the hospital reception area. Me and Cassady.

The reception area was a large oval room with a mirrored ceiling (don't ask me why, but it made looking upwards a dizzying experience) and a hexagonal purple and green virtual monitor hovering at its heart. It also had the standard SNG pastel—wishy-washy-coloured walls of the kind that always made me want to start shooting a projectile gun full of primary-coloured paints. There were of course, carefully embedded in the walls, micro-cameras that covered every single area in the room. But it was a fair bet no-one in the surveillance centre was looking at us. Not *now*. Not with all the shit that was going down.

"The riot's started?" asked Cassady.

I consulted my retinal display. "You bet your arse," I confirmed.